FRANK

and the Unidentified Flying Blob

Look out for more Frankly Frank books:

**Frankly Frank and Little Crumb's
Really Big Footy Game**

Frankly Frank

and the Unidentified Flying Blob

dAMoN BuRnArd

■ SCHOLASTIC

For Poddzo

Scholastic Children's Books,
Commonwealth House, 1-19 New Oxford Street,
London, WC1A 1NU, UK
a division of Scholastic Ltd
London ~ New York ~ Toronto ~ Sydney ~ Auckland
Mexico City ~ New Delhi ~ Hong Kong

First published by Scholastic Ltd, 2004

Copyright © Damon Burnard, 2004

ISBN 0 439 97343 0

Printed and bound by AIT Nørhaven A/S, Denmark

2 4 6 8 10 9 7 5 3

CHAPTER ONE

One ordinary kind of night, Frankly Frank was hanging out with his great friend Watson...

They were watching TV and sharing a huge Bucket o' Fizz.

Bucket o'Fizz

SuddeNLY

a man wearing enormous glasses appeared
on the screen.

And now...

It's time for...

SPACE NEWS!

6

"All right! I *love* Space News! It's all about space and stuff!" said Frank.

"Check this out!" said Space News Guy. "Later this week the Great Cosmic Caramel Popcorn Shower will be whizzing by our planet for the first time in **100 YEARS**. Yes, you heard me – **the Great Cosmic Caramel Popcorn Shower!**"

"Well..." said Space News Guy.

WOW!

said Watson, who was excellent at baking, boiling, frying and poaching, and loved to taste things in general.

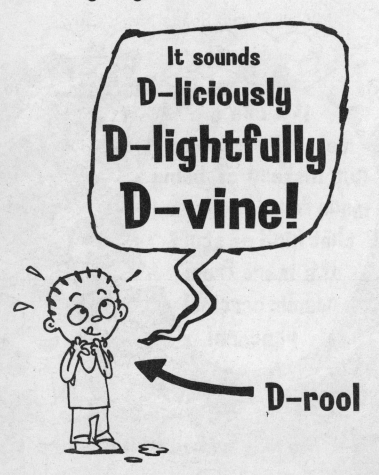

It sounds **D-liciously D-lightfully D-vine!**

D-rool

"Unfortunately," Space News Guy continued, "it'll be passing by too high up to see with the naked eye!"

"Hee hee!" chuckled Watson and Frank. "He said naked!"

A chucklesome picture popped up in their heads.

But then they stopped their chuckling.

"DARN! I really wanted to see that Cosmic Caramel Popcorn Thingummy!" said Frank.

"Double-darn! Me too!" said Watson.

And then...

Frank had an idea!

"Wait, I've got an idea!" said Frank.

"What is it?" asked Watson.

"I'll tell you in Chapter Two!" said Frank.

CHAPTER TWO

"Okay, so now we're in Chapter Two," puffed Watson, "what's your idea?"

"Listen up!" said Frank.

> Why don't we build a space rocket ship type-thing so we can see the Great Cosmic Caramel Popcorn Shower really close up?

"That's a fantastiologicallyriffic idea!" said Watson.

> And I'll bring some bags and napkins so we can taste it, too!

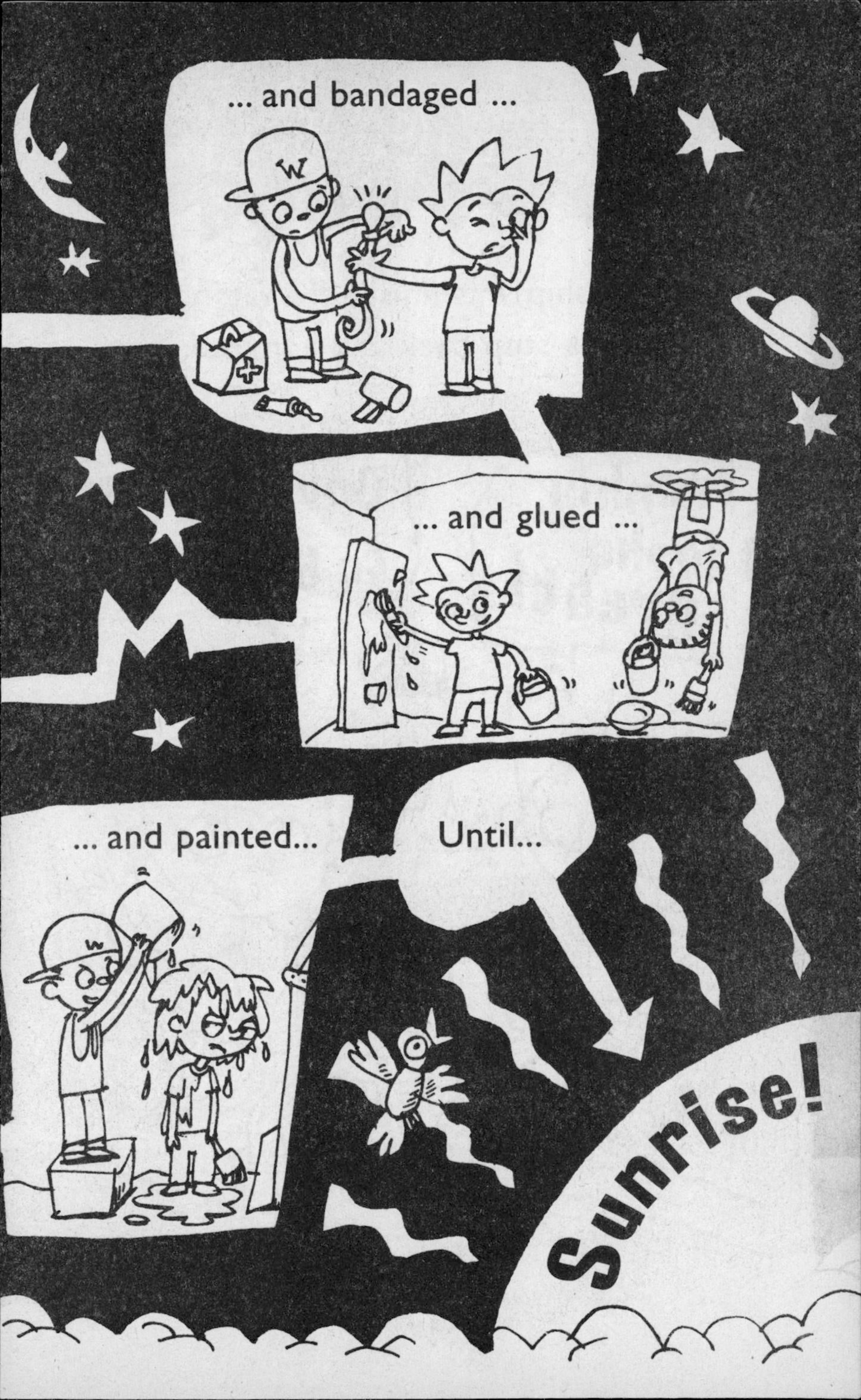

... and bandaged ...
W
... and glued ...
... and painted...
Until...
W
Sunrise!

AT LAST

the rocket ship was finished! Watson and
Frank took a step back and admired their
work.

Frank and Watson shook hands and grinned from ear to ear and back again.

They were so proud, they decided to invite all their friends over at lunchtime to see it.

CHAPTER THREE

By lunchtime, most of Frank and Watson's friends had arrived...

"Welcome!" said Frank and Watson,

"Please be seated," said Frank.
Their guests sat down...

The air exploded with a roaring rolling raspberry sound that made everyone jump from their seats and cover their bottoms and look very, very embarrassed indeed!

Out from behind a Miscellaneous
Tree popped Big Hair.

"Hee hee!" she chortled
gleefully. "There ain't
nothing like a whoopee
cushion for loads of
loud lunchtime-
launch-type laughs!"

Everyone said "Tsk!" and gave Big Hair an extra-specially cross look that made her chuckle even more.

Frank decided to ignore her (which was a sensible thing to do). "Ladies and gentlemen," he declared.

Watson whipped the sheet from the

MYSTERIOUS OBJECT!

Ta-da!

whip!

Everyone gasped...

Except
Big Hair.

Great.

What
is it?

"It's the ricket shop," said Frank, "which we'll fly up into space so that we can see—"

"And taste..." interrupted Watson.

"—The Great Cosmic Caramel Popcorn Shower!" continued Frank.

"And now..." declared Frank.

CHAPTER FOUR

"**H**elmets on!" said Watson, seriously.

"Helmets?" said Frank.

"These helmets," said Watson.

Frank and Watson bravely put on their buckets – I mean, helmets ...

... and boldly took their seats in their fabulatastical rocket ship!

 yelled Watson.

yelled Frank.

yelled Watson.

 yelled Frank.

yelled Watson.

BLAST OFF!

Frank pulled a lever.

STOP

GO

AND...

Nothing happened.

"Oh dear!" said Frank sadly.

It doesn't work!

Pooh!

Never mind, old chaps!

Maybe it needs an engine?

said Posh Norris kindly.

sang Grungy Rockette helpfully.

Hey!

It's, like, totally cute-a-licious, anyways!

said Gurly-Gurl thoughtfully.

It was all rather disappointing to say the least.

Frankly, my adventuresome spirit feels like a deflated balloon!

Hey! Mine too! Sort of like a soufflé that didn't rise in the oven!

Tsk!

"Oh, cry me a river!" said Big Hair, who was still hanging around.

Stop feeling so sorry for yourselves!

"Here!" she said. "Smell my flower!"

"Thanks, Big Hair!" said Frank. "I think I will!"

He bent down for a whiff, and...

"Thanks a bunch," grumbled Frank, wiping his face.

"Come on Frank," chuckled Big Hair. "Snap out of it!"

If you **really** want to see that Caramel Popcorn Thingummyjig, all you need is a **telescope!**

"A teleposcope!" said Frank. "Of course! But where can we get one of those?"

"You could try Tina's Everything Shop," suggested Big Hair. "She sells everything!"

"You're right!" agreed Watson. "It's so much better than Micky's Almost Everything Shop, don't you think?"

CHAPTER FIVE

Frank and Watson rushed into
Upsan Downs ...

... and dashed into Tina's Everything Shop.

"Hello!" said Tina.

Can I help you?

You bet!

We'd like a teleposcope please!

A teleposcope?

Yes, a teleposcope.

So that we can see the Great Cosmic Caramel Popcorn Shower close up!

"Oh!" said Tina. "You mean a telescope!"
"That's right!" said Frank. "A teleposcope!"

Wait there! I've just the thing!

Frank and Watson waited while Tina rummaged around in her store room.

AND THEN

Here!

OPEN WITH CIRCUMSPECTION

Tina opened up the box, to reveal...

"Can you taste things through it?" asked
Watson.

"I'm afraid not," said Tina.

"That's a shame!" said Watson
thoughtfully. "But we'll take it anyway!"

"You bet we will!" said Frank. "How much?"

"That all depends," said Tina, "upon what you've got!"

Frank and Watson emptied their pockets.

"Great! It's a deal!" grinned Tina, whose favourite thing ever was collecting string, buttons, twigs, bent paper clips, and best of all, fluffy mints.

Tina helped Frank and Watson put the telescope back in the box ...

... and away they happily went, off to Chapter Six.

CHAPTER SIX

Frank and Watson rushed back to Frank's house and set up the telescope.

"Can you see any stars?" asked Watson.

"Pooh!" said Frank. "I can't see a thing."

They looked and looked for an hour, and then Watson had an idea.

Maybe it'd work better if we set it up outside!

Good idea!

Frank and Watson carefully carried the telescope outside.

They looked and looked for about two hours, and then Watson had another idea.

"Perhaps we should wait until it's dark?" he suggested.

"Good idea!" said Frank.

When at last it was dark, Frank looked again.

"Let me see! Let me see!" said Watson,
hopping about on one foot.

Watson took a look.

DOUBLE-WOW!

he gasped. "Awesome!"

"Any sign of the Great Cosmic Caramel Popcorn Shower?" asked Frank hopefully.

No...
Not yet...

They searched the sky for a while, but there wasn't a nugget of popcorn in sight, so Watson decided to go home.

DIAGRAM ONE

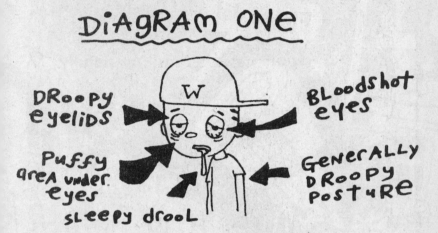

DRoopy eyelids

BLoodshot eyes

Puffy area under eyes

GeneRALLy DRoopy PostuRe

sleepy drool

As you can see in Diagram One, staying up all night to build a non-working, not-so-fabulatastical-after-all rocket ship and then waiting all day for it to get dark had left him rather sleepy. (Also, the fact that it was a non-tasting kind of telescope had taken away some of his excitement for the whole Cosmic Caramel Popcorn Shower thing.)

CHAPTER SEVEN

Meanwhile, Big Hair was out on her nocturnal constitutional.

She was busy blowing little bubblegum bubbles and popping them with her teeth, when she caught sight of Frank's telescope.

"Did you get that at at Tina's Everything Shop?" asked Big Hair.

"I certainly did!" said Frank.

As Big Hair looked through the telescope, a Big-Hair-type idea popped into her head.

When Frank wasn't looking, Big Hair took the gum from her mouth and stuck it to the telescope lens!

Big Hair nimbly jumped back down and peered through the telescope.

"There's a flying blob heading for the town!" shouted Big Hair. "Look, Frank!"

Frank looked.

Gulp! It was

TRUE!

A big dark blob was
hovering in the sky ...

... and wherever Frank moved
the telescope, the blob
moved, too!

"Gasp! It's heading for Watson's house!" gasped Frank.

And then he pointed the telescope at Gurly-Gurl's house.

"And now it's heading for Gurly-Gurl's house!" Frank cried.

Goodness gracious! We're being attacked by a UFB!

A UFB? What's that?

chuckle! snort! Giggle!

CHAPTER EIGHT

"**Q**uick!" shouted Frank. "We've got to do something!"

He grabbed two dustbin lids and ran off through the streets of Upsan Downs.

"Wake up!" he yelled, clanging and banging the dustbin lids.

We're being attacked by a UFB!

While Frank was running and yelling and clanging and banging, Big Hair peeled the gum from the telescope lens.

This has got to be my best joke ever!

59

Before long, Frank had woken up
the whole town.

"A UFB?" said Gurly-Gurl,
rubbing her eyes.
"Where?"

Up there!

I saw it through my teleposcope!

Sounds fishy!

What's all the racquet?

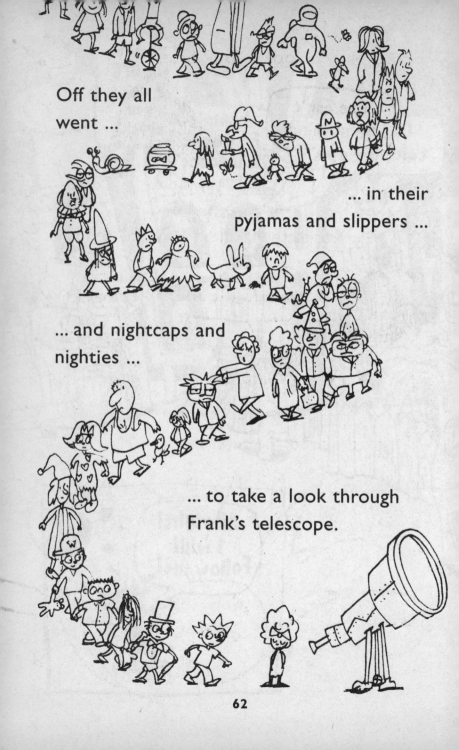

Off they all
went ...

... in their
pyjamas and slippers ...

... and nightcaps and
nighties ...

... to take a look through
Frank's telescope.

Posh Norris took a look first.

Grungy Rockette was next to sneak a peek.

Frank grabbed the telescope.

"There was no UFB..." said Watson, kindly.

Everyone trudged back home. Big Hair
went with them, chuckling and chomping
and rubbing her hands together with glee.

CHAPTER NINE

The next day, some people poked fun at Frank about the Unidentified Flying Blob.

"I did see it, I swear!" swore Frank.
But no one believed him.
Not even Watson.

That evening, as soon as nightfall fell, Frank went back to his telescope, determined to prove everyone wrong.

But this time, Frank didn't see a UFB...

He saw something else altogether.

It was an incredible sight...

A thousand pieces of giant popcorn blazed across the sky, each followed by a fiery tail.

But then Frank noticed

SOMETHING

that made him say...

The popcorn had stopped blazing across the sky, and had started blazing down it!

YIKeS!

It's heading for Upsan Downs!

Frank looked again.

Frank's heart beat like a big bass drum. He ran over to Big Hair's house as fast as his legs could carry him...

"Big Hair! Quick!" he shouted, hammering at the door.

Big Hair's head popped out of a window.

"Honest! It's TRUE!" insisted Frank. "You've got to get out of there..."

"True schmrue!" said Big Hair.

Big Hair nodded proudly.
"My best ever!"

Frank glanced up at the sky and began to walk backwards.

Skyward glance

Backwards walking style

"You're right, Big Hair!" he said. "There is no popcorn shower! I was making it all up. Totally."

"I knew it!" said Big Hair.

You need to get up pretty early in the morning to pull one over on me!

SUDDENLY...

In seconds, Big Hair's house was buried under a mound of Cosmic Caramel Popcorn!

"Help!" cried Big Hair's muffled voice, from somewhere sticky deep inside.

"Well, I don't know..." said Frank.

"Please Frank! I'll do *anything*!" whined Big Hair.

"Like what?" asked Frank.

"Like I promise never to play any tricks again! Honest! Now, please help!" she pleaded.

"I'll see what I can do," said Frank, and he ran round to Watson's.

Quick! Follow me to Big Hair's house...

You again?

What is it? An Unidentified Hovering Glob?

Come on! Trust me! And bring some napkins!

When Watson saw what had happened to Big Hair's house, he thought that he was dreaming.

Pinch me! I must be dreaming!

Okay then....

Youch! But not that hard!

Sorry.

"Okay, so I'm awake," said Watson, rubbing his arm, "and that means that the popcorn must be real!"

Yippee!

80

They climbed to the top of the Cosmic Popcorn pile ...

... and began to munch in a downward direction.

CHAPTER 10

an hour later, Frank and Watson still hadn't reached Big Hair's roof.

Phew! I never thought I'd say it ... but I'm getting full!

Me too!

"We need reinforcements!" said Frank. While Watson carried on chomping and munching, Frank gathered together as many friends as he could.

And bring your appetites!

One hopes he's not imagining things again!

He'd better not be ... for his sake!

That'd be like, totally too much!

Tragic indeed!

With the extra help, things went a lot more quickly, but no less deliciously ...

... and before long they'd munched and crunched down to the roof.

... and munched and crunched her sofa clean!

"Hey! Look what I've found!" Watson suddenly shouted.

They slipped a movie into Big Hair's VCR and made themselves comfortable in a sticky kind of way.

HEY! yelled a voice from under a sticky drippy mound of popcorn by the window.

What about ME?!

"We're coming!" said Frank.

Grrr!

Just as soon as we can!

Frank and his
friends munched
and crunched and
watched their
favourite movies
until the popcorn
was mostly all
gone ...

... and they had no choice but to start on the big, sticky, grumbly mound...

At last, Big Hair was

She was sticky and gooey and viscous,
but at last she was

"Thanks a lot, everyone!" she said.

"Don't thank us, Big Hair!" said
Gurly-Gurl.

Big Hair blushed. "Thank you, Frank! And sorry about the trick..."

I deserved to be buried under a mound of Cosmic Caramel Popcorn for seven hours!

Yes, frankly, you did!

Frank reminded Big Hair of the promise she'd made.

"Promise?" said Big Hair. "What promise?"

"The one where you promised not to trick anyone ever again!" said Frank.

"Oh, *that* promise..." said Big Hair. "I'll try my very, very best to keep it!"

"That's what I'm afraid of!" said Frank, who didn't have very high hopes for Big Hair's very, very best.

"Hey! You two! Shhh!" shushed Watson.

And so everyone sat down together and munched popcorn and watched *Space Monster Death Battle Six*, *Seven* and *Eight*, until the sun came up...

And Big Hair's promise? She kept it as long as she could, which was about until the sun went down again ...

... when she had a brilliantly pranktastic Big Hairish idea...

Don't miss Frankly Frank's second
stupendalicious story...

Teaching as learning

This book follows the success of *Action Research: Principles and Practice* which urged teachers to develop and improve their own classroom practice by taking educational research out of the confines of academia and conducting it themselves as part of their normal work.

In *Teaching as Learning: An Action Research Approach* Jean McNiff continues her study of her own professional development and argues for the necessity for practitioners to hold up accounts of their own practice for public criticism. She challenges the traditional approach to the initial and continuing education of teachers and offers personal action enquiry as the basis for their ongoing professional development. The author's radical ideas are already being put into practice by schools and local education authorities who encourage teachers' own action enquiries and school-based research groups.

Jean McNiff is an independent author and consultant in education, and a visiting Fellow at the University of Bath.

Teaching as learning

An action research approach

Jean McNiff

With a foreword by Jack Whitehead,
Lecturer in Education
University of Bath

London and New York

First published 1993
by Routledge
11 New Fetter Lane, London EC4P 4EE

Simultaneously published in the USA and Canada
by Routledge
29 West 35th Street, New York, NY 10001

Reprinted 1995

© 1993 Jean McNiff

Printed and bound in Great Britain by
Mackays of Chatham PLC, Chatham, Kent

British Library Cataloguing in Publication Data
A catalogue reference for this book is available from the British Library.

Library of Congress Cataloging in Publication Data
A catalog record for this book is available from the Library of Congress.

ISBN 0–415–08980–8 (hbk)
ISBN 0–415–08390–7 (pbk)

Contents

Each one should use whatever gift he has received to serve others . . .
Always be prepared to give an answer to everyone who asks you to give the reason for the hope that you have.

(1 Peter 4:10, 3:15)

Acknowledgements

I wish to thank a number of people who have made this book possible.

First, the teachers. Thank you to the inspirational teachers in Dorset whose words appear in Part IV, and to the two staff development officers for sharing their thoughts. Thank you to Terry Hewitt, Margaret Hine and Kevin Eames in Avon for permission to publish their work in Part III. I know their support is valued by the colleagues with whom they are working as much as it is valued by me.

I acknowledge with gratitude permission to publish the Avon Local Education Authority Policy Statement that appears in Chapter 6.

I am grateful to the *British Journal of In-Service Education* for permission to reprint the work of Kevin Eames in Chapter 8.

I with to thank Denis Vincent of the Polytechnic of East London for his initial faith in the idea; and Jack Brook of Portsmouth Polytechnic for his painstaking review of the manuscript which has helped strengthen the book significantly.

Three people in particular are the creators of this book as much as I am: Roda Morrison, my editor, who has been a constant source of encouragement and good cheer; Jack Whitehead, my friend and colleague, caring and generous in time and spirit – thank you, Jack, for enriching the lives of so many of us; Alan Hyde – many of the ideas in the book came out of the laughter of our lives. It is good to share the joy.

Foreword

Jack Whitehead
School of Education, University of Bath

The crisis of confidence in schooling has pushed education to the top of the political agenda. The crisis has extended to higher education because of the low level of access relative to that of our European neighbours. There is also the lack of a national organisation to promote 'education at work' as a way of improving the quality of our productive lives. Each of these problems is contributing to our present anxiety that the economic and cultural foundations of our society are declining.

It is one thing to see the need to do something about such problems. It is a different matter to move ourselves and our political, educational, commercial and industrial institutions in a desired direction. Education is fundamental to social regeneration, yet there is a danger that it will fail to play its part because the traditional view of educational knowledge is still dominant in our educational institutions. This is the view that educational knowledge is created by researchers in faculties of mathematics, history, philosophy, psychology, chemistry, etc., in institutions of higher education. The alternative put forward in this book is that educational knowledge is created by individuals at work as they answer questions of the form, 'How do I live more fully my values in my practice?'

In this book, Jean McNiff presents an account of her own education at work. This text follows the success of her *Action Research: Principles and Practice*, which has become a standard text on many education programmes. I believe this current book will fulfil its aim of encouraging practitioners to have faith in their own creative powers to understand education from the point of view of making sense of their own practice, while exercising their critical powers in evaluating the contributions of other thinkers to this understanding.

The first texts in the field are going to provoke a range of emotional and intellectual responses. The profession is not used to educational researchers who are willing to submit their own professional practice to

public test in the formative process of generating and testing an educational theory which can describe and explain their own form of life in education.

We are certainly not used to an educational researcher offering an account of her own educational development which includes both the results of years of profound reflection together with examples of the naivety of first encounters with new ideas. The text and author are vulnerable to criticism. Jean is open to and learns from criticism. She sees it as a necessary part of her educational development. It will be interesting to read the comments of readers to see whether they respond with a sensitivity and quality of criticism which does not violate her integrity.

The book is a form of resistance to the imposition by academics of their conceptual structures onto educational theory. It does this by inviting teachers and academics to offer descriptions and explanations for their own educational development as part of the process of generating and testing a living form of educational theory. I share Jean's belief that such accounts open up a new, dialectical form of educational knowledge. This form is openly constructed through a process of question and answer and requires individuals to ask questions related to living their own values more fully in their workplace. In such questions they acknowledge their existence as a living contradiction.

Rather than encouraging teacher researchers to remove their own 'I' from the enquiry on the spurious grounds that statements containing 'I' are necessarily subjective and therefore of less value than 'objective' statements, the dialectical form enables individuals to acknowledge themselves as living contradictions in an educational enquiry of the form, 'How do I live more fully my values in my practice?' The success of Jean's earlier book on Action Research has been attributed to the fact that teachers and students identified with the experience of those teachers who explained how they held educational values while at the same time recognising that they were not living them fully in practice. In other words, teachers recognised the experience of being living contradictions as they engaged in practical attempts to improve the quality of practice. While retaining her commitment to the fundamental importance of the individual researching her or his own practice, Jean extends her understanding of action research as a form of collaborative network which can transform institutional structures into forms of good order which can promote the educational development of individuals. We still have much to learn about these processes of educational transformation. The fact that Avon Education Authority and

Wiltshire schools such as Wootton Bassett and Greendown are supporting their teachers' action enquiries into the quality of pupils' learning
in collaboration with higher education gives some grounds for opti-
mism that the ideas developed in this book are not grounded in speculation. The ideas are grounded in the concrete practices of individuals
and groups of professionals who are showing what it means, within our
present social context, to work towards improving the quality of education with pupils and students. I have more faith that the living explanations embodied in the practices of these professionals will constitute
educational theory than I do in the conceptual structures of my academic colleagues in higher education.

I cannot think of one Professor of Education in this country who has
made a systematic study of her or his own educational development
and offered for public criticism a claim to know this development. I see
academics offering lectures on the expert teacher without subjecting
their own teaching to critical scrutiny. I see academics running educational development research groups without subjecting their own
educational development to research.

I do not want this criticism to be seen as a blanket condemnation of
the work of my colleagues in higher education. I value their contribution to the philosophy, psychology, sociology, history and management of education. These contributions, however, are all made from
within a language and logic which denies the existence of contradictions within educational theory. I believe that the omission of any systematic analysis of their own educational development is preventing
them from seeing the dialectical nature of educational knowledge, and
hence their work serves to promote a view of this knowledge which is
now harmful to the processes of social regeneration. I hope this text
serves to strip away some of these crippling influences.

At a time when the Conservative Government sees the process of
improving standards of education in terms of imposing a national curriculum, national assessment and local financial management of
schools, it may do some good to emphasise that the quality of education is ultimately dependent upon the professional quality of the
teaching force. One of the crucial elements in a profession is its practice
of 'practice guiding theory'. This text is focused on the nature of the
educational theory which can produce valid descriptions and explanations for the educational development of individuals. I would argue
that the production of such a theory, grounded in professional practice,
is an urgent political necessity for all those who wish to improve the

quality of education in this country. This is why I think Chapter 8 is so important, where Kevin Eames describes the development of a school-based research group.

While Jean does not approach her work in education from an explicitly political perspective, in Chapter 13 she acknowledges the importance of collaborative networks of practitioners for ensuring that educational values are lived in practice. She is also offering a way of understanding her educational development which she affirms as true to herself and is 'rational' in a way which challenges the rationality of traditional ways of thinking about educational knowledge. In grounding her views in personal knowledge she is following Polanyi's view that no one can utter more than a responsible commitment of her own, and this completely fulfils her responsibility for finding the truth and telling it. Whether or not it is the truth can be hazarded only by another equally responsible commitment.

I hope that this text captivates your imagination and moves you into a form of collaborative action in which you will recognise a new way of thinking about education – a way which corresponds to the way you think about your own education and yet has not been acknowledged in the world of educational theory. I believe that you will find Jean's text comprehensible in the sense of moving us into a new, dialectical form of rationality in thinking about education. This is not to say that you cannot judge her work in terms of the criterion as to whether or not she adopts a rigorous approach in ensuring that her assertions are adequately grounded in valid evidence. In hoping that Jean will captivate your imaginations I am conscious of the values which are embodied in her educational development as she shows their meaning in the course of their emergence in practice. This is, of course, very different from the view in many books and journals that the meaning of values can be clearly communicated through the propositional form of text. It is a contention of this book that an understanding of educational values and hence educational knowledge requires the educational researcher to show the meaning of the values as they are embodied and emerge in practice. If this is not done it is difficult to understand in what sense the research can claim to be 'educational'.

The majority of work on educational theory is presented in terms of conceptual structures rather than a form of enquiry. Educational theory is still seen as a traditional form of theory which contains a set of determinate relationships between variables in terms of which a fairly extensive set of empirically verifiable regularities can be explained. An alternative view to this, set out by Jean in her earlier work and devel-

oped here, is that you and I should take the lead in generating a living educational theory by producing descriptions and explanations for our own educational development in our professional work in education. Rather than conceive theory in terms of a set of conceptual relations, this text offers a view of theory in terms of embodied explanations for the way of life of individuals. The explanations are embodied in the sense that they are part of the individual's practical responses to questions of the form, 'How do I improve my practice?' It is possible to judge the adequacy of the theory through the formation of better quality questions and improved practice and understanding. Such an educational theory is a narrative in which individuals examine their lives in relation to questions of the form, 'How do I live more fully my values in my practice?'

In the course of such an enquiry, individuals can explain how they are assimilating, accommodating and integrating the insights of other thinkers in making sense of their own way of life. Such explanations will not be reduced to those of other thinkers. In other words the form of educational theory proposed in this book can integrate the unique contributions of individuals as they strive to improve the quality of their own way of life. The dialectic of question and answer permits an openness to the possibilities which life itself permits. It is not closed off by any conceptual structure. This characteristic of the dialectic stresses the importance of education as a process of transformation in which traditional theories can exist as transitional structures which are open to modification, rather than a process in which conceptual structures are imposed on our thinking as in earlier accounts of eductional theory.

A final criterion which I know Jean would want applied to her work is that of authenticity. In a world where the values of freedom, rationality, justice, democracy, integrity and community, are much needed, I think you should take the opportunity offered by this text to engage in a critical dialogue with the author in a way which will help to take her enquiry forward. In the course of such a conversation you may find that a reciprocal relationship is established that helps to take your own enquiry forward too. I think you will find in these pages an individual's commitment to give meaning and purpose to her professional life through the quality of her relationships and productive work, together with an expression of faith, based in experience, that such work in education is of value in the search for human betterment.

Introduction

Let us consider the nature of educational knowledge – specifically, my own.

This presentation is part of my on-going project, in which I seek to understand my own educational development, and to offer an account of that development in explicit form, in order to support my claim that I have improved the quality of my own education.

I believe, as Polanyi tells us (1958), that development is a transformational process. A person may hold certain views and sometimes make dogmatic assertions about them. However, when she presents these views for public scrutiny and criticism, she may change her mind about them, because of several influences: by engaging in the analytic process of writing which focuses her thoughts more precisely; or by the feedback from other people as they critique her work; or in the light of her own developing experience; and so on.

In this sense, this text represents my present best thinking about the nature of educational knowledge. It is not a final answer. It is a firm but temporary intellectual platform on which I am standing to create new, more mature structures. I began to understand this process of my own learning from Polanyi, that I must not shrink from taking a firm stand in order to give me the security to move forward; but that this firmness should be fluid, provisional, part of my conscious intent to transform my own thinking, and subject to dismantling when the time is right to move on. The general framework of my intellectual life is that, like Rogers (1961), I hold my concepts loosely; but at critical transitional times, such as in synthesising my ideas in written form, I narrow the focus in order to 'freeze' the intellectual action and crystallise the ideas.

This is the point of this book: it is an articulation of my present best thinking of how people – myself and those who have contributed to the text – are continually engaged in transforming our own lives through a process of question and answer. The book is part of the developing story of my life.

While the focus of this text is on the professional development of

teachers, ultimately the value of this work must be judged in relation to the quality of clients' learning. This concept is still in embryonic form in this book and continues to develop.

Personal experience

I often reflect on the bitter-sweet experience of my own professional development. I took early retirement at the age of 46 because of a heart problem. At the time I was deputy headmistress in a large secondary school; I had been intensively involved in the continuing education of colleagues; I had written my first book on personal and social education; I was already five years into a part-time PhD study. Retirement put an end to it all.

At the time I felt cheated. My career was in full swing. I knew it all. What would I do now?

The first thing to get out of the way was my thesis. I set about writing; it would be finished in three months.

It wasn't: not for the next two years. Those years were the most formative of my professional life, and the time in which I began to think – actively think – creatively and critically. My real education began here; my real professional development began when I left institutionalised education; and I am concerned that it should now never end.

It is ironic that I came to see the importance of personal freedom through the process of being free. I am currently institution-unbound. I like it that way. At first it was frightening. I, like most people, I suppose, enjoy the security of a structured environment. I like to know what is going to happen next; and, as a teacher, I had lived by a time-table for a long time. Now I was not responsible to, or for, anyone.

When I set about writing my thesis I employed the same thought-structures that I had used all my working life. I thought in propositional terms (see Chapter 2). My teacher-education work had always reflected this: 'If I do X to these teachers, then they will do Y. And I will tell them that if they do Y, then Z will follow. I will be successful in my institution's terms, and so will they in theirs.' This logic caused me to write up my practice in school on an 'if . . . , then . . .' basis. I still felt that I had to adhere to the received format for writing an academic treatise.

As it was, I had to rest for some months, and I took up some reading that looked attractive. I read several books that were to have a lasting influence: Polanyi's *Personal Knowledge* (1958); Pring's *Personal and Social*

Education in the Curriculum (1984); Bernstein's *Beyond Objectivism and Relativism* (1983); Fromm's *To Have or To Be* (1978); and others. I began to relate these books to myself: not only to my professional practice, but to the total practice of my life.

I began to see that the institutionalised pressures on me as my functional self had left no space for my personal self's development. I had always been concerned to meet others' expectations: what of my own desire to think for myself? The enforced freedom demanded that I now do just that. I had no choice but to fall back on my own resources, to create my own life from now on.

The acceptance of freedom, both social and intellectual, was difficult, at times harrowing (Fromm, 1942). But survival is at the root of existence. I became virtually better a year after retiring. I went into business, started writing seriously, and took up consultancy work. I work very hard, but I am free to think and act as I please.

I am intensely aware now that yes, I was cheated, but not in the sense I had originally perceived. I had been cheated of timely professional and personal development because I was a child of the empiric initial and in-service training that cripples the individual by the straitjacket of institutionalised expectations. I had *served* as a teacher. I had fitted my practice into others' forms of thought. I had accepted their claim that knowledge was theirs, not mine, and that I had to perform in a certain way in order to acquire knowledge.

Now I am concerned that other teachers are also, systematically and deliberately, being cheated by the expectations of the policy makers. I regard my work now as a mission that will help teachers to be free, *in spite of* the policy makers. I want to influence the policy makers, themselves servants of the institutionalised machine, that there is another way, another life, that rests on the creative understandings and intersubjective agreements of caring individual professionals, that they can work things out together through a policy of love, not domination.

I want to institutionalise user-friendly systems of thought and communication. I want to communicate how my quality of life has improved beyond all recognition since I was put into the position of losing the opportunity actively to teach in a conformist environment, and how instead I opened the doors to my own learning. I want to encourage other teachers to abandon formal instruction-based teaching and try out a way of life that is based on their own willingness to learn about themselves.

I am now quite involved in continuing teacher education. The more I go on in my own work as a teacher, the more convinced I become of

the need to organise it as a learning process rather than as a teaching objective. I am compelled to believe that my work as a supporter is focused on the self-education of teachers. I am increasingly aware of my own role as a resource that may provide an appropriate environment in which people may grow, of my need to resist offering glib answers that are based on my own insights and experience rather than encourage them to find their own answers.

I am convinced of the need to encourage people to appreciate the power of the self, when that self engages in the process of her own development; of the power of the self to create her own understanding. This power allows us to apply our educational practices to the process of transforming our lives. If we are not happy with a situation, we change it. Our educational knowledge is the process whereby we know why and how we transform our lives.

In order to do this, we must be free, socially, intellectually and spiritually. I am concerned in my work to break with our current traditions of teachers' intellectual dependence. Teachers must regard themselves as free thinkers, as creators of their own lives, in order to regard themselves as part of the educative process. If they do not, teachers remain as implementers; and that, to my mind, is wasteful and immoral.

Creating educational knowledge

I will state at the outset that I do not think education is intrinsically concerned with behaviour, or the study of behaviour, and I do not believe that knowledge is to do with bodies of statements that aim to control behaviour.

I want to explore the idea that education is concerned with the process of growth of an individual whereby the individual's life is formed and informed by the values that she holds and the knowledge that she develops. Values, or beliefs, are aspects of an individual's thinking and practice. Throughout this book I want to look at how the nature of values and the way in which they are realised could constitute a particular way of life. The realisation of values may be seen as offering reasons for acting in the way that we do. Our way of life may be understood as an expression of 'values in action'.

If we regard our enquiries as the process of seeking reasons for action, we are working towards explanations. The form of this life process may be seen as a commitment by an individual to move an unsatisfactory situation, in which values are denied in practice, towards

an improved situation, in which values are more fully realised in practice. The enquiry itself follows the process of improvement, grounding itself in the intentional actions of the individual who was initially dissatisfied with a situation, and who made a personal commitment to work systematically towards improving her practice in order to improve the situation.

I am concerned to work towards changing the currently popular focus and status of educational enquiries. At present there is a predominant view in the literature that education is to do with behaviour, and that educational enquiries are to do with the control of behaviour (e.g. Wilson, 1989).

Let me characterise the nature of an enquiry as a search for knowledge. The dominant focus in the literature is that educational enquiries are enquiries into education: that is, a researcher is involved in acquiring knowledge about education from sources outside herself. I would like to see the focus of educational research as appertaining to the creation of knowledge: in which case, a researcher is involved in creating knowledge of education. Education is not a field of study so much as a field of practice.

I am trying to show here two different approaches within two separate parameters. Let me picture one parameter as being the focus of educational enquiries, which may be approached by (1) the dominant view, that knowledge about education generated by researchers is imposed upon teachers; and (2) an alternative view, that educational enquiries are processes that enable teachers to create their own knowledge.

The second parameter concerns the status of educational enquiries, which may be approached by (1) the dominant view, that educational enquiries are the property of researchers who enquire into, and make statements about, the professional practices of teachers, and (2) an alternative view, that teachers own their own knowledge, and are seeking to understand their own professional practices with a view to improving them.

The diagram overleaf illustrates the two parameters.

Here we are considering the question of the ownership of knowledge: whether knowledge is mainly the property of an external knower who may use it to control others; or whether it is the creation of the individual.

The educational factor in teachers' educational enquiries needs nurturing. An enquiry that qualifies as educational may be characterised by the fact that it may be seen to be personally educational for the enquirer: that is, that it has enabled the practitioner critically to evaluate

focus of enquiry	status of enquiry
(1) – training of teachers	(1) – about education – derivative – access to knowledge
(2) – education of teachers	(2) – educational – personal – creation of knowledge

and improve her own professional life. At the heart of this process of improvement is that person's own conscious understanding of her practice.

This use of the term 'educational' is not necessarily the same as its 'normal' use. Much of the literature accepts as 'educational research' enquiries that are to do with the management of classrooms, the organisation of the curriculum, teaching skills, and other aspects of pedagogy. I see a sharp distinction here. For me, such enquiries would be better labelled 'managerial' or 'sociological'. I will attempt to use the term 'educational' in a consistent fashion, as to do with the process of the development of individual rationality. I hope to show my conceptualisation of the term 'educational enquiry' as the search by individuals for their own knowledge – not 'knowledge about education' but 'knowledge of education'; that is, knowledge that is of itself educational. I hope to show my perception of the nature of educational enquiries as being this creation of personal knowledge; and of the use of educational enquiries as helping practitioners to bring about an improvement of practice through the development of critical awareness.

So I may say that my enquiry in this book gives rise to three basic questions:

1   What constitutes educational knowledge?
2   How is educational knowledge acquired?
3   How is educational knowledge put to use?

(see also Chomsky, 1986)

I shall attempt to offer answers to these questions in the form of descriptions and explanations of the work of real teachers and learners, including my own. I hope to demonstrate within the book the reasons

for my present intensified concerns about the status of educational knowledge, as it is perceived and used within schools and other institutions. I feel there is much pressure on teachers to conform to a perceived need to justify their pedagogic practices rather than to investigate how their personal and professional conduct affects learners.

I must reinforce here my position statement: that I am using this text to work out these ideas, and that they are presented as provisional hypotheses which are subject to public evaluation. In presenting my tentative answers I hope to highlight some central issues in my work to date, and the work of colleagues, particularly in Avon and Dorset, who are active in related areas.

Form of the book

This text is itself an enquiry into the nature of educational knowledge. I hope to demonstrate the systematic nature of educational enquiry by outlining the framework I intend to use, and by showing how my preferred procedure can lead to an improvement of a problematic situation.

I shall employ the strategy of question and answer as outlined by Jack Whitehead:

1 I identify a problem when some of my educational values are denied in my practice;
2 I imagine a solution to the problem;
3 I implement the solution;
4 I evaluate the solution;
5 I modify my ideas and my practice in the light of the evaluation.
(Whitehead, 1981, 1989)

This outline acts in its general form as a strategy for working through the book.

1   I identify a problem when some of my educational values are denied in my practice (Part I)

The educational values I am focusing on in this book are those of my intellectual freedom; my status as a teacher within current bureaucratic constraints; my desire to engage personally in the improvement of my own education; the desire to see (and have seen) my practice as my personal creation. These values – of myself, and of colleagues who share

them – are in danger of being eroded by power groups who think differently. They seem to aim at controlling me rather than encouraging me to develop. I feel required to receive others' educational knowledge instead of engaging in the creation of my own.

2   *I imagine a solution to the problem (Part II)*

I look at the problem as a number of issues. I consider how these issues are being tackled within the procedures of 'traditional' models of teacher education, and I conclude that those procedures do not constitute a strategy of improvement that solves my practical problems as an independently-thinking practitioner, either as a teacher in class, or as a teacher-educator. I suggest alternative ways of tackling my problems, as an individual and as a collective exercise.

I formulate this question as a series of needs, and possible answers to those needs.

3   *I implement the imagined solutions (Part III)*

There is a very powerful movement afoot in the United Kingdom, instigated largely by the activities of practitioners who are engaged in action research. I am thinking specifically of personnel, currently or formerly, at the Universities of Bath (Jack Whitehead) and East Anglia (John Elliott; Jean Rudduck and Jon Nixon – now at the University of Sheffield; David Hopkins; Clem Adelman – now at Bulmershe College of Higher Education; Rob Walker and Stephen Kemmis – now at Deakin University, Australia). Because of the persistence of these people, and others who have been caught up in their vision (people such as myself), there is now a clear committed voice which demands a national forum for the recognition of the need for a research-base for professionalism, a strategy that encourages teachers critically to identify the problem areas of their own practice and to work systematically towards solving the problems.

Such an approach has already been adopted and implemented by some funding bodies and institutions; and I outline how they are managing change through dialogue between administrators, advisers, teachers, children, parents, and national government.

4   *I evaluate the outcomes of my imagined solutions (Part IV)*

The notion of evaluation, as used in this book, is the process of reaching a position of shared values and understanding through dialogue. In

this process, individuals make explicit and public their tacit educational values, and show the systematic nature of their enquiries as they try to realise their values in their practice. In telling their stories they are inviting other people to consider their particular way of life; in making public how they have become critical, as they try to realise their values in practice, they are inviting others to comment on the efficacy of their process of self-improvement; and in asking others to evaluate what they are doing, they are inviting those others to consider sharing that particular way of life – or they modify their way of life according to their acceptance of others' better arguments.

In this section I present some of the work that we are doing in Dorset, where support personnel (field tutors) are working with teachers on an individual basis in a collaborative enquiry. I present a dialogue between teachers, and with advisers, which shows how we try to evaluate the quality of our work within our various locations; and how we attempt to justify our claims that we have improved the process of education by undertaking our living enquiries.

5 I modify my ideas and my actions in the light of my evaluation (Part V)

In my view, the evolution of society is grounded in the same values as those that underpin our lives as teachers, in the morality of an educational epistemology of practice. It is not enough to aim for the realisation of our educational values only as our objectives; it is essential to engage in the present realisation of our educational values in and through our lives as teachers. Professional practices are the living out of the educational values of the community of reflective practitioners as they engage in their own educational development in an attempt to improve the process of education.

Educational development implies an on-going process of expanding consciousness, and an improvement of practice that has its basis in the consciousness of the individual. I would like to see the institutionalisation of such an individual-centred research-base as applied to on-going professional development. As I see it, the evolution of a rational society is grounded in the evolutionary practices of self-reflexive practitioners.

In the United Kingdom we are working towards the legitimation of academic accreditation for teachers carrying out classroom/workplace research; we are introducing diplomas for professional development in various forms, such accreditation to be made available through all types of higher education institutions. Such flexible programmes of accreditation for research strengthen the view that 'research as practice'

may be seen as the foundation of a society that is open to the reflexive control of its own process of evolution.

Audience

This book is intended for teachers at all levels of institutionalised and non-institutionalised life. One of my educational values, as articulated throughout, and particularly in Parts III and IV, is that teachers will see the need for, and feel confident to initiate, school-based programmes of practitioner-centred enquiry in action; and that teacher educators will encourage their initiatives. This book is intended to provide support for those teachers who are concerned to improve the quality of education for themselves and for the people (teachers and learners) in their care.

Improving the quality of teaching as learning

I believe that the best teaching is done by those who want to learn. I reflect on my own work, as a teacher and as a writer, and I consider how I have transformed my own life through critically reflecting on what I am doing in all aspects of life. I recognise myself as a changing individual in a changing world; I change my thought as my thought changes me. I am open-minded to life, and delight in my own learning. I feel crucially that this is what teaching is about: the ability of an open-minded individual to bring her learners to the point where they, too, may be open to their own process of self-development. I feel this may be done by the efforts of teachers to establish the frameworks of care in which learners may develop their own understanding of their own experiences. Teaching transforms into learning, and back again to teaching. I think teachers have the key to their own process of self-improvement by acknowledging that they, too, are travellers, and still have far to go.

PART I I EXPERIENCE A PROBLEM WHEN SOME OF MY EDUCATIONAL VALUES ARE DENIED IN MY PRACTICE

Chapter 1

The Professional Education of Teachers

The nub of the problem, as I see it, lies in the currently dominant approach to the initial and continuing education of teachers. There are certain assumptions in this approach that do not always see teachers at the centre of the educational enterprise. These assumptions need careful reconsideration and judicious replacement by another set of assumptions that put teachers in charge of their own learning and development.

I believe profoundly in the need for on-going education. I shall reiterate this belief throughout. What causes me concern is the way in which most teacher education is conducted. I am concerned about the methodology, including the assumptions (theories) which form and guide the methodology. It is high time for a new methodology and a new theory; for a new epistemology of practice.

In the last few decades there has been an evolution in patterns of teacher education in the UK. There has been a shift of emphasis in the control of education recently. There appears to be a tension between a centralised control of the curriculum and the devolution of power to individual schools through the local management of their finances.

Let me give a brief outline of the ways in which continuing teacher education has developed over recent years. I shall then put forward a new set of assumptions which could replace the old.

Two sections follow here. Both comment on the assumption that research is the basis for professional improvement. I shall suggest that there is a need for a shift in status and in focus. This shift expands a view of research as the basis for improved practice to a view of self-improving practice as research.

Within the debate about the relationship between theory and practice, there are currently two somewhat polarised positions in the United Kingdom, two 'visions of professional development' (Elliott, 1989), which I shall term here 'Theory into practice' and 'Practice into theory'.

1   Theory into practice

The dominant tradition for teacher education has been, and still is, a 'line mangement' approach in which an informed person offers guidance to teachers. This model usually operates through specific strategies which are intended to help a teacher to improve a particular educational situation.

STATUS

The status of research, in this view, is methodological; its focus is the practices of others. The nature of research is that it is conducted by an observer, who will offer the results to the practitioner.

Various strategies are used by the observer to make certain standards available. House *et al* (1989) have identified the five most common: (a) technical rationality; (b) study and prescribe; (c) practitioners as role models; (d) vicarious experience; (e) action research. I shall draw on their work here.

(a)   Technical rationality

The assumption in this approach is that what works well in one situation will work equally well in another. I have identified this view (McNiff, 1988) as belonging to the empiricist-positivist tradition, and have critiqued it as resting on a mistaken interpretation of the creative nature of human potential. It is assumed that the methods of experimentation in the fields of botany, in which one variable is likened to another, may be transferred to the fields of human experience. It operates on an 'if . . . , then . . .' basis, with standardised input and output.

When applied to teacher education, it could be interpreted that what worked well in one educational setting will be successful in another. One set of teacher actions in one specific situation will produce similar results if another teacher acts in a similar fashion in another situation. Most of the literature of teacher education rests on this assumption.

I will accept that this approach is useful in many pedagogical situ-

ations: a standardised model of standardised actions will often provide like results in like situations. I cannot accept, however, that this is an appropriate foundation for the professional learning of teachers. Learning involves the evolution of understanding, and professional development involves considered reasons for action. All these aspects involve the critical reflection of individual teachers within their own context-specific situations.

The same criticism applies to strategies (b)–(e) that follow (House *et al*, 1989).

(b) Study and prescribe

This strategy requires someone to study what teachers do and prescribe ways in which the teachers might improve. Shavelson and Stern (1981) have collated such research, and have drawn up a possible taxonomy of teacher decisions and subsequent actions.

(c) Practitioners as role models

In this view, teachers are seen as the experts in their own classrooms. The best practices are held up as models to be emulated by colleagues. House *et al* (1989) cite the work of Scriven (1985), arguing that this view offers us a practical science of education, rather than a theoretical one.

The problem then arises, they go on to say, whether it is possible to abstract the significant features of good practice, and generalise from those; as well as the underlying problem of whether teachers ought to reformulate their own practice through emulating that of others.

(d) Vicarious experience

House *et al* consider the work of Stake (1985) in presenting case study material as the basis for others' improvement. There is a danger in this interpretive case study approach that teachers will feel that they have to adapt what they are doing to the recounted practices of others. I have argued (McNiff, 1988, and below) that the way to improvement is not through trying to copy what other people do, but by the critical understanding of one's own practice. Copying someone else does not move forward my own understanding of why I do as I do. It might make my immediate situation better, but, unless I understand why I am acting in the way that I am, I will not develop, personally or professionally.

(e) Action research

This is a strategy of research that passes the control of practice over to the individual teacher in a specific setting. The conventional view of this strategy is that practitioners may follow a certain action-reflection procedure that will allow them to improve an unsatisfactory situation. This procedure is one of identification of a problem, and subsequent resolution of the problem through a process of observation – solution – action – reflection – modification (e.g. Kemmis and McTaggart, 1982; Elliott, 1981).

In my view (see also McNiff, 1988), this approach to action research still assumes the primacy of the observer who, in this case, is offering a course of action for others to follow. Granted that the teacher is in control of the action-reflection cycle; but it seems still the case that a certain theoretical course of action guides the practical decisions in action of teachers in each and any situation. (I will discuss another approach to action research in Chapter 3.)

The nature of research, in this dominant tradition, is that theory forms and informs practice. Researchers propose certain hypotheses which are then implemented by others within practical situations. Theory comes before practice. The form of the theory is propositional (see Chapter 2).

An extreme form of this approach assumes that the most credible research is undertaken by academics who pass on their findings to teachers (e.g. Wilson, 1989). This view is being vigorously challenged, particularly by those keen to promote the image of teachers as researchers (e.g. Stenhouse, 1975; Elliott, 1987), and by those who regard teachers' attitudes as a vital component in the education of learners (e.g. Sockett, 1989).

My personal view here tallies with that of Denis Vincent (personal correspondence) that 'in-service providers tend to be opportunists and will use "experts" for entertainment value but generally see the real work being done in much more reflective, problem solving modes.'

FOCUS

It is interesting, too, how the focus of research has changed over recent years. I have so far indicated a shift in a conceptualisation of the nature of research, from being the property of the external researcher to becoming the property of the individual teacher. It is also possible to

identify a shift away from a focus on the institution to a focus on the individual.

(a) Institution-based research

In the last decade there has been a massive endeavour to move away from the disciplines approach to educational research as applied to teacher education. In this view, teachers' practices were seen largely in terms of implementations of the curriculum in relation to the insights from the philosophy, history, sociology and psychology of education; and where learner performance was judged in terms of how well aspects of the curriculum had been internalised. Good practice was seen as the integration of the separate disciplines within a curriculum.

(b) Classroom-based research

The work of Lawrence Stenhouse and his colleagues at the Centre of Applied Research in Education, primarily through the Humanities Curriculum Project, did much to promote the idea of the teacher as researcher. From focusing on the institution, research now moved into the classroom. Interest centred on the practices of teachers, and there was an initiative to 'take the lid off the black box of teachers' practices' (Eggleston *et al*, 1976).

(c) Practitioner-centred research

In the 1980s, the teacher-researcher movement gathered more and more adherents. Advisers and consultants took on an enabling role. It is important to note two aspects, though: (1) the nature of research was still grounded in method (how classrooms should be run); and (2) the form of this method was still arranged by external agents (e.g. Kemmis and McTaggart, 1982). Granted that the research in question was about the activities of individual teachers, and conducted by those individual teachers; the *status* of research was still derivative (controlled externally), and the *focus* was still concerned with descriptions of what other people were doing.

So now we are at a point to move into a discussion of the emergence of a new paradigm; a form of research that enables teachers to develop their own understanding of their own practice, and to turn their practice into a form of research.

2   Practice into theory

This section deals with the need for the development of teachers' personal theories of education (Whitehead, 1983), drawn from the experience of their own 'reflection in action'. It emphasises the need for teachers' conscious understanding to be placed at the centre of explanations.

Whereas the dominant paradigm operates in terms of collectivism, this approach regards the individual practitioner as the centre of the research study. In philosophical terms, it is the development of knowledge of self, the integrity of the living 'I' as the focus of educational enquiries; in educational terms, it is the concern by the practitioner to focus critically on areas that need attention and, through a systematic cycle of critical reflection in action, to work towards improving the situation.

Again, let me consider here the status and the focus of enquiries from this perspective.

STATUS

Let me adapt a concept from Chomsky (1986) of E- and I-status. Let me say that E- (externalised) enquiries are those conducted by one person into the practices of others. This is the traditional pattern of INSET research. Someone observes and describes teachers' classroom actions and gives advice on how they might be improved. An I- (internalised) enquiry is that conducted by the individual into her own practice. She reflects critically on her work, either privately or through discussion with others, and aims to think of original ways that will help her improve. The status of an I-enquiry is personal. Any improvement in the practice involves a commitment by the practitioner.

FOCUS

In E-enquiries the focus of the research is the practices of others. In I-enquiries the focus is the practice of the self. If I say that practice is part of an individual's way of life (how I act, and why I act this way), I may say that the focus of an I-enquiry is the self.

It is interesting now to note the difference of perspective in the concept of research, as it is applied within these two paradigms. In E-enquiries the purpose of research is to observe, describe and explain what other people are doing. Its status is derivative – that is, the accounts given of the research are those of the recorder, but not always

of the practitioner. The accounts themselves aim to offer explanations to others through an 'objective' study of the data, to see if those data (facts about the study) fit the recorder's theory. In this conventional INSET research pattern, the observer has reasonably clear ideas about how a pedagogical situation ought to be; he watches the teacher, and advises the teacher on her action plans.

In an I-enquiry the purpose of the research is to explain what I, the practitioner, am doing. Its status is personal. The accounts rendered are those of myself, and aim to offer an externalisation of my mental processes as I try to bring about change; that is, I try to show how I was dissatisfied with personal practice, and why, and the steps I have taken in order to improve. By this, I mean to overcome a situation in which my values are denied; so I aim to improve my thinking (an improvement of mental processes) with a view to improving my practice (an improvement in my actions in the world). My practice is an outcome of my thought, and my improved practice is an outcome of my improved understanding.

The status of my I-enquiry is explanatory because its focus is the self. My explanations are based on personal reasons for personal actions. I may be assisted in the formulations of my explanations by critical friends who question me on why I do as I do; it is my answers to those questions which give an explicit account for my reasons in action.

In this view, educational research aims to encourage the development of personal understanding that will lead to an improved form of practice. It becomes an enquiry by the self of the self; and, rather than aim to fit personal practice into another person's theory, it concerns itself with enabling individuals to develop their own personal theories.

Let me formalise this process of personal 'enquiry in action'. Let me suggest that many personal enquiries begin with a sense of vision. The origin of the enquiry lies in the vision of the enquirer which embodies her values. For example, I wish that all children had equal opportunities; that we all cared for each other; that we enjoyed peace and freedom – these are some of my (educational) values.

The vision is of a satisfactory state. This satisfactory state is an expression of the realised values of the enquirer, in which statements of fact and statements of value blend in the same form, both linguistic and conceptual, in a steady state. My statement, 'I wish that all children were loved', may be seen as an expressed value of the vision of the enquirer. The practice of the enquirer may not be within a location in which all children are loved, however, nor may it have such an expression; resulting in the statement of fact: 'Not all children are loved.'

Statements of fact are separated from statements of value, and therefore form separate realms of discourse. The vision of the enquirer is of the day when the negation may be negated, and the situation transformed into one of stability.

The slippage rests in the experience of 'I' as a living contradiction, in that my values are not fully realised in practice (Whitehead, see below Chapter 3). This denial, itself an unsatisfactory state, causes tension in the mind of the enquirer. The sense of crisis occasioned by the lack of stability causes her to want to act in order to restore the balance.

Seen from this perspective, the process of an enquiry in action aims to draw a theory out of practice. Contrary to the traditional form of INSET research, where theory acts as the basis for others' practices, this approach that centres on an individual's understanding sees practice as the ground for the development of the process of theorising.

There are two very important points here: (i) I am trying to show that each individual may legitimately theorise about her own practice, and aim to build theories; (ii) an individual may offer a tentative theory which she openly accepts as subject to change: the action of theorising as a process is a concept more appropriate to educational development than the state of referencing a theory. In this view, people change their practices, and their practices change them. The interface between person and practice is the process of theory building, which involves a critical reflection on the process of 'reflection in action', and which legitimates the notion of a changing individual interacting with a changing world.

Implications for teacher education

The two approaches described have both taken research as the basis for the professional learning of teachers, but the approaches have involved different sets of assumptions which have influenced the perception of the nature of teacher education. These assumptions proceed from a view of the use of educational knowledge (Chapter 2), and may be formalised as follows.

THE TRADITIONAL APPROACH: A 'LINE MANAGEMENT' MODEL

Assumptions

(a)   There is a standard model – a theory, or a set of procedures. Teachers are invited to adopt or adapt this theory to themselves.

(b)   The teacher educator advises on the best course of action.

(c)   The model is institutionalised. The focus is teachers' activities within institutions. The aim is usually the improvement of pedagogical situations, and often the improvement of institutionalised procedures: curriculum, management, communications, etc.

(d)   The model involves an objectives approach. The research programme is predetermined as working towards specific outcomes within institutionalised procedures.

(e)   Research is seen as the basis of teaching (pedagogy). It operates in terms of skills, offering checklists of expertise.

AN ALTERNATIVE APPROACH: A SHIFTING CENTRES MODEL

Assumptions

(a)   Teachers are regarded as experts, who empower themselves to offer accounts of their own practice, these accounts to be legitimated through the validation of peers and clients. Teachers are encouraged actively to draw out theories, and to develop these personal theories through their accounts.

(b)   Teachers, teacher-supporters and clients are awarded equal status and responsibility for helping the other person's process of understanding to evolve. In this collaborative view, all practitioners at all levels (learners, teachers, supporters) are involved in the process of the development of their own, and each other's, rationality: they are improving the quality of their own learning. Teaching and learning are interchangeable terms, existing as processes that regulate the interrelationships within a network of thinking practitioners.

(c)   The model is personalised. The focus is the understanding by the individual of her own life (the understanding of the self by the self). The intent is to improve the process of education within a particular present situation.

(d)   The model is based on a process-view of learning. There is no end product in sight, other than an 'end product' of 'no end product'; a final answer that there are only new questions; an end state that is the beginning of a host of new states.

(e)   Research is seen as a form of teaching which explores new ways of life that promise to be beneficial to the community of which the

researcher is a part. The act of teaching involves the concept of bringing about improvement. Seen in this light, self-reflective research not only provides a proper base for teaching (Rudduck and Hopkins, 1985), but *is* teaching. Teaching becomes an 'enquiry in action', in which the teacher constantly endeavours critically to evaluate and improve the process of education for herself and for the people in her care.

Teaching as learning

This final section is to explain clearly how I see the concept of teaching as grounded in the concept of learning; and the process of others' education as grounded in the education of self.

If I take teaching as a process of 'enquiry in action' – reflection into the on-going process of current practice – I may say that I am open-minded to my own development. My teaching situation is the scenario for my own spirit of learning to emerge; the process of my teaching is the process of my learning, in which I give free rein to my intellectual curiosity.

I have said above that the focus of learning, and the focus of an enquiry into learning, is the individual practitioner. Instead of the traditional model in which someone advises on another person's performance, the individual is encouraged to be critical of personal practice, and use her deepened insights to move forward.

The act of teaching, in a traditional view, involves the passing on of skills and concepts to learners. Let me suggest that this view is pedagogical rather than educational. Education, as I have suggested above, is to do with the development of the process of individual rationality. If we apply the 'shifting centres' approach to the processes in classrooms and other workplaces, it is possible to see the teacher's job as facilitating the same critical awareness of personal practice to be available to her clients as to herself. It is a sort of chain reaction within a network. In this process we are seeking to educate, to involve ourselves in helping others to improve themselves.

At the end of the day I am left with the notion that teaching implies the process of opening the doors in my clients' minds that will make them aware of their own processes of development, and of their own potential for unlimited acts of creation. I can bring my clients to the point where they will want to learn; and I can enquire into the most effective way of making the awareness of such discoveries available to

my clients. This scenario is the same for myself in the role of teacher to pupils or teacher to teachers. I am an agent. I can attempt to make my agency a facilitating one. But first I have to understand the nature of that agency before I can use it.

As I see it, this view of teaching constitutes an attempt to formulate an emergent epistemology of practice (see Chapter 5): the knowledge base of professional development, and the ethical form of that practice. What I am suggesting here is the construction of a community of self-reflective practitioners, learners at all levels of the community exercise, who are concerned for each individual's realisation of his or her own potential, and who care enough first to make an unqualified commitment of self to the education of self, in the interests of the education of others.

Chapter 2
The Problem of Educational Knowledge

Inherent in the choice of model for teacher education is the underlying problem of educational knowledge: the nature of its constitution, its acquisition and its use. I have already highlighted a parallel problem to do with the nature of education, in the discussion about models: whether we are seeking knowledge *about* education or knowledge *of* education. If we look for knowledge *about* education, we assume that education is something 'out there', not our own property, but to which we must gain access. If we look for knowledge *of* education, we assume that education is a personal process, of which we have immediate, direct experience.

This chapter is to do with knowledge, specifically educational knowledge. I want to show that there are several different forms of knowledge; that people think about knowledge in different ways; and that the way they think about knowledge influences the way they think about other people's knowledge. I shall first outline different aspects of knowledge, and then relate these views to the current discussion about approaches to teacher education.

Aspects of knowledge

'Epistemology' is the word used to refer to issues concerning the nature of knowledge. In studying epistemological issues, we are focusing on problems that have occupied philosophers since time immemorial.

Within the current literature that deals with questions of epistemology, there are two somewhat polarised positions, and the debate is described succinctly by Marjorie Grene (1966) as 'the knower and the known'. One school of thought (e.g., Ayer, 1956) suggests that knowledge is reified or becomes fixed. It exists 'out there', independent of an agent-knower. The person who aspires to knowledge must gain

access to this body of knowledge. Popper (1972) uses the term 'objective knowledge': that is, knowledge that exists as a separate 'world', and to which we must gain access for knowledge of things and institutions.

There is another school, represented by Polanyi (1958) and Grene (1969), who accept that some knowledge exists independently of the knower; but there is a more important form of knowledge – personal knowledge – that enables the knower to know that she knows. This is a fundamentally crucial point.

I shall now expand these brief reviews of theories of knowledge, and try to show how they influence theories of education. I shall then look at the implications for teacher education.

OBJECTIVE KNOWLEDGE

This view suggests that knowledge exists independently of individual knowers. It is a reified body of explicitly formulated ideas about the world. It is often expressed as 'know-that' and 'know-how', or propositional knowledge and procedural knowledge, though there is some debate as to whether there are these two, or only one, form.

Propositional knowledge

The usual expression here is 'I know that P', where P is a proposition about the world: 'I know that today is Friday', 'I know that he lives there'.

Procedural knowledge

The usual expression here is 'I know how': 'I know how to drive a car', 'I know how to speak German'. The 'how' element of procedural knowledge is usually regarded as an acquired skill, but this is by no means always the case. There is much debate in the literature whether 'know-how' automatically incorporates 'know-that'; the argument goes that if we know how to do something, this procedural knowledge may well contain elements of knowledge about that thing; 'know-that' could become redundant.

Whatever the state of the debate, the main point is that this type of knowledge is grounded in explicit statements about the world, statements that are assumed to be true, and that may be verified by recourse to data.

The organisation of explicit knowledge

The usual way of thinking about propositions is in a formal sense, usually following an 'if . . . , then . . .' formula: 'If I do X, then Y will follow'. This is the usual form of reasoning used in enquiries which attempt to test a given hypothesis.

Propositions about education

Most of the literature on education accepts the dominance of propositional knowledge as the basis for theories of education. I will refer again to my questions regarding the nature of the constitution, the acquisition and the use of theories of education.

(a) The constitution of education

There seems to be a prevailing view in teacher education provision (and educational provision in general) that education is an object, a 'desirable stuff' (Warnock, 1977), that we aim at, and, once acquired, will result in the production of the 'educated person'. This view is being reinforced by aspects of current legislation that emphasise criterion-referenced schedules of attainment, and by aspects of teacher-appraisal schemes that operate in behavioural terms – how well teachers do in specific tasks, for example. In this view, education is a thing to be acquired by a learner.

(b) The acquisition of education

In this view, the way that education is acquired is through the processes of assimilation and accommodation. It is supposed that learners assimilate what is presented to them in various ways: they acquire certain mental sets which dispose them to form habits, or otherwise organise their mental faculties to accommodate the structures of knowledge on offer. The acquisition of education is seen as a structured process of input and output, where the acquisition of education as input is manifested in terms of behaviour as output.

(c) The use of education

In this view, the use of education might appear as an instrument of control. Speaking of teachers, Pring says (1984) that, being in control, they *do* things to other people. In classrooms, teachers can use their

educational knowledge to control the practices of their learners; and in teacher education provision, providers can use *their* educational knowledge to control the practices of teachers. At best, such a concept of education can be used to strive towards an identified objective for the common good. At worst it can be used as an instrument of coercion in the domination of one will by another.

Propositions about educational knowledge

A parallel situation is apparent when we consider teacher education, and the way in which this propositional view is implemented.

(a) The nature of educational knowledge

Currently dominant approaches towards teacher education seem to rest on a characterisation of knowledge as a body of theories, or statements, usually in a propositional form: 'If I do X, then Y will follow'. This corpus of propositions is often seen as a fund on which teachers may draw in order to improve their expertise. It is sometimes presented (e.g., Skinner, 1968; Wilson, 1989) as a technology of teaching, a series of guidelines that will help teachers become more skilled in imparting subject matters to their learners. The corpus of propositions is seen as reified, existing independently of practitioners. The idea is that a body of knowledge is there for people to use, as and when they need.

(b) The acquisition of educational knowledge

In this view, knowledge is something to be accessed. The body of knowledge exists in reified form in libraries and other institution-bound systems of communication.

An extension of this mythology is that the method by which knowledge is accessed is also reified. There are certain procedures which practitioners need to follow in order to gain knowledge. There is currently a tension between courses that are trying to reflect in their organisation and legitimation procedures the view of the teacher as a free-thinking professional, and courses whose legitimation procedures are grounded in propositional rather than dialectical forms of knowledge.

Knowledge, then, is seen as an input: the acquisition of knowledge is seen in terms of output. The 'knowledgeable person' is judged in terms of the amount of knowledge she has accumulated.

(c) The use of educational knowledge

The dominant view of knowledge that I am outlining here seems to have its main use in controlling others' practices. Knowledge is seen as presenting certain norms, both in its acquisition and use. If we aspire towards reified knowledge we are aiming to reach certain standards of intellectual excellence; and if we aim to implement the concept of reified knowledge, we are aiming to reinforce certain established norms. Our practices as aspiring knowers are controlled; and we aim to control the practices of other aspiring knowers. Ours is a closed shop of normative controls on the normative practices of normative individuals in a normative society.

PERSONAL KNOWLEDGE

This view of knowledge has been suggested mainly through the work of Michael Polanyi. In 1958 he published *Personal Knowledge*, which stressed the need for a personal commitment in any act of knowing. To speak with any sort of sense about the concept of the act of knowing, he says, I have to accept that I am an *active* knower.

This view incorporates two dimensions: the need for an acceptance of self as knower, and the creative aspect of knowledge.

The self as knower

Any claim to knowledge, says Polanyi (1958), involves an individual knower's passionate commitment. I am the owner of my own knowledge. My knowledge exists because I exist. If I cease to exist, so does my knowledge. This does not mean the cessation of other people's knowledge – Polanyi's view of the world of explicit knowledge, the sharing by people of their pooled knowledge – but it underscores the essentiality of an individual's knowledge.

This knowledge takes two forms, what Polyani calls 'focal knowledge' and 'subsidiary knowledge' (1958), or 'tacit knowledge' (1969). What he says, basically, is that we may acknowledge the existence of an explicit body of knowledge – the propositions of objective knowledge. But, in order to accept this notion, we must know that we know.

> What is usually described as knowledge, as set out in written words and maps, or mathematical formulae, is only one kind of knowledge, while unformulated knowledge, such as we have of something we are in the act of doing, is another form of knowledge. If

we call the first kind explicit knowledge, and the second, tacit knowledge, we may say that we know tacitly that we are holding our explicit knowledge to be true. (Polanyi, 1969).

So, if I say, 'I know that today is Friday,' I am making a claim to knowledge; but that claim involves my awareness that I am making that claim. This awareness of knowledge, this critical consciousness of consciousness, is the personal, tacit knowledge that underlies our knowledge about the world.

The creative aspect of knowledge

In 'Understanding ourselves' (in Ornstein, 1973), Polanyi says that it is not enough to regard knowledge as a capital sum outside ourselves; for the act of knowing that we know is an additional piece to the lump sum. So the sum continues to grow commensurate with the acts of individual knowing.

> Man must try for ever to discover knowledge that will stand up by itself, objectively, but the moment he reflects on his own knowledge he catches himself red-handed in the act of upholding his knowledge. He finds himself asserting it to be true, and this asserting and believing is an action which makes an addition to the world on which his knowledge bears. So every time we acquire knowledge we enlarge the world, the world of man, by something that is not yet incorporated in the object of the knowledge we hold, and in this sense a comprehensive knowledge of man must appear impossible. (Polyani, 1973)

In this sense, knowing is an on-going act of creation by the person who makes a personal commitment to his own ability to know.

In my own work (see above) I have drawn on the work of Chomsky (1957, 1965) to help me understand the nature of the state of mind of a knowing practitioner. In particular I have adopted Chomsky's formulation of levels of mind. Competence is the level of mind that enables an individual to know rules, and performance is the level of mind that enables the knower to use rules in concrete situations. I have recently (McNiff, 1990) linked the notions of

competence – tacit knowledge
performance – explicit knowledge

suggesting that tacit knowledge is part of the vast pool of underlying potential that every individual possesses, and that explicit knowlege is the externalisation, or realisation, of that tacit knowledge.

I shall rely on this formulation within this book, for it is my belief, as I shall continue to demonstrate in this section, that education is to do with helping individuals make explicit their tacit knowledge; to raise aspects of competence to performance level.

At this point, let me consider the nature of the organisation of personal knowledge, the forms of thought we use when thinking about personal knowledge. I will go on to consider the constitution, acquisition and use of educational knowledge, when we admit that the concept of knowledge includes the personal, tacit dimension.

The organisation of personal knowledge

I have suggested above that traditional attitudes towards knowledge are expressed in a propositional form. I will say that the organisation of personal knowledge may be expressed in a dialectical form.

Present day perceptions of dialectical logic have evolved over the last 2000 years and have been increasingly synthesised via the Hegelian and Marxist-Leninist systems (see Comey, 1972). It may be characterised by three aspects:

1 – it recognises the inherent harmony of contradiction;
2 – it balances the tension between quantitative change and qualitative change;
3 – it proceeds via an evolutionary cycle.

1 It recognises the inherent harmony of contradiction: the Law of the
    Identity and Conflict of Opposites.

Every thing contains within itself aspects and processes which are contradictory to each other. This polarisation provides a balanced tension; the opposing forces offset each other in providing for dynamic development. The natural tendency of the thing is to overcome the state of tension by evolving into a new balanced state.

In this view, a thing is never static; what appears to be a new balanced state already contains within itself the potential for the new tension that will enable it to continue evolving. If this potential is denied, the thing atrophies and dies.

2 It balances the tension between quantitative change and qualitative change: the Law of the Transition of Quantitative into Qualitative Change.

Any given thing may be recognised in terms of its essential aspects. Quantitative changes do not usually affect the essential nature of a thing – water remains water, even if I subtract or add amounts of water to the original volume. However, quantitative change in one aspect of the thing – for example, if I heat the water – will effect a change in the quality of the thing – the water will evaporate.

In this view, every thing depends for the realisation of its essential nature on the effects of the world about it.

3 It proceeds via an evolutionary cycle: the Law of the Negation of the Negation.

The rhythm of life may be seen within the process whereby a thing changes into a new form of itself under the two laws so far discussed. The world we inhabit is a non-static entity, consisting of a myriad of sub-entities, all evolving in time and space. In order to evolve, an entity must have within itself the ability to change, to develop into a form different from the form of the present moment. In this, an entity contains within itself its own process of change. Change may be seen as evolution, a process in which a less mature form transforms into a more mature form of itself.

A dialectician sees relationships between parts that bind the parts as a synthetic whole. In doing so, she can see new patterns and convergences. It is possible to focus on one element, while recognising that other elements will affect the original one. Everything exists side by side, each element with its own essential integrity, yet accommodating to its own change within a changing world of other changing elements.

Consider, for example, the process of question and answer. In dialectics, the nature of the answer is not the end phase of a previous question, but the beginning of a new question. The process of question and answer is not to lead to a fixed 'truth proof', but to lead to a continuing dialogue, in which the understanding of each party moves forward (Collingwood, 1939).

A characterisation of educational knowledge

(a) The constitution of educational knowledge

In this view, educational knowledge is not only knowledge *about* education, but knowledge that is educational: that is, it moves the

practitioner's understanding of her own practice forward. It is the property of the individual knower, and constitutes the basis of her *claim* to educational knowledge (see below). In terms of teacher education, the focus of the exercise is to empower the individual enquirer to externalise the intuitive, tacit understanding that underpins her practice; to air and share the values that form and inform her practice; and publicly to acknowledge her commitment to those values by indicating why and how she has adopted them as a way of living.

(b) The 'acquisition' of educational knowledge

I am using the term 'acquisition' loosely, to fit in with the general framework I have outlined. In fact, I regard this aspect as individual creation. In my view, each person is born with the potential for an unlimited number of acts of creation; and teachers, by accepting the responsibility of their vision to transform the world – initially by transforming their personal bit of the world – deliberately engage in a critical, creative process of 'reflection in action' in order systematically to work towards a situation of recursively improving practice. By 'recursively improving practice' I mean a cycle of cycles; when an individual cycle of

identification of problem – imagination of solution – implementation of the solution – evaluation of solution – modification of practice

may be taken as the germ of a system that generates an unlimited number of cycles that operate in similar fashion.

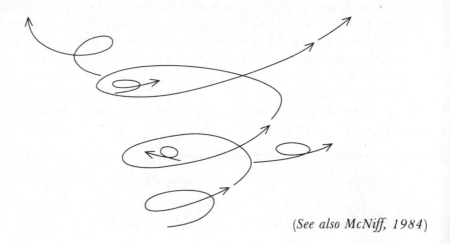

(*See also McNiff, 1984*)

(c) The use of educational knowledge

In my view, an individual may use her educational knowledge to make explicit and continue to improve her own process of educational development. In doing so, she helps others to do the same thing for themselves. In making explicit the process of her own educational development, she demonstrates the realisation of her educational values through the form that her life takes; and she invites others to validate (or not) her claim to knowledge, if they wish, by sharing in, and adopting, a similar form of life.

In this way, individuals may establish communities of self-reflexive independent practitioners, whose method is the dialogue of question and answer, and who aim to share understandings. In this view consensus is not the aim, nor necessarily desirable, for we are all individuals living in a pluralist society. What is important is that we agree to agree: we agree, not with a specific content in mind, but a process. We agree a process of dialogue that will enable us to move forward; and part of the process is the skill of asking the right questions that will enable individual enquirers to discover the questions latent in their own minds (Collingwood, 1939).

Aspects of justification*

I have said that the use of educational knowledge is to enable individual practitioners to account for their own personal and professional development; that is, that they may show how they turned an unsatisfactory situation into a satisfactory one, or how they realised their educational values in and through their practice. Such accounts amount to a claim to educational knowledge, and have to be justified.

If an individual's account is not justified, the account stands as an empty claim. I may say 'I know', but I must anticipate and accept the challenge, 'How do you know? Demonstrate to me that you know!' My justification for my knowledge will validate my claim to knowledge: I will produce an authenticated explanation.

Now, there are different kinds of knowledge claim, and different conditions involved in justification. I will suggest that there are several forms of justification to knowledge claims, such as through inference,

---

* I am indebted to Brian Haymes for helping me to understand many of the issues treated here through his book, *The Concept of the Knowledge of God* (Macmillan, 1988).

through the way a person lives, through individuals engaging in intersubjective agreements; and that there is a mistaken emphasis in the literature that justification rests mainly in inference and verification.

Let me consider these two aspects now.

Verification conditions and truth conditions

I believe that we are mistaken if we equate verification with truth, as much of the current educational literature does: that is, if a thing may be verified by the data, it must be true; if it cannot be verified, its truth is in doubt.

In my view, claims to propositional knowledge ground their truth conditions in verification. The utterance, 'I know that today is Friday', is true because it can be verified by looking at the calendar. The utterance by Golfer B in the conversation:

> *Golfer A*:   Do you know you look exhausted!
> *Golfer B*:   I only know my legs ache.

is true because his form of life bears out his personal knowledge in that he is limping; his claim cannot, under any circumstances, be verified by recourse to someone else's knowledge of his state; his truth is not open to verification or question, but it is essentially true to him.

The dominant tradition in the literature is that claims to knowledge may be justified by inference. A.J. Ayer (1956) equates verification and truth conditions in his definition '. . . first that what one has said to know be true, secondly that one can be sure of it, and thirdly that one should have the right to be true'. Now, this arrangement may be appropriate to claims of the form 'I know that P'. As I write, I know that P is true – yes, this is a pen in my hand. I am sure that P is true – this is a pen and not a pencil. I have the right to be sure – I have the evidence to say that this is a pen and not a pencil.

However, if truth and verification conditions are the same, Polanyi's problem goes unanswered; for I may verify that I know that P, but I cannot verify that I know that I know. I may verify my explicit knowledge to demonstrate its truth, but I cannot verify my personal knowledge that underpins my explicit knowledge. The way that my personal knowledge may be demonstrated is through the way that I live.

I shall elaborate this concept presently, but, before I do, I wish to consider the need for justification. In doing so, I need to consider the notion of truth (and I shall return to this in Chapter 3). As a teacher,

when I used to regard my practice in propositional terms – as an object, an abstraction that was not my personal creation – I believed that there was an external, reified Truth. This was a kind of standard towards which we all must strive. I have come to the view that caring individuals, in all walks of life, create their own, mutually agreed and acceptable truths, grounded in a shared sense of vision (see page 105; Habermas, 1981). In this sense, truth may be expressed in the form of the mutually agreed values system of individuals in agreement.

Incorporated within this principle is the notion of language game. Wittgenstein used this phrase to indicate the 'rules' of an area of discourse: that is, context-specific semantic-specific utterances. An area of human knowledge may not be justified unless participants of that form of knowledge share the same realm of discourse. Consider, for example, the conversation:

A   I saw a UFO last night.
B   You couldn't have. It was dark.

Or perhaps, when the visitor to the spiritualist's meeting hears the spiritualist say, 'I see you have brought someone with you', he might say, 'No, you're wrong; I have come alone.' As Haymes says (1988), for a non-believer to ask a believer to prove the existence of God simply does not make sense.

In the examples, the participants are engaging in different fields of discourse. They do not share the same language game. They cannot achieve intersubjective agreements in order to establish a mutually agreed truth.

Let me return to the question of the need for justification.

When, as children, my sister and I talked to the fairies in our shed, the exercise was true for us. It was not true to father who thought we were playing in the shed. Nor did he share our field of discourse.

The truth of the shared beliefs of individuals in agreement provides, for them, a way of life. We children did not attempt to draw father into our shared truth, but that did not invalidate that particular truth for us. Nor did it need justification. When father finally banned us from the shed we took our shared knowledge to other locations. The locations changed; the knowledge did not. Nor did it change until we agreed to change it – probably by changing our views about the existence of fairies.

Ways of life based on agreement are not vested in the objects of discourse (our childhood fairies) but in the heritage of mental states that

give rise to such agreements (Gadamer, 1975). As I have indicated before, consensus is not the aim of discourse, but an agreement to share understandings that will provide the 'right' answers to move forward individuals' ability to question (Collingwood, 1939). Habermas (1981) indicates that societies develop in agreement because they share in a view of the ideal that they have the potential to agree. The sense of vision that has led a society to its present state of evolution is the very aspect that enables that society to strive towards continuing forms of evolution which themselves are grounded in the evolution of forms of agreement.

Knowledge as a way of life

I am suggesting that the act of intersubjective agreement is an act of creation, a realisation in action of dynamically evolving knowledge, whereby individuals join together in forging their particular way of life in accord with their sense of vision of a life grounded in a notion of good order.

At the basis of this notion is the formulation:

> I claim to know something;
> I am committed to that knowledge – that is, I believe it is true;
> I take this knowledge into my values system;
> I am committed to my values system;
> I show my commitment in my actions;
> My claim to knowledge is apparent through my actions;
> My 'values in action' result in a particular way of living;
> My knowledge is manifested in my way of life;
> My claim to knowledge is justified by my way of life.

I am not here speaking about the veritude of knowledge. I am speaking about the justification of an individual's claim to knowledge. Knowledge by definition cannot be in error (Haymes, 1988). The question of whether other individuals subscribe to the particular values of the individual who professes to own that knowledge is another matter, and one to be resolved by dialogue. What I am speaking about is an individual's right to claim justification for her particular knowledge claim through a way of life that reflects the knowledge that is her property.

Conclusion

I now need to draw together the several threads of this chapter.

I have touched on several issues concerning the nature of the constitution, origin and use of educational knowledge, pointing out that a practitioner's understandings of these aspects will depend crucially on her perception of the concept of knowledge, as well as the concept of education.

My own view is that knowledge begins and ends with the individual knower. When the knower makes a passionate commitment to the act of knowing – that is, eagerly accepts the responsibility for the activity of her own mind – she engages in the creation of a process of knowing that moves her forward. She consciously and deliberately opens her mind to the possibility of new beginnings. In this case, the act of knowing becomes educational: through her conscious knowing, the individual engages in the development of her own rationality.

As Marjorie Grene points out (1969), knowing is essentially something that we do. In my view, the creation of educational knowledge is a critical process in which we engage to improve the quality of our own lives, personally and professionally.

Now, I need to relate all this to teacher education. In Part II I shall explore the implications in depth. I will highlight the fundamental difference in the approaches to teacher education which I have presented: a 'line management' approach which is grounded in the notion of propositions that are external to the individual practitioner; and a 'shifting-centres' approach which is grounded in the personal understanding of individual self-reflexive practitioners.

PART II I IMAGINE A SOLUTION TO THE PROBLEM

Chapter 3

The Notion of a Living Educational Theory

In this chapter I want to outline some of the central issues in the work of Jack Whitehead of the University of Bath. His work has been instrumental in promoting the idea of action research as a way of improving personal practice, where practice takes the form of critical 'reflection in action on action' by the individual practitioner. The implications inherent in his system of ideas offer a possible answer to some of the problems identified in Part I. The strength of his contribution, in my view, is that he is offering a form of educational enquiry that empowers practitioners to generate and control their own process of change.

I stated in the Introduction that this book is an enquiry into the nature of educational knowledge. It shows in action the conscious development of understanding that leads to an enhanced practice by the contributors. In this sense, the book is a case study of a collaborative enquiry involving individuals who are presenting their personal case studies. The content and process of the book may be seen as a demonstration in action of the themes I shall now discuss.

1 The living 'I'

Educational enquiries have as their centre of interest the individual practitioner who is conducting the enquiry. This person is not an abstraction, but a living, thinking human being.

In this sense, Whitehead established a precedent in the literature of

educatonal research and theory, challenging the view that the individual researcher was someone who was written *about* (e.g., Peters, 1977; O'Connor, 1957).

The introduction of the concept of the living 'I' established a new genre in the literature. A small army of teacher-researchers followed the pattern by presenting accounts of their own practices from the standpoint of themselves as researchers who intervene critically in their practice with a view to improving it (e.g., Green, 1979; Larter, 1987).

In the later 1970s and early 1980s, action research became increasingly popular as a method that enabled teachers to claim ownership of their own research enquiries. This movement was substantially a reaction against the disciplines approach that had enjoyed popularity during the 1950s to 1970s under the leadership of Professors Peters and Hirst of the London Institute. The reform was supported and popularised through the work of Lawrence Stenhouse of the Centre for Applied Research in Education (e.g. Stenhouse, 1975).

Two branches of action research developed concurrently in the United Kingdom. One branch was based at CARE, at the University of East Anglia. The researchers there developed a model that aimed to guide teacher-researchers as they carried out their enquiries into their classroom practices (see Hopkins, 1985; McNiff, 1988). The other branch was developed by Whitehead at the University of Bath, who adopted an alternative strategy.

Instead of offering a specific *method* (blueprint) with which to guide teachers' practices (e.g., Kemmis and McTaggart, 1982), Whitehead developed a methodology (strategy) aimed to move forward teachers' understanding of their practices, this being a sequence of ideas that reflect the mental states of the individual practitioner, when that individual practitioner is the living 'I' who is conducting the enquiry (see Introduction). This sequence is dialectical in nature, being grounded in the notion of question and answer; and it is open ended, recognising the fact that individuals will control the process of their own development. In this sequence 'I' at the same time am the subject and object of the enquiry (see also Stronach, 1986).

2   The creation of personal theories of education

Whitehead indicates that it is not enough for teachers to speak about experience. We have to experience experience for ourselves (Whitehead, 1983).

If we speak about experience as if it were abstracted, 'out there', and not part of the development of our own lives, we regard experience in its propositional sense. If we accept experience into our own space and time, that we are conscious of what is going on, that experience becomes part of us as changing persons, and it changes us *because* we are open minded.

In this sense, says Whitehead, it is a mistake to expect teachers only to read about, or accept otherwise vicarious experience, as the main resource for their professional development, for that abstracted knowledge will not help them to experience things for themselves, or develop deeper insights into their own experiences. This form of enquiry encourages a propositional form of discourse, where theory is more important than practice.

What is necessary, says Whitehead, is that teachers should be encouraged to develop their own theories of education from, and through, their own practices: that is, they should be encouraged critically to examine aspects that they feel need improving, and to work systematically to thinking how (building theories) to carry out the improvement. What is crucial is that teachers themselves form theories about their own practices. This process of theorising – that is, forming and re-forming theories – is an integral part of good practice (see, for example, Eames, 1987, and Part III; Larter, 1987).

The traditional approach to teacher education sees theory as an input that influences practice; and that practice is seen as the end product, an outcome of a theory successfully implemented.

$$\text{THEORY} \longrightarrow \text{PRACTICE}$$

Whitehead's view is that theory is an outcome of practice, and is part of an overall strategy of *theorising* which is a form of practice.

$$\text{practice} \longrightarrow \text{theory} \longrightarrow \text{re-formed practice} \longrightarrow \text{re-formed theory}$$

PROCESS OF THEORISING

This process of theorising, in which practice and theory fuse and interchange, is the foundation of a creative practice which is an aspect of the creative pattern of life of an aware, critical person who is concerned to improve the quality of life for herself and for the people in her care.

3   The knowledge base of educational theorising

If we regard the idea of practical theorising as more in tune with creative teaching than the idea of theory-driven practice, it is necessary to
abandon a solely propositional view of knowledge. Instead of describing our practices in the format of 'I know that P', it is more appropriate
to accept that much of our personal and professional life is based on
tacit, intuitive knowledge. This knowledge, sometimes inaccessible to
conscious reflection, is tied in closely to our values, the things we
believe in. The fact that this knowledge is not articulated explicitly does
not deny its force in leading us to a particular way of teaching that is a
direct reflection of those deep, underlying values.

The way in which we are helped to make our personal knowledge
explicit is by engaging in the dialectic of question and answer. This
question and answer may be of an intuitive form, where I, the practitioner, am convinced of the value of my intuitions, and grope my way
forward through the process of trial and error, constantly homing in on
what my intuitions tell me are the significant features of my practice.
The process of question and answer may also take the explicit form of a
dialogue between practitioner and another individual, this process of
dialogue constituting the spur to initial reflection that will move the
understanding of both parties forward in the process of dialogue (see
Part IV). The purpose of this process of question and answer is to raise
tacit knowledge to consciousness.

The aim of teacher education and on-going professionalisation
should be to help teachers make explicit their tacit understanding, so
that teachers may show, in a rigorously scientific manner, how they
may improve that understanding, and the practical situations which are
grounded in that understanding, in order to improve the quality of life
for themselves and for the people in their care.

4   Educational enquiry as a negation of the living contradiction

A dominant theme in Whitehead's work is the notion of the self existing as a living contradiction (see Elliott, 1989; see also Chapter 2 for the
criteria for dialectical forms). Let me explain.

When I say I believe in something, and then I do the opposite, I exist
as a living contradiction. When I say I should not lie, and then I do, I
am denying my values in my practice. We often do this in our society
with others. I would like the world to be more peaceful, but, for a vari-

ety of reasons – usually human frailty – I contribute to the lack of peace in the world.

As a teacher engaged in the business of education, I hold a number of educational values. Within my practical, everyday classroom situations those values are often denied in reality. For example, I would like to teach in an empathic style: I find I am teaching in a didactic style.

I can be aware of this process of contradiction by externalising for my own observation what is going on in my daily life. I can achieve this externalisation in a number of different ways: I can video my practice and observe it; I can write down my thoughts; I can discuss my actions with critical friends; and so on. So far, my enquiry exists at observational level.

I can then move forward by describing what is going on. I can describe how I feel I am not living up to what I believe in. I can capture a moment in time and space, and show the living reality of how my educational values are being denied. Now my enquiry exists at a descriptive level.

I may then move on to show how I attempt to overcome the problem. I can capture moments of time at intervals: I can show how yesterday my values were negated (my children were hostile), and how today those values were in process of realisation (my children were more friendly). I can show what I did, and why I did it, to improve the situation. In this case I am actively demonstrating how I changed my thinking in order to improve my practice. I explain: I give my reasons for action. My enquiry is at an explanatory level.

In this way, by engaging in the process of systematic critical enquiry, individual teachers are enabled to proceed, albeit sometimes by minimal steps, with the realisation of their educational values in and through their practices. They may overcome the contradictory elements of life, and show how enquiry may be used as a positive force in improving their own, and others', process of education.

5 Educational enquiry as a learning process

When an enquiry aims to describe a situation, it does not always qualify as educational. In order to be termed educational, an enquiry needs to show the process of the improvement of the enquirer's understanding (that is, it is explanatory); and in order to be termed 'research', the systematic nature of that process needs to be made public, and subjected to others' validation (see 6 below).

In this sense, the use made of the terms 'education', 'research' and 'educational research' by much of the literature does not coincide with the use of those terms by Whitehead or myself.

In our use of the term 'research' we follow the aphorism of Stenhouse (1983) that 'research is systematic enquiry made public'. An individual's commentary on her practice may lead to developed insights, and the process of the development of these insights may be termed educational, for they will lead to a better practice. For that enquiry to qualify as research, however, the individual needs to make apparent the systematic nature of her enquiry, how she followed a coherent process in her attempt to make sense, and how she made public and held up for others' validation the process of the enquiry itself. The airing of an enquiry is the first step; the sharing of the enquiry is the on-going process. In seeking validation for her claim to knowledge, the practitioner is aiming to legitimise the status of her enquiry as research.

Whitehead uses the theme of an individual's claim to educational knowledge to encapsulate the notion of an individual's process of 'coming to know'. Educational knowledge, for Whitehead, is not an object. It is a creative process in which an individual attempts to construct her own life. If an individual may demonstrate in practice the changes in her practice, and also indicate why and how these changes were effected (that is, account for altered states of mind that generated those practices), then the individual may claim that she understands her own educational development. This improved understanding in explicit form constitutes an individual's claim to educational knowledge.

From the beginning of his project, it has been Whitehead's mission to legitimise the notion of academic validation for individuals' claims to knowledge: that is, for practitioners to make public their accounts of how they came to know, and for these accounts to be accepted for academic accreditation (e.g., Jensen, 1987; Foster, 1982; Gurney, 1989).

My own project has offered the notion of the generative transformational power of educational research, and I have put forward the idea that the form of Whitehead's dialectic offers the potential for an infinite number of original educational practices (McNiff, in preparation). This present text shows that generative power in action, in that teachers may undertake their personal enquiries into how they may best support others who are in turn undertaking personal enquiries. One person's practice is generated by, and embedded within, that of another's.

6 Validation as a shared way of life

In traditional models of teacher education, the validation of a practitioner's project is usually in its acceptance by a supervisor or other agent who approves the work. Whitehead follows the views of Habermas (1972, 1979) that validation, or legitimisation, is in part a social process. One person may present an idea, which she regards as part of her personal truth, for acceptance by her peers. In presenting her idea, she also fulfils certain criteria for the justification of her idea: she shows that it follows certain standards that ascertain its internal validity (for example, it is pertinent to the individual; it is systematic; it is honest). These standards of judgement are determined by the peers who are sharing in the validation process. They decide the criteria, and then they examine the idea to see if it meets those criteria or not. In the validation process itself there are also certain criteria to make sure that communication between individuals is not distorted. These criteria may be those developed by Habermas (1979), that speech acts between individuals may be authentic, sincere, honest, and appropriate to the situation.

In this sense, if a person presents her idea to others, this idea, or knowledge claim, represents a claim to personal knowledge – that she knows why she is as she is. If the other persons accept what she says, they validate her claim. Their acceptance of the idea in making sense of their own lives indicates that they are willing to adopt her idea and adapt it to their own lives.

The idea of truth, following this line, is that it is a process shared by reflective, caring individuals. If you and I agree about something, we share the idea of a version of truth. It must be stressed that sharing an idea does not mean arriving at a consensus. There is a difference between structure and process, and the transformational tension between the two. Traditional forms of enquiry emphasise the need for structures of knowledge, usually in the form of hypotheses or end products, and the need for a consensus about those structures. In Whitehead's formulation, structures of knowledge are rapidly transformed into new structures by the transformative process of developing understanding. What is important is the agenda, the transformative process itself. Agreement about such a process takes the form of a willingness to negotiate about the processes involved. We are all individuals in a pluralist society, and the freedom of the individual mind is central. Freedom must be cherished and nurtured. This very freedom is what guides dialogue: the agreement by individuals to agree – not to

reach a consensus about structures, but to reach an understanding about processes. We agree to agree, even though that agreement means we may differ. Truth is not arrived at through coercion, but by the agreement by individuals that this is an appropriate way of life that is beneficial to one and all. If an individual disagrees with commonly held understandings, it is up to her to attempt to prove her case over time; and it is up to the community of individual thinkers to validate her idea (a claim to knowledge) by accepting her idea and its demonstration, or not, as the case is agreed to be.

In this view, on-going professionalisation is the intervention by the individual practitioner in her own life, and the validation of her knowledge claim is in the acceptance of her claim by the community of peer practitioners who are sensitive and caring of her project. Lomax (1990) makes the point that, in processes of validity, the community needs to protect the emergent thinking of the individual practitioner, while still providing critical support that will move the thinking forward (see Part IV).

7   The creation of dialogical communities

Following the philosophy of Bernstein (1983), Whitehead believes that what qualifies communities as constituted of free individuals is their willingness to enter into dialogue. This, he feels, is the way for the development of society.

The establishment of a critical educational science lies in the recognition and legitimation of the need for the establishment of dialogical communities. 'A critical educational science' indicates an epistemology of practice (see Chapter 5), a framework for educationalists to develop practices that are themselves educational, such practices being developed by open-minded criticism that will facilitate altered states of consciousness to improve practice. Improvement may be effected by dialogue.

Agreement takes the form of seeking questions that will move the dialogue forward. In traditional forms of teacher education, the judgement of the supervisor often is final. In dialogical communities, nothing is final. What is vital is the on-going recognition for on-going dialogue, to sustain on-going development. The notion of reciprocal dialogue is in the willingness of individual members of the community to ask the 'right' questions. Collingwood (1939) says that there are no 'true' questions or answers; there are only 'right' ones, 'right' being the idea of

appropriate reciprocation that will enable the dialogue to continue in order to enable understanding to grow.

In educational communities, professional support may be regarded as the establishment of dialogical communities. Such communities comprise peer-practitioners who are concerned to move each others' understanding of practice forward by engaging in dialogue.

Teachers are the owners of their own educational knowledge. They may share this knowledge with others, by demonstrating its internal validity in that they are able to live out their educational values. Peers may accept (or not) this knowledge as valid, by discussing the claim to knowledge of the individual, and sharing in it by adopting or adapting it (or not) to themselves. In this way, those peers also create their own educational knowledge. In this way are constituted dialogical communities of self-reflexive practitioners who share the same values base as a shared way of life.

Chapter 4

The Educational Enterprise

In this chapter I wish to consider the major implications of the foregoing, which I express as a series of perceived needs.

Educational enquiry may be seen as concerned with the realisation of a good order, or a good way of life. I shall attempt to explain this notion more fully throughout this chapter: that educational enquiry is an enterprise whereby we try to make our contribution to a more peaceful world: and that 'the sovereignty of good' (Murdoch, 1970) is the fundamental aim of educational endeavour.

1 The need for educational enquiry to be seen as a cognitive science

I take the meaning of 'cognitive science' as that used by Gardner (1985), in that it involves itself with efforts to explain human knowledge. I am concerned to endorse and popularise the concept that education is what goes on in the individual mind, and that the study of education constitutes a science of mind. For me, education is not what goes on 'out there' in classrooms or other institutions, other than in the other minds that are 'out there' (see 6 below).

Let me propose that what goes on in the individual mind may be termed 'intrinsically educational'. Factors 'out there' that contribute to the improvement of what goes on in the individual mind might be termed 'extrinsically educational', factors such as the skills of pedagogy and management, that will lead to an enhanced situation among persons that will foster and nurture intrinsic elements. Much of the literature of educational research and theory assume that education is to do with sociological or management factors (see 2 below). This approach appears to me mistaken because (a) it minimises the importance of individual rationality; (b) its methodology is based on collectivism

rather than individualism: the 'I' in society, rather than the 'I' in its essence; (c) it is concerned with behaviour and the control of behaviour, rather than the state of consciousness that enters into behaviour (see also Chomsky, 1986).

I suggested earlier that the mind operates at several levels, and that there are several levels of consciousness, or awareness; levels that are the organisational, functional elements of mind. There is a random, haphazard level of consciousness, a level that is open to experience, a 'scanning' operation that trawls indiscriminately; there is also a focused, specific level that homes in on experience, that enables the individual to be aware of experience.

In my view, the process of education is the self's knowledge of the self, the workings of the organisational elements of mind that raise intuitive levels of mind to rational consciousness. The process of *educating* is essentially concerned with the development of one's own rationality, with a view to enabling the development of another person's rationality.

I think that teacher researchers need to spend a lot more time and energy in investigating such issues, rather than concerning ourselves over-much with issues of behaviour and the control of behaviour. We need to commit ourselves to the development of our own understanding, as part of the good order of our own educational practices.

2 The need to distinguish between theories of schooling and theories of education

Theories of education need to be grounded in a valid explanation of what education is. The dominant assumption in the literature is that education is to do with schooling, and that educational research should be focused on an improvement in the management of schooling.

I believe that education is not necessarily to do with school. I accept that efficient management of schools and schooling is necessary for a promotion of an improvement in the quality of education (extrinsically educational). An improvement in schooling, however, does not of itself imply an improvement in education (instrinsically educational), and research into schooling does not imply research into education. Schooling is, to my mind, to do with the turning out of people who will adopt appropriate standards which will entitle them to a legitimate place in a given society (Hamilton, 1989). It is not to do with helping them to think, to be aware of states of being and states of awareness,

that will help them rationalise which standards they want to adopt, nor explain why they should.

3 The need to break with propositional forms of knowledge

Speaking about experience results in descriptions of practice, either in terms of other people's practice or one's own. What is needed, I feel, is for researchers to use research as a means actively to demonstrate how they have come to know – to show how they have moved in time from a less satisfactory state of being in which values were denied to a more satisfactory state of being in which values are in process of being realised. Practitioners in all sectors need to demonstrate publicly how they have come to know – that is, to justify their claim to understand their own personal development – by making their reports available to a wide audience, and using that public scrutiny as a means of validating their claims to educational knowledge. We need to build up a body of literature devoted unashamedly to the positive power of educational enquiry, to a view of teaching as the most optimistic endeavour available to human enquirers.

4 The need for individual enquirers by teachers

I have suggested in Chapter 1 that there has been a significant shift in the focus of teacher education during the 1970s and 1980s. The emphasis in most of the literature, however, is still on schools and their organisation, rather than on teachers' understanding of practice. Teacher education is still more to do with schooling than education (Hamilton, 1989).

At present the dominant paradigm for in-service education is still grounded in the notion of the control of educational knowledge. This knowledge is seen as a reified body of accumulated knowledge, which teachers are required to accept. Educational research is still seen in the light of the application of this body of knowledge, in terms of a clear process (know-how) of the application of a specific content (know-that). Provision for teacher education is grounded in propositional knowledge. So long as this situation obtains, teachers are in a service role of technicians.

I broke out of the mould. I am a practising teacher, but I have rejected the view of controlled knowledge and the control of my prac-

tice, and I exercise my right as a 'person claiming originality and exercising [her] personal judgement responsibly with universal intent' (Polanyi, 1958). I feel very strongly that teachers should be given the support and encouragement to do the same.

For me, personal enquiry is the best way to improve personal practice. I have attempted to demonstrate this throughout the text. There is an urgent need for teachers to be encouraged to see the control of their practice as resting within themselves, as well as influenced by social structures; the need to give reasoned justification for that practice in making public their claims to knowledge; the need to have ratified in public forum the legitimacy of those forms of knowledge.

5 The need for individual enquiries by learners

I am advocating the establishment of a new tradition of educational enquiry that focuses on the integrity of individuals in the living reality of their own locations. I have suggested that teachers need to be encouraged to take on the role of researchers, but that their field of enquiry should not be in the propositional sense, as traditional models suggest, of applying reified theories to what they are doing. Rather I am saying that teachers need to take on the responsibility of investigating their own practice through their own action-reflection, in order to produce personal theories of education (Whitehead, see Chapter 3 of this text) to provide explanations for their way of life, and provide publicly agreed substantiation for their claim to knowledge.

In this sense, teachers become learners, in that they may come to know themselves – that is, engage in their own personal process of education. This in turn has enormous implications for traditions of teaching methodologies.

I am drawing a comparison here between the control of knowledge by writers of the literature, and by teachers, consumers of the literature. Throughout this text I have challenged the view that legitimate knowledge rests in the academy or in the literature, and is not generally viewed as a creation of individual teachers. I am now saying that teachers also need to relinquish their vested interest in the control of their clients' knowledge.

My own case study traces my educational development as a teacher (McNiff, 1989). I noted how, in 1981–3, I engaged people in their own learning with a view to bringing them, by their own volition, to my interpretation of the truth. As I learned more about myself through

critically examining my work, I came to understand that I was guilty of deception and manipulation, of myself as well as of them.

I believe my later practice of 1984–6 was beginning to qualify as educational. I began to relinquish control, in that I genuinely afforded validity to my children's views, rather than attempted to distort them to fit my own. I did this by encouraging enquiry learning, by encouraging the children to engage in their own systematic action-reflection. In so doing, I attempted to move away from the image of the courtroom, in which they were on trial and I was the judge, to the image of a dialogical community, in which we intentionally set up the framework for a foundation of intersubjective agreement that would allow us genuinely to communicate as persons of integrity. I understand now that I was moving away from content-based styles to client-based styles, and from an objectives approach to a process approach (Stenhouse, 1975).

This is, in my opinion, an area that needs urgent attention by researchers. I conducted my own action research into my pupils' action research. What is needed, I believe, is published accounts of enquiries which encourage learners' enquiries, to see if such an approach will contribute to teachers' perceptions of how to encourage learners to learn; to build dialogical communities of enquiring practitioners, from the ranks of teachers and learners, and work together to improve the quality of life for themselves and for others.

6 The need for educational research to be educational

I have indicated throughout my belief that much of what goes on in the community of researchers in the name of educational research often does not qualify as educational. I have suggested that the term 'educational' is often used when the term 'sociological' would be more appropriate. There seem to be two tendencies in the literature: first to use the terms synonymously, and second to confuse the characteristics of the two terms.

'Educational' and 'sociological' tend to be used synonymously when commentators are referencing the activities involved in schools and schooling, such activities often classified under the term 'management'.

We need to be clear about the dangers of terminological confusion when we claim that we are engaging in educational research. If, in the name of educational research, we undertake an evaluation of others' practices, for example, we need to accept that we may do so only as part of our own practice which itself has to be subject to evaluation. It

should not be as an exercise of management, whereby we make statements about the way that other people act.

In my view, educational research has to demonstrate the understanding of an individual's 'enquiry in action' for that individual to claim legitimate educational status for that enquiry. I believe, with Torbert (1981), Walker (1985), Stronach (1986) and Whitehead (1989), that educational research needs to be educational. The person doing the research needs to be prepared to shift ground, because her intentions, in embarking on her enquiry, are (a) to change her thinking, and (b) to change actions in line with new thinking. Such change constitutes the nature of education; the creation of new forms of being is the implicit notion of 'education'. I have come to this conceptualisation precisely because, when I first embarked on my study, I was not prepared to change; and I was forced to change in view of the innovative aspects I had to adopt in order to stay true to the emergence of my own personal knowledge. Polanyi's aphorism (1958) that personal enquiry is a hazardous journey was never so true. But it was worth it.

7   The need for a paradigm of research-based professionalism

Educational research may be seen as a process of systematic enquiry made public (Stenhouse, 1983), in which an individual's life takes the form of the minimal steps of trial and error, in which successive triumphs lead, in an iterative fashion, to a more satisfactory situation when educational values are more fully realised in practice.

I now wish to dwell for a moment on the notion of frustration as an essential creative part of the research process – the sense of tension in the mind of the practitioner when values are prevented from being actively realised.

In a bread-and-butter sense, I may say that I must experience sadness in order to recognise happiness when it comes. In order fully to appreciate a thing, we need to have knowledge in some measure of its opposite. In order for me to be successful as a teacher, I must have experienced a less successful form of practice than the one I am currently enjoying.

Rudduck and Hopkins (1985) highlight the need in teacher education of the recognition of failure as a vital part of learning. I share this view but I do not like the word 'failure'. I do not believe that teachers 'fail' within the terms of their own practice.

To be explicit: within dominant traditions of INSET there are clearly

defined standards of measurement by which to judge success. These standards of judgement are various – national documents, institution-alised examinations, advisers' checklists – but all take the form of an ultimate standard that will indicate the required level of professional development. In this view, teachers pass and fail consistently, on an 'either . . . , or. . .' basis.

Let me suggest that 'failure' is an inappropriate concept here. What we are doing in teacher education is engaging in a creative learning process. The notion of creation does not mean something out of noth-ing: it was not, and suddenly it was. For me, creation is something out of something. Education does not mean a process of $A \longrightarrow B \longrightarrow C \ldots$ N, in which N is the ultimate, and anything short of N is failure. For me education is the creative process of $A < B < C \ldots$ N, in which intermedi-ate stages themselves are nearer approximations to N, the satisfactory state in which values are realised in practice. These intermediate stages are not criteria of success/failure: they are states of being which are a present realisation of the practitioner's struggle to realise her values. The process itself is a journey towards self-fulfilment. The journey itself is the objective, not just the elusive goal at the end.

For me, the function of teacher education is to enable teachers to become aware of their own sense of process. The way to develop this sense of process is through critical reflection on the innovative nature of personal practice. Supporters need constructively to encourage teachers to recognise the moving nature of their own life towards the situation of success in which educational values are realised.

I take the view that we are all equal in terms of our human value. We all develop individual strengths according to our own interests and capabilities. In this book I do not regard learners, teachers and supervi-sors as existing on separate planes. Such categories I view as man-made social categories, which of themselves have nothing to do with personal potentials. For me, the educational enterprise is concerned with the process of the development of individual rationality, not the construc-tion of social status.

What is necessary is that we all, as a community involved in edu-cation, recognise the need to evolve our individual and collective prac-tices through the process of critical reflection. Teacher education, and the educational enterprise as a whole, is not the domination of one will by another, as in our currently favoured 'line management' approach. It is the 'shifting centres' of focus that emerge through the areas of con-cern of caring people: today you and I might focus primarily on mov-

ing forward *my* understanding, but tomorrow we might shift attention to you.

In order to bring about such a community of creative practitioners we need to agree the knowledge base for our practices: and that in itself requires us to identify and agree the values that we share in our lives as teachers.

Chapter 5

Towards an Educational Epistemology of Practice

In this chapter I shall be considering the nature of process as structure. At first sight, process and structure might seem to appear as opposites, like considering movement as static, or stasis as moving. I do not see the ideas as contradictory: rather, in dialectical fashion, I will attempt to show that the notions are complementary and interdependent. I will explain my view that process may become structure, and that structure is inherently mobile and is also part of a wider process: and I will continue to explain that epistemology – the functional ideas base for practice, traditionally associated with process – may become the object of study – a structure; and that educational practice, usually viewed as an object, is inherently developmental and should be regarded as process.

Let me refer to work in related fields to illustrate this: to the idea expressed by Bertanalffy (1952, in Ornstein, 1973), that structure is a process wave of short duration placed on a process wave of long duration: to Stephen Tyler's (1978) concept of language, that it is a means to establishing relations rather than an object consisting of relations; and to Lawrence Stenhouse's (1975) view of education, that it is not an end that contains knowledge about the world (an objectives approach) so much as a means for getting things done in the world (a process approach).

Sharing as a way of life

To make the discussion more explicit, let me draw up an analogue.

I, the individual practitioner, am a preciously unique person. I have my own knowledge about the world which I inhabit with others. I have my own personal knowledge about myself within the world, and I have my values which have been shaped largely through my involvement with others. Because I live in a society I cannot operate alone. I would

be then like a worm-thread cog, which has the potential for movement, but, because nothing sets me off, I am stationary.

Let me recognise another person. This other person, herself a preciously unique person, inhabits the same world. She is an object in the time and space of my world, as I am in hers. We regard ourselves as 'I-It' (Buber, 1937). We are like two worm-thread cogs, existing separately, both with the potential for separate movement, and for corporate movement, but, because nothing sets us off, we are stationary.

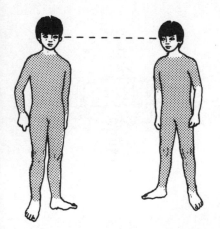
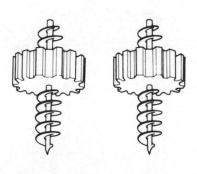

I and the other person, unique that we are, want to get to know each other. We are human, and we are drawn to one another by our need for love. We tentatively formulate a commitment; we touch each other's lives. We hesitate, for commitment is full of hazard. Our wheels move together and interlock. The potential is there: shall we set it in motion?

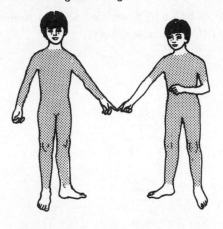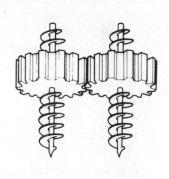

We come togther. We are 'I-You'. We are committed to each other, be it ever so lightly to begin with; and we are open to the possibility that the commitment will grow. Our wheels are turning and spinning. More, by their own separate momentum, they are moving themselves and each other up the worm-threads. They are moving forward into new forms. They are realising their innate potentials as fully operational organisms.

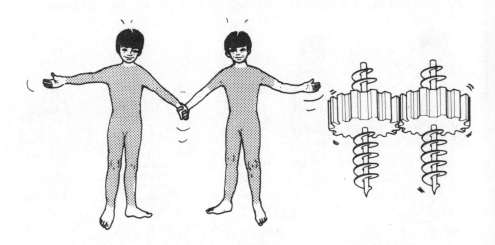

I now need to pause, and temporarily shift to another plane of thought. So far I have described what is happening, with only occasional hints as to why it is happening. In a description, I can use practical heuristics: 'Who? What? Where? When? Which?', and the answers will give me practical information about the current situation.

But if I want explanations for that situation, I need to ask 'Why?' and 'How?' I need reasons for the action.

I will now become a little more fanciful, and let my cogs think. I need to ask, with I and You, 'Why did we come together? How will we continue our commitment? How will we improve our relationship, make it last?' My thinking machine can ask the same questions: 'How is it that we are moving: moreover, why are we moving?'

Let me suggest that I and You, while in no way forfeiting our individuality, have joined together because we want to communicate. It is part of our innate endowment as persons that we need to realise our potential. We are born with the innate potential to speak, to walk, to think – and we naturally do these things, as persons. Our cogs are made with the specific innate potential, as cogs, to function as cogs, and they do.

The answers to 'What? Where? When? Who? Which?' give us descriptions of practice. Traditionally, descriptions are seen as structures – the thing as it is, the state of the art. I and You can describe our relationship. Our machine can describe itself as moving. But we need to look at the answers that explain the process: the reasons for the actions. 'How?' and 'Why?' are questions about the epistemology: 'What is the knowledge base for the action? What are the states of mind behind the behaviour? What is the vision that causes I and You to engage in communication?'

Let us stay for a moment with the cogs. By engaging in corporate independent activity – cog-communication – they are moving themselves and each other forward. They are making progress. This is the action of cogs who are realising their full potential as cogs. What, though, is the nature of the driving force that enabled them to set themselves into motion? In my fancy, I can say that it was the *desire* to realise their full potential that urged them to go, their cog-sense of vision that they would move forward to the very top level of their existence – to the utmost form of their being.

To return to I and You, I can ask, 'What caused us to come together? What is the nature of our interpersonal dynamic?' I can answer that the driving force – loosely translated as the epistemology, or knowledge base – that made us join forces, was the human personal desire to share. I as an individual have to live out my life as a creative entity by engaging fully in the kind of life of which I am capable: I am forced to realise my full potential, just as surely as I have to eat and drink. But I can realise that full potential only through you. I have to accept you, and commit myself to you, in order to understand me; and you have to do the same.

Epistemology and practice

The purpose of my science fiction about cog wheels is to illustrate the need to consider reasons for action as much as the actions themselves. The current literature of educational theory emphasises the need to describe actions, but fails to give importance to the reasons. I have said in Part I that I-enquiries may qualify as educational, because they inevitably involve giving the reasons; and 'educational' in this book means the process of moving the development of understanding forward. So I am saying that an educational enquiry will focus on the epistemology – the reason for the driving force – as much as the practice. Further, it may focus on the epistemology *as* practice: and this is where I will refer to the introduction to this chapter, that structure and process are interdependent.

In Part I, I indicated my view of the nature of educational research as a process of iterative (or recursive) processes. It is means and end, in that the process of the research becomes the practice that is under investigation. What, though, of educational *practices*, the actions within pedagogical settings which are the locations of the research? This is another matter altogether, and one which has traditionally been approached either through the social sciences (e.g., Young, 1971), or ignored altogether. In my view it is probably the most urgent charge on the educational enterprise altogether, but one of the most difficult to tackle.

I would suggest that much teaching – and this includes the professional development of teachers – is a case of 'Do as I say' rather than 'Do as I do'. I believe that it is essential for teachers to be encouraged to make explicit their knowledge base – their educational values – to justify both what they are hoping to achieve for their learners and for themselves. If I want to help my learners to appreciate what a just society is, I must make the learning situation itself a just society. I must act in accordance with the values that I am attempting to communicate to my learners.

Let us return to I and You. I have said that the driving force that enables us to make contact is our need to share our own personal knowledge. In the terms I expressed in Chapter 1, I may say that we are turning our respective competences into a shared form of performance.

In talking about practice, or intentional actions, I need to characterise the nature of those practices that are a realisation of our values as sharing individuals, persons who are intentionally engaging in a com-

municative form of life. How will we ensure that communication will continue? What is the nature of the values that underpin our practices?

The person who has probably done most to characterise the nature of communication is Jürgen Habermas. He has identified four separate criteria that are essential for effective communication: that I am sincere in what I say, that what I say is comprehensible, that it is true, and that I have chosen an appropriate situation in which to say it (Habermas, 1979). Effective comprehension is based on and reflects our *intention* to share. Our intentions are the trigger that turn our values into actions: in my formulation of Part I, my values at the level of competence are transformed into the action of performance through the transformatory nature of my intentions.

Let me relate this to the need, as I see it, for the explicit articulation of an educational epistemology of practice. I have characterised education as the process of the development of an individual's rationality, and I have defined educational practices as those which encourage that process. An educational epistemology of practice is one which allows teachers to undertake an enquiry that is focused on the development of personal understanding with a view to engaging others in the development of their personal understanding. The 'aim' and the 'process' here are the same. Teaching and learning are two sides of the same coin; they are two perspectives of the same process. The process of practice becomes the object of the enquiry; practice becomes enquiry. The practice of teaching others becomes the process of learning about oneself. The process of learning about oneself becomes the object of the research.

I am saying that we need to see research as practice, and that pedagogic practice should be viewed as a constant process of enquiry. If we view teaching in this light, it is no longer an activity geared toward passing on information; it becomes a shared communicative exercise which is focused on generating intersubjective agreements about the nature of being.

Towards an epistemology of love

I will take my argument a final step further. First I will review here some of the formulations that I have put forward.

I have said that intentional action is often a living out of personal values. Educational practices constitute a certain way of life, in itself often a living out of educational values. I have said that communicative action is

based on our desire to share, and that an educational epistemology of practice will result in pedagogical actions that lead to a development of the personal potential of all parties in the enterprise. I have said that recommendations in the current literature approach the improvement of practice as a social exercise: I have indicated my view of the need for the improvement of practice as a personal exercise. An improvement of personal understanding will lead to an improvement of social situations. Instead of approaching educational research through the social sciences, I prefer to approach it through the reconstructive sciences: that is, making explicit what is implicit.

I need to highlight now the pivotal aspect of the educational process, and that is the transformative nature of our intentions. I believe that if we want something badly enough, and care enough and work hard enough, we usually will get it. It is our intentionality that is at the base, that can transform our potential into actuality.

What is at the foundation of our intentional educational practice is love – that is, care, understanding, commitment. In my desire to realise my own potential I treat myself with care; in my desire to help others to realise their potential, I treat them in the same way. My intentions are those of best interest; my aim is the best interest of those in my care. My educational practices blend and merge with my social practices. Mine is an educational epistemology of practice which is based on a personal epistemology of love.

I will return to these ideas in Part V. For now, let me close with an articulation of the need for love to shine through everything we do; that we require our learners to do as we do, and ourselves to do as we say, in the best interests of us all.

PART III I ACT IN THE DIRECTION OF THE SOLUTION

Chapter 6
The Answer of Avon

There are a number of developing and on-going initiatives across the country that are taking practitioner-centred research as the basis for schemes for professional development.

The foundation for the adoption of this approach as a policy framework is that professional development is the responsibility of individual practitioners, who will then aim to share their collective practices in order to build communities of critical practitioners. The emphasis is initially on the improvement of individual practice – the nature of this improvement being the realisation of educational values in practice – with a view to bringing about improvement at a community level, in which shared educational values are realised in institutionalised practices.

I am currently involved in several such initiatives, and in this section I want to outline how some institutions at local and regional level are implementing their responses to their perceived problems.

This section focuses on work going on in Avon. I am in touch with this work because of my association with the University of Bath. There is much work going on elsewhere, such as in Nottingham, and some in Dorset (see Part IV).

Implementation presupposes concurrent evaluation: as I do something, I am already considering if it is worthwhile; and the processes of my action and evaluation fuse. At a notional level of abstraction they maybe seen as separate; but, in reality, my actions are in a constant process of modification because I am always considering what I am doing and acting upon that consideration, from one moment to the next. The reports that follow include this aspect of 'reflection on action in action'.

Three separate reports constitute the chapters in Part III. In this Chapter I outline the planning involved in a large-scale initiative. In Chapter 7 I present a report by Terry Hewitt, who is committed to establishing action research as a strategy for professional development across a group of schools. In Chapter 8 Kevin Eames reports how he moved from being a lone action researcher to involving his whole school. I have used this presentation of narrowing the focus to show how action research may be used as a device that generates shared educational practices, in that it may focus on the one and the many at the same time, engaging individuals in their own and each others' best interests.

The first report presented in this chapter is part of an Avon policy statement. It represents the adopted county ethic that individual practitioners should engage in their own enquiries into their educational practices, and it also reflects the ethic of engaging in dialogue in order to bring about a community framework of care and best interest. The production of this document signals an outcome of a long process of negotiation and shared understandings.

I am grateful to Avon Local Education Authority for permission to reprint extracts from this report.

Supporting your professional development

This pamphlet explains some of the changes in professional development which are planned to ensure that the classroom teacher's contribution to education in Avon is fully recognised and valued.

1   How do I get time to think about my teaching and plan what I need to do next?

In future the majority of LEA-provided INSET will be directly linked to what goes on in your school and classroom. On a typical in-service programme you will spend two or three days away from school, accompanied whenever possible by a colleague from the same school. You will be given the opportunity to reflect on your teaching and to identify the areas you want to develop. You will receive support in working out a plan to try out your ideas back in your school and classroom. Time for you to work with your colleagues to carry out your plans and record the results will be provided in the school. After a period of time you will get together again with members of your initial group for another day away from school. On this day you will review your progress, exchange experiences and make further plans for development. This process forms part of an action-research approach to professional development.

2   How do I get recognition for my school-based professional development?

In future all teachers will receive recognition for their development activities through a personal professional record of achievement to be known as *The Avon Professional Portfolio*. Teachers will be able to use their Professional Portfolio as they wish. In addition you will be able to submit your action-research development work for accreditation by Higher Education. The work you do can then count towards Higher Degree, Diploma and Certificate awards.

3   Where does the non-contact time come from?

FINANCE

A greater proportion of staff development funds will be given to schools to manage. This money can be used to increase the school's staffing. In this way the non-pupil contact time for school-based development activities will be made available. The school's staff development budget can be used to cover any course fees, travelling and subsistence expenses. It can also be used to fund the support of external providers and training.

PLANNING

During the Summer Term, Headteachers and Staff Development Co-ordinators will be involving you in discussion about the school's development priorities and how those priorities will be achieved using the funding you have available.

Your school will then produce a Staff Development Action Plan describing how your school's allocation of staff development funding will be used to meet development needs during the coming year. This Action Plan will aim to make the best use of all the available resources – the non-contact days, directed time, enhanced staffing and staff development funds.

PROGRAMMES

The LEA will provide your school with a full year Professional Development Opportunities programme at the beginning of the Summer Term. This will allow your school to plan development a full year ahead.

4   What support do I get in developing my classroom practice?

LEA SUPPORT

Teachers involved in the process of action-research in their schools and classrooms will receive support from specialist LEA staff working in curriculum and sector teams. These staff will be available to support teachers who are following a negotiated plan which is worked out with participants and would form the basis of a 'contract' for development.

IN-SCHOOL SUPPORT

Within school you will be asked to help to identify and nominate a colleague who can act as a Staff Development Tutor.

The Staff Development Tutor's role will be to help you and your colleagues to decide which aspects of your teaching you wish to develop through action research. They will also support you in carrying out your classroom focused development.

Staff Development Tutors will need to be given non-contact time to carry out their role. The time they need can be funded through the school's staff development budget. They will also be provided with training opportunities to help them to develop the skills and understandings required to support development in your school.

HOW DO WE CHOOSE OUR STAFF DEVELOPMENT TUTOR?

In order to be effective, Staff Development Tutors need to be readily accepted by their colleagues as equal partners. They need to be able to work alongside teachers in an open and supportive way. It is suggested that the staff of the school decide amongst themselves how to identify and nominate a Staff Development Tutor, bearing in mind what the role entails. It is also important that Schools leave themselves room to review their nomination process in the light of experience.

5   What about the specialist support I will need?

The LEA does not intend to remove or reduce support for specialist areas. The LEA programme will still contain opportunities to work on specific curriculum issues in order to develop your expertise. The aim in the future is to help you to implement your developing specialist expertise in your own school and classroom. Specialist curriculum programmes will therefore use the action-research approach as part of the process of development.

6   What about my own personal professional development needs?

It may well be that your personal professional development needs are not the same as your school's development priorities. If this is the case then you will be able to apply for central funding to support what you want to do. A special budget will be held centrally for those who are unable to get the support they need from their school's budget. This budget will be 'cash limited'. You will be informed of how and when to apply for support in the next few months.

7   Why are these changes being made?

All of these changes are intended to enable you, the classroom teacher, to have more control over your professional development and to make sure that the development work you undertake is of clear benefit to you and your pupils.

Chapter 7
Action Research for Groups of Schools

The second report is written by Terry Hewitt, co-ordinator for Avon's STRICT (Supporting Teachers' Research into Classroom Teaching) programme. This programme ran from 1986–90, and is now subsumed under the general Avon professional development scheme, as outlined above. The report shows how a group of schools implemented action research as a foundation for professional development, and the dialogical nature of its evolution. The report also indicates the importance of on-going and concurrent evaluation as a focal part of the action strategy, and the importance that Terry places on having his own practice seen as a form of enquiry in action.

How can I provide evidence to support my claim that my work is helping to improve the quality of education for pupils in the classroom?

Supporting Teachers' Research Into Classroom Teaching is a programme of in-service support in Avon which has aimed to encourage a collaborative approach to professional development. In its title we see an emphasis on: support for teachers, teachers as researchers, a classroom focus. Teachers carry out classroom based research into a concern that they have about their teaching strategies and course delivery using a systematic form of action enquiry which traces the following route:

Stage 1   Discuss your concern. What are you wanting to improve?
Stage 2   Decide on a strategy for change and improvement.
Stage 3   Put the strategy into effect – act!
Stage 4   Evaluate the outcomes of your action.
Stage 5   Modify your statement of concern in the light of the evaluation.

Repeat the cycle from Stage 2.
Write a report at the end of the year.

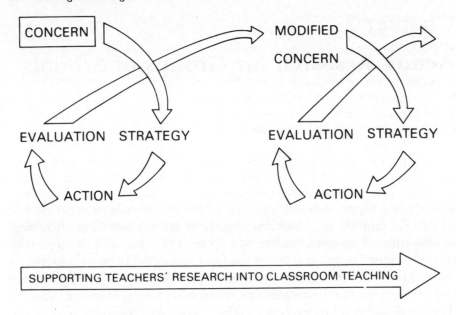

```
CONCERN ─────────────────→ MODIFIED
                            CONCERN
        EVALUATION  STRATEGY        EVALUATION  STRATEGY
              ACTION                      ACTION
```

SUPPORTING TEACHERS' RESEARCH INTO CLASSROOM TEACHING

The acronym STRICT is intended to highlight the rigour which collaborative action research demands as teachers seek to provide answers to the question:

> "What evidence can you provide to support your claim that your work has improved the quality of education for the pupils in your classroom?"

School based work combined with attendance at workshops and dialogue between teacher colleagues and professional supporters from outside the school are the main elements of a process which is characterised by its impact on pupils. Pupils in 18 secondary schools and 1 primary school in Avon have worked with their teachers on issues such as:

- What precisely happens in the first twenty minutes of a lesson?
- Are active and experiential learning strategies improving the quality of students' learning?
- Introducing electronics into the third-year modular CDT course.
- How effective are teaching techniques in the first year?
- Is it possible through English lessons to enable students to appreciate the value of oral discussion as a means of learning?
- Alleviating stress arising from GCSE coursework demands.

The two teachers from local secondary schools who have acted as part time co-ordinators of this programme have found it useful to offer support including:

- A series of workshop days at Teachers' Centres to work on research, reflect on progress and plan each stage;
- Supply time to facilitate meetings of colleagues, mutual classroom observation and discussions with learners;
- Access to the expertise of a support team including consultants from H.E.;
- Collaboration with other teacher researchers;
- Technical and other support in classroom observation techniques;
- Assistance with the critical evaluation of evidence.

Teachers clearly appreciate having time in their own classroom to pursue their own research, and one wrote 'This form of research would be impossible without it'. The workshop sessions have been described as 'Vital – otherwise research would have slipped off our list of priorities. We also gained space and time away from school'. One teacher saw them as 'very useful opportunities to interact with teachers from other schools and subject areas'. These meetings may become less important as teacher groups form within schools, and the main problem appears to be the tendency for teachers to feel guilty about leaving classes with a supply teacher, a fact highlighted by the teacher who wrote: "It is difficult to reconcile the idea of leaving your classroom with a supply teacher so as to improve the quality of pupils' learning!!"

The part played in action research by written reports has been the focus of some debate recently, and it may be worth spending some time considering the emphasis which the STRICT support team has placed on the written reports. These reports are not intended to be polished research documents. They are the working papers of classroom-based research in action. They are written for two purposes:

- to help the process of reflection;
- to provide a permanent record and means of dissemination.

Over the past four years the 'permanent record' has proved a useful resource to colleagues. It has also been an effective means of dissemination within the LEA and beyond. But it is the part which writing plays in helping the process of reflection which is more significant. Evidence to support this view comes through hints contained in comments such as that made by one of the teachers: 'getting one's thoughts on paper helped crystallise ideas concerning future actions or initiatives'. More powerful was the comment made by one of the teachers involved in 1987 who wrote in an evaluation of the part played by the workshop sessions, where one aim was to 'help develop self criticism in the secure environment of a sympathetic but challenging group':

> "The workshops have actually developed a self-critical climate, but it was more the preparation and writing of the report which developed our self-criticism."

Significant this year was the way in which participants built on previous experience and integrated pupils' work into the text of their reports. It is no longer appropriate (if it ever was) to relegate pupils' work to the separately bound appendices of earlier

phases. The styles range from the highly structured formal report to the more informal 'user friendly' account; they are all characterised by their quality. They are also characterised by the attempt to cope with the demands of a support team who wrote in July 1986: "If we are successful in developing this form of in-service support we would expect to be able to show that we had been of some assistance in helping you to improve the quality of education with your pupils".

Techniques used in the collection of evidence to support these claims have included:

- Examination of pupils' work
- Observation of pupils
- Mutual observation by teachers
- Questionnaires to pupils
- Questionnaires to teachers
- Video tapes of lessons
- Diaries
- Written accounts
- Photographs
- Audiotapes of interviews
- Case studies

Traditional educational research has tended to measure the easily measured and report the easily reported. In Avon we see teachers 'measuring' improvements in the quality of pupils' learning and reporting the sights, sounds and feelings of their shared experience through the necessarily limited medium of the printed page. We are unable to include the taped recordings of pupils' interviews or the video tapes of lessons, but we hope that the reports of our 'systematic enquires made public' (Stenhouse, 1983) made a contribution to the growing body of knowledge of the ways in which teachers may communicate their work to a wider audience. Incidentally, we may meet the challenge of Ebbutt (1983) that 'If action research is to be considered legitimately as research, the participants in it must . . . be prepared to produce written reports of their activities.' As the drafts are critiqued by the group as critical friends we may also satisfy Hopkins (1985) who has stressed the importance of reports being open to critique by other teacher researchers. Distribution within the LEA leads, hopefully, to a public critique and the 'discourse among teachers which is research oriented and committed to action and the improvement of practice' which we join Hopkins in encouraging.

The experience of the last four years has made me feel reasonably secure in the belief that through LEA support the action research teachers will be able to provide evidence to support their claims to have helped improve the quality of learning in the classroom. I am confident that teachers will respond imaginatively and creatively and that such evidence will take a variety of forms. As a member of the support team I see in these most recent reports evidence of the success of our involvement in this form of in-service support. This leads me to have some confidence that those who are one step removed from the main focus of action may also be able to provide evidence that

stands up to critique to support the claim that their work has been of some assistance in helping to improve the quality of education for the pupils in the classroom. It may, therefore, be appropriate that this is the last collection of case studies presented under the banner STRICT as the LEA moves into a dramatic expansion of an action-research approach to professional development.

Section 9 of the Local Authority Training Grants Scheme 1990-1 – Joint Report of the Director of Education and County Treasurer of the County of Avon – opens: "It is proposed that staff development provision be improved to support teachers carrying out action research in their own schools and classrooms". Action research is subsequently described as a way of developing classroom practice which leads to staff development having a greater impact on students' learning experiences. A booklet for teachers – 'You and your professional development' [see Chapter 6] – refers to changes which are planned.

In the majority of LEA provided INSET teachers will be encouraged to undertake classroom focused action research, supported in school by a colleague who will act as a Staff Development Tutor. The teacher and the Staff Development Tutor will receive LEA support from an Advisory teacher who will assume the role of Sector Consultant working with primary, secondary and special schools in a geographical sector. The likely impact of this shift in emphasis in uncertain and the extent to which action research on the scale envisaged can be supported is untried. I have to confess to one or two concerns. The first is that if others are persuaded by my assertion that writing is a crucial element in the process of action research, the LEA is likely to be confronted with a significant problem in what to do with pieces of reflective writing from 12,000 teachers. Libraries? Databases? Journals? Newsletters? What happens to non-written material? How do we access video/audiotape? There are a few storage/retrieval issues to be resolved!

My main concern, however, is that the further one moves away from the pupil in the classroom the more difficult it is to provide "evidence that my work is helping to improve the quality of education for pupils in the classroom" [see also Chapter 10]. I do not doubt that the teacher will be able to provide 'evidence', possibly as we have done by developing the written reports of teachers. I suspect, however, that the Sector Consultant will find the search for "evidence that my work is helping" far more difficult. I do not know what this evidence may look like, how it may be presented or how it will be validated. It is this question that I would like to explore.

There is a growing body of evidence to support claims that classroom based research has a significant contribution to make to improving the quality of childrens' learning. Ultimately, however, I am sure that many of us agree with Hopkins' (1985) view that "It is the sharing of our experiences and the social and intellectual benefits that emanate from it, not the meeting of some abstract academic criteria, that provide the logic for publication and critique in classroom research". Lomax and McNiff (1989) have suggested that teacher researchers "use writing in a creative way as part of creating knowledge and publish it so that others can share in the process and not just in the end result". This paper represents one individual's attempt to share with others the process of developing an action research approach to professional

development in Avon. I hope that it may be possible to use it as a basis for discussion among teachers and other groups addressing the question: How can I provide evidence to support my claim that my work is helping to improve the quality of education for pupils in the classroom?

Chapter 8

Whole-School Development

This chapter is written by Kevin Eames, Head of English at Wootton Bassett School, Wiltshire. In it he analyses his own development as an action researcher, while encouraging the professional development of his colleagues.

Growing your own
Supporting the development of action researchers within an action-research approach to whole-school development

WHAT IS THIS PAPER ABOUT?

It's an attempt to illustrate, for teachers who may be new to action research, how I became an action researcher over the past few years. I hope that my experiences will provide some short cuts for those who are setting out on the same path – and their number will grow strongly, I think, owing to the commitment of LEAs like Avon to action research, especially in the light of the Department of Education and Science's 'Planning for School Development' (December 1989), which suggests an action-research approach to school development plans, and their evaluation. The focus in the paper is primarily upon myself, because action research demands that the researcher should examine his own practice and educational development, rather than anyone else's.

WHY BOTHER?

Because I think that action research is of immense importance to the professionality of teachers. It's a form of knowledge produced by teachers, and primarily aimed at communicating with teachers, and at being used by teachers. Although it's 'home-grown', it also satisfies legitimate demands for accountability, since it constitutes a demonstration that teachers are evaluating and improving their classroom practice in a methodical and rigorous manner.

BECOMING AN ACTION RESEARCHER

Although all teachers are potentially action researchers (and I think I was one for a long time without realising it) action research as a methodical, professional approach

to developing and evaluating classroom practice doesn't just happen of its own accord; it must be supported by the structures and personnel of each institution and of the local authority, and each teacher involved must do it, and talk about it, if he or she is to understand the power of the form, and the possibilities for its use. In the following account, I hope that the ways in which my own development as an action researcher were supported will become apparent.

Stage One: Learning about Learning

Ten years ago, as a newly-appointed head of English in a large comprehensive school on the outskirts of Swindon, I became involved in the 'Learning about Learning' project, organised by Pat D'Arcy, the Wiltshire English adviser. This was a cross-curricular, cross-phase initiative which brought together teachers from all over the country for a series of meetings where they would teach a characteristic lesson from their own specialist area to the rest of the group. The discussion and writing which followed each presentation focused on the reactions of the other teachers as learners: how did they respond? What difficulties did they have as learners? How might learning be clarified and made easier?

By trying to understand their own learning processes, the teachers on the project were encouraged to develop and share classroom strategies for supporting learning. This exploration of classroom practice was further encouraged by a residential 'summer institute', in which members of the project worked together for a week or so with teachers from a neighbouring county. The residential institutes were backed up by writing weekends, which gave participants the chance to write about and discuss accounts of their own classroom strategies for improving learning, as well as sharing the writings of other teachers and academics; where possible, the accounts were published by Wiltshire County Council as booklets in the 'Learning about Learning' series, and have proved interesting to those teachers who have come across them, if my own experience is reliable, in that the accounts of practice given in the booklets have suggested strategies to adapt and try out in the classroom. The booklets have also been noted in the more academic press[1], and have been used by teachers as far afield as West Germany, Hong Kong and California; they have proved an effective method of sharing practice.

How did this stage move me towards being an action researcher, though? It did so in the following ways, I think:

- I reflected on my own learning processes, and tried to apply my growing understanding to improving my classroom practice.
- I tried to use the theoretical insights of academic writers[2] to help me understand what was happening in my own classroom practice.
- I began to realise the power of teachers working and talking collaboratively to help each other develop their own classroom practice.
- I wrote accounts of my own classroom practice, and read the accounts of other teachers. Through this, I came to see the importance of defining my own under-

standing in writing, and of learning from the writing of other teachers and writers about education.

I wasn't yet an action-researcher, although I was moving in that direction. I was giving accounts of my classroom practice, trying to explain why the things I did worked (or not), and these accounts were available to be discussed and adapted by other teachers. However, there were a number of elements missing, which I want to deal with in the next section. I must emphasise, though, the role of the English adviser and the opportunities she provided for collaboration, exploration, discussion, and publication. Without such practical and firm support, I wouldn't even have got this far.

Stage Two: Bath University

As a development from the 'Learning about Learning' project, a group of participants was encouraged by the Wiltshire English adviser to submit proposals to Bath University for research leading to an M. Phil. degree. I was one of the two teachers who actually went through with the application, and it was through the research that I did at Bath, and through the support and advice of Pat D'Arcy, Andy Larter (my fellow researcher from the 'Learning about Learning' group), and Jack Whitehead, that I gradually made the transition to being an action researcher.

My first two research reports were along the lines of my booklets in the 'Learning about Learning' series. They were narrative, descriptive, and focused in detail on the learning of one pupil. They tried to integrate a discussion of academic theory with my developing perceptions of what was happening in my own classroom.

It wasn't until I had presented my second report to a validation group meeting, that I understood what was lacking. Fundamentally, I needed to clarify why I was taking the actions that I did. Teaching is a value-laden activity, and we take action to improve our classroom practice, when we see that what is happening doesn't fit in with what we want to happen. In my case, I was teaching in a school which, at that time, was very transmission-oriented. Pupils were like so many little vessels to be filled with knowledge by their teachers. I wanted to give them more control over their writing than the dominant learning climate allowed, since I held autonomy in learning to be an important aim of education, and I felt that pupils would learn more effectively if they were allowed greater control over decisions affecting their writing. As a result of my increased understanding, which came about through discussions with Pat D'Arcy, Jack Whitehead, Andy Larter, and others, my next two reports used the five-part action-reflection cycle, and took the following form:

- a specific description of the problems I had identified, where what was happening didn't correspond to what I wanted to happen;
- a description of a possible solution (or solutions) to the problems identified;
- an account of what happened when I tried to put my solution(s) into action;
- an evaluation of how successful my solution(s) has been, in the light of the evidence I had collected;

- a modification of my understanding as a result of this process, and a restatement of my ideas and actions to enable me to continue the process of improving my practice.

I learned from this stage that:

- the five-part cycle help me to maintain the detailed case-study element of my research, while giving shape and clarity to the context-rich data which emerge from classroom action and reflection;
- the five-part cycle, as part of its form, made it necessary for me to clarify my developing understanding of what I was doing and why I was doing it;
- the cycle, as part of its form, made it necessary to take action in order to improve my teaching, and to redefine and replan problems, solutions and actions in the light of the action taken.

Thus, I realised how the form could have a direct effect on my classroom, and could lead to a continual and methodical process of improving practice and understanding. Again, though, I could not have reached this point on my own; the support of the local authority was essential in terms of funding for fees and remitted time; the English adviser was continually supportive in terms of positive criticism of the work I was doing; the university gave support through Jack Whitehead's attempts to get me to see how I might present my research using the five-part cycle; Andy Larter provided me with an example of an action-researcher who got there well before I did, and showed me how to do it.

Stage Three: The School Research Group

Once I had grasped the power of the five-part cycle of action and reflection, I was able to begin supporting other researchers. After a break following my M.Phil., I had started some further research at Bath University, and I became aware that there were other teachers in the school who were also involved in research at the university. Four of us formed the nucleus of a research group, which was intended to provide mutual support by circulating relevant reading material and through meetings to discuss drafts and future directions.

The others, apart from myself, were the deputy head, who was writing a dissertation as part of his M. Ed. studies; a teacher from the design faculty who was carrying out an M.Phil. by action research, and a teacher from the English faculty, who was working as part of a cross-phase group towards an Advanced Diploma in Educational Studies at Bath University. Jack Whitehead was the superviser for both Paul Hayward, the design teacher, and Daniela De Cet, the English teacher. He also gave his time willingly to advise Chris Kirkland, the deputy head. The kind of work produced by the group is illustrated by publications such as 'How can we improve professionalism in education through collaborative action research?'[3]

I learned from this stage that:

- a group of researchers in a school could support each other effectively;
- this mutual support created a climate in which members of the group felt able to discuss their research and their teaching openly and honestly;
- the presence of an experienced action researcher was valuable, since I could advise on problems similar to those I had already encountered myself.

We were supported by:

- the English Adviser, who provided supply cover for Daniela on an occasional basis so that she could attend meetings at the university, or spend some time writing up research reports;
- the local authority, who provided help with fees and remitted time for the other three members of the group;
- the university, through Jack Whitehead;
- the recently-appointed headmaster of Wootton Bassett School, who was strongly supportive of the individual and collaborative work done in the group.

Stage Four: Action research in the English faculty

If action research is to do the things I claimed for it earlier in the paper, it's got to be more than just a way of working for a few privileged academic researchers. In June and July 1989, therefore, the English faculty tried using an action-research approach to evaluating its policy on reviewing and profiling, taking advantage of the time created by the departure of our examination groups. (Each teacher was kept free of exam investigation for four consecutive forty-five minute periods, to help with writing his/her report.)

We produced a case-study, based on our evaluaton, which was presented at a one-day conference on action research attended by Wootton Bassett School's heads of faculties and senior management. In the case-study, I tried to demonstrate how our evaluation worked, using an action-planner which the conference was considering.

The evaluation demonstrates, I think, the five-part cycle in action:

- We had a concern (to find out how our policy was working) which we wanted to investigate.
- We worked out a way of doing it, by clarifying once more the principles and intentions of our policy. At the same time, we decided how we were going to collect the information.
- We took action by looking at pupils' written work and their review sheets, and by carrying out interviews.
- We wrote our reports and reflected on what we had learnt about the operation of our policy.
- We planned changes to our practice which we felt were needed to bring it into line with our principles and intentions.

I learned from this stage that:

- action research was useful in clarifying our ideas about what we were doing, and by following the five-part cycle we were able to plan and carry out improvements in our practice;
- it was collaborative, and involved the whole faculty;
- time needed to be made available for teachers to write their reports, as you can't ask teachers to do it on top of all the work they have to do normally.

The headmaster was fully supportive of what we were trying to do, and all members of the faculty found it a worthwhile exercise.

Stage Five: Action research in the whole school

As a result of the experience gained in the first four stages described above, the headmaster decided that an action-research approach to implementing and evaluating the National Curriculum would best serve our purposes. This decision was reinforced by the publication of 'Planning for school development' (DES, December, 1989).

So far, the following steps and decisions have been taken:

- A one-day conference for heads of faculties and senior management was held in Feb. 1990, to discuss the principles of action research, and the experiences of the research group and the English faculty; to formulate preliminary concerns for investigation by faculties; to consider practical ways of making action-research work as a normal part of curriculum development and evaluation.
- The research group is being enlarged. One member of each faculty will receive 0.05 FTE remitted time per week to work as the faculty's 'designated researcher'. He/she will investigate his/her own practice within contexts decided by the faculty as a whole, using the five-part action reflection cycle. He/she will be registered at Bath University for an advanced diploma, with fees paid by the LEA, and will contribute his/her growing experience of action research to the faculty's understanding and practice as a whole.
- The present system for curriculum development, consisting of standing committees and development groups, is to be dismantled. Co-ordinators for each area (e.g., information technology, assessment, active learning) will have 0.1 FTE remitted time per week to work with faculties, to plan and review action reflection cycles with them.
- Two of the five teacher-development days per year are to be given over to producing and discussing action-research accounts of practice within faculties.
- Time needs to be found to enable teachers who are not members of the research group to examine aspects of their practice using the five-part action reflection cycle. This will come from a combination of teacher-development days; individual supply days built into each faculty's allocation; time freed by examination classes leaving; curriculum co-ordinators and/or 'designated researchers' taking over individual teachers' timetables for a morning or an afternoon.

At this stage, support from the headmaster is fundamental; nothing can move without it. The LEA is also providing financial support, and Bath University will support members of the research group. Teachers will be able to support each other, though, in these first steps towards making real the collaborative, methodical professionalism that teaching needs.

Conclusion

I hope that this account of my own development as an action researcher has clarified some possible methods of supporting and encouraging action research within schools. Ways need to be found to enable teachers to use the five-part action reflection cycle; to circulate and use the accounts produced; to work collaboratively; to be aware of, and use within their practice, already published educational theory. If we can do it, we will have evolved a powerful form for improving and understanding our practice, which will have immense significance for the professionality of all teachers, not just the ones in our own schools.

NOTES

1   For example, in references in Martin, N., *Mostly about writing* (Heinemann, 1983) and Protherough, R., *Encouraging writing* (Methuen, 1983).
2   For example, the work of James Britton, Frank Smith, Donald Graves, Donald Murray, Nancy Martin, Janet Emig, Ann Berthoff, etc.
3   Eames, K. (ed.) 'How can we improve professionalism in education through collaborative action research?', Bassett Action Research Group, Wootton Bassett School, Swindon, Wilts.

And . . .

I met Margaret Hine, a teacher in a school in Bristol, who told about her delightful approach to introducing Action Research to colleagues. Here is her strategy.

When I was asked to be a Staff Development Tutor and realised that this meant talking to colleagues about improving practice through action research, I was anxious not to present this in a negative way. I didn't want staff to start feeling inadequate, when so many new ideas are already taxing their time, energy and confidence.

So I searched for a positive way to introduce the idea of staff development, and came up with the vision of our 'classroom' as a beautiful garden. As we look at that garden, it is not in any way displeasing, but there are always things which could be added to make it even more beautiful. I introduced the idea of planting a magnolia tree in the middle of the lawn. We therefore began with the premise, 'I want to improve my garden', and went on to ask the questions:

1　What is there already?
　　(A beautiful garden with a big lawn)
2　How can I make it better?
　　(Buy a magnolia tree)
3　Who or what can help me?
　　(Garden Centres, gardening books, tools, etc.)
4　Am I happy with the results?

We then looked at this in action research terms as:

1　Reflection
2　Planning
3　Action, and
4　Evaluation

The allegory was well received and I had some positive and enthusiastic reactions from staff members wanting to 'improve their garden'.

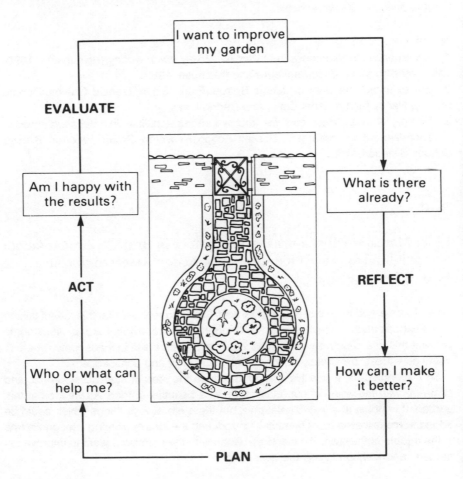

PART IV I EVALUATE THE IMAGINED SOLUTIONS

Chapter 9

Evaluating Practice

In April 1990 I, along with some twenty colleagues, was invited to become a field tutor within the modular Bachelors and Masters degree programmes organised by Dorset LEA and Portsmouth Polytechnic. Several of the modules would be Practitioner Based Enquiry (PBE), in which individual teachers would follow through a particular educational interest, supported by the field tutor, with a view to producing a written report to contribute towards accreditation.

For some months now I have been working with six teachers on a one-to-one basis, and I have also arranged for them to meet as a group. These meetings have become support sessions, with colleagues helping each other decide on how best to take their enquiries forward. The teachers also act as validators of each other's claims about the improvements they believe they are bringing about in their practice.

My role varies according to expressed need. I offer a point of information or clarification; or suggest a different focus to a colleague's thinking; or draw out critical points from the discussion and reflect them back.

From the beginning, I decided to turn my work into a research project and I started keeping records of my own practice as a supporter.

My practice needs to be evaluated, as much as my colleagues need to evaluate theirs. The processes of those evaluations need to be made public, and the claims that we are making (that we have improved the quality of education for ourselves and for our clients) also need public substantiation.

I have undertaken in-service support in a number of forms over the years, often in a transmission mode. I have sometimes been left with a

vague feeling of emptiness, that my work has not significantly contributed to a deep understanding of the nature of improvement, either for
myself or for the people I have been helping. I believe I have contributed to an improvement of educational situations, in terms of management and pedagogy; but I have never before been so intensely concerned to reach the people with whom I have been working, really to
strive to establish a rich empathic relationship.

My colleagues and I held a validation meeting in July 1990. My four
colleagues are:

Beth, a teacher of religious education, and personal and social education, in a secondary school. Beth is also head of year.

Liz, a newly appointed head teacher of an infants' school.

Dee, a newly appointed head teacher of a junior school.

Susan, a teacher who has been working with hearing-impaired children,
and who has now left teaching to follow her own inclinations. She wants
to take up some form of educational research.

Our conversation falls into two parts. In the first part, which constitutes this chapter, we concentrate on evaluating our practices. We take
as a base line the issue of whether we have improved the quality of education within our immediate locations. In the second part, which constitutes Chapter 10, we focus on an evaluation of support, both in terms
of my support to them, and of their support to colleagues in school and
to each other within our research project. In Chapter 11 I record the
transcript of the conversation I had with two Staff Development Officers (also field tutors), which looks at the fundamental values which
guide us as teachers, and how and why these values are being realised
through this form of teacher-education provision.

We pick up the conversation where we are discussing the notion of
evaluation, and the popular view that it is to do with measurement, a
characterisation which we feel is inappropriate to the ideas which our
research is generating.

Jean   Dee has been saying that, as part of her action plan – you used
the word 'measure', and said it was inappropriate.

Dee   I am looking at the change that has happened within school as a
result – may be or not – of what I have changed myself. I wanted to
change my practice in order to achieve certain things. I now want

somehow to 'measure' the success of the change in my own practice by what has actually happened within my school.

Beth Would 'prove' be a better word? For example, I know what I've done, the mistakes I've made, and how, if I were doing it again, what I would do differently. I also know what I want to go on to do next. This seems to me to be the next logical step; I know what I've done, but I've now got to show it.

Jean How are you going to show it?

Beth In the piece of written work I'm going to do, where I shall be referring to the bits of evidence I have collected along the way. For example, the videos to show classroom practices. I've got the journals of the pupils, which we kept week by week. I've got my journal.

Jean Can you actually point to other people involved in the project and say that their practice has changed because of your practice? I'm thinking here of colleagues and pupils and parents . . .

Beth That particular group of pupils, definitely. I feel there have been spin-offs, but those would be more difficult to show.

Jean You are making a claim to say that you have improved the quality of the pupils' education. How can you demonstrate this in practice?

Beth The interviews that I've got on tape, and from their journals.

Jean Can you give us specific instances of the action of improvement?

Beth Yes. My naughty boys. The ones that were really difficult and couldn't be trusted. One of them was very naughty and disrupted the whole lesson, playing around. I've got it on the tape, him playing around. And then, very gradually, in some way or another – not altogether successfully – they've been won over. The best example is Sam who, for just one week out of a whole eight or so weeks, worked – but that was just a major achievement for him. I have his written piece of work that Sam has taken an interest. He's thinking about what he's doing – not taking the soft option.

Jean So we have concrete evidence to say that he believes that you have improved the quality of his life.

Beth Yes. This evidence backs up my claim.

Dee I don't think I have the confidence to make that claim. It may be one of the major differences when you move out of the classroom

where you can see evidence of what you're doing fairly adequately. Certainly as a class teacher, I think I would often have felt able to make a claim that I had achieved something, that by what I had done, a child's education had improved. It's much more tenuous when you get to our level as heads. Would you agree, Liz?

Liz   Absolutely.

Dee   I like this expression, that you are making a claim. I am simply not sure that I can make that claim. That goes back to my need to 'measure', that I actually want to find out whether there's anything that I can claim, and I have to evaluate first of all.

Liz   I don't think your research into your own practice as a headteacher is measurable. How do you judge it? Do you judge it by pupil performance? Do you judge it by improved relationships? It's so vast, and you're making tiny steps all the time. So in the end, because you're constantly striving, you'll never get there simply because you're constantly striving and moving on. You are developing all the time. You need to demonstrate that process of development – which you are doing here in your project.

Jean   When we first discussed your project, Dee, you said that one of your ambitions was to introduce a new ethos, an ethos of care. You were very concerned to generate this feeling of care. From recent conversations, it sounds as if you're succeeding.

Dee   I feel as though it is, and that's why I really want to have a look to see whether it really is. I need to involve other people in my evaluation. This will be the focus of my next enquiry. I have worked very hard to get across the idea of *preventing* unacceptable behaviour, and not only punishing it. Staff and children seem to be talking in those terms now. We need to find out if we all agree if that's the case.

Jean   So now, at the end of this term, you're going to reflect on what you've been doing; and then next term you're going to start a new cycle of action reflection by involving colleagues.

Dee   Yes. Obviously one talks to the staff about this all the time. If you have any sort of relationship with people, then your whole moral background must come out, nurture it. I genuinely try to understand my staff, and it is how much your staff are prepared to understand you that I think determines how successful you are.

Liz By your being more caring for them, they actually reflect that back by caring for the children.

Dee That's what we hope.

Liz Wouldn't it be hard to go and measure that, in a conventional sense?

Susan It would be impossible to go and quantify that.

Liz Because all the time you're inside it yourself, and you can't take yourself outside it because you're part of the change, and you're part of the ethos, aren't you. I did some evaluation once about something we were doing, and when I actually looked at it afterwards, because I knew what responses I wanted, and because I knew that I wanted certain changes to happen, the whole way I set the evaluation up was going to actually effect change. It wasn't going to actually evaluate what we were doing and where we were; but it did effect change, beautifully.

Susan If you're talking about measurement, you've got to have some sort of record whereby you can say, there is some of 20 per cent happening . . .

Liz But is that necessary? Is measurement necessary?

Beth Maybe only in the sense of giving proof.

Dee Yes, or even encouragement.

Liz To yourself.

Dee Yes. Beth said she wanted to prove to other people – to her audience – that . . .

Beth I think I've just really got to show that the enquiry has in some way moved things on. And there are a lot of things that I would have done very differently, especially in so far as collecting the evidence. I think the important thing about the enquiry is the difference it has made to me.

Dee I immediately see evaluation as the next step through, because presumably if you feel very strongly that the way that you've changed your practice is good for the children, then one of the things that you would want to see is other members of staff taking on board those changes. I can see that you want to offer proof, so that you can say to other members of staff, 'Look, this actually worked'.

Beth   I think I will get the opportunity, because I've already been asked to help with some INSET to do with active learning and group work. Now I will actually be able to use the proof, the evidence, that I've collected. But I think the important thing about the enquiry now is this: I started off small with just one small group – and it has made me realise, inside the interviews, the honesty was really beginning to come through. The children weren't just saying, 'Oh, yes, it was really good and we really enjoyed that', as they tended to do at the beginning. They are being very honest, and they are saying, 'Yes, it's been really interesting, but could we try it this way?' So they are evaluating my practice, and we are negotiating together a shared practice. That's the way that my enquiry is moving us all forward at the moment.

Chapter 10

Evaluating Support Practices

We then went on to talk about the evaluation of our practice as supporters. We are all claiming to have improved our support practices: are those claims justified?

Jean What we're looking at is evaluating our own education. Now, when I say 'education', I mean the attempt to improve the quality of life for an individual. I have tried in my work as a field tutor to improve my practice by carrying out a systematic evaluation with yourselves. I've asked you to comment and reflect back to me so that I can modify my practice, and in turn you have done the same; so we have set up this dialogue, on a one-to-one basis, and also on a one-to-many basis, where we have all shared ideas to move forward our joint practice. Now, by the word 'evaluation', I suppose I mean 'Does it work?' – that is, has the quality of life been improved for me and for the other individuals in this group? From my point of view, it has been improved. I can point to the evidence to my own life, in that I feel I have helped you to improve your understanding of what you are doing, so that you have now been articulating the fact that you have assisted other people in improving their understanding. So my claim is that I have improved my own education, in that I've helped you. Am I correct in making that claim? Would you substantiate it?'

Everyone: Yes

Jean In that case, what evidence can you show in your life to substantiate my claim?

Beth My journal shows how our discussions have helped me to clarify my thinking, to move on in the enquiry. And also about the first meeting we had as a group.

Jean What benefit did you get out of that?

Beth   It helped me really to clarify my thinking, to narrow the focus of my enquiry. You made me go back to the beginning and say 'What do I want to enquire into?'

Dee   Yes, I think that's exactly the same for me. After we met the first time, I was anxious to get things down on paper and start things off. I had all sorts of thoughts about where I would go then. And then when we met in a bigger group – it's always helpful, isn't it, to talk with others because conversation actually raises one's own awareness: the thought processes one goes through oneself. You often hear somebody else reflecting, and airing what you are saying, even if you haven't actually articulated it yourself.

Jean   Have you noticed any difference in your thought processes?

Dee   Just got slower and slower as the years have gone on!

Liz   I feel much freer. I think after being on taught courses for so long, and the only research that I've ever looked into or known was a research with a definite outcome. Until now I have been totally strung up because there was nothing about what I really wanted to study that I thought could be measurable. Now, we're back into our 'measure' again. And it was only after I'd talked to Jean after that first session that I started to think that whatever happens, I'm growing, the situation around me is growing – and I'm sure there will be a lot of things I can put down on paper – and I feel it would be a good enquiry. As to it being any use to anyone else, I'm not sure about that, but my enquiry certainly is effecting change in my school. And it's only after speaking to you, Jean, that we talked about making an effecting of change the tangible part rather than more evidence about four-year-olds – the whole thing got into motion, and, as you say, Dee, after our discussions, I was quite prolific on paper. There is a lot coming through and I start putting down. It wasn't till we'd had those individual meetings, though, sharing our own viewpoints, that I've got to that stage.

Jean   Can we pick up this idea that, in fact, we have formed a support group? Now clearly you're finding this small support group very valuable in terms of friendship, in terms of sharing anxieties and successes, sharing ideas . . .

Dee   Yes, I think so. Liz talked about freedom. This is really freedom, because I feel instinctively that I can trust the members of the group. I have large amounts of things that I cannot talk with anybody else about. I found that immensely valuable, that trust.

Liz It's the time factor involved as well, isn't it? In lectures, everything's tightly programmed. I feel, if necessary, we'd sit here, if somebody had got an urgent problem, we would sit here and listen.

Dee I felt that very much last time when we met with Anne. She was really struggling, wasn't she? I don't think either you or I spoke about what we were actually doing at all, Liz. I gained tremendously by just talking through with her about where she was going to go.

Jean Dee, you've just said, 'I gained tremendously by helping Anne'. In what way did you gain?

Dee I think by actually having to suggest ways in which she could sort our her own problems. One actually is drawing on one's own experience and in a sense solving one's own problems even if they haven't been mentioned at that time. You can always see a related incident.

Jean You were teaching her.

Dee Yes.

Liz I think it may be something to do with the fact that we're all practising at a high, rapid level, and I don't think we stop to rationalise our practice. You're involved as you are living it. But when someone else has a problem suddenly something in your mind says, 'Oh, I remember that in my situation, and I . . .' You then actually start to clarify what you actually did in that situation. You never stopped to clarify at the time . . . and that's what's really useful about the whole process, isn't it? It's a matter of reflecting on your actions as you do them.

Jean So you're learning through teaching, and teaching through learning.

Liz Yes. Things happen. And when you look back they've actually worked. I suppose it's a form of evaluation of our own practice, isn't it, when we actually go and help someone.

Dee When we advise.

Jean Someone said to me the other day about a 'cascade model', and I said, No, absolutely not, because a cascade model implies the drip feed . . .

Dee And the person at the top ends up with nothing. It's all going down, isn't it? But that doesn't happen with us.

Jean   Right. I said that I was very much into developing networks. And I feel that that's what we've done because – perhaps the original impetus came from our original individual conversations, but now a real network has begun, in that this support group has developed, which in turn has generated further support groups, such as in the individual schools in which we're working. You've involved colleagues, children and parents, so it's anything but a cascade. It's very much networking.

Liz   Yes, because we're taking – a cascade implies that you're giving out all the time, but we're actually taking all the time as well as giving out, aren't we?

Jean   It's reciprocal. And you're doing this through setting up dialogue.

Dee   And recognising need. That's what we do intuitively as teachers, isn't it? We have children in our care. And I think that's what we do as a small group. I suppose in a class situation it's more one way, whereas in our group each of us is demonstrating a need at different times, and others are moving in to offer that support. It's a constant exchanging of strengths and weaknesses and everything else.

Jean   Beth is the only one of us who is working in a classroom situation as such and from what you've been observing recently, in fact that's happening in your classroom situation as well. We were talking about peer tutoring the other day, which is what we're doing here.

Beth   Two things have just occurred to me really. First is the difference in my relationship with the particular group that I've been teaching in this different way. I've just been given my own office, and the children who are buzzing in and out are the children from this particular group.

Liz   Now that's just what I was saying to Dee, that all these things are happening, and it's not until someone triggers off something and you start rationalising that you actually pick out key points and key issues.

Beth   The other thing that occurred to me was the fact that in a way the best results for me have been occurring with other groups. It's as if the confidence that I'm getting as a result of my relationship with the one group is having an effect on other groups, because I've got the confidence to go in and do things slightly differently with other groups and to be far more effective: for example, the net curtain incident with another group when we were talking about the difficulties if you belong to another faith. Previously we've always done this towards the end of

the second year; and we've always read the chapter, made notes, done some drawing. I thought, 'We'll do it differently'. We didn't even read the chapter together – they read the chapter in groups, and they then had to present in some way to show the difficulties. They all chose a drama way. They really showed empathy with people of different religious faiths in this country, and some really good drama came out of that. As a result of that lesson, I thought, I'll try in that way with the other group. It's a knock-on effect, because the other group – I suppose it's because of my enthusiasm – were much more enthusiastic than the first group. When it actually came to showing their productions they all pulled out these net curtains and they swathed themselves in them because they were being Muslims – they really went to a lot of trouble. It made the point so much more – there couldn't have been a house on the estate that had any curtains! All these girls were swathed in net curtains from head to foot! Afterwards they sat down and talked about it. 'It's difficult to know – we felt so enclosed – what it must be like to be those girls!'

Dee Don't you think that absolutely illustrates – I think the first time we met as a group I was telling you that I had done the West Sussex maths course which was purely maths – it wasn't about anything else at all, but it completely changed my classroom practice. You're saying this kind of thing has a knock-on effect – if you start changing the whole outlook, then you can't say, 'I'm only going to do it with this group', because it changes *you*, doesn't it, and the way that you walk into the classroom. I think if you actually change something fundamental then everything changes. You can't put it into a compartment and say, 'For the rest of the day I'm going to be different.' I think that's something that's quite difficult to explain to staff who haven't actually experienced that themselves, because they think that they can do something here and something there quite differently. It's all to do with your basic philosophy, isn't it, and if you are feeling that the right way to talk with young people is to open it up – to allow them to experience – then you can't switch that on and off.

Jean So are you saying, Dee, that fundamentally you change you, and therefore you change your whole life? Are you saying that the fact that you've undertaken your personal enquiry has changed you?

Liz You can't actually become involved in anything without effecting some sort of change in yourself, can you really? Even if – perhaps this is a bit naive – even if it was something such as always shopping at the

same shop – if you make a decision to start shopping at the small shop instead of the large shop, that actually changes you. You become more talkative in the shop. There's very little you can do in life, is there, that doesn't actually change your being?

Jean   So the research that you've undertaken is part of your life.

Liz   It becomes very current in your thinking. All my technique is focused now, because the project has become such a major part in my thinking and it has a number of offshoots. I don't think I have ever really concentrated like this till now.

Jean   You're constantly critical.

Liz   Yes, that's right. So from seeing this research as a problem a year ago, as to how to start looking at problems of receptions, coping, thinking 'That's not right, we're not succeeding', I'm beginning to get into such a heavy programme. I don't think even at the end of this year it's going to stop, even if I wanted to now; although I can't say that the second sets we have now will be the same as the ones we have next year, because we don't know what our staffing is going to be. From looking at Fours, looking at playgroups, we've gone into staff development in a different way – the staff are beginning to monitor it. They have suggested things – they've got time to start a base-line assessment of the Fours with the parents, which is something that's been hanging around everywhere, but suddenly it's central.

Jean   So you've turned that into a collaborative research issue?

Liz   Yes, even to the fact that last week I suddenly realised that we were in this position where we were a popular school and our planned admission limit is 30. This year there are going to be about 78 applicants for my 60 places, and so for the first time I found I had to say No. So I've actually been to the Appeals Court. I've spent the whole day at the Appeals Court fighting now for something which I've always known is an issue. I've always known that Fours shouldn't be in large classes, but suddenly there's so much thought being turned into action, I felt I had to do something about it, and I'm trying.

Jean   Going back to the idea of our claim, our claim to educational knowledge – we have improved the quality of our lives in order to and because of our concern to improve the quality of other people's lives. We have set up dialogue, we have generated networks of enquiring practitioners, we are describing a community ethic of enquiring minds.

Beth's classrooms are going in that direction. Dee's and Liz's schools are going in that direction, and we've set up this community of reflective practitioners because of our determination to do something about an unsatisfactory situation. We have individually found ourselves in an unsatisfactory situation. Our locations were quite different, to begin with, but we've engaged in a process of dialogue to share our views about the process of improvement that we have all deliberately undertaken, the action reflection which is helping us to improve the quality of education for ourselves, for the people within our locations; and we're doing this by sharing our views about the nature of those improvements that we're trying to bring about. Is that a fair assessment?

Liz   Yes.

Dee   I think the difference that I particularly noticed was, when we were talking to Anne, we were offering advice because we were seeing in what she was saying a reflection of things that had happened to us, but we had never thought about it. Perhaps the difference is that we're actually starting to think about things as they actually happen, rather than almost instinctively. When something occurs, we don't just react instinctively, but we actually reflect on it as we go along. And that might be the difference – instead of being on auto-pilot, we're being critical.

Jean   You consciously reflect.

Dee   Yes. Something that's always been fairly sub-conscious has been raised much more into consciousness now.

Jean   We are making it explicit to ourselves and to others.

Dee   And, I suppose, when I start to feel that I'm going under is when pressure becomes such that I go back into that auto-pilot mode which is no longer satisfactory.

Jean   Can we summarise? I have made my personal claim that I have improved the quality of my own education by working with colleagues, and you have approved that claim. Are you prepared to make similar claims for yourselves – that you have improved the quality of education for yourselves?

Dee   Yes, I think so, in those terms. I go back to what I said before – I'm not sure that I have the confidence yet to claim that I have improved for other people.

Jean   You have for me, and for Liz, and for Beth, and we can all say the same, I think, of each other. It's this knock-on effect, the ripples in the pool. What I'm concerned to do in my project is to show the process of education as operating as a network for all of us, whereby I don't make social distinctions between teachers, supporters, pupils, learners, whatever role. Each one of us is improving the quality of her education with a view to improving the quality of other people's education.

Liz   Really, Jean, what you're saying is what we very much are striving for in the classrooms. Not the didactic way – we learn together; and increasingly teaching in the classroom is going this way. Why shouldn't it go right the way through education?

Susan   The better learners we are, the better teachers we are.

Chapter 11

Evaluating Provision for Continuing Teacher Education

I then spoke with two Staff Development Officers. I wanted to investigate with them the nature of the values they held that prompted them to initiate the courses that their LEA was running in conjunction with an Institute of Higher Education, and particularly when there was an increasing emphasis on Practitioner Based Enquiry (PBE).

Both Officers operate as field tutors, and the views that they have expressed in this chapter are their individual opinions as teachers who are engaged in examining their own support practices as well as administrators of teacher education provision. They are both involved in evaluating the impact of the scheme so far.

We pick up the conversation where I have just asked Steve to identify the educational values which place such emphasis on the PBE element within the scheme.

Steve Inasmuch as the initiative towards a scheme like this really rests upon a particular view of a teacher, as an independent, freestanding professional person. That's a basic value. A teacher isn't the deliverer of a National Curriculum which comes in a set of books or as a set of ring binders. This view of the teacher as the independent, freestanding professional goes back to a view which has been developed over many years. It isn't coincidence that we see it like that. That's the result of the approach to training teachers over the years, really. We are looking to strengthening the partnership between the LEA and the Higher Education institution. Any shortcomings we may feel that courses leading to higher degrees may have had in the past reflect really the extent to which they were prepackaged, delivered courses. In that respect they didn't match this notion of teachers as independent, freestanding professionals who were themselves involved in their own professional development, and who make choices about what they need to do, and who actually give coherence to what they do on the basis of their own background and their current professional concerns.

Pat   Our original intention was actually to accredit teachers for considered research efforts of their undertaking in terms of their teaching methods. The way in which it has developed, I think, is that we've got much more involved with empowering teachers to realise that the decisions they make are the crucial ones, more than the decisions they're asked to make via some authority.

Steve   Some of the staff development that comes from the higher degree course is to raise their confidence to take that on. There are currently powerful forces which would press the teacher into becoming a narrower, more regimented individual, because of the nature of the developments that are coming along now. Teachers could be seen as the deliverers of the National Curriculum. They need considerable confidence and stature to be able to combat that. In a way it's always been difficult to try to develop that, but in teaching you've had a lot of independent people. The best teachers have always had that sort of distinctive element to them, haven't they – a very wide variety of individuals of all sorts who have all brought their individual contribution to what they are teaching. It's that that has produced quality in their work, very often. If you believe that it is still the practitioners who must make decisions on the basis of their own critical self-reflection about what and how to teach, then you are bound to plan along these lines.

Pat   One problem we've had, I think, is that the medium is the message. If you're trying to say to teachers, 'The work that you're doing in the sense of your planning, your thinking, your management, your own classroom practice, deserves recognition and accreditation' – if you're managing that, then our INSET opportunities must grow on this experience and not on the tutor's experience. In our evaluation so far we've discovered that the way the field tutor system works very positively is that the field tutors are encouraging them to look very closely at their practice, more so than on a course in the traditional way.

Steve   Yes, it is that the medium is the message, and that's why, if I'm operating as a field tutor, the overriding message that I have to say to the teachers is that they're not actually searching around for topics to study. Really they've got to look into their own practice. We want them looking inwards to what they're doing every day, and that again goes back to that original initiative. They are, in fact, dealing with lots of problems every day, at the moment more so than they ever have, I suppose, with implementing the National Curriculum, and so on.

Pat   It's interesting, isn't it, as a field tutor, when you actually talk to

the teachers involved, they seem to assume that there has to be some taught element before they can get on to their piece of research. That's why I think that the evaluation course mounted through the local university has gone well, because the teachers get three days' taught programme, and they feel very confident because academic university lecturers have delivered something to them, and they feel they can then get working from there. It's quite different, isn't it, really, on a one-to-one basis, to persuade them that they've got all the skills, they've got all the knowledge they need to go about their piece of action research.

Jean But you see that as the road to improving the quality of education in the classroom?

Pat Yes. I think that's our basic aim with this scheme. A lot of INSET that's delivered is really 'short stab' stuff – maybe six hours on one particular curriculum area, and I doubt that this experience affects practice. With an on-going programme like this, one looks at the change in classroom practice. It reflects the notion of the continuing professional development of teachers.

Steve That's right. I think that again shows strengths and weaknesses of types of in-service, doesn't it? Change is going to come about because teachers have greater confidence to examine what they're doing in depth and at the same time see that as a valuable exercise and have that message reinforced both by H.E. and by us. Because we're supporting it we get rid of this notion that undervalues the actual practice in the classroom, which is part of the problem. Part of helping teachers develop is that you do value their experience in the classroom, and you can't underrate that as part of their development. If you're continually giving the cues that you don't value the experience they're having in the classroom by looking always outwards – taking them out all the time – looking at other experiences all the time, detached from what they're doing in the classroom, you're continually reinforcing this notion of undervaluing the practice in the classroom. If you're going to show value for the practice in the classroom, which is what we feel is important, what goes on with children, what they do every day, and how that can be changed to improve it, then this has got to be the focus of what you're doing. That again is a most important message. That's why the scheme seems to be meeting a need which a lot of in-service doesn't.

Pat That's why we've converted a lot of our cash into advisory teachers, to work alongside the teacher in the classroom, and to enable the

teachers to feel much more confident and much more positive about the work they're doing.

Steve   And in that respect, the role of the advisory support teacher may not be very different from the field tutor's role. If an advisory teacher sees himself as focusing on practice, then he is very much like the field tutor. And part of what he would want to be there for is to be promoting confidence in the teacher in looking at the development of practice. This is part of the whole philosophy of the school-based approach in the county, isn't it – linking training with follow-up supported by the advisory teacher which follows up the development in the classroom and throughout the school.

Pat   That's one thing we need to talk about, is how to make this action research much more significant in the individual institution. It goes beyond classrooms, doesn't it?

Steve   Inasmuch as you can do that, yes.

Jean   Do you see that as part of your evolving programme?

Pat   I see that part of my role as a field tutor is to initiate whole school involvement. Let's imagine someone in a school is researching, say, using IT in a particular way, and if they can, they facilitate other teachers in the school to work in a successful way. Now, if they just do a closed piece of research only to do with them and their own classroom, that's missing a golden opportunity. In some of our in-service courses, some of our projects, we do spend time on how to write for a particular audience, or how to present their ideas in that sort of positive role. That's a second stage we've got to get on to.

Steve   I think if I understand it correctly, the development of a PBE – and action research more generally – has a gradation between looking at your own practice and then broadening it out to the extent to which that involves colleagues and involves the management of the school and so on. There is that development in the PBEs, and I think that's an important ingredient. It doesn't just come about. You've really got to structure it into what you're doing.

Jean   Actually building up a community of enquirers.

Steve   Yes. If you just take a single example: if you take developing a skill, say, in the IT way – there are definitely problems associated with that being taken on board by an individual teacher as a result of a piece of in-service and then going back into their classroom and practising

that and developing that – becoming more skilled themselves. There are definitely problems associated with that – but there are further problems associated with that individual actually passing that on to other colleagues and disseminating that with colleagues. That takes you into some quite significantly different problems which have to be systematically approached. In the past we just assumed that teachers would come out of the course, go back into school and somehow they would disseminate that to their colleagues; whereas it doesn't happen like that.

Pat   We have trained staff development co-ordinators in schools now, and where they work effectively is where they reap the benefit of people doing various bits of in-service. They use documentation to do this. They say to people, 'You've been on this course, and now you need to think of what you're now doing in school. What do you need in terms of time – resources, help in school? Do you need to visit another school?' What we need to work on now is the individual teachers on our scheme who are working individually in the school, and who aren't being supported by an INSET co-ordinator in the school.

Steve   So in terms of their development through their PBEs, it would be better if, in a later PBE, they were involved with a colleague or with groups of colleagues, as part of the structure which brings them into the whole set of problems which surrounds disseminating and working with colleagues. What I would like to see – and we've been trying to do this in all sorts of ways – is what we have on the evaluation course. It is structured in such a way that they have three days' taught course and five days' research based in their school. The notion there is that the project-based element is an activity in school. It will require that teacher to be talking to colleagues. They can't do it simply on their own. They've got to interact with everyone else.

Pat   Part of the three days' training basically is who do you aim your report or your feedback at – do you actually ask for time in a governors' meeting to talk about it, or do you go to a senior management meeting, or do you talk to a year team? How can you make this piece of research active in changing things in a school?

Steve   A number of the management courses that we've been running have been structured in such a way that after each session we have two or three weeks when the teacher is required to pursue a piece of project work which again involves them in going back into school and working with colleagues. That is a deliberate attempt to get into the school con-

text. We are trying to do that in all sorts of ways. This approach to action research is another way really; and this gives credit to that, because we regard it as important. It is as important an element of the staff development programme as the course itself. And perhaps it hasn't been sufficiently valued in the past as a part of the course. If you take the course requiring a year's secondment, often it didn't bring very much back to the school at all. It operated at really considerable expense, and, at the end of it, the individual obtained the credit for it in terms of a higher degree, but it wasn't really paying off very highly in terms of them going back into their institution to do things within the institution.

Pat   Often they'd do research about the school they'd left and because they'd have the year out they'd have time to look through the '*Times Ed*' and apply for posts, and they wouldn't go back to that particular school. One particular example of us as co-ordinating this scheme – a positive thing – is that we've both been concerned about the isolation of some of the teachers on it. It's important that they know what other people are doing; so what we have been doing in the last couple of weeks is getting a list of all the first PBEs that will be circulated to all of them, so that they may well find that there are other groups that are looking at, say, special needs in a small group in a classroom, and will try and set up a facility whereby they can work together. So we are encouraging the field tutors to set up support groups with the teachers they are working with, with a view to networking at a wider level.

Steve   I don't think it always can happen. I think it depends on where they are and how they're situated, and how the field tutor can operate and so on – but I think that's the beginning of networking – something perhaps which is very difficult to sustain although we can get tremendous spin-offs from it. I think we are hard pressed to compete with the sort of community provision that the university as an institution can provide to resident students. I think that's part of the difficulty with teachers anyway, isn't it? If you look at the isolation of some of the teachers in the county in terms of professional development, it's quite difficult to combat – again this is what we want this scheme to be partly overcoming, really – to provide the basis for networking.

PART V I MODIFY MY IDEAS AND MY PRACTICE IN THE LIGHT OF THE EVALUATION

Chapter 12

Perspectives on Practice

We have seen that a critical reflection on practice may bring about significant transformations in individual and community practices, both on personal and professional levels. I now want to consider some implications for our educational systems if we (a) accept the need for a paradigm of on-going critical reflection on practice, that is, research-based approaches to teacher education, and (b) acknowledge the fact that, once we do fully accept this paradigm, we will critically set about changing our educational systems, that is, we will not only work intentionally to change our practices, but aim also intentionally to change ourselves.

I will look at some of the implications from the perspectives of personal, professional and political practices.

Personal

I have said throughout that teachers' conscious understanding should be placed at the heart of educational explanations. Without understanding, practice is meaningless.

This may seem a very bold statement to make. Let me clarify my meaning by drawing an analogy with another current vigorous debate: that is, the extent to which artificially intelligent machines may be said to think. Much of this debate centres on a definition of 'think'. It is proposed that there is 'weak AI', where a programme is designed to imitate, or replicate, the possible ways in which humans think; and 'strong

AI', where the computer itself is supposed to think (McCorduck, 1979; Newell, 1983). The argument goes that, if we are prepared to judge the level of human intelligence by the behaviour that the human exhibits, then we may do the same with a machine. The operations that the machine may perform will indicate the degree of 'thinking power' that the machine possesses, and its parity with human capabilities.

John Searle, among others, has attacked the 'strong view' of AI (Searle, 1980, cited in Gardner, 1985), by his 'Chinese Room' conundrum. Put very simply, Searle's compelling argument runs as follows.

Suppose that I, a native English speaker who does not know any Chinese, am locked away and given a large amount of Chinese writing. I am then given another batch, and rules in English on how to correlate the first batch with the second. I am systematically given more and more Chinese writing and English rules which will teach me to correlate one set of formal symbols with another set.

Over time, I am able to decipher the writing, and, indeed, to use it correctly as answers to given questions. Would I then be said to 'understand' Chinese? Searle thinks not, for I am here following specific rules to help me produce answers by 'manipulating uninterpreted formal symbols. As far as the Chinese is concerned, I simply behave like a computer. I perform computational operations on formally specific elements.' (Searle, 1980)

Let me refer again to the work of Michael Polanyi (see also Chapter 2). In my view, Polanyi's formulation of primary and secondary knowledge is an answer to the problem of whether machines (and persons) are 'thinking'. The comparison between AI and human intelligence may hold as long as we are talking about information processing; indeed, computers are often far superior to humans in terms of the speed and quantity of information they are able to process. Under no circumstances, however, can a machine know that it knows. No machine can be aware of its own knowledge, can have a consciousness that lets it critique its own thought. No machine possesses the tacit knowledge of its values, this tacit knowledge allowing it to generate the explicit knowledge of its information. Humans do.

My argument is intended to highlight the shaky premise that is the current foundation of the dominant teacher-education paradigm: that teacher education is a matter of information processing. So long as this situation persists, it is difficult to see how teachers may be encouraged to regard themselves as reflective practitioners. The basis of good professional practice, says Schön (1983), is that practitioners understand what they are doing, and use their cognitions intentionally to improve

their practice. In my view, traditional 'line management' approaches to professional development actively discourage teachers from taking on the responsibility of thinking for themselves.

Parts III and IV of this book have indicated the tremendous advantages to be gained by individuals who are given the personal freedom to think for themselves, to explore the novelty of their practice. It is not only a case of transforming practice: it is also a transformation of self. Part IV encapsulates in practice the arguments of Part II: a society is more than a group. It is a collection of individuals; and when each of those individuals is consciously aware of what he/she is doing, their individual practices actively transform the society which they constitute. A critical concentration on personal practice moves the individual beyond his/her own self; it actively serves as the catalyst whereby community practices are transformed.

Professional

John Elliott (1989) has referenced the work of Maxwell (1984) in what he calls 'the philosophy of knowledge' and 'the philosophy of wisdom'. I shall draw on these ideas here.

Elliott criticises the form of educational research that regards theory as superior to practical actions. This form, he says, assumes that, 'the primary concern of the teacher educator should be to help the student or teacher utilize specialised knowledge, helping him or her to apply it to real educational problems and issues. There will always be a point . . . when some element of dissociation, from the practical topic in hand, is necessary for depth of understanding.' He has a problem with this view, which he places within the 'philosophy of knowledge', and leans rather towards 'the philosophy of wisdom'. Here, he surmises, the focus is that of *practical enquiry*, 'precisely the philosophical perspective which has informed the growth of educational action-research as a form of educational enquiry (see Elliott, 1987). Educational inquiry is not a separate process from the practice of education. It is a form of reflexive practice. Teaching can be construed as a form of educational research rather than its object.'

I will return now to the notion I aired in Chapter 2, that educational theory is not an object consisting of relations so much as a means of establishing relations. It seems to me that a philosophy of knowledge stresses the need for educational research to be an accessible structure, an 'end product', which may be defined in terms of specific significant

features. This view, critiqued so pungently by Elliott, allows the notions of education and educational research to be broken down into constituent disciplines, each with its own set of theories. The form in which this knowledge is communicated is through instruction. Educational research becomes a way of applying the theories in which the student teacher is instructed. On the other hand, a philosophy of wisdom stresses the value of practical knowledge, gained through first-hand experience of strategic action, and reflections on that action.

In Part III of this book we have seen how a transformation of professional practices may be generated by operating within the framework of a philosophy of wisdom. We have seen how professional teacher educators have deliberately and systematically transferred the responsibility of educational theorising from themselves to their student colleagues. This transference has not resulted in an abdication of responsibility; rather it has allowed teachers to be prepared to learn, rather than be prepared to be taught. From a paradigm of instruction, this community has moved to a paradigm of education. From regarding educational knowledge as resting with outsiders, the community has come to regard educational knowledge to be created by individual practitioners. The whole has become a community exercise, in the sense of individuals working together in each other's best interests. One example of where this approach is being developed is in the review and developmental process of Greendown School, Swindon, Wiltshire. In their report of this process, Andy Larter and Erica Holley (1990) make explicit how they support each other and colleagues in the school in their separate and joint enquiries.

Happily, this pattern of teacher education is being acknowledged more and more by LEAs and other advisory bodies. The movement needs to gather momentum, not only initiated by teacher educators, but by teachers themselves. This brings me to the third section – the politics that influence the dissemination of educational knowledge.

Political

I have stated my belief throughout that education is not only something that teachers wish to bring about in their learners, but also something which they hope to bring about in themselves. To this end, I have said, education should not only be the aim of enquiries, but also be the process of the enquiry. Teachers need to be open to learning about themselves in their efforts to learn about others.

In this book I have pointed to certain efforts, both on a personal and professional plane, to effect this educational revolution. Yet this is only the beginning. The problem is how most effectively to persuade funding bodies and policy makers of the value of this approach.

I believe that the efficiency of our educational system today is judged in terms of the normative-analytic type: a certain percentage success rate within an identifiable skill. This framework is applied to children in schools – how many pass national examinations, for example; to teachers in institutions – how many pass institutionalised, standarised tests; and to teacher educators – how many get how many of their teachers through the examinations. I have said throughout that such a system is far from educational, and is not concerned with assessing the quality of education. What it is concerned with is measuring the amount of information-processing ability individuals have developed, and how efficient institutions are in producing operators capable of processing information.

Systems are kept going by dominant interest groups within the system. Systems are changed because groups holding alternative views become bolder in challenging the current state of the art. The challenge is given direction and strengthened by vocal members within the emergent group. Directors of the dominant system needs must heed the voice, for their existence depends on it; in democratic systems, politicians are elected by the people, and, if the people begin to think differently, politicians have to listen to the emergent opinions, or fall from popularity.

What is needed is people power, and, in terms of this book, teacher power. I will repeat that teachers are teachers at all levels – classroom, home, institution, academy: we are all teachers in our own way and in our own location. What is needed is for more and more people to stand up and speak their mind. This process of making explicit needs to go on in as many locations as possible, and through as many media: in schools and colleges, in professional discourse, in printed documents, on radio and TV, in the home. It is not enough to talk about education, although this is a first step; we also have to engage in educational talk – to engage in a dialogue of question and answer that will help us move our individual and collective understanding forward.

What is also needed is for such talk, such enquiry, to receive some form of public recognition or accreditation. A growing number of institutions and authorities are making research diplomas and other forms of accreditation available to teachers involved in classroom research. Current shrinking funding for academy-based research is throwing

schools more and more on their own resources. This presents an opportunity for political initiative. Long has there been pressure for a national scheme for institution-based teacher research, for the establishment of a General Teaching Council (Whitehead 1989). Such an apolitical council could set up and monitor accreditation, the standards of judgement for such accreditation to be agreed by peers. By this I mean that classroom excellence should be judged in terms of strategic action; that the focus of educational enquiry should be the development of personal insight that will generate such strategic action in an effort to improve the quality of education; and that the success of that action – that is, an identifiable improvement in the quality of education – should be validated through the intersubjective agreements of individuals who are sympathetic to the efforts of the enquiring practitioner.

All this may seem like a vision. If so, then I am a practical visionary. It can be done. But it cannot be done alone. It can be done by teachers who are prepared to make their views public. No revolution ever succeeded because the revolutionaries were quiet. Nor am I suggesting a noisy, combative process of effecting this revolution. I am requiring my fellow teachers to accept the dignity of the responsibility of their own professionalism. I require them to stand up with confidence and claim that they understand, and to be prepared to back up that claim with the justification of evidence. This is the way to effect the revolution, a revolution that is not about defining education in behavioural terms, but that is in itself educational for all the individuals in the community of enquirers.

Chapter 13

Education and the Society of Tomorrow

In this chapter I want to explore an idea that the way in which the values which move education forward may provide insights into the nature of social evolution.

I believe, like Habermas (1981), that the development of society is grounded in the collective understandings of individuals as they strive to enhance the quality of life for themselves and for each other. I do not believe that the development of society lies in individuals' practices being directed by 'knowing' others, any more than I believe that teachers' practices develop through being directed by external agents.

Let me review some ideas that I have put forward. The process of education, I have said, is the process of an individual's development as she engages strategically in the expansion of her own consciousness.

Education, I have said, is something that is implicit in the way that the individual conducts her life. While we recognise that we are, to a certain extent, restricted by role, social situation and status, it is possible for us constantly to engage in the process of living our values more fully in our practice. Some individuals find themselves in the role of learners, as children in classrooms or teachers on degree courses; some find themselves in the role of teachers, as in classrooms, or institutes of education. Some are in schools and in other institutions where the process of education is accelerated by the conscious and willing involvement of other committed individuals. Some are institution-unbound.

The values that move education forward are those of our own and others' best interest. Best interest involves the willingness by one to allow the other to be free to develop as and how her potential leads her, while she in turn still acts in the others' best interest.

This may seem like a circular argument, and indeed it is, for social intercourse is both reciprocal and recursive. Let me explain more fully.

I, an individual, am engaged in education – that is, improving the process of the development of an individual's rationality. So, in the first instance, I am concerned to develop this individual, myself.

I am a teacher. As such, my business is education, and my job is to educate. So I facilitate the process whereby another person engages in the process of developing herself.

My education (trying more fully to realise my values in my practice) is concerned with developing my ability to facilitate the development of another person (trying more fully to realise her values in her practice).

I can undertake this exercise on a one-to-one basis, or I can extend it to one-to-many.

My values are always those of the other's best interest, where I am concerned to develop the latent potential in each and every one of my clients. We live in a pluralist society, and I must ensure that each person maintains her integrity to develop according to her own individual potential – always with the provision that she will act in the other's best interest.

Let me now move forward from one-to-one, and develop a network, whereby I help someone to help someone else.

It may be said that I am fostering peer tutoring, and indeed I am; and I need now to examine the nature of the values that underpin collective practices such as teaching for peer tutoring.

Best interest implies generosity and care. I am prepared to care for you. In turn, your 'I' is prepared to care for mine – you act in my best interest. We aim to share, both values and intentions. We are prepared to love each other, in word and deed.

I may formalise this by saying that the development of collective awareness is based on individuals' own conscious awareness. The situation in which individuals share their awareness comes about through a process of intersubjective agreement, where individuals air their values with a view to sharing them with others as a potential way of life.

I believe that individuals' critical awareness is encouraged to emerge because of the practices of caring, wise others: the evolution of society may be said to be grounded in the morality of an educational epistemology of practice. It is not enough to aim for the realisation of our educational values as the objectives of our practices; it is essential to engage in the present realisation of our educational values in and through our practices. In this way, I believe that what goes on in classrooms and workplaces may be seen as the living out of the educational values of the reflective practitioners who constitute those communities as they engage in their own educational development in an attempt to improve the quality of the process of education for the people they care

about. The evolution of a caring rational society has its base in the evolutionary educational practices of self-reflexive practitioners.

I am drawing a parallel here between two systems, and I am suggesting that one system is embedded within the other. I am talking about the development of society and the professional development of teachers. It is my firm belief that the future rests in the hands of teachers, and that the title 'teacher' may be applied not only to those who have a formal teaching accreditation, but to anyone who is involved in the business of helping others to develop, provided they are prepared to develop themselves. 'Teacher' is not a licence to instruct; it is a licence that proclaims the status of a professional learner.

I am also suggesting that the nature of the professional development of teachers influences the nature of the development of society. Democratic forms of teacher education will encourage like forms of client education. Democratic forms of client education will go far towards establishing a moral epistemology of practice as the foundation of society, and as the basis of the on-going actions of that society.

This is not just so much wishful thinking. I came to these ideas through my own research. In my teaching in school I moved away from a situation in which I implemented a programme of care within the lesson, through conducting a programme of personal and social education with the children, towards a situation in which I cared enough to implement a programme of community sharing, through being critical of my own practices and encouraging the children to do the same (McNiff, 1989).

Education, and particularly teacher education, is not concerned with finding laws so much as meanings. Educational theory is not a static body of knowledge that constitutes a description of teachers' ideal practices so much as a creative story, always transforming, always expanding, that reflects the critical awareness that teachers develop of their work. Educational research is not a standard procedure whereby findings are put into practice, but the process of testing out tentative theories that provide a basis for the living out of values.

I think this view is becoming accepted today. There are many trends that show the shift away from E-enquiries to I-enquiries. What I am trying to do in this book is give a firm philosophical and epistemological foundation to the educational revolution. I am saying that, as a profession, we need to make explicit the need for such a turn, and make equally explicit the processes and procedures involved. In making our

knowledge explicit, we need to make an impassioned commitment to the pursuit of teachers' intellectual freedom, not just by talking about it, but by doing it.

Appendix

Sometimes I cannot find the right words to express my ideas. This happened when I came to write Chapter 10. At the time, instead of struggling to articulate the thoughts in analytic form, I relaxed and wrote a poem.

I have decided to include the poem as an appendix, for two reasons:

1 I feel the poem speaks more directly for me. However, the form of poetry in a book like this might seem inappropriate, so it is not in the main text.

2 I believe teaching, like poetry, is an art form. I believe that teachers should be encouraged to express their intuitive thoughts in a diversity of ways, in order to help them more fully understand the workings of their own minds. Teachers' creativity needs to be nurtured throughout all aspects of the educational enterprise. Creative, non-transactional writing is just one mode to be explored in our efforts to help teachers realise the potential of their creative lives. Painting, dance, music are other aspects of the creative arts which, I feel, should be more widely available as part of programmes of professional and personal development.

The publication of this poem is the realisation of the values I am expressing. It is an important part of the book, not only in the sense that it communicates my inner thoughts, but also in the sense that the publication of this form of communication will strengthen the view of education as a generative enterprise, and the movement toward the development of the professional creativity of teachers.

Stars

Tell me, teacher, tell me –
Why am I here, within these barren walls?
What do you know, that you ask me to learn?
What do you care?

For I am a child of dreams,
I am a child of light,
Who lives and yearns for light.
I was born from infinity into infinity;
Mine is the power of the universe.

Tell me, teacher, tell me –
Do you seek to trammel me with books,
Bind up my knowledge into swaddling clothes?
Do you hanker after trophies? Notch your pen,
And stab red darts into the soul of my invention?

Tell me, teacher, tell me –
For I fear your power, I fear your mighty power,
Omnipotent, omniscient, teacher only knows.
Where will you lead me? Will you force me in,
In to your world of dark inverted stars?
Will you take my life of dreams? Will you chain me down,
Bind my mind to yours with countless facts,
Each fact a nail, each nail a crucifixion?

Tell me, teacher, tell me,
For I need to know, I need to know.

My life depends on my knowing.

● ● ●

Hush, my child, hush. Be still.
Be brave. Be of good cheer.
I cannot do you harm, for I know no harm to do.
Let me walk with you, for I, too, am a traveller.
I, too, am a harvester of life;
I taste the sweetness of a thousand mornings.
Let me find with you the jewels of the earth,
And share with you the song of crystal springs,
And seek the secrets of the magic mountains
That we but glimpse within these concrete walls.

Have no fear. You are a child of light,
As I am a child of light, and dreams, and laughter.
Let us grow together, each on our separate path,
Yet sharing the same journey.
Let us play among the ageless stars,
But let us play to win, and not to conquer.

Peace, my child, be still.
I will give you courage. I am here.
I will not fail you. I will help you grow,
As you will me.
I am your friend in need, as you are mine.
Let us explore together. Let us taste the joy, and share,
Each with the other, the loveliness of our new tomorrows.

Good morning, Mr Smith. I see you there
With checklists out and big guns standing by.
I see the heavy judgement suit you wear,
The cold glint of appraisal in your eye.
What will you do to me, when you see my class?
Will you consult your book, and let me pass?

Have mercy, please, I cannot know it all.
The more I try, the more there is to know.
I've read your book. I've rallied to your call.
I'm still quite new. I still have far to go.
What will you do to me, when you see me teach?
Should I assume success is out of reach?

I'm just a teacher, just a human being;
I have my weaknesses, I have my strengths.
Your trouble is, believing lies in seeing,
Your observation lists go to great lengths.
What will you do to me, when you see I'm worried?
Will you ignore me, just because you're hurried?

Please help me, Mr Smith. I need a friend,
Not an evaluator, not a judge.
I'm trying to understand the means, the end.
Will you accommodate me? Will you budge?
What will you do to me, if I'm not like you?
I wanted to be a teacher. Will I do?

● ● ●

Welcome, my friend, to the land of tomorrow.
Look for the answers within your own mind.
Drink of the cup of your joy and your sorrow.
Seek, and be open to what you might find.
You, more than I, are aware of your living –
Yours for the asking, and yours for the giving.

See how you stand on the edge of decision,
See how you act, and consider, and plan;
See how your practice is honed to precision,
See how you weigh what you can't and you can.
You, more than I, may judge your own ability,
How to turn chaos to easy stability.

You have the questions to some of my answers,
I have the questions to some of your own.
Consciously tuned dialectical dancers,
We are the knowers of that which is known.
Yours is the key to your own education.
Open your mind to the power of creation.

Hustle, bustle, quick, quick, quick!
Get me the results! I need them!
Here's the battery, take your pick!
Mark the tests, don't stop to read them.

Time is money, every second,
Get statistics, crunch the numbers.
Dream-time's over, ready-reckoned,
Wake the princess from her slumbers.

Gone the sweetness, gone the passion,
In the matrix, in the grids.
Measured thought is out of fashion –
Only measurement of kids.

Where's commitment? Where's endeavour?
Where's my soul? I had it once.
Who is average? Who is clever?
Who is an abandoned dunce?

Free me from this structured jungle!
Loose my strictured intellect!
Let me fumble, let me bungle,
Think, creatively reflect.

Let me learn from each mistake;
Let me turn the bad to good.
Free me! Let me make the break!
Let me lead the life I should.

Leave my spirit of enquiry unfettered.
Leave my sense of awe and wonder free.
I as individual cannot be bettered.
Politician, let me be the person that I want to be.

● ● ●

This office is the centre of the Universe
In terms of power, status, money and career.
I keep a watchful eye upon the public purse,
And say which economic course we ought to steer.
I am a politician; I decide. The fact is,
I alone dictate what you do in your practice.

Mine is the awsome task to tell you what to do;
Yours is to implement in practice what I say.
Do not think to question what I'm telling you.
I do not question, either, in my loyal way.
Let's work for standardised agreement, all of us,
Obedient to the system without any fuss.

I am a father figure. I have a lovely child.
I have a social conscience. I have been seen to try.
Why do you rise against me, militant and wild,
Reforming zealots, why the impassioned battle cry?

Are you the crazy people who would teach my son?
Not likely. He's in private education, out of reach.
I am well pleased with how the schools are being run;
Thank you for your opinion. Now please get on and teach.

Come dance with me among the dancing stars,
Centre to glittering centre, ray to ray.
Infinite power, infinite love is ours.
Infinite time in timelessness. Come and play.

Bibliography

Ayer, A.J., *The Problem of Knowledge* (Penguin Books, 1956).

Bernstein, T.J., *Beyond Objectivism and Relativism: Science, Hermeneutics and Praxis* (Basil Blackwell, 1983).

Bertanalffy, L. von, *Problems of Life* (New York: Wiley, 1952).

Buber, M., *I and Thou* (trans. R.G. Smith) (Edinburgh: T. and T. Clark, 1937).

Chomsky, N., *Syntactic Structures* (The Hague: Mouton, 1957).

Chomsky, N., *Aspects of the Theory of Syntax* (Cambridge: MIT Press, 1965).

Chomsky, N., *The Generative Enterprise* (Foris Publications, 1982).

Chomsky, N., *Knowledge of Language: Its Nature, Origin and Use* (New York: Praeger Publishers, 1986).

Collingwood, R.G., *An Autobiography* (Oxford University Press, 1939).

Comey, D.D., 'Logic' in Kernig (ed.) *Marxism, Communism and Western Society*, Vol. 5 (New York: Herder and Herder, 1972).

Davies, P., *God and the New Physics* (Penguin Books, 1990).

Department of Education and Science, *Planning for School Development* (1989).

Eames, K., *The growth of a teacher's attempt to understand writing, re-drafting, learning and automony in the examination years* (Unpub. MPhil, University of Bath, 1987).

Eames, K., 'Growing Your Own' in *The British Journal of In-Service Education*, Vol. 16, No. 2 (1990).

Ebbutt, D., 'Educational action research: some general concerns and specific quibbles', mimeo (Cambridge Institute of Education, 1983). Also reprinted in Burgess, R. (ed.) *Issues in Educational Research* (Falmer Press, 1985).

Eggleston, J., Galton, M. and Jones, M., *Processes and Products of Science Teaching* (London: Macmillan, 1976).

Eggleston, J., Galton, M. and Jones, M., 'Characteristics of Educational

Research: Mapping the Domain' in *British Educational Research Journal*, Vol. 5, No. 1 (1979).

Elliott, J. 'Action research: framework for self-evaluation in schools', TIQL working paper No. 1, mimeo (Cambridge Institute of Education, 1981).

Elliott, J., 'Educational theory, practical philosophy and action research' in *British Journal of Educational Studies*, Vol. xxxv, No. 2 (June, 1987).

Elliott, J., 'Educational Theory and the Professional Learning of Teachers: an overview' in *Cambridge Journal of Education*, Vol. 19, No. 1 (1989).

Elliott, J., 'Educational Research in Crisis: performance indicators and the decline in excellence (BERA Presidential Address)' in *British Educational Research Journal*, Vol. 16, No. 1 (1990).

Foster, D., *Explanations for Teachers' Attempts to Improve the Process of Education for their Pupils* (Unpub. M.Ed, University of Bath, 1982).

Fromm, E., *Fear of Freedom* (London: Routledge and Kegan Paul, 1942).

Fromm, E., *To Have or to Be* (Jonathan Cape, 1978).

Gadamer, H.G., *Truth and Method* (New York: The Seabury Press, 1975).

Gardner, H., *The Mind's New Science: A History of the Cognitive Revolution* (New York; Basic Books, Inc., 1985).

Green, B., *Personal Dialectics in Educational Theory and Educational Research Methodology* (Unpub. MA, University of London, 1979).

Grene, M., *The Knower and the Known* (Faber and Faber, 1966).

Grene, M., 'Introduction' in Polanyi, M., *Knowing and Being* (Routledge and Kegan Paul, 1969).

Gurney, M., *The Development of Personal and Social Education through Action Research* (Unpub. PhD, University of Bath, 1988).

Habermas, J., *Toward a Rational Society* (trans. J.J. Shapiro) (Heinemann, 1971).

Habermas, J., *Knowledge and Human Interests* (trans. J.J. Shapiro) (Heinemann, 1972).

Habermas, J., *Theory and Practice* (trans. J. Viertel) (Heinemann, 1974).

Habermas, J., *Communication and the evolution of society* (trans. T. McCarthy) (Heinemann, 1979).

Habermas, J., *The Theory of Communicative Action, Volume Two: The Critique of Functionalist Reason* (Trans.T. McCarthy) (Basil Blackwell, 1981).

Hamilton, D., *Towards a Theory of Schooling* (Lewes: Falmer Press, 1989).

Haymes, B., *The Concept of the Knowledge of God* (Macmillan Press, 1988).

Hopkins, D., *A Teacher's Guide to Classroom Research* (Open University Press, 1985).

House, E., Lapan, S. and Mathison, S., 'Teacher Inference' In *Cambridge Journal of Education*, Vol. 19, No. 1 (1989).

Jensen, M., *A creative approach to the teaching of English in the examination years: an action research project* (Unpub. MPhil, University of Bath, 1987).

Kemmis, S. and McTaggart, R., *The Action Research Planner* (Geelong, Victoria: Deakin University Press, 1982).

Larter, A., *An action research approach to classroom discussion in the examination years* (Unpub. MPhil, University of Bath, 1987).

Larter, A. and Holley, E., 'Work on school-based action research groups': a paper presented to the British Educational Research Association annual conference (1990).

Lomax, P., 'An Action Research Approach to Course Evaluation' in Lomax, P. (ed.) *The Management of Change* (BERA Dialogues 1) (Multilingual Matters, 1989).

Lomax, P., 'An Action Research Approach to Developing Staff in Schools' in Lomax, P. (ed.) *Managing Staff Development in Schools: An Action Research Approach* (BERA Dialogues 3) (Multilingual Matters, 1990).

Lomax, P. and McNiff, J., 'Publish or be Damned' in *Research Intelligence* (BERA Newsletter, No., 34, Winter, 1989–90).

Martin, N., *Mostly About Writing* (Heinemann, 1983).

Maxwell, N., *From Knowledge to Wisdom: a revolution in the aims and methods of science* (Basil Blackwell, 1984).

McCorduck, P., *Machines Who Think* (San Francisco: W.H. Freeman, 1979).

McNiff, J., 'Action Research: a Generative Model for In-Service Support' in *British Journal of In-Service Education*, Vol. 10, No. 3 (Summer 1984).

McNiff, J., *Personal and Social Education: a Teacher's Handbook* (Hobsons Press, 1986).

McNiff, J., *Action Research: Principles and Practice* (Macmillan Education, 1988).

McNiff, J., *An Explanation for an Individual's Educational Development through the Dialectic of Action Research* (Unpub. PhD, University of Bath, 1989).

McNiff, J., 'Writing and the Creation of Educational Knowledge' in Lomax, P. (ed.) *Managing Staff Development in Schools: An Action Research Approach* (BERA Dialogues 3) (Multilingual Matters, 1990).

McNiff, J., 'Generative educational research and the development of the concept of education' (in preparation).

Murdoch, I., *The Sovereignty of Good* (London: Routledge and Kegan Paul, 1970).

Newell, A., 'Intellectual Issues in the History of Artificial Intelligence' in Machlup, F. and Mansfield, U. (eds) *The Study of Information: Interdisciplinary Messages* (New York: John Wiley, 1983).

O'Connor, D.J., *An Introduction to the Philosophy of Education* (Routledge and Kegan Paul, 1957).

Ornstein, R. (ed.), *The Nature of Human Consciousness* (San Francisco: W.R. Freeman and Co., 1973).

Peters, R.J., *Ethics and Education* (Allen & Unwin, 1966).

Peters, R.J., *Education and the Education of Teachers* (Routledge and Kegan Paul, 1977).

Polanyi, M., *Personal Knowledge* (Routledge and Kegan Paul, 1958).

Polanyi, M., *The Tacit Dimension* (Routledge and Kegan Paul, 1967).

Polanyi, M., *Knowing and Being* (Routledge and Kegan Paul, 1969).

Polanyi, M., 'Understanding ourselves' in Ornstein, R. (ed) *The Nature of Human Consciousness* (San Francisco: W.R. Freeman and Co., 1973).

Popper, K., *Objective Knowledge* (Oxford University Press, 1972).

Protherough, R., *Encouraging Writing* (Metheun, 1983).

Pring, R., *Personal and Social Education in the Curriculum* (Hodder and Stoughton, 1984).

Rogers, C.R., *On Becoming a Person* (London: Constable, 1961).

Rudduck, J. and Hopkins, D., *Research as a Basis for Teaching: Readings from the work of Lawrence Stenhouse* (Heinemann Educational Books, 1985).

Schön, D., *The Reflective Practitioner* (Basic Books, 1983).

Scriven, M., 'Evaluation as a paradigm for educational research' in House, E.R., (ed.) *New Directions for Educational Evaluation* (Lewes: Falmer Press, 1985).

Searle, J., 'Minds, Brains and Programs' in *The Behavioral and Brain Sciences*, 3 (1980).

Shavelson, R.J. and Stern, P., 'Research on teachers' pedagogical thoughts, judgements, decisions, and behaviour' in *Review of Educational Research*, 51(47), (1981).

Skinner, B.F., *The Technology of Teaching* (New York: Prentice Hall, 1968).

Sockett, H., 'A moral Epistemology of Practice ?' in *Cambridge Journal of Education*, Vol. 19, No. 1 (1989).

Stake, R.E., 'An evolutionary view of program improvement' in House, E.R., (ed.) *New Directions for Educational Evaluation* (Lewes: Falmer Press, 1985).

Stenhouse, L., *An Introduction to Curriculum Research and Development* (Heinemann, 1975).

Stenhouse, L., 'Research is systematic enquiry made public': Site lecture presented at Simon Fraser University, Vancouver, 8/1980 (cited in Skilbeck, M., 'Research methodology – "Research is systematic enquiry made public" ' in *British Educational Research Journal*, Vol. 9, No. 1 (1983. See also Rudduck and Hopkins, 1985).

Stronach, I., 'Raising Educational Questions' (mimeo: Cambridge Institute of Education, 1986).

Torbert, W., 'Why educational research has been so uneducational: the case for a new model of social science based on collaborative inquiry' in Reason, P. and Rowan, J. (eds) *Human Inquiry* (Wiley, 1981).

Tyler, S.A., *The Said and the Unsaid: Mind, Meaning and Culture* (New York: Academic Press, 1978).

Walker, R., *Doing Research* (Metheun, 1985).

Warnock, M., *Schools of Thought* (Faber & Faber, 1977).

Whitehead, J., 'A practical example of a dialectical approach to educational research' in Reason, P. and Rowan, J., *Human Inquiry* (Wiley, 1981).

Whitehead, J., 'Developing Personal Theories of Education' in *British Journal of In-Service Education*, Vol. 9, No. 3 (Spring, 1983).

Whitehead, J., 'An analysis of an individual's educational development: the basis for personally orientated action research' in Shipman, M. (ed.) *Educational Research: Principles, Policies and Practices* (Lewes: Falmer, 1985).

Whitehead, J., 'Creating a Living Educational Theory from questions of the kind, "How do I improve my practice?" ' in *Cambridge Journal of Education*, Vol. 19, No.1 (1989).

Whitehead, J., 'Can I Improve My Contribution to Practitioner Research in Teacher Education? A Response to Jean Rudduck' in *Westminster Studies in Education*, Vol. 13 (1990).

Wilson, J., 'Authority, Teacher Education and Educational Studies' in *Cambridge Journal of Education*, Vol. 19, No. 1 (1989).

Young, M.F.D. (ed.) *Knowledge and Control: New Directions for the Sociology of Education* (Collier Macmillan, 1971).

Index

good order, x, 34, 46-7
Green, B., 38, 115
Greendown School, x, 102
Grene, M., 22-3, 35
Gurney, M., 42

Habermas, J., 33-4, 43, 58, 105
Hamilton, D., 47-8
Haymes, B., 31-4
Hewitt, T., viii, 62-70
Hine, M., viii, 77-8
Hirst, P., 38
Holley, E., 102
Hopkins, D., 8, 19, 38. 51, 68-9, 115
House, E., 12-5
Humanities Curriculum Project, 15

I-It and I-You, 55-7, 80, 106-7
identification of problems (see problems),
individuals' rationality, xii-iii, 46-7, 52
individuals' research, x, 16, 61, 67, 71, 94
institutional practices, 61
interpretive paradigm, 13
intersubjective agreement, 3, 32-5, 45, 53, 59, 104, 106-7

Jensen, M., 42
justification:
    forms of, 33-4, 82
    of claims to knowledge, 9, 31-4, 82-4, 104
    of educational practices, 7, 58, 71

Kemmis, S., 8, 15, 38
knower and known, 22, 26, 35, 105
knowledge as creation, 26-7, 35, 100
'know-that' and 'know-how', 23, 48

language game, 33

Larter, A., 38-9, 73-7, 102
latent questions (see also tacit knowledge), 31
legitimation procedures for claims to knowledge, 19, 25, 31, 41, 43-4, 48-9, 85-92
levels of mind (see also competence and performance), 27-8, 47, 100
life process as personal creation, 3, 44, 100
living contradictions, x, 17, 40-1
living educational theory, x-xii, 9, 37-45
living 'I', x, 16, 37-8
Local Management of Schools, xi, 11
Lomax, P., 44, 69
love, 3, 56, 59-60, 106-7

management of schooling, 6, 18-9, 46-8, 50
Martin, N., 77
Maxwell, N., 101
McCorduck, P., 100
McNiff, J., ix-xii, 12-3, 27, 38, 49, 69, 107
McTaggart, R., 14-5, 38
meaning of values through practice, xii
modification of practice (see also problem solving approaches), 9, 99
moral practices (see also epistemology of practice), 9, 20, 107
Murdoch, I., 46

National Curriculum, xi, 76, 93-4
national teaching council (General Teaching Council), ix, 8, 104
networks, xii, 20, 62, 88, 92, 98, 107-8
Nixon, J., 8

MILLIONAIRE'S WEDDING REVENGE

by
Anna DePalo

Dear Reader,

I love writing about intelligent, resourceful, strong women, and Megan Simmons, the heroine of this book, is no exception. Megan's trying to hold her life all together – the child, the job, the family move – until Stephen Garrison walks back into it.

To say these two have been dancing around each other for a long time is the least of it! Stephen owns *the* trendy hotel in South Beach, and now he's out to discover Megan's secrets.

Have you ever had a hotel stay that made you feel as if you're getting away from it all for a while? Now imagine getting involved with a guy who knows how to provide you with that kind of luxurious pampering all the time. I hope you enjoy!

Wishing you the best,

Anna

For Susan Crosby and Barbara Daly.
Thanks for the mentoring.

ANNA DePALO

discovered she was a writer at heart when she realised most people don't walk around with a full cast of characters in their heads. She has lived in Italy and England; she learned to speak French, graduated from Harvard, earned graduate degrees in political science and law, forgot how to speak French and married her own dashing hero. A former intellectual property lawyer, Anna lives with her husband and son in New York City. Her books have consistently hit bestseller lists and have won a *Romantic Times BOOKreviews* Reviewers' Choice Award for Best First Series Romance and been published in over a dozen countries. Readers are invited to surf to www.desireauthors.com and can also visit Anna at www.annadepalo.com.

THE GARRISONS

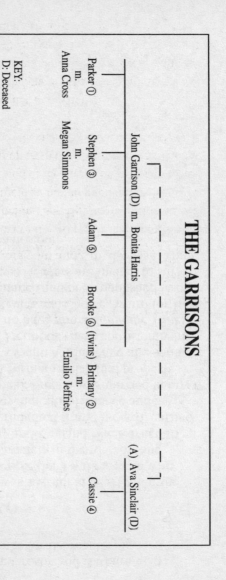

John Garrison (D) m. Bonita Harris

Parker ①
m.
Anna Cross

Stephen ③
m.
Megan Simmons

Adam ⑤

Brooke ⑥ (twins) Brittany ②
m.
Emilio Jeffries

(A) Ava Sinclair (D)

Cassie ④

KEY:
D: Deceased
A: Affair

① *The CEO's Scandalous Affair* by Roxanne St. Claire
② *Seduced by the Wealthy Playboy* by Sara Orwig
③ *Millionaire's Wedding Revenge* by Anna DePalo
④ *Stranded with the Tempting Stranger* by Brenda Jackson
⑤ *Secrets of the Tycoon's Bride* by Emilie Rose
⑥ *The Executive's Surprise Baby* by Catherine Mann

One

When Megan Simmons left Miami four years ago, she'd struggled every day to regain her equilibrium and put the past behind her. But her equilibrium had eluded her, and the past had dogged her every step.

Now, at the sound of the knock on her open office door, she glanced up from the documents on her desk and into the eyes of the man she'd once thought she'd never see again.

Her breath left her in a whoosh.

She put down the papers she was holding.

"Your new partner is hard at work already, Conrad."

His voice went through her like fine cognac. It *always* had. Particularly in bed.

This time, though, she immediately sensed the danger. Stephen's words held a note of cynical amusement.

Her eyes traveled to the second man at her door. Conrad Elkind's offer of partnership in the interior design firm she used to work for as an employee was the reason she was back in Miami.

"Good news, Megan," Conrad said heartily. "We've got an assignment to redesign part of the Garrison Grand. Stephen here was so impressed by the job you did on the Garrison, Inc. building four years ago that he requested you work on this new project."

Her eyes shot back to Stephen. From the look on his face, she knew this was no mere coincidence.

Stephen's lips twisted. "I asked Conrad not to let the cat out of the bag until we'd sealed the deal."

She felt the blood drain from her face. If she hadn't already been sitting down in a chair, she'd have collapsed into one.

When she'd moved back to Miami, she'd known she might run into Stephen, but she hadn't expected to be working for him within weeks of being back at her old firm.

Someday, in the not too distant future, she hoped to be a *senior* partner. Her firm would be Elkind, Ross, Gardner & *Simmons*. Now, however, Stephen loomed like an immovable obstacle in that path.

She composed herself and stood, even as her eyes

shot daggers at the man who'd haunted her days and not too few of her nights.

"What an *unexpected* compliment," she announced as she came around her desk.

She was dressed in a sand-colored skirt suit paired with an emerald blouse that echoed the color of her eyes. She was glad now for the professional armor, though—in a nod to the hot, sunny weather—her feet were encased in strappy tan sandals.

The end of summer in Miami was still *hot*. The September sun radiated outside Elkind, Ross & Gardner's cool offices, and its rays filtered through the blinds on her office window, hitting her back.

Still, though her sandals lent another two inches to her five-foot-nine frame, the boost wasn't enough to counteract Stephen's intimidating presence. At six foot three, he loomed over her, radiating a charisma and sex appeal that were palpable.

He was the epitome of tall, dark and handsome, with jet-black hair and coffee eyes, and a body that looked as if it would make military basic training seem no more rigorous than a stroll in the park.

She'd seen evidence of his effect on women four years ago. They'd *swooned* over him. *She'd* been stupid enough to swoon over him, too.

Even now, she felt a tingling that went all over.

She wondered whether it was the cleft chin—a Garrison family trait—that did it for some women.

But unlike screen idol Cary Grant, Stephen was a living, breathing playboy nonpareil.

A quick glance at his left hand was enough for her to confirm he was still single.

Conrad glanced at his watch. "I've got a phone conference starting in five minutes, so I'm going to leave the two of you to talk and get reacquainted."

Getting reacquainted was the last thing she wanted to do with Stephen Garrison, ever, but she forced herself to nod. "Thanks, Conrad."

When the older partner had retreated, her gaze came back to Stephen, and of its own volition, her chin rose a fraction.

Then she caught herself. It was ridiculous for her to feel defensive. *She* had nothing to feel defensive about.

"Hello, Stephen. Won't you have a seat?" She turned to head back to her desk. "I'm sure we can help you with whatever it is you're looking for."

"That's what I'm counting on," he said silkily.

She heard him close the office door, and she couldn't help but think of the sound as the opening bell in a boxing match.

She turned to face him. "I suppose it's too much to hope that your appearance here today is a mere coincidence."

"You guessed right," he drawled. "It's taken a while, but I plan to get the answers I'm looking for."

"Why do I get the impression we're not talking about the Garrison Grand?"

"Four years ago, you left Miami without a backward glance."

"You mean I left *you*."

A muscle jumped in his jaw.

"No one leaves a Garrison, is that it?" she said, hands braced on hips. Hips that now had experienced childbirth.

Motherhood had instilled in her a newfound courage, changing her from the woman she'd been four years ago. She'd do anything to make sure her daughter had the future she deserved, including struggling with the demands of single parenthood.

Including coming back to Miami.

Last month, she'd uprooted herself and Jade from her hometown of Indianapolis, and returned to Miami, though she knew it was the Garrisons' town. She'd been lured by the promise of a lucrative junior partnership in her old design firm.

Now, looking more closely at Stephen, she realized the intervening years had wrought a change in him, too. She knew he was thirty-one now, only a year older than she was, but he had a physical maturity he hadn't possessed the last time she'd seen him.

It wasn't that he looked different. He was still as good-looking as ever.

It was more that he wore his power more easily.

His air of command had lost its harsh shine and achieved a subtle luster.

Subtle, but more dangerous, she reminded herself. With that thought, she blurted, "How did you know I was back in town?"

He shoved his hands in the pockets of his bespoke suit and sauntered closer, completely comfortable in an office that should have been her domain.

She thanked her lucky stars that she hadn't set out any photos or revealing mementos. She also prayed Conrad hadn't mentioned anything too revealing about her private life.

"How did I know you were back in Miami?" he repeated, as if taking his time to consider her words. "Now that's the central question, isn't it?"

For all his smoothness, she couldn't miss the quiet danger in his voice.

His eyes held hers, and she felt as if she were drowning in their dark depths. "It seems you never mentioned to your friend Anna that you and I used to be lovers."

Oh, Anna, Megan wailed silently. Why, oh why, did you have to mention me to Stephen Garrison?

Yet, she could hardly blame her friend. She'd kept Anna in the dark—she'd kept *everyone* in the dark—about the debacle in her life four years ago.

Stephen's lips twisted sardonically. "If you wanted your return to Miami to remain a secret, you should have sewn up that hole with the brand-new Mrs. Parker Garrison."

He was right, of course, but it didn't make the pill any easier to swallow.

"You know, it's funny," Stephen went on, his tone implying it was anything but humorous, "there we were sitting around Sunday dinner at my parents' estate in Bal Harbour a few weeks ago when I happened to mention I was looking for an interior design firm to update the Garrison Grand." He paused. "One guess as to what Anna said."

Megan compressed her lips, but Stephen apparently wasn't looking for a response.

"She mentioned her friend Megan Simmons had just moved back to Miami to be a partner at Elkind, Ross." Stephen rubbed his jaw, then paused as his eyes focused on her again. "I didn't even know you and Anna were friends."

"That's how Anna got her start at Garrison, Inc. four years ago," she said tightly. "I'd gotten to know people in the HR department at Garrison headquarters when I was working on the redesign there, and I recommended her for a job. She was ready to leave Indianapolis."

She braced her fingertips against the top of her desk. Her legs felt rubbery, but since Stephen had yet to mention Jade, she guessed Anna had left out she had a daughter now.

"Right," Stephen said, sauntering even closer. "Four years ago would be right about the time you skipped town."

"I *decided* to leave Miami, yes." She'd *fled,* but these days she'd learned when to run and when to stand her ground.

"Of course," Stephen went on, seeming not to have heard her, "if you hadn't run off like a scared rabbit when I headed your way at Anna and Parker's wedding reception recently, we could have had this conversation elsewhere."

She'd hoped he hadn't spotted her mingling among the guests at Anna and Parker's lavish beach wedding, but clearly it had been a false hope despite her quick departure.

Her fear of coming face-to-face with him had almost kept her from attending, even without Jade, but loyalty to Anna had ultimately won out.

Still, she wasn't about to concede an inch. "I did *not* run away."

He quirked a brow disbelievingly.

"I just refused to sully Anna and Parker's wedding day with an unpleasant conversation."

He laughed humorlessly. "Spare me the drama."

"Is it so hard to believe there are women who don't want to flirt with you?" she retorted, her temper igniting.

"I haven't found any who've turned down an invitation to my bed, sweetheart," he shot back. "Including *you*."

"Yes, but I was the one who ultimately walked away," she countered, then went on the offensive. "Does it bother you, Stephen? Did I ruin your perfect record with women when I dumped you?"

A muscle ticked in his jaw.

She tilted her head. "You know, I promise not to tell...."

His eyes narrowed, his lips becoming a thin line, and for a moment, she worried she'd gone too far.

They'd always been good at pressing each other's buttons. It was what had added an element of exhilarating excitement to their short-lived affair.

She reminded herself, however, that nothing *she* could do now could match *his* betrayal at the end of their affair.

He searched her face. "Did you run because I was getting under your skin?" he mused, his voice lowering. "Were things getting too hot in the bedroom for you? Was your cool facade in danger of melting?"

She sucked in a breath.

"You know it was good," he murmured.

"Don't flatter yourself!"

She hadn't wanted an ugly confrontation four years ago, so she'd walked away without an explanation—without a goodbye. She'd been afraid that if she faced him with her knowledge of his betrayal, he'd convince her to stay.

Because she knew she was weak where he was concerned. Because she was intimately acquainted with just how charmingly persuasive he could be.

He shifted a step back suddenly, laying off some of the pressure. "Why did you leave?" he asked bluntly.

"I told you in the last conversation—"

"A phone message."

"I wanted a clean break," she lied again.

"After dodging my calls for days," he accused.

"You were out of town on business."

"Yeah, and then you were—supposedly."

"I was never good at breaking up," she countered, "and it was clear to me our fling was coming to an end."

As clear as the woman whom she'd seen leaving his yacht, she added silently.

His jaw clenched. Evidently, he didn't like her response, but he also wasn't going to dispute her belief.

She read his silence as confirmation, and her stomach dropped sickeningly. Obviously, if she hadn't called it quits first, Stephen would soon have been giving her his "it was good while it lasted, babe" talk.

"There, that wasn't so bad, was it?" he taunted finally. "A simple explanation for why you ended the affair. You could have given it to me at Anna's wedding without an ugly scene."

Perversely, she felt her temper rise again. "Are

you suggesting that if you'd had a chance to talk to me before now, you wouldn't be here today with a brand-new project for Elkind, Ross?" she demanded. "Because if so, I don't believe it. I know you too well, Stephen."

"You *used to* know me well, sweetheart," he responded silkily. "About as well as any woman who's shared my bed."

She was just one in a crowd, Megan thought bitterly. *As if she could ever forget.*

Yet one more reason Stephen must never, *ever,* know about Jade.

She could bear working for him if she had to. She just couldn't bear having him jeopardize what mattered most.

Stephen stared at the woman who'd walked away from him four years ago without a second glance.

He'd wanted her from the moment he'd seen her, coming out of a conference room at Garrison, Inc., right after her firm had inked a deal with his older brother, Parker, to refurbish the offices at Garrison headquarters.

She'd been laughing at something Parker had said, and the laugh, combined with everything else, had hit him like fine aged whiskey burning a path to an empty stomach.

She'd been intoxicating. A tall redhead with legs

that went on forever, and a body that was all curves. A Jessica Rabbit come to life in all her bombshell glory.

He'd pictured her beneath him in bed, those long legs wrapped around him as he lost himself inside her.

And the reality had lived up to the billing—for the first time in his jaded experience with women.

Their five-month affair had been explosive. They'd spent weekends aboard his yacht, just enjoying each other, then had sneaked away in the middle of the workday for lunchtime sex in a hotel room.

Fortunately, he'd owned—and still did—the most luxurious hotel in Miami's trendy South Beach, and he kept a private suite there for his own use.

On days when he was done meeting and greeting the high-rolling hotel guests who'd come to frolic in the sun and party in nearby nightclubs, and he didn't feel like heading back to his four-bedroom villa and estate near South Beach, he could crash at the hotel.

This particular day, however, was supposed to be about putting a coda on unfinished business. Instead, he was irritated to discover, she still had as much an effect on him as ever.

The urge to touch her was irresistible, despite the fact that *she* had chosen to end their affair four years ago with a curt phone message.

He'd tried to contact her, always getting her voice mail, until he'd discovered from the receptionist at her design firm that Megan had given two weeks' notice and skipped town to go back home to Indianapolis.

To hell with it, he'd decided. His male pride had been stung, and he'd already put it on the line enough by breaking his cardinal rule: don't look back.

He'd never been dumped before. He was used to leaving women, not having women leave him. His breakup with Megan had been the first time he'd experienced being cast aside, and he hadn't liked it.

"Why are you here?" Megan demanded now, her green eyes flashing.

To get some answers, and as it happens, I need to hire an interior designer. He'd figured he'd enjoy having Megan on his payroll, playing it until he got some answers, and in the meantime, keeping the pressure on—letting her see just what she'd walked away from.

Now, he shrugged. "Isn't it obvious? I need an interior designer to update the look of the Garrison Grand. Your firm has done work on various Garrison properties in the past, including the Garrison Grand."

"Why ask for me?" She gestured around her. "Any number of people in this office could help you."

Because I'm going to enjoy seducing you back into my bed. "Because you're one of the best interior designers in town, and you're the one who's most familiar with the Garrison account."

He hadn't shown up with the intention of reigniting their affair, but now he'd seen her again, the idea appealed increasingly.

Her response as to why she'd ended their relationship had been only a little more satisfying than the one she'd given him by phone, and he wasn't sure he bought it: their affair had been so hot, he thought his fingers would be singed.

Now that she was back in town—and back in his orbit, by his own doing—he intended to dig a little deeper.

Conrad had told him he and the other partners had lured Meghan back to the firm. They needed new blood, and she was that good.

Megan opened and closed her mouth. "But we—"

"—slept together?" he finished for her.

At her indrawn breath, he arched a brow. "You have a problem working for former lovers?"

"This is the first time I've had to face the situation!"

"What? Worried about maintaining your professionalism?"

"It's not *my* professionalism I'm worried about," she retorted.

He swept her a look, letting his gaze linger on her chest before coming back to meet her mutinous gaze.

He smiled slowly. "Then you have nothing to worry about."

She raised her chin. "I'll ask that someone else be assigned to work on the Garrison Grand."

"Careful, sweetheart. The Garrison property is one of the most lucrative accounts your firm has going. You wouldn't want to be the one who caused your firm to lose it."

Her eyes widened, and color seeped into her face, masking the dusting of freckles there—freckles that he'd spent one memorable night kissing, one by one.

"You wouldn't dare," she gritted.

He shrugged. "Since you're just back in the office, I'm assuming you've got the most time to devote to a new account. You're going to find it hard to explain to your partners why you can't."

Her shoulders heaved, and her lips compressed.

"Fine," she said finally.

He looked back at her blandly.

"But our relationship this time is strictly business."

He inclined his head. "Whatever you say…Meggi-kins."

He was going to enjoy coaxing Megan Simmons back into his bed. And this time, she'd leave only when he asked her to.

Two

Megan stepped past the liveried doorman and into the cool lobby of the Garrison Grand.

The change was a welcome respite from the heat outside. She'd dressed for the hot weather in a lime-green sheath dress with a short matching jacket, her feet encased in strappy sandals.

A couple of men sent appreciative looks her way.

She knew that as a tall redhead in heels, she was hard to overlook—even if she wore her hair tied back and constrained, as it was today.

What she *wasn't* used to, she thought, as she looked around at the hotel guests in the lobby, was the cool sophistication of Stephen's world.

She'd almost forgotten what this world was like, having spent the past few years variously wiping baby food off her shirt, reading nursery rhymes and teaching Jade how to use the potty.

Now though, as she surveyed the women with lithe tanned bodies dressed in halter tops or less, and the men projecting a chic style in khakis and designer shirts, she knew she had to gird herself for today's meeting.

Glancing to her left, she noticed Stephen walking toward her from across the lobby.

She watched as he was waylaid by an employee, then as his progress was halted again by someone who appeared to be a familiar hotel guest.

When he finally approached, she said, "I thought I was meeting one of your executives."

"Change of plans," he said, cupping her elbow and gently steering her with a subtle pressure.

He slanted her a look. "That is, unless you *mind* it's me."

"No," she responded automatically. Since she had been the one to call their relationship strictly professional, she had no choice but to stick to the script. "Of course I don't care."

Of course I care. Just being in the same room with him was enough to make her tense and jittery.

As it was, little shock waves coursed through her from the casual contact of his hand at her elbow.

They walked across the majestic soaring lobby

toward the elevators. One end of the lobby led to the street, and the other end, with columns alternating with billowing white curtains, opened onto the Garrison Grand's private beach. The smell of surf and sand wafted in.

She hadn't been able to stop herself over the years from reading the occasional news article about Stephen and the Garrison Grand. The hotel had kept a fantastic reputation while she and Stephen had been dating, but it had surpassed itself since then, becoming the *it* place for the rich and famous who flocked to South Beach.

Walking through the lobby now, she could understand why. Stephen seemed to keep everything new and cutting edge.

"I'm looking to redesign some of the meeting rooms on the second floor," Stephen said. "Then we can talk about other changes—what else needs to be revamped and updated."

His deep voice buffeted her like the warm jets of a hot tub.

This is not going to work, she thought. How could she stand to work with him when she couldn't even think straight?

Yet, she had no choice. After Stephen had left her office yesterday, she'd gone to see Conrad. The meeting had confirmed everything Stephen had said: everyone else in the office was too busy with other projects to be the lead person on the Garrison Grand, and they were looking to her to be a team player.

Now, as Stephen called the elevator and they rode up together, she felt the air between them fairly crackle with tension.

When they stepped out on the second floor, they walked down a hallway with recessed lighting along either side of its carpeted floor.

He gave her a quick tour of the business center and various conference rooms. They ended up at the end of the hall, where Stephen opened a set of double doors and ushered her inside the last empty conference room.

As she walked past him, she was careful not to brush against him. She didn't think she could stand it.

This conference room contained a long, rectangular, glass-topped table that looked as if it could seat twenty. Like the others, the decor was modern, with high-backed office chairs and all the proper business amenities: phones, a flat-screen television with a DVD player, and a projection screen that appeared as if it was normally hidden behind a wooden wall panel.

"I find it hard to believe," she observed after looking around and turning back to Stephen, "that anyone can work in paradise's playground."

It was a thought that had increasingly hit her during their brief tour.

A smile slashed across Stephen's face. "*I* do," he

said, then added drily, "That's why you can't see the beach from this room or the others."

She walked farther into the room, trailing her fingertips along the top of the table before setting her purse down, putting together the thoughts and ideas that had been formulating since the beginning of their tour.

He watched her.

"Very modern," she mused.

"Very," he agreed, "but I'm not looking for merely modern. I want different—unique—and that means changing to stay ahead of our competitors."

She turned to face him. "Are you thinking of the Hotel Victoria?"

"Just back in town, and you've heard of it already," he quipped.

She lifted her shoulders. "I'm an interior designer. Of course I'm interested in news of a hotel opening."

"Well, don't be too impressed," he advised. "Jordan Jefferies is an imitator, not an innovator, and I'm more than ready for a fight."

Stephen's comments reminded her of everything she knew about him from four years ago. He was still strong-willed, powerful and competitive.

Seeking to change the direction of the conversation, she said, "The conference rooms are different from the rest of the hotel. They don't have the same white theme—"

His lips quirked. "We were looking for something a little more professional for the business rooms. White is the ultimate indulgence."

"Decadent luxury," she agreed.

It was what his celebrity guests came for. She could only imagine what his cleaning bill amounted to for the hotel. She knew most of the guest rooms were decorated in white, with splashes of color lent mostly by fresh flowers and marble accents.

But then again, given the room rate at the Garrison Grand, she could well imagine Stephen seeing healthy profits.

She thought about the suite at the hotel that Stephen kept for his personal use. It had also been done in white, she recollected. But unlike the other suites in the hotel, the room rate there had been a night of passion in Stephen's bed.

She felt herself heat at the thought.

"What are you thinking?" he said, and she jumped.

"I was just mulling the possibilities," she said quickly, trying to cover her lapse. "It occurred to me to do a takeoff on the decor in the rest of the hotel. White and dark blue. White leather, midnight-blue velvet. Different textures, different fabrics."

She spoke rapidly, sketching her idea for him, the thoughts spilling from her. "White to echo the calming relaxation of the rest of the hotel, midnight-blue for business. Navy is a business color, but we'll subtly undermine it by casting it in sinful velvet and giving it a unique hue."

His long-ago familiar lopsided smile appeared. "Tell me more."

It was easy to think *sinful* in his presence, she wanted to tell him.

Her heart beat rapidly.

There was a time, four years ago, when they'd been so hot for each other, they'd have abandoned their business meeting to sneak away upstairs and have frantic sex in his hotel suite, kissing and holding hands in the elevator as soon as the doors closed.

Or he'd have locked the door, and taken her right here.

Not anymore.

And she shouldn't be having such lascivious thoughts about a client, she reminded herself. Particularly him. She was mommy material now.

She glanced around. "We'll replace the wood paneling with sound-soak material to help with the acoustics and lighting. It comes in an off-white color, but with a suede finish, so it'll blend with the decor."

He smiled. "Sounds good."

"It'll sound even better when I've had time to draw up plans," she responded as she walked back toward him. "We'll need to move the business center, too. It should be convenient but less obtrusive. Right now, from what I saw, it has too much glass, in my opinion."

"I'm liking it even more," he replied.

"Aren't you lucky, then, that you got me before Jordan Jefferies did?" she joked, then could have bitten off her tongue as Stephen's eyes darkened.

She watched as his gaze traveled over her. "Yeah, I *got* you," he drawled before he met her gaze. "The question is, when will I have you again?"

Her stomach flipped. *"Never."*

"Never is a long time, sweetheart."

"I thought we agreed to keep this relationship strictly professional."

"We did?" he murmured.

"That would put sexual innuendo on the wrong side of the line," she informed him.

"How about dinner?" he asked, his voice flippant even as his look heated her all over. "Would having dinner together be on the wrong side of the line?"

"Mo—" She stopped to clear the catch in her throat. "Most definitely."

"Too bad," he murmured.

Yes, too bad. Then she caught herself.

No, not too bad. He was lying, cheating vermin, and she'd be three kinds of fool to fall under the spell of his seductive charm—again. What was wrong with her?

He looked at her hair. "Why is your hair up?"

"It's hot."

Outside. It's hot outside. But she felt as if she was burning up right in here.

Before she could stop him, he reached up, and with an efficient move, released the barrette holding her hair in place.

A cascade of dark red hair followed.

"Much better," he remarked. "I always liked it better down."

"Stop it." She didn't know whom she was angrier with, him for putting the moves on her, or herself for her breathless reaction.

"It was good four years ago," he stated.

"Yes, and it's over now."

"Easily rectified. Have dinner with me."

Stephen being Stephen, it was more a command than a request.

"I can't. I need to go—"

She clamped her mouth shut. He'd gotten her so discombobulated, she'd almost said she had to go relieve the babysitter. It was an excuse that came effortlessly to her lips. She'd grown accustomed to using it over the past three years.

"You have to go, what?" he asked.

"Nothing," she responded. "When I have something down on paper for this project, I'll call you."

Then she grabbed her purse and brushed past him in her haste to get out of the room.

Stephen stood looking out his office window, his suit jacket hanging open and bunched above the hands shoved in his pockets. He had a rare moment for calm introspection.

He'd come on strong with Megan earlier. Maybe too strong, he admitted to himself now.

She'd reacted like a deer caught in headlights. It was far different from the way she'd reacted to his pursuit four years ago. Then she'd flatly refused to go out with him, but the unaccustomed taste of rejection had simply spiked his interest.

He'd made up reasons to show up at Garrison, Inc. headquarters, even recruiting Parker so he would know when Megan was due to show up there.

He'd engaged her in casual conversation, and eventually discovered they'd both been captains of their high school swim teams and they were both football fans, though she followed her hometown Indianapolis Colts while he was a Miami Dolphins fan.

More importantly, he'd liked the fact she was ambitious without taking herself too seriously. It was something he could relate to.

He'd discovered she'd left her home in Indiana and come down to Florida because of the career opportunities in the interior design field. She dealt with the aesthetics of workplace and hospitality environments, while his aim was to make his hotel the premier accommodation in Miami by focusing on cutting-edge design.

To his chagrin, he'd also discovered his reputation

as a player had preceded him and Megan was understandably wary.

"Why won't you go out with me?" he'd asked her one day, bestowing one of his trademark killer smiles. He'd found from experience that the direct approach often worked best. "It's been rumored I'm actually a reasonable dinner partner, decent arm candy and even a fairly good kisser."

Her lips had twitched. "Yes, and that's not *all* apparently. I know about your reputation."

"Rumors of my prowess have been exaggerated," he parried, not averse to shamelessly self-serving comments.

She laughed. "Can I quote you? It's rare to hear a guy like you argue for once that his image has outstripped the reality. Still, I noticed you didn't say *greatly* exaggerated."

"A guy like me?" he repeated, pretending to look wounded.

"Mmm-hmm. Exactly like you," she said archly, turning back to her work.

Still, he'd eventually caught her at a weak moment one day and coaxed her into having an overdue lunch with him at a corner bistro. She'd relented, and their affair had taken off from there.

Yet, back then she'd never had that apprehensive quality around him that she'd exhibited earlier today.

People changed, of course, but he wondered what could have triggered it in this case.

Still, he didn't intend to let the pressure off Megan.

He wanted her—sooner rather than later.

Three

When Stephen showed up at her office two days later, Megan was prepared to act as if their encounter in the Garrison Grand's conference room had never happened.

She gritted her teeth now as she led the way down the hall to Elkind, Ross's storage rooms, where they kept fabrics, carpets and wall coverings.

She was determined to keep this an all-business relationship even if it killed her.

She could feel his presence behind her—authoritative, confident, all male—and wished now she'd worn something more severe than a wrap dress and heels to work today.

They stepped into the secluded and very empty storage room, and Megan couldn't help thinking that there were some requirements of her job that she could easily do without right now.

Stephen looked around at the shelves surrounding them. They were all piled high with materials.

"So this is what things really look like around here," he said, his voice tinged with amusement. "I was beginning to think, judging from your austere office, that this was a place where even a paper clip wouldn't dare to be out of place."

"I haven't had a chance to settle in yet," she responded.

Let him think what he liked, she thought. She didn't want him getting any hints of her life as it was now.

She walked toward the back of the room to search for the samples she was looking for, and he followed, then stopped beside her. In his dark pin-stripe suit, he pulled off the look of restrained power effortlessly.

Retrieving a small chip from a cardboard box, she said, "This is a sample of the type of wall covering I'd like to use in the conference rooms."

As he took the chip from her, their hands brushed, sending awareness shooting through her.

"As you can see," she went on, determined to ignore the sensation, "it's not quite white, but close enough, I think."

"Right," he muttered, but his eyes were focused on her, not the sample in his hand.

She scooted over to another shelf. "And these are examples of the fabrics I'd like to use. This is the white leather—" she tapped a bolt of fabric "—and this is the midnight velvet."

She watched him feel the leather, his tanned hands dark against the lightness of the fabric, and an erotic charge went through her.

Cursing her wayward mind, and seeking to distract both him and herself, she yanked the bolt of velvet fabric forward with more force than necessary.

"As you can see, the color has a depth and a richness to it that make it more than merely navy-blue. It's plush, and at the same time, fairly easy to clean thanks to the wonders of new industrial processes."

He reached out and touched the fabric, his hand slowly stroking over it.

She nearly gulped. It was impossible, she belatedly realized, to have this conversation *without* a sexual subtext.

"You're right," he said, gazing directly at her. "It's…sinful."

She could see amusement lurking in his eyes. Damn him. He knew exactly the effect this conversation was having on her.

The sudden ring of a phone made her jump and broke the spell.

Stephen arched a brow.

"We keep a phone in the supply room," she explained, hurrying over to a nearby cabinet, "in case anyone needs to be reached while they're working."

While they're being seduced by the look in a client's eyes.

Picking up the phone, she said, "Hello?"

"Megan, it's Tiffany."

What a time for her babysitter to call! Maybe it hadn't been such a great idea to tell her secretary to forward any important calls. She cast an involuntary look at Stephen from the corner of her eyes.

"Is anything wrong?" she asked.

"Just checking in."

She groaned inwardly. "Thanks. That's thoughtful."

"Jade wants to go to the park," Tiffany continued, "so we might not be here when you arrive home. I didn't want you to worry, so I thought I'd call now. If we don't beat you back, we'll be on the way."

"That's fine."

"We might stop for some ice cream."

"Just remember what she's allergic to," she responded in a lowered voice.

"Will do."

When she hung up, Stephen asked, "Is everything okay? I heard you mention the word *allergic.*"

She thought frantically, even as she struggled to appear composed.

"Ah, it's a client I'm taking to lunch," she fibbed. "I was just reminding my secretary to bear in mind what the client is allergic to when making reservations." She waved her hand around. "You know, ah, ethnic cuisine and all."

"Right."

She cleared her throat. Time to get out of the pressure cooker that the storage room had turned into. "If you follow me back to my office, we can consider the layout of the Garrison Grand redesign in greater detail."

What was Megan hiding? She'd appeared furtive when speaking on the phone in the storage room earlier in the day.

Stephen stared out the window of his office, his fingers steepled, his feet crossed on his desk.

He knew she wasn't married. She didn't wear a ring, and he figured Megan would be one to change her surname when she got married.

Maybe there was a boyfriend in the picture.

His lips thinned at the thought of Megan with another man. Still, her reaction to his asking for a date *hadn't* been to say she was seeing someone. She'd been about to say something, but he was fairly sure it wasn't that. She would have finished her thought otherwise, because a steady boyfriend would have afforded her an easy excuse to turn him down.

Still, he wondered how many lovers she'd had since their breakup. He'd hardly been celibate himself. They're were plenty of beautiful women in South Beach who were only too happy to hook up with the wealthy and good-looking owner of one of the trendiest places in town.

But none of those relationships had gone as deep as the one with Megan. When his mind had slipped its leash and he'd compared those women to her, they'd come up short.

He thought back to Megan's accusation. *No one leaves a Garrison.*

Yeah, it had irked him to be dumped. Particularly since, as far as he was concerned, their relationship had been just fine. The sex had been great, and she'd challenged and fascinated him out of bed, too.

She was the one woman he'd actually given thought to settling down with.

"You look severe."

He looked at his open office door and noticed his new sister-in-law, Anna, holding on to the doorjamb.

He pushed away from his desk and lowered his feet.

Anna walked into the room. "What were you thinking? I could practically see the storm clouds."

"Nothing," he said, standing. "What brings you to the Garrison Grand?"

He kept his personal life private, including the particulars of his short-lived affair with Megan.

Still, now he knew Anna and Megan were friends, he figured his new sister-in-law could be useful to him. He wasn't averse to doing some subtle digging.

"Parker and I are having dinner at the Opalesce Room," Anna responded.

He flashed a smile that more than one woman had characterized as devilish. "Come to invite me along?"

Anna laughed. "Hardly. Parker and I are still honeymooners."

"Yeah, how can any of us forget?"

The change in his brother had been extraordinary. The guy actually seemed to be in love, which—given the train wreck their own parents' marriage had been until their father had died—was some feat. It also spoke volumes about the woman before him.

His parents' marriage had been marred by Bonita Garrison's drinking. Still, after John Garrison's sudden death from a heart attack, everyone had been shocked to learn he'd fathered a love child.

"Actually," Anna went on, "since your brother is going to be late, I thought I'd stop by on the off chance that Megan might be around. I know she's working on the business center renovation."

"She came by yesterday." He didn't add she'd hightailed it out of there after his thwarted pass.

Anna looked momentarily disappointed, then

shrugged. "Oh, well. I suppose I'll catch up with her soon." After a moment, she added impetuously, "I'm glad you hired her."

"Yeah," he said, coming around his desk, "I didn't know until you mentioned it that you were close friends with one of Miami's best up-and-coming designers."

"In fact," Anna admitted, "I have Megan to thank for my start at Garrison, Inc. four years ago. She'd gotten to know people in the HR department while she worked on renovations at Garrison headquarters."

"So she said. What are friends for?" he remarked flippantly as he made his way to a side cabinet that held a small refrigerator and beverages.

Recently he'd suspected Anna of corporate espionage, but he'd been proved wrong. Someone, though, *was* leaking secrets to the damn Jefferies brothers. Last month, editorial coverage and a photo spread in *Luxury Traveler* that he'd been working hard to negotiate for the Garrison Grand had somehow fallen through, and the magazine had instead—by strange coincidence—decided to profile Jordan Jefferies's soon-to-be-opened Hotel Victoria.

Fortunately, Parker had asked the family's private investigator, Ace Martin, to ferret out the traitor. It didn't help matters, though, that one of his younger twin sisters had just decided to get herself engaged to Emilio Jefferies.

"Drink?" he offered.

"No, thanks. Parker should be here any minute."

Stephen poured himself some bottled water. After watching his mother drink herself silly, he was careful with the heavy stuff.

"Anyway, I'm glad you hired Megan after I mentioned her for the project here at the hotel," Anna continued. "I'm glad I was able to return the favor she did for me."

"I'm sure she can't thank you enough," he responded tongue-in-cheek, thinking of Megan's reaction when he'd shown up in her office.

"I also convinced her to take over the cute little house I was leasing in Coral Gables."

He turned back toward Anna, and took a sip of his drink. "You don't say?"

Parker appeared in the doorway behind his wife, and Anna turned.

"Great, you're not as late as I thought you'd be," Anna said.

Parker gave his wife a quick kiss.

"Leave it for dessert," Stephen said to no one in particular.

Parker flashed him a grin, and Anna looked embarrassed.

Stephen raised his glass in salute. "Enjoy your meal."

Thanks to Anna, he had more important matters to attend to, starting with calling over to HR at Garrison headquarters and finding out his sister-in-law's old address.

Four

He scanned the house numbers, and when he found the modest little home in Coral Gables, he pulled up at the curb and parked his Aston Martin convertible.

As Stephen strode up the well-kept front lawn, he scanned the home's facade. It was hard to tell if anyone was home.

The house was painted white, with light blue shutters and trim providing vivid contrast. Flower boxes spilled over from the front windows, and some small bushes dotted the lawn before them.

He pocketed his sunglasses before finding and ringing the doorbell.

It was a late Saturday afternoon, and the temperature hovered modestly in the mideighties. Megan could be anywhere, he thought. She could be out running errands or seeing friends. If she wasn't home, his plan was to try another time.

He rang the doorbell again.

He knew just calling Megan up and asking for a date wouldn't work. She'd already turned down his invitation to dinner.

So, he'd decided to show up on her doorstep unannounced. He figured he could offer his help for what remained to be done moving in, and in the process, he might even persuade her about dinner.

She was bound to be more relaxed outside of work.

On top of it all, he was more than a little curious about what Megan was hiding. At the Garrison Grand the other day, when she'd abruptly cut herself off, the alarmed look that had crossed her face had been telling.

Showing up at her house would give him a good opportunity to discover any secrets.

With that thought, he rang a third time.

After waiting for a few moments, and again receiving no response, he resigned himself to trying again another time.

He turned to leave when a distant laugh suddenly stopped him.

The laugh came again, and this time he thought it was coming from the rear of the house.

Changing direction, he cut across the lawn, then

turned the corner and walked along the concrete path that ran along the side of the house.

As he neared the backyard, he could tell from the sound of movement that there were definitely people outside.

"Mommy, the green."

"Okay, Jade. Just a minute, honey."

He recognized the second voice as Megan's.

Even as his mind roared to life trying to make sense of the conversation—*Megan, a mother*—he turned the corner into the backyard.

His eyes rapidly took in Megan, her back to him, sitting at a plastic picnic table opposite a little girl. They were finger-painting and wearing matching smocks.

The little girl looked up suddenly and stared at him.

He stared back—and felt the breath leave him.

The girl had dark brown hair, pulled back in a ponytail, and her large brown eyes stared at him innocently.

But the characteristic he zeroed in on was her cleft chin.

He was all too familiar with the trait. He viewed it every morning when he shaved, and he saw it in the faces of his siblings.

All the Garrisons had cleft chins.

The girl looked to be around three, which would make her the right age....

His mind froze.

The little girl smiled and pointed. "Mommy, there's a man here."

He watched as Megan looked over her shoulder.

When she saw him, her eyes widened and her lips parted. Color drained from her face.

She owed him some answers big time, Stephen thought grimly.

He could read the truth in Megan's reaction, could see it in his daughter's face. *His daughter.*

"Hello, Megan." Given his fury, he was surprised by how even his voice was.

Not in front of Jade, her eyes seemed to beg him as he stepped forward.

"And who is this pretty girl?" he asked, looking over at Jade.

The little girl giggled. "I'm Jade."

A door opened and slammed. "Sorry, I'm late—"

Stephen turned to see a woman—a cute blonde who looked to be in her early twenties—stopped in front of Megan's back door.

Megan rose. "That's okay, Tiffany. I was just entertaining Jade with some finger-painting."

Stephen noticed Tiffany gazing at him as if she recognized him.

More likely than not, she did. If she and her friends partied at the Garrison Grand or one of the other hot spots among the Garrison properties, chances were good she would have seen him. Or maybe she recognized him from the newspapers.

"My name is Jade, and I like green!"

Despite the charged atmosphere, Stephen couldn't help smiling at the little girl's outburst. The tyke had personality.

Megan looked down at her daughter. "Time to clean up, sweetie."

"But, Mommy, we're not done!"

"Why don't I finish painting with Jade?" Tiffany offered, stepping forward, though her eyes remained on him.

Doubtlessly, Stephen thought, she was wondering what he was doing standing in Megan's yard.

"Yes, Megan," he drawled, "why don't you let Tiffany take over, since you and I *need to talk*."

His tone said she wasn't getting rid of him. He wanted answers *now*.

Their eyes met and clashed until Megan broke contact.

"All right," she said finally, then raised her arms to untie the smock from behind her neck.

Because Tiffany continued to look at him curiously, he said smoothly, "Aren't you going to introduce us, Megan?" Then without waiting for a response, he held out his hand. "Hi, I'm Stephen Garrison."

Jade's father. Megan's former lover. The guy who just found out he has a child.

"I thought I recognized you!" Tiffany exclaimed. "You're the owner of the Garrison Grand, aren't you?"

"Yes," he acknowledged, then shook Tiffany's hand.

He was used to women stating the obvious when meeting him for the first time.

He knew his effect on the opposite sex. He was tall, well-built and rich. Three qualities women loved. When they weren't slipping him their phone numbers or hotel keys, they were finagling an introduction from friends.

His image blended with that of the Garrison Grand: life in the fast lane.

"Get around, don't you?" Megan remarked drily.

He arched a brow as he stepped toward where she stood, waiting for him. "I'm locally known, if that's what you mean."

He could tell Tiffany was following their exchange avidly, which made it all the more imperative that he and Megan find a place where they could speak privately.

"Listen to what Tiffany says, sweetheart," Megan said to her daughter before turning to walk toward the back door.

He followed, watching Megan's hips swing in tailored shorts and a light blue T-shirt, her feet in flip-flops.

She could have been any suburban mother trying to entertain her kid on a hot weekend afternoon.

Except now he knew she was the mother of *his* kid.

He trailed her through the house to a cozy living room furnished with tropical-print furniture and strewn with toys.

She stopped and turned to face him.

"Why the hell didn't you tell me I had a daughter?" he began without preamble. "And don't bother denying it. She's got the Garrison features, right down to the cleft chin!"

She folded her arms in front of her, almost hugging herself. "I thought it was best."

"You…thought…it…was…best?" Fury made him enunciate every word. "Best for whom? *You?* Because I can already tell you, honey, it sure as hell wasn't best for me." He stabbed his finger in the direction of the yard. "And it's questionable whether it was best for that little girl out there to be raised by you alone and denied all the advantages I could have provided for her."

He'd just given voice to her own niggling doubts over the years, Megan thought.

There were times when she'd thought about contacting Stephen. Times when she'd wondered whether she was doing the right thing by not telling him of Jade's existence.

And then she'd thought about his betrayal and his playboy lifestyle, and realized all over again he wasn't father material. There was no way he'd be happy to learn he'd accidentally fathered a child.

Now, though, he'd found out about Jade in the worst possible way.

Still, she rebelled at his judgment of her.

"Why?" he asked.

"It was clear to me our affair was coming to an end."

"Try again," he snapped. "You've used that line before. It may have sufficed as a reason for breaking up, but it doesn't explain why you kept my daughter from me."

"What would you have done if I'd told you?" she flung back at him. "Would you have accused me of deliberately getting pregnant? Of trying to trap you?"

He stared at her hard. "My reaction is beside the point. I had a right to know."

"You gave up that right when you proved yourself untrustworthy."

"Untrustworthy? What the hell is that supposed to mean?"

"It means you were seeing other women. *Having sex with other women.*"

He didn't move a muscle.

Just let him deny it, she thought angrily.

"You're crazy," he said finally.

"I saw *her,*" she responded, dropping her arms. "I saw her leaving your yacht the night I was coming—"

She cut herself off.

"The night you were coming to tell me you were pregnant?" he finished for her, guessing.

"She said you were the best she'd ever had."

"A nice compliment if it had been *true*," he retorted, "but I wasn't sleeping with anyone else."

She threw up her hands. "What was I supposed to think? She was straightening her dress while she spoke to me! She was leaving your yacht, it was late, and you had a reputation as a player."

A reputation that she'd been well aware of. She'd only gone out with him after he'd pursued her persistently while she'd worked on the renovation of Garrison headquarters. Even then, it had been against her better judgment. Of course, once she'd found out about his cheating, she'd castigated herself for her naiveté.

"I can hardly remember who you're talking about! Women have thrown themselves at me—"

"And that's the problem," she retorted. Definitely not Daddy material. Not then, and not now. "You're the Garrison Grand's owner. You operate in a sophisticated world."

A heartless world.

A muscle worked in his jaw. "Even if I'd slept with someone else, it doesn't justify your hiding Jade."

"Oh, yes, it does," she responded. "It meant as far as you were concerned, we weren't serious. It confirmed you were still a player. I knew you wouldn't be thrilled to discover I was pregnant."

If she couldn't trust him with her heart, how could she trust him with her baby?

At least, that's what she'd told herself whenever she'd had doubts about keeping Jade's existence a secret.

"How can you be so damn sure of my reaction when I'm not even sure what the hell my reaction would have been?" he tossed back, then raked his hand through his hair. "How could you have gotten pregnant? We used protection."

She'd wondered the same thing for a time. Now, she shrugged her shoulders. "I took some antibiotics for a sinus infection. They must have interfered with the pill."

He just continued to look at her fixedly.

She steadied herself. "The question is, where do we go from here?"

She dreaded raising the issue, but it was a question that had to be asked.

"I'll tell you where we're *not* going, and that's back to you excluding me from Jade's life."

His words chilled her. The thought of Jade somehow, someday, being taken away from her was her biggest fear.

"What do you mean?" she breathed.

"I mean," he said, his expression flinty, "you're going to marry me and publicly acknowledge I'm Jade's father."

"*What?* You can't be serious!" Even as her heart thudded, she tried to wrap her mind around the idea and couldn't.

"But I am, *sweetheart*," he responded implacably.

"And if I say no?"

His face closed, hardening, and she got a glimpse of Stephen, the ruthless businessman. "Then I'll take you to court to establish my parental rights. I'll use every means at my disposal to give you the legal battle of your life and to get access to my daughter."

She knew those means were formidable. Stephen had wealth, power and political influence, not to mention the Garrison empire to back him up.

Still, she managed to find her voice, and say evenly, "I'd probably win a custody battle. The law is on my side as Jade's mother and the one who's raised her."

"You couldn't afford a fight, and even if you could, would you want to risk it?" he shot back.

No, she acknowledged, if only to herself. She knew Stephen had the money to hire the best lawyers in town, which would make for a protracted and messy battle. He could very well win generous visitation rights, at the least.

"Think about it," he said, seeming to read her mind. "One way or another, I'm in your life."

"I *could* fight you." She wasn't without some means herself. But she knew she was out of her league with Stephen.

And that was the heart of the matter. He'd always been out of her league, in every way.

"Yeah," he acknowledged too quietly, "but think about your career. You just got a new start in Miami. You don't have the time for a legal battle, and your professional reputation will take a hit."

She hated that he was right. Her professional reputation *would* suffer. Interior design was such a fickle business. Who would want to hire a woman whose personal life was a disaster? Who might be trailed by reporters to their doorstep?

Stephen had influence in this town. He was a trendsetter and more. She knew there would be people who'd want to keep on his good side—and that would include not doing business with the former lover with whom Stephen was involved in a messy child-custody fight.

"Why are you doing this me?" she whispered, distraught.

"Isn't that my line?" he countered. "Why did you do this to me?"

She opened and closed her mouth.

"No matter what," he said flatly, "we're joined at the hip."

"Oops, sorry to intrude!"

Megan turned and saw Tiffany standing in the doorway from the hallway to the living room. She had no idea how long the sitter had been there.

"I didn't realize you were still here, Megan," Tiffany said, "but I thought I'd check because you usually tell me when you're leaving." Then glancing from Stephen back to her, she added, "Didn't you say your dinner was at seven?"

Megan closed her eyes. She'd almost forgotten about her business dinner!

Opening her eyes again, she looked at her watch. It was nearing six. She'd have to hurry.

Tiffany looked from her to Stephen, and evidently judging that she'd walked in on a heated conversation, she took a step back. "I left Jade in the kitchen. Call me if you need anything."

When the sitter had retreated, Megan looked back at Stephen. "I have a business dinner in a little over an hour to court a potential new client. That's why Tiffany came over."

She'd made an exception to her rule not to let business intrude on her weekends with Jade because Conrad had asked her for a favor. She was supposed to meet Conrad and the potential client at a downtown Miami restaurant—and she wasn't even dressed yet.

Stephen looked at her coldly. "I'm giving you until Monday to make up your mind. And I'm only giving you that amount of time because I know you're scheduled to come by the Garrison Grand and we can talk then without having Jade around." He paused. "You already got *four* years."

Megan watched then as Stephen strode to the front door and slammed out of her house.

But *not* out of her life, she thought with a pang.

Five

The Mediterranean-style Garrison estate in Bal Harbour should have felt like home, but it didn't.

Still, Stephen reflected, even now with John Garrison gone, and his extramarital affair and its illegitimate child exposed, not to mention Bonita's heavy drinking, they all still felt obliged to maintain the illusion of a happy family gathering over Sunday dinner.

Yet, it was rare for all the Garrison siblings to be present, and tonight was no exception.

Stephen looked around the room. Bonita sat at the head of the dining room table, and his younger brother, Adam, and younger sister, Brooke, sat across from him.

Missing were Parker and Anna, and Brooke's twin, Brittany. Stephen figured the newlyweds had better things to do, lucky dogs. And since Brittany had recently decided she was in love with Emilio Jefferies, she preferred avoiding tense family dinners.

Now, as they chewed dinner mostly in silence, Stephen reflected on how an outsider might perceive tonight's gathering.

Valuable artwork hung on one wall, and in front of the opposite wall sat a china closet displaying various crystal pieces. Potted ferns sat in two corners of the room, and Greek columns flanked an arched entry. Overhead, a magnificent chandelier hung from a painted domed ceiling.

The room, like the rest of the estate, was majestic—and cold as ice.

His gaze came back to his family. Better to bite the bullet, he thought grimly.

"I just found out I have an illegitimate child," he announced into the silence.

Brooke gasped, and Adam froze.

Bonita stopped in midmotion, her wineglass halfway to her lips.

Given the shock waves that the discovery of John Garrison's illegitimate child had recently sent through the family, he had no illusions about how his news would be received.

Suddenly Bonita gave a raucous laugh. "Just

like your father, except you don't have a wife to trick."

He ignored the outburst, though it was uncharacteristic. He was the only one of the Garrison offspring that his mother didn't criticize, but he knew his news was a bombshell. "There's a three-year-old little girl named Jade."

"How?" Adam asked, raising the question he knew must be in everyone's mind.

He held his brother's gaze. "I had a relationship with her mother, Megan Simmons, when she did some interior design work at Garrison headquarters."

Bonita shook her head. "Just like your damned father!"

He heard the note of betrayal in his mother's tone, and felt his face tighten. "I'm planning on publicly acknowledging Jade as my daughter as soon as possible."

And marrying Megan, he added silently, if he got his way. He planned to do everything in his power to get his way.

Bonita's hand came down, her glass hitting the table with a thud and sending red wine across the white tablecloth. "You will do no such thing, do you hear me? I will not have the child of another tramp in this family! I will not tolerate another slut getting her hands on the Garrison fortune!"

He faced his mother. "You have no say in the matter," he ground out.

"I'm disappointed in you, Stephen," Bonita said, her voice frigid despite her inebriated state. "First your father betrays this family, then you do. Don't we have enough turmoil to deal with?"

In fact, he'd been thinking the same thing, but he rebelled at putting Megan in the same category as his father's faithlessness.

His fling with Megan may have been careless, but it sure as hell hadn't amounted to marital infidelity.

And it wasn't the fact that he had fathered a child out of wedlock that bothered him. It was having a child and not acknowledging her for years that, for him, created uncomfortable parallels with his father.

The longtime housekeeper, Lisette, appeared in the archway, no doubt having heard raised voices.

Bonita knocked a wine bottle to the floor, sending more wine, as well as glass this time, everywhere. Then she rose unsteadily to her feet.

Stephen stood, and Adam did the same.

Immediately, Lisette moved to Bonita's side. "Let me help you, Mrs. Garrison."

Stephen watched, along with Adam and Brooke, as Lisette helped Bonita from the room.

His hands bunched at his sides. He figured Lisette, as well as the missing Garrison family members, would find out soon enough what caused tonight's ruckus.

"Well, another rockin' Garrison family dinner!" Adam said, then picked up his glass and raised it in a mock salute before taking a swallow.

"Why don't we continue this conversation outside on the patio where the wet bar is?" he said to Adam and Brooke. Outside, they would be away from any prying eyes and open ears among the household staff. "We can let the staff clean up in here."

They'd almost finished with dinner, anyway. He looked down at the spilled wine and broken glass in distaste.

"Sorry," Brooke demurred. "I think I'll pass."

Stephen noticed his sister continued to look pale.

"Is something wrong?" he asked. "Did my news shock you that much?"

"N-no," she stammered.

He searched her face. "You look upset."

"I'm concerned about Mother's drinking." She lowered her voice. "Did you notice she drank almost a full bottle of wine at dinner—before she spilled the rest?"

Yeah, he had, and he hated to think how much his mother had imbibed *before* dinner.

Still, he had to admit that sometimes *he'd* felt the need for a fortifying drink before a Garrison family dinner.

They'd all moved to one end of the dining room, and he gently chucked Brooke under the chin. "Don't worry, kid. Let our mother deal with her own problems. But if it makes you feel better, I'm planning on having a talk with her."

Fat lot of good it would do, but he'd try. For some reason, today's dinner aside, Bonita usually held her tongue with him, and he figured that gave him some leverage. He'd also have to make clear that he wouldn't tolerate his mother taking any more cheap shots at Megan.

After he and Adam had said goodbye to Brooke and had retreated outdoors to the patio, he went to the marble-topped wet bar to pour himself a Scotch on the rocks.

The patio was dominated by an Olympic-size pool and lined with queen palms that swayed in the cool breeze. There was an unobstructed view of the ocean.

Their surroundings were serene, which made the recent tumult inside the mansion seem all the more out of place.

"Drink?" he asked Adam, who'd taken a seat on one of the bar stools.

"Booker's Bourbon, thanks."

From there, the conversation quickly moved to local business and politics. By an unspoken agreement, he and Adam put the ugly scene inside behind them as quickly as possible.

"The president of the Miami Business Council is

retiring next year," Stephen found himself observing after several minutes.

"Yeah, I know," Adam said. "I've been thinking of running to be his replacement."

Stephen shook his head. "The Business Council wants to uphold a certain image. Only married men have ever won election." He raised his glass and took a sip of his drink. "And you and I, little brother, are far from the image they want."

He and his brothers had well-earned reputations as players. Except now, Parker was married, and he'd probably be heading the same way soon, too, though he didn't feel the need to share that news with Adam just yet.

"So, what are you going to do about Jade? I'd like to meet her." Adam paused. "I'm an uncle, and I didn't even know it!"

"Try finding out that three years ago you became a father," Stephen replied ruefully. "And don't worry, you'll get to meet her."

All the Garrisons would, even if he had to move heaven and earth to make it happen.

His brows snapped together as he recalled Megan's accusation that he'd cheated. He could barely remember the night she'd referred to, or the woman who may or may not have tried to come on to him. But he knew he'd never two-timed anyone.

Still, he'd have to jog his memory somehow about

the night she was talking about. It infuriated him even now that she had continued to be skeptical even in the face of his denial.

"How *did* you feel when you found out you had a child?" Adam asked, curiosity lacing his words.

Stephen considered his brother's question. As he looked out at the water, Megan's words came back to him. *You wouldn't be thrilled to discover I was pregnant.*

Four years ago, he'd been happy to live in the moment. Yes, he'd given a passing thought to the fact that Megan was the one woman he could settle down with, but he hadn't taken any concrete steps in that direction. The truth was he'd have been blown away to discover he was a father.

Now, though, he thought about the little girl he'd seen yesterday. She looked like him, and he'd felt an instant connection.

He knew he wanted to be a father to Jade.

"It was unbelievable," he said, his gaze moving from the ocean to his brother. "She looks just like a Garrison, and the protectiveness automatically kicked in."

In fact, he was mad as hell at being shortchanged on the past three years.

"I've heard having a daughter changes everything for guys," Adam commented. "Suddenly you can't look at women the same way."

Tell me about it, Stephen thought, his mind traveling over all the women who'd blended into his past. Adam was right. He wouldn't want Jade to grow up and fall for the kind of smooth operator he'd been for most of his adult life.

"So, you're going to publicly acknowledge her?" Adam shook his head doubtfully. "I hope you know what you're getting into. As much as I hate echoing our mother, what do you know about Megan Simmons?"

"Enough," he said shortly.

"I remember meeting her when you dated four years ago," Adam went on. "Think she's one of those women who believes getting knocked up by a rich guy is like hitting the jackpot?"

"Shut up, Adam."

"No, really," his brother pressed.

"You don't know anything about it. She was hiding the kid's existence from me. I found out *accidentally* when I showed up at her house unannounced."

Adam whistled. "Well, that puts a different spin on things. I won't bother asking why you showed up at her house without an invitation." His brother gave him a sly look. "Still carrying a torch?"

"Shut up," he said, and downed some more of his drink.

It was late Sunday afternoon, and she and Anna Cross—no, Anna Garrison now, Megan corrected herself—sat at her dinette table enjoying some coffee and sinfully good Tres Leches cake.

Jade was playing in the living room, where they could hear and sometimes see her.

The house was big enough for Jade to play in, but small enough for just two people. Megan was glad now she'd taken up Anna's lease when she'd moved back to Miami. At the time, Anna had no longer needed the house in Coral Gables because she was marrying Parker Garrison.

Jade's uncle.

Of course, that meant Anna was Jade's aunt.

She really needed to 'fess up, Megan thought, looking at her friend.

She steeled herself and took a deep breath. "I have something to tell you."

"Mmm?" Anna responded, cutting off another piece of cake with her fork. "I shouldn't, but this is so—so yummy—"

"Jade is a Garrison."

Anna stilled for a moment, then her fork clattered against her plate. *"What?"*

Anna stared at her in disbelief, a dozen questions flitting across her face.

Megan rubbed clammy hands against her shorts. "Before you came to Miami four years ago, I dated Stephen Garrison."

"Stephen—?"

Megan nodded.

"I didn't even know the two of you had been involved!"

"It wasn't a long relationship." Though it had left its permanent mark. "It ended badly, and once it did, I was reluctant for a long time to share the details with anyone."

Now, though, she decided to fill in Anna on her past relationship and recent conversations with Stephen. Once she was done, she said, "He's threatened to go public. And he demanded I marry him."

"I can't believe you didn't tell him about Jade," Anna said. "Not that I'm passing judgment. It's just that I think I'd have found it hard to keep it secret."

And that was why, Megan thought, she hadn't confided in her closest friend about the details of Jade's paternity. She knew Anna would be working at Garrison, Inc. headquarters, and she didn't want to burden her friend with an explosive secret about the boss's brother.

Of course, she'd been tripped up by *not* having confided in Anna.

Anna looked thoughtful now that she seemed to have recovered from the initial shock. "I *knew* there was something between you and Stephen. I got some hints from Stephen's reaction when I mentioned you at dinner once. You also seemed to have a funny reaction at my wedding when he was heading our way."

"Actually, Stephen discovered I was back in Miami when you mentioned it to him," Megan said.

Anna's brow furrowed. "Oh, Megan, I'm *so* sorry! I didn't know how it would cause problems! All I wanted to do was send some business your way."

"Thanks." She reached out and patted Anna's hand soothingly. "I know you had the best intentions."

"And you know," Anna went on, "you *can* help Stephen. The Jefferieses are pressing *hard,* helped along by what Parker thinks is a corporate spy within the Garrison organization." Her lips twisted. "For a while, Parker—and, I guess, Stephen, as well— thought *I* was the spy."

"Yes, you explained it to me." She withdrew her hand and waved it around vaguely. "But now look at you. You're the glowing newlywed."

Anna laughed self-consciously, then murmured, "Parker…"

"*Believe me,* I'm very familiar with the charms of the Garrison men." Megan nodded her head toward the front room. "I have a daughter to prove it."

"But you don't regret Jade, do you?"

"No, of course not. She's wonderful. But now I have Stephen to deal with."

"All the Garrison men are alike," Anna observed obliquely. "What are you going to do?"

Megan sighed. "I'm not sure. Any suggestions?"

"Why don't you agree to marry him?"

"Are you serious? I can't!"

Obviously, Anna's eyes were clouded by love, Megan thought.

"Why not?"

Two simple words, and yet they dredged up a wealth of emotion, Megan thought. She was dangerously weak where Stephen was concerned, despite *everything*.

She'd seen that herself since he'd walked into her life again. It had been the same old feeling of excitement and overwhelming awareness—as if she couldn't stop arguing with him, and the only way to deal with it was to give in to the itch to jump his bones.

"He's a cheat," she contented herself with saying.

"Are you sure?" Anna pressed.

"You mean, am I sure I saw a woman with disheveled clothing emerging from Stephen's yacht, claiming to have seen more of him than his famous cleft chin?" Megan asked sarcastically. "Then, yes, I'm sure."

Anna cocked her head. "Well, even if he did cheat, that was four years ago. Now you have a child together. Think about Jade."

In fact, she had been thinking about Jade. Until now, Jade hadn't had a father in her life—though her own parents and family had been around in Indianapolis to shower her with love.

"You know," Anna went on, "being married to Stephen might not be so bad. It would take away some worries. Jade would grow up with everything money has to offer. You wouldn't have to worry about arriving at some complicated arrangement with Stephen for him to see her."

Yes, she thought, but she didn't know if *she* could take living under the same roof with Stephen. Sharing his bed…

Just being in the same room with him made her tense, jittery, and acutely aware of herself as a woman.

And she definitely couldn't risk her heart again. She'd cried for days, heartsick, when she'd discovered his betrayal four years ago.

At the time, she hadn't told him she was pregnant because she was sure a marriage between them would have been a disaster: he'd have cheated—he'd already proven himself capable of it—and she'd have wound up divorcing him to save herself.

There was *no way* she could marry him.

No way…no way…no way…

Unless…unless, of course, she could marry him without risking her heart again.

She paused.

Now, *there* might be a way out of her dilemma….

Six

Stephen stepped out of the elevators at Garrison, Inc., and the receptionist gave him a wide smile.

"Hi, Sheila."

"Hello, sugar." Sheila batted her eyelashes at him, and purred, "Come to make my day?"

He laughed. "I wish I could, honey, but duty calls."

Sheila pretended to pout.

The blue-eyed, blond, ex-Playboy bunny was his type, but this time, he knew his heart wasn't in their customary banter.

Damn Megan.

"Parker in his office?" he asked.

Sheila nodded.

"Thanks," he said, then walked down the hall.

He greeted Mario, who was pushing a mail cart and had been with the company since John Garrison's day, then a human resources person named Roberta, who was a recent hire.

All the while, he keenly observed every employee he passed. Someone in the firmament at Garrison, Inc. was passing along information to the Jefferies brothers, and until they discovered who it was, he and Parker and every other executive had to be careful about what they said and did within range of others.

Just last month, someone had accessed Parker's office computer and forwarded an e-mail they'd planted to Jordan Jefferies.

At his brother's partially closed office door, he rapped with his knuckles.

When he strode in, Parker said, "I hear congratulations are in order."

Closing the door, Stephen made for one of the leather chairs positioned before his brother's desk. "Thanks, but save it for after the wedding."

He was here because he and Parker had a Monday-morning appointment scheduled with Brandon Washington, the Garrison family lawyer. Brandon was always punctual, so Stephen knew he'd be here soon.

He caught his brother's raised eyebrows as he settled into his chair. "Somehow I knew the news would reach you one way or another."

Parker leaned back in his mesh swivel chair and tapped his fingertips together. "Maybe not the way you expected. Anna."

That caught his attention. "Anna?"

"I guess it's all right to disclose this now, since I also discovered you've been letting the news be known yourself." His brother paused. "Anna was over at Megan's place yesterday afternoon, and they had a little powwow."

Stephen felt his nostrils flare. "Tell me the wife encouraged Megan to do the sane thing."

Parker chuckled. "Define *sane*."

"Stuff it, Parker."

"Whoa, whoa, go easy here. I just discovered I'm an uncle."

Stephen let go with an expletive.

Parker eyed him. "You know, I should have known the minute I hired Megan four years ago that you'd find her irresistible. Of course, a redhead with flashing green eyes would send you down for the count."

"Yeah, well, I'm up again, and I intend to win this match. Why the hell didn't you tell me Anna and Megan were friends?"

His brother shrugged. "I had no idea myself until recently. It never came up. In fact, the first time I saw Megan again was at the wedding."

"You haven't reacted to my news with the same

suspicion it's been greeted with in other quarters," Stephen observed.

"Well, I *did* hire Megan, and I *am* married to Anna."

Just then a knock sounded, and both brothers turned to look at the door.

"Come in," Parker called.

Brandon walked in. "Good morning." He shut the door behind him. "I'm glad to see you're both here."

Stephen and Parker stood, and the men all shook hands.

Brandon took the other chair facing Parker.

"So what do we have, Brandon?" Stephen asked, as he and Parker sat back down.

"Cassie Garrison is still refusing to deal," Brandon stated matter-of-factly.

Stephen suppressed a snort of disgust.

At the reading of his father's will two months ago, he, along with the rest of the family, had discovered John Garrison had fathered a daughter during an extramarital affair with Ava Sinclair, a local he'd met in the Bahamas.

On top of it all, it turned out that the daughter was Cassie Sinclair, the manager of the Garrison Grand-Bahamas hotel, and that she, along with the five legitimate Garrison siblings, had inherited shares in the family business.

Stephen's lips twisted. Cassie Sinclair now chose to go by the name Cassie Sinclair Garrison.

Something had to be done.

So far, Cassie had resisted Parker's overtures and refused to turn over her shares in the Garrison empire.

"She apparently just wants to be left alone to run the Garrison Grand-Bahamas," Brandon said.

"No dice," Parker responded.

Brandon sighed. "I'm not getting anywhere by phone. Frankly, our best option is if I go down there and try to negotiate in person for a deal to buy her out."

Parker laced his fingers together. "I have no problem with that plan." Parker glanced over at Stephen for his assent before looking back at Brandon. "We're willing to pay—within reason."

Brandon named what he'd offered as a reasonable price for Cassie's shares, and Stephen's hand flexed on his armrest.

"You lowballed her first?" Stephen heard himself ask.

"Of course," Brandon said.

Stephen trusted Brandon like a brother. The Washingtons—Brandon and his father before him—had been the family legal advisors for years. Still, it was vitally important they get this problem with Cassie wrapped up soon and to their satisfaction. They couldn't let the future of the Garrison empire rest with an unknown quantity—a potential loose cannon.

"And if she still refuses to sell after I approach her in person?" Brandon asked, voicing the question on all their minds.

"Everyone has their price," Parker said grimly. "We'll have to think about how much more we're willing to offer."

Stephen arched a brow. "Or we can borrow a page from the world of celebrity." He looked over at Brandon. "When you get down there, why don't you first see if you can dig up some dirt on Cassie's past? It'll give us some leverage to force her hand."

Parker nodded thoughtfully. "With stakes like this, I'll take any ammunition I can get."

When Megan walked into Stephen's office at Garrison, Inc., she had some design plans in hand. But more importantly, she had a decision.

Stephen stepped around his desk and strode toward her.

"I've drawn up some preliminary plans," she said. "You can take a look at them at your leisure, and then we can discuss them. Anything can be changed, of course."

He took the plans from her and dropped them on a nearby table. Then he shut his office door and braced his arm there. "Well?"

They both knew the real topic of this meeting.

She told herself she wasn't afraid of him. She

wasn't afraid of the vast Garrison family wealth and influence. But she had to face reality.

She chewed her lip. "I've thought about your proposal."

His *proposal* had been a far cry from her girlhood dreams, but those she'd buried along with their relationship four years ago.

"Good. I expected you to."

She walked farther into the room, and he followed.

Stephen's immense office had a view of the beach and endless blue water. His desk stood in front of floor-to-ceiling windows, and off to one side were a sofa and chairs arranged around a low table.

Like the rest of the hotel, the office was light and airy. The only thing she'd change was the abstract artwork. Though she was sure it was all very valuable, she'd prefer to see something less geometrical and more soft, maybe impressionist.

But more importantly, the view from Stephen's windows said everything, and *that* she couldn't change. She watched as a toned blonde walked past to head into the hotel.

She turned toward Stephen.

His too-handsome face gave nothing away.

Nervous energy thrummed through her. She rubbed a palm against her taupe linen skirt. "I've decided to accept your proposal."

His eyes shot dark fire, and she could read the

triumph in them. "We'll have the wedding next weekend."

Her stomach flipped over. "*Next weekend?* That's not enough time!"

She'd thought she'd have more time to adjust to the idea of being Mrs. Stephen Garrison.

"You've already had four years," he said in a clipped voice, as if he'd read her mind.

"A week is not enough time to plan a wedding—"

A grim smile slashed his face. "It is if we have it here at the Garrison Grand, where *conveniently* I'm the boss. In fact, I just put together Parker and Anna's wedding in a short time."

"I have a job I just started," she began.

"You won't need to do anything but show up."

She stared at him doubtfully.

"Let's seal the deal." He looked at her innocently. "I hope that's okay?"

Then before she could react, he pulled her into his arms, and his lips came down on hers.

First there was the warm pressure of his mouth, then he slipped inside, his tongue touching and coaxing hers.

Hot, sweet sensation flooded her, and a rainbow of colors danced behind her eyelids.

When he eventually pulled back, he gave her a heavy-lidded look. "Just like I remembered," he murmured.

She touched her fingertips to her lips, feeling him there still.

Ordinarily, the stolen kiss might have sparked her ire, but under the circumstances, it reminded her of what she had to do.

She dropped her hand. "I forgot to mention something," she said hoarsely.

"What's that?"

She took a breath. "I have a couple of conditions of my own."

His look turned guarded. "Shoot."

"I want to wait until after the wedding to explain to Jade that you're her biological father."

He looked ready to argue, so she rushed on. "I want to give her time to adjust. It's enough for the moment that I'm springing this wedding on her."

"Aren't you just drawing this out when it would be better to explain the whole thing at once?"

She shook her head. "I want her to get used to you…get to know and—and like you, first, without putting any sense of obligation on her three-year-old shoulders."

"Fine," he said, though she knew he still wasn't thrilled with her idea.

And now for the hard part, she thought.

"I'm agreeing to this marriage for Jade's sake," she said. "I know there'll be lots of advantages to growing up a Garrison and with you there to help raise her."

He nodded, as if he was glad she saw reason.

"That's why," she went on, her chin coming up, "this will be a marriage in name only. I'm doing this for Jade. I won't sleep with you, Stephen."

Something in his eyes flared, and his lips curled. "Strong words from a woman who just melted into my kiss."

"Those are my conditions," she repeated.

Their eyes held for one drawn-out moment.

"You'll get your own bedroom," he said finally.

She relaxed. She was thankful for the walls of a bedroom. Now she just had to work on shoring up the ones around her heart.

When she pushed back the tissue paper, Megan felt the breath leave her.

A short while ago, a messenger had delivered several boxes. She'd taken the delivery, puzzled but knowing from the sender's information that it came from Stephen. She'd wondered why he hadn't bothered to bring the boxes himself, since he was due to arrive in a short time.

Now, Megan let her fingers stroke over the smooth white satin revealed when she'd opened the first box.

A multitude of conflicting emotions stormed her.

She understood now why Stephen may have chosen to send the boxes by messenger before he arrived. Once she'd seen what he'd bought for her, he'd known she'd find it hard to resist.

Carefully, she lifted the gown from the box and examined it.

It was a backless sheath dress with a small swallowtail train made of satin overlaid with lace. The bodice, which had a sweetheart neckline, was held up by two spaghetti straps.

Simple but sexy, it would be spectacular with her flaming red hair, as well as show off her generous chest to advantage.

Stephen knew her so well. And *that,* she realized, was part of the problem.

She'd told Stephen she'd be wearing something practical—something she already owned—for the wedding. Instead, he'd overridden her.

He'd sent her this dress, and its message was clear: she was being served up as a delicious dessert he intended to savor.

Still, the dress was so beautiful, it brought tears to her eyes.

She'd once wished for happily-ever-after. Instead, she was getting an illusion.

A sham wedding leading to a fake marriage.

Tamping down a sudden well of emotion, she forced herself to open the rest of the boxes.

One box contained a pair of stylish stiletto sandals. Another held an adorable sleeveless flower girl's dress with a high ribbon waist and matching white sandals.

Her heart squeezed as she thought of Jade and how delighted she'd be.

When she opened the last box, however, her reaction changed, and she felt heat course through her.

The box contained a white bustier, matching lacy underwear and thigh-high hosiery.

Unbidden, images of modeling the sexy concoction for Stephen went through her mind.

Then, annoyed with herself, she let her hand drop away from the box.

Of course, Stephen had no trouble picking out her size. He was a connoisseur of the female form, she reminded herself. A playboy extraordinaire.

She was torn from her thoughts by the sound of the doorbell.

Moments later, she heard the sound of running feet.

"Mommy, there's someone at the door!" Jade called out.

"I'll be right there."

She and Stephen had agreed he'd come over on Wednesday night in order to ease the transition for Jade to the upcoming marriage.

She'd already explained to Jade as well as she could that she'd be getting married to Stephen and they'd be known as Megan and Jade Garrison.

Now, she prayed Stephen's get-to-know-you session with his daughter went well.

When she opened the door, with Jade peering around her, she was presented with an incongruous sight. Stephen held a bouquet of flowers in one hand, and a large brown-haired, brown-eyed baby doll in the other.

As annoyed as she'd just been with him, she couldn't help reacting with a laughing gasp.

His eyes met hers, and she saw laughter lurking within them. "She rode in the front passenger seat."

Wide-eyed, Jade stared at Stephen.

Megan covered her mouth.

Not a word, Stephen's eyes mockingly warned her. Then he stepped forward. "Hello, honey."

Megan stared at him—dressed as the consummate corporate executive in a charcoal business suit—before he bent forward and kissed her on the lips.

"We need to make this good for Jade," he murmured as he straightened.

She gave him a startled look, then closed the door behind him. What was he up to?

But Stephen was already looking down at his daughter. He smiled. "Hello, Jade."

Jade edged closer to her, and Megan put a comforting arm behind her.

"Hi," Jade said hesitantly.

Megan realized with a start that Jade was uncharacteristically shy. Apparently, it was one thing to enthusiastically point out a stranger—as Jade had done when Stephen had appeared in their backyard on Saturday—and another to welcome someone more permanent.

Megan prayed again or all their sakes that tonight went well.

Stephen held out the baby doll, which was dressed in pink and purple and wore a headband. "I have a present for you. This is Abby, and she's looking for a home."

Jade eyed the doll, then looked back at Stephen.

Megan saw a flicker of uncertainty in Stephen's eyes, and her heart went out to him. He was clearly lost.

"Stephen bought a gift for you, isn't that nice?" she said to Jade.

They'd agreed Jade would call him Stephen until she got used to him in her life.

Jade stepped forward, then took the doll and hugged it to her. "Thank you."

Megan watched as Stephen's eyes went to her again. "And these are for you."

The bouquet that he held out to her contained lilies mixed with lavender. Her favorite. He'd sent the flowers to her when they'd dated, and he'd remembered still.

"Thank you."

Their hands brushed over the flowers, and a sizzle

went through her. And though her mind flashed danger, her heart beat rapidly.

She steadied herself. "Why don't we go into the living room? Dinner is almost ready. Would you like anything to drink, Stephen?"

"A beer would be great."

Jade was already playing with her doll, and Stephen planted himself halfway between the kitchen and where the little girl sat.

Megan felt a small smile rise to her lips. Big, bad Stephen Garrison was in unfamiliar territory, rendered helpless by a three-year-old.

She could see the headline: Playboy Beaten by Child's Play.

When she came out with Stephen's beer, she noticed Jade looking at him from the corner of her eyes.

The little girl stood, then blurted, "Would you like to see my toys?"

She watched the play of emotions on Stephen's face, before he responded casually, "Sure. Let's see what you got, kid."

Her heart constricted as she watched Stephen follow Jade, and a variety of emotions swept over her.

Finally, she headed back to the kitchen. She had chicken Kiev in the oven and potatoes and broccoli on the stove.

Dinner would be a far cry from what Stephen was used to at Miami's top-tier restaurants, including the ones within the Garrison Grand itself. She had to give a nod to kid fare, but she reminded herself that Stephen was better off finding out sooner rather than later what parenthood was about. He was determined to come into her life and Jade's, and she wasn't going to sugarcoat it for him.

When she'd gotten everything on the table, she went to find them—the most important person in her life, and the one around whom her world had revolved four years ago.

She located them in Jade's room.

"…and this is Holly, and that's Caroline," her daughter said.

Megan watched as Stephen nodded. "Quite a crowd."

Jade had all her dolls and stuffed animals lined up, and apparently had been introducing them all to Stephen.

"Dinner's ready," Megan heard herself say.

Stephen and Jade both turned to her.

"But, Mommy, I still need to introduce my dolls!"

"Later, sweetie."

Stephen winked. "I promise I'll come back after dinner, pumpkin."

Jade pulled a face but trudged in the direction of the kitchen.

Pumpkin?

It was a big turnaround from where Stephen and

Jade had been a mere thirty minutes ago, and Megan was reminded again of the fact that a three-year-old's worldview could do a one-eighty in a minute.

She watched Jade leave, then looked back at Stephen. "Quick work there."

He gave her a lazy smile. "Charm upsets you?"

She forced herself to shrug indifferently. "Your *legendary* charm. Why should I be surprised?"

"Afraid you'll fall under it again?" he challenged.

"I've been inoculated for life."

He chuckled as he sauntered toward her. "Don't worry. I leave my best for someone…special."

She sucked in a breath, but he didn't try to steal a kiss or make a pass.

Instead, he walked out of the room and followed Jade's lead.

She expelled the breath she was holding, then followed him out.

In the house's little dining area, she saw Stephen eyeing the floral display in the center of the table.

She'd set his bouquet there in a clear glass vase.

"Very nice," he commented, "if I do say so myself."

"I put them there so we wouldn't have to stare at each other across the table through dinner," she muttered in a low voice as she went past.

He had the audacity to laugh, which just sent a shiver through her because she remembered how much she'd always liked his laugh.

She felt his arm snake around her, and he gave her a quick kiss on the neck. "Glad you like them so much."

"You know flowers that stand for *devotion* are my favorite," she retorted.

At dinner, Jade kept up a steady stream of conversation with Stephen. She seemed openly curious about him now.

He handled her questions well, simplifying but never talking down to her, and it was clear that though he was still feeling his way, he was gaining confidence with every passing second.

Megan watched the interaction and thought they could all be any family having dinner together. Except this was a pretend family with an upcoming sham marriage.

Seven

So far, Stephen thought, things were working out as he'd planned.

Jade was warming to him, and while he had further to go with Megan, he knew at least that she was far from being immune to him.

"Want to see the rest of my dolls?" Jade piped up as soon as dinner was over.

"Sure."

Jade's face lit up. She ran around the table to grab his hand and tug him forward as he stood.

"Jade, we don't drag guests around like toys," Megan warned. "Stephen isn't Barney."

"Yes, Mommy," Jade responded without looking at her mother.

Stephen felt a smile pull at his lips.

She reminded him of himself when he was a little kid—full of boundless energy and enthusiasm. He wondered which parts of herself Megan saw in Jade.

It was still hitting him that this little girl was *his*. He wouldn't—couldn't—let her down.

Twenty minutes later, Jade was instructing him on tea party etiquette using her table-and-chair set and toy kitchen when Megan appeared in the doorway.

His eyes ate her up. He'd discarded his jacket and tie before dinner, but she was dressed even more casually in a flower-print short-sleeved blouse, tailored beige cropped pants and espadrille sandals.

Memories tugged and he remembered the way they used to dance together at some of Miami's hottest nightspots.

Their bodies had brushed, swayed and come together again. They'd tantalized each other before heading home to make passionate love on silk sheets.

Realizing he'd been staring at Megan and she'd begun looking back at him questioningly, he suddenly felt ridiculous.

It was absurd to be having sexy thoughts about Megan while he was sitting in a girly pink bedroom, waiting to drink pretend tea from a toy cup.

Covering his lapse, he said, "Have you shown Jade her flower girl dress?"

Megan hesitated, but Jade perked up, "Dress? What color?"

"Pink, of course," he informed her.

Jade squealed and clapped her hands. "Can I see? Can I see?"

Megan sighed. "It's on my bed, Jade."

Stephen noted Megan didn't seem too happy with his gift. He was doubly glad now he'd let the cat out of the bag and gotten the jump on her.

They followed Jade to Megan's bedroom, which was decorated in tropical colors of lime-green, peach and pink. White wicker furniture blended with a couple of antique pieces.

His eyes fell to the bed, where some of his purchases from yesterday lay in and out of their boxes. The lingerie he'd sent was nowhere to be seen but a tulle-and-satin flower girl dress with a wide sash and little rosebud embroidery along the neckline lay spread out across the bed.

Jade oohed and aahed over the dress before announcing, "I love it!"

"I wasn't sure of the size, so I had to guess."

"It's her size," Megan said gloomily from next to him.

He tossed her an amused look, and she raised an

eyebrow at him. Clearly there'd be a battle later, but he was more than up for it.

After Megan gave in to Jade's pleas to try on the dress, and the little girl had twirled around for them, Megan announced it was time for dessert.

They all went back to the dining room to have what Stephen discovered was Jade's favorite: mint chocolate chip ice cream with chocolate syrup.

Afterward, the three of them cleared the table and Megan said it was Jade's bedtime.

Jade put up some resistance, but gave up the fight when Stephen agreed to read a bedtime story.

Only after he'd read three of Jade's favorite stories were he and Megan able to head back to the living room.

Once there, Megan folded her arms. "I can't accept the gifts you sent."

"Then I suppose you're really not going to like this." He reached into his pocket, then picked up her hand and slid a ring onto her finger.

He heard her breath catch, hitch.

Yesterday, he'd gone to one of Miami's most exclusive jewelers and bought an engagement ring with a large Canadian diamond in the center flanked by two emeralds.

"The stones signify our yesterday, today and tomorrow," he told her. "I chose emeralds for your eyes."

"We're not having much of an engagement," she said, staring at the ring.

"We're just condensing the steps."

She looked up at him, then started to pull the ring off, but he stopped her.

Her chin came up. "Do you want a symbolic reminder of our yesterdays, Stephen?"

His mouth tightened. "Do you regret having Jade?"

"You know that's not what I meant!"

"Then what did you mean?" he challenged her. "Do I want to remember nights of mind-blowing sex? Do I want to remember the way we were so hot for each other, we couldn't be in the same room without getting turned on?"

Their eyes locked.

He'd opened the door, and their past came flooding back. One touch, one kiss, right now, and Stephen knew they'd both be swept away.

"I was waiting to discuss the packages with you, but now that you made her aware of the dress, Jade is all excited."

"Yeah, well, consider yourself outmaneuvered."

The air between them shimmered with sexual energy.

"And what about that kiss when you first walked in?"

He gave her a rakish smile. "What about it?"

"What did you mean by 'we need to make this good for Jade'?"

He sobered. "I mean, if this marriage is about doing what's best for Jade, then we need to make her believe we're happily married."

She stalked away, then whirled back. "You're just using Jade as an excuse."

Busted. "For what?" he asked innocently.

"You know what. To put the moves on me, hoping to get me back in bed."

"When we wind up back in bed, it'll be because you'll want it as badly as I do."

"You're not even going to try to deny it, are you?"

"In fact—" he glanced back toward Jade's room "—since Jade's asleep now, I'm going to suggest we practice." He took a step toward her.

Her eyes widened. "Definitely not necessary," she said sharply.

"But oh so enjoyable. Did you like the lingerie I sent?"

She flushed. "Strumpet & Pink. You *do* know your lingerie, and why am I not surprised?"

He was close enough now to see the pulse jump at the side of her throat.

He smoothed a lock of her hair with the back of his hand, and her eyes sparked before his gaze dropped to her mouth.

He'd always liked her fire. As much as he liked

her mouth, in fact. It was full and made for kissing. He remembered all she'd done with that mouth, and nearly groaned aloud.

"You had an amazing collection," he muttered against her lips, "and a fabulous body to go with it."

Then he kissed her, sinking into her with a hunger that surprised even him. There was a moment when she didn't react, but then her mouth opened to him.

He deepened the kiss and brought his hand up to cup her breast, feeling the nipple harden through the thin fabric of her bra and top.

Lust slammed into him, and just like that he was aroused.

She'd always been able to turn him on faster than any woman ever had, and apparently nothing much had changed.

He had to have her. In bed and out. He *would* have her.

It gave him some satisfaction to be in control—to be calling the shots. It was what he was used to.

But if he didn't stop this make-out session soon, he was in danger of losing it. Tonight wasn't the night for seduction—just for giving her a taste.

Jade was sleeping nearby, and he didn't want to scare Megan off a wedding when he almost had her where he wanted her.

He eased back from their kiss. When he raised his head, he met her lambent gaze.

"Was that kiss supposed to prove something to me?" she asked.

"Yeah. We won't have any problems convincing Jade." Hell, his body still raged for her, and it was only with effort he got it under control.

Her brows drew together. "Of course not. You're a playboy of mythical proportions."

He refrained from gibing about what proportions she was talking about. Instead, he said, "I won't cheat because my father was a cheater."

That got her attention.

"What?" She stopped, and her brow puckered again. "What do you mean?"

"I mean, my father had an extramarital affair, and we only found out about his twenty-seven-year-old love child at the reading of his will recently. Suffice it to say, the news wreaked havoc on the family, particularly my mother."

He filled her in on his family's discovery of the existence of Cassie Sinclair Garrison and her claim on the Garrison fortune.

"You do have problems, don't you?" she said. "The Jefferieses on one hand, and now your father's illegitimate child."

"Don't forget *my* illegitimate child, but I'm about to fix that situation."

Megan folded her arms. "So I'm supposed to conclude from the Cassie story that you've reformed?"

Her coolness and continued skepticism ate at him. He picked up his jacket from where he'd thrown it on the back of a chair at the beginning of the evening. "You're supposed to conclude we'll have a *real* marriage."

He gave her a lingering look—sparks shooting back and forth between them—before he let himself out of the house.

The wedding ceremony was held on a private slice of beach behind the Garrison Grand, where Parker and Anna's wedding had taken place the month before.

A floor had been laid over the sand, and folding chairs had been set up on either side of a makeshift aisle. Off to the side, adjacent to the hotel, was a canopied area that would serve as the location for an indoor-outdoor reception.

Because of the short notice, and the small number of guests, the local media had not caught wind of the pending nuptials.

Now, as Megan stood behind Jade and next to her father in the shade of the hotel's lobby, waiting for the string quartet to strike up Pachelbel's *Canon,* she was profoundly grateful for the relative privacy.

She was nervous enough as it was.

This week, she'd had to break the news to both her family and her employer that she was about to have a hasty wedding to Stephen Garrison.

Her parents and younger sister had known at least that Stephen was the father of her child, though they'd kept a vow of secrecy for the past four years.

She'd simply told them that she and Stephen had reconnected when she'd moved back to Miami and that the two of them had realized they were destined to be together.

Her mother had nonetheless worried about whether Megan was making the right decision, but Megan had kept a determined, upbeat front. Her entire immediate family had decided to fly down to Miami for the weekend for the ceremony.

Breaking the news to her coworkers at Elkind, Ross had been a trickier matter. They'd been surprised and even astonished to discover she and Stephen were going to marry. None of them had even been aware that she and Stephen had been involved in the past, because she'd been discreet about her affair with the middle Garrison brother four years before.

She'd had to explain that she and Stephen had reconnected over her work on the Garrison Grand and known immediately they'd made a mistake by parting ways.

Once she'd assured everyone that Elkind, Ross would continue to have the Garrison account, and she'd continue to work on it with the utmost professionalism, everyone's initial curiosity at least had been satisfied. Conrad Elkind was even attending the ceremony today along with his wife.

By far the hardest disclosure for her to deal with had been the announcement to the media. She'd helped Stephen draft a public statement that would be released right after the wedding. She'd combed over every word of the announcement of her marriage and the disclosure that Jade was Stephen's child.

She was suddenly recalled from her reverie as the instrumentalists struck up Pachelbel's *Canon*.

The assembled guests turned to look at her, and she in return surveyed them. Even Bonita Garrison was in attendance, though Stephen had warned her that his mother had drawn unpleasant comparisons between their situation and the hurt caused by her late husband's philandering.

Her eyes drifted to Stephen, and she only had eyes for him as she started down the aisle created by the partitioned guests.

His expression was carved in granite—except for his eyes. As she drew closer, she saw that his eyes shone with sensuous promise.

She had to remind herself it was a well-practiced look for him and she shouldn't attach too much significance to it.

Still, when she reached his side, and they turned to face the officiant, tears pricked her eyes and she trembled.

There were times when she'd wished Jade had had a father around, and now Stephen had stepped up to the plate—whether she wanted him to or not.

She handed her round bouquet of tightly packed roses to Jade.

"We have been called here today to witness Megan and Stephen being joined together in holy matrimony…"

As the officiant went on, she was very aware of Stephen standing by her side and she stole a look at him. He was steady as a rock, facing forward, his expression serious.

Maybe because he felt her observation, however, he turned his head and glanced down at her.

She blinked rapidly to clear the mist from her eyes.

"Who gives this woman to be wedded to this man?"

"I do!" Jade piped up, and the guests laughed.

She and Stephen laughed, too, and then her breath caught. She hadn't seen Stephen laugh like that in four years.

And all at once, it was time to say her vows.

"I, Megan, take you, Stephen, to be my husband…" Her voice came out a little unsteady, but Stephen held her gaze, refusing to let her look away.

When it was his turn, he looked into her eyes and spoke in a sure and clear voice. "I, Stephen, take you, Megan, to be my wife…"

His words gave her goose bumps, and the goose

bumps turned to a fine tremor when it was time to exchange rings.

She wondered if Stephen could feel her unsteadiness as he took her hand and slipped a filigreed platinum band next to her engagement ring.

"Take this ring as an eternal symbol of my love…"

She couldn't look away from him as he said the words and then it was her turn to repeat them back to him.

"…I now pronounce you…"

Married. The word echoed in her head, and she felt the full effect of its heady power.

Stephen had changed the course of her life already, and now he was her husband.

Her husband, and he was bending forward, a dark glimmer in his eyes and lust in his soul.

"Let's make it good for Jade," he murmured.

His lips touched hers, and before she could react, he'd deepened the kiss to a long and lingering one she felt down to the toes. Her hands curled into his upper arms.

The guests hooted and clapped.

Stephen straightened, and she took a deep breath. Then she hooked her arm through his and they walked past their guests and toward the hotel to the tune of "Ode to Joy."

Fortunately, once the reception started under tents set up on the beach, she was able to mingle among the guests and push aside—at least for the moment—the disturbing feelings Stephen aroused in her.

As she watched Jade dance with Stephen, Anna come over to congratulate her.

Her friend gave her a quick hug. "I'm so glad you married into the family, even if I have selfish reasons. The Garrisons *can* be intimidating."

"Tell me about it," Megan muttered. She'd met all of the Garrison siblings when she and Stephen had dated, so she had an inkling. Then she thought about how hard a time she had handling just Stephen.

Anna searched her face. "So are you satisfied with your decision?"

"Thanks for dispensing with the word *happy,*" she responded. They both knew this forced marriage was anything but a joyous occasion.

"You should give Stephen a chance. He might surprise you."

"It'll be difficult to surprise me. This time I won't be shocked if I find another woman in his bed."

Stephen was still dancing with Jade, who was twirling around. It wasn't hard to see how they were related—the dark-haired little girl who was smiling and laughing, and the darkly gorgeous father who somehow managed to look comfortable dancing with an unpredictable partner.

"You shouldn't be such a cynic," Anna admonished.

Megan looked back at her. "It's precisely because

I don't think he can be faithful that I made sure this would be a marriage in name only."

"What do you mean?"

"I mean—and this is confidential—we won't be sleeping together."

Anna's eyebrows shot up. "Stephen agreed?"

She recalled Stephen's challenges, then his gambit regarding making things look good for Jade. "He agreed to separate bedrooms."

Anna looked at her shrewdly. "Uh-huh."

Megan glanced over at the man who'd sent her life careening off course ever since he'd stepped into it four years ago. "I won't lose my heart to him again," she said adamantly.

Eight

He was, Stephen decided, a masochist.

Looking at Megan in the wedding gown *he'd* picked out, all he wanted to do was spirit her away to a place where they could get naked and find feverish deliverance.

His yacht would serve the purpose well. He kept it nearby, and it was somewhere he could relax and get away from it all. Its satin-covered bed was his favorite place to make love, rocked by the soothing waves lapping the sides of the boat.

His body had been at a steady hum ever since he'd seen Megan start down the aisle. He hadn't been able to peel his eyes off her. She'd looked incredible in the simple but sexy gown he'd picked up for her at a high-end Miami boutique.

He was getting what he wanted, but he wanted her *willing*. Despite her attempt to make this a marriage of convenience, he planned to seduce her back into his bed—as the first step toward making them the family unit they should be.

He'd seen tears in her eyes during the ceremony, and had wondered whether they signaled sadness or happiness. When she was in his arms, he'd make sure she was beyond sadness or happiness. They'd just *fit,* as they had from the very beginning.

He absently twisted the ring on his finger.

"Still getting used to the feel? Don't worry, you will, faster than you can believe."

He turned at the sound of his brother's voice. "Hey, Parker."

"What are you thinking?"

"Nothing."

"*Nothing* is a lot when you're the groom, and it's your day," his brother commented.

Stephen watched Megan float among the guests. She stopped to speak with Conrad and his wife and accept congratulations.

"Be careful," Parker murmured, following the direction of his gaze. "At this rate, you'll be falling for her all over again, and she'll have you eating out of the palm of her hand."

"Not gonna happen."

He wanted Megan, but he was done with surprises coming out of left field. This time he was in control.

He scanned the guests, then gave his brother a lopsided smile. "I pulled this thing together in a week. I'm getting good at it. Think any of our other siblings wants a spur-of-the-moment wedding?"

Parker groaned. "Don't even think it. It's bad enough Brittany thinks she's getting hitched to a Jefferies."

"Speaking of which," Stephen responded, spying Brittany and her fiancé, Emilio Jefferies, "looks like some guests are heading our way."

"Yeah, *Jefferies,*" Adam grated as he joined them from where he'd been standing a few feet away.

Parker turned in the direction of their gaze, and watched, too, as their younger sister approached with the darker of the Jefferies brothers.

Stephen had gotten a chance to size the man up when Emilio had crashed Parker and Anna's wedding. Unlike his brother, Emilio was dark haired and olive skinned, his green eyes a startling contrast to his complexion.

From an investigative report that Parker had ordered, Stephen knew Emilio had been adopted. His mother had been the Jefferies' nanny, and he'd been born in Cuba.

"Hola," Brittany said, smiling as she came toward them holding Emilio's hand.

Emilio, in contrast, looked as guarded as he and his brothers probably did, Stephen noted.

"We just wanted to say congratulations, Stephen." She stepped forward and brushed his cheek with a quick kiss.

"Thanks, kiddo." Then he looked up, and said in acknowledgment, "Jefferies."

Emilio held out his hand. "Congratulations."

It was a bold move, and after a split second, he reached out to grasp Emilio's hand. "Thanks."

He and his brothers had their suspicions, but while signs pointed to corporate espionage by the Jefferieses, they'd yet to uncover the trail and, more importantly, find the culprit.

In the meantime, it was clear Emilio was devoted to Brittany, and Stephen figured that had to count for something—at least for a cool but civilized exchange of pleasantries at a wedding. And, if there was one thing he'd learned in the corporate world, it was never to let the competition see you sweat.

Parker looked narrow-eyed. "Good to see you, Jefferies."

Adam nodded his head in acknowledgment.

Brittany beamed, and Parker caught the look.

"It's easy to be charitable when this is one wedding Emilio isn't crashing," Parker said to his sister wryly.

Adam coughed to hide a laugh, and, if he wasn't

mistaken, Stephen thought, a glint of humor appeared in Emilio Jefferies's eyes.

As he turned to say something more to Brittany, however, he spotted one of his hotel employees wheeling in the table with the wedding cake.

He grasped his brothers' arms, and nodded at his sister and Emilio. "You'll excuse me. Business—of the pleasant variety—calls."

She'd visited Stephen's private estate near South Beach four years ago, but this time around it was home—and Megan found herself adjusting to the idea.

She and Stephen had agreed she'd give up the lease on the cute little house in Coral Gables and move into his four-bedroom Spanish Mission-style home. She knew the grounds of the estate included a pool, while the house itself had a gym and a home theater.

Even a little girl as active and rambunctious as Jade would have a hard time making a dent in such a place.

Megan consoled herself with that thought now, as she prepared to get out of her wedding gown and get ready for bed in the bedroom next to Stephen's.

Her room and Stephen's were separated only by a connecting bathroom, and Stephen had explained that while his bedroom was the master suite, hers had been set up as a baby's room by the house's previous owners. Since Jade was occupying the third bedroom, which was ideally configured for use as a child's room, and the fourth was being used by Stephen as a guest bedroom/upstairs office, there was no place else for her to stay.

She sighed now as she looked around the room, toying with the bouquet she'd held earlier in the day as she'd walked down the aisle.

The room was outfitted with Spanish colonial-style furniture, in keeping with the house's architecture. Rich, sturdy wood furniture contrasted with white walls and wrought-iron accent pieces.

Four years ago, when she'd spent nights at Stephen's estate, she'd imagined this room one day being used as a nursery for their child. Now Jade was already past the need for a nursery, and she and Stephen wouldn't have any more children.

The thought inexplicably depressed her, just as the entire day had been an emotional maelstrom for her.

After the wedding reception, she and Stephen had headed back to his estate and put a very tired Jade to bed. Jade had promptly fallen asleep in her new bedroom, down the hall from hers and Stephen's.

There hadn't been time to move all their possessions from the Coral Gables house to Stephen's place before the wedding, but since she'd already paid the current month's rent, she knew she had some time to move out, though she'd given notice she'd be giving up the lease.

With any luck, Jade would settle right into their

new routine. She'd still drop Jade off at preschool, and Tiffany would pick her up and babysit until Megan or Stephen got home from work.

Her thoughts were interrupted by Stephen's appearance in the open doorway of the connecting bathroom.

His eyes were shadowed in the low lighting afforded by her bedside lamp, and though she couldn't read his expression, her breath caught.

His tie hung loose around his neck. "Need some help?" he asked.

She dropped the bouquet of roses onto the bed. "Even if I did, asking you would be like asking a wolf to shepherd a lamb."

He flashed a smile and sauntered into the room. "Are you a lamb?" he murmured. "You're dressed in white…but not devoid of sin, from what I recall."

She tossed her hair, and moved to the bureau to remove her watch and earrings. "Spoken like a true scholar of the subject."

He laughed. "That's my girl."

"What do you want, Stephen?"

"In a word, you."

A tremor went through her at his words, despite her best attempts to steel herself against him. "Do I already need to remind you this is a marriage in name only?"

"I'm a patient man. I'm willing to wait for the pleasure of seeing you in that lingerie I sent you earlier in the week."

He moved up behind her and his hands clasped her shoulders. She stared at their image in the mirror in front of her.

She could feel the imprint of his body behind her, the male heat emanating from him and branding her. She picked up his masculine scent, one she recognized from four years ago and one which predictably awakened her senses.

He bent his head to nuzzle her neck, and her body reacted to remembered passion, as well as the image of the two of them together in the mirror.

His dark good looks were a perfect foil for her red hair and pale creamy skin.

His hands stroked up and down her arms, his mouth caressing the curve of her neck, then the shell of her ear…and the wisps of hair at her temple. Always teasing her.

Her nipples hardened, thrusting against the fabric of her gown.

She felt herself succumbing to him with mind-numbing ease, pulled under by a seductive undertow.

She turned in his arms, breaking free and intent on telling him off, but his mouth claimed hers before she could speak.

His lips moved over hers, taking control of the kiss, slipping past her barriers to touch her tongue with his and invite her to duel with him. Mate with him.

Her defenses came crashing down as the past

stormed back to greet them in all its passion and un-fettered need.

His mouth moved over hers with greater urgency, and his hands roamed her back, bringing her closer to the flame of his desire.

She felt his erection press against her.

Sexual need ate at her. It was even hotter than before. Even hotter than she remembered.

She felt his hand at her back, tugging the zipper of her gown downward.

With a last desperate effort, she pulled her mouth from his and pushed away from him.

He took deep breaths, his eyes dilated from arousal.

Her breaths matched his, and she ached all over. Especially in her heart.

She hugged the sagging bodice of her dress to her.

He reached for her again, and she took a step back.

"You can't deny we both want it," he said in a quiet voice.

She raised her chin. "I'm wise enough to know now that *wanting* doesn't mean *having*."

They locked eyes, and she watched his expression shutter.

"One of these days, you're going to realize you're not the only one who's changed in the past four years," he said evenly.

They both stood there for a moment, not moving, before he strode out of the room.

She watched him leave, fighting to slow her pulse. Then she turned toward the vanity table to pick up her brush—and the broken pieces of her shattered four-year-old control.

Stephen arrived home on Monday to relieve the babysitter. He and Megan had decided to try out staggering their workdays as much as possible so that one of them would almost always be with Jade and they'd use their babysitter only to fill in small gaps.

"Hi, Stephen," Tiffany said, giving him a bright smile.

The sitter couldn't be more than twenty-two or twenty-three, he'd concluded when he'd first met her. Today, she wore hip-hugging denim shorts and a sleeveless tee with the words Baby Phat in rhinestones across the chest. Her straight blond hair was pulled back in a ponytail.

He was familiar with Tiffany's type. Women like her roamed at the periphery of his world—through the Garrison Grand's celebrity-hosted events, and at hot spots like his brother's nightclub, Estate.

"Hey," he said in acknowledgment. "Everything go okay today?"

Tiffany nodded, looking a little tongue-tied, and Stephen recognized the reaction. In some ways he was even used to it.

He wasn't a movie star or rock sensation, but with

his looks and wealth, he'd inspired reactions ranging from no-holds-barred come-ons to stolen glances and coy smiles. As the owner of the Garrison Grand, he was considered the epitome of cool—as much as it amused him sometimes.

Like everyone else, Tiffany had reacted with surprise when he and Megan had announced they were getting married. Still, she seemed to accept the explanation Megan had given—that the two of them had realized when they'd reencountered each other that they wanted to be together.

If Tiffany had caught on that he and Megan had begun their marriage sleeping in separate beds, she hadn't said anything. And frankly, Tiffany's presence was another reason he'd put Megan in the room next to his—aside from the obvious one of wanting Megan close by. He didn't want the babysitter to be the source of idle gossip. There'd been enough speculation out there among the public and the press about his lifestyle.

He loosened his tie just as Jade bounded into the room, holding what he'd come to know was her Baby Alive doll.

"Hello, gorgeous." He crouched and opened his arms, and Jade threw herself into them.

He'd recently been instructed by his daughter, in a very important voice, about all the cool characteristics of Baby Alive.

He seemed to recall Brittany and Brooke having a similar doll when they were little—one that, as a prank, he'd put in the pool to see if it could swim—so the toy apparently had staying power. Go figure.

He also decided it was best if he didn't mention that particular prank to Jade—though his sisters might rat him out at some point. Old stunts like that could tarnish his budding reputation as a great dad.

After a moment, Jade pulled back from his embrace. "Hi," she said, somewhat shyly.

He noticed that, despite her initial exuberance, Jade seemed to be hesitant.

One step forward, two steps back, he thought. But he was in this for the long haul.

After Tiffany left, he and Jade played with some puzzles and simple board games in the den until Megan arrived home.

They went out to greet her in the foyer.

One look at Megan, and his body tightened, the way it always did around her.

A short brown skirt showed off her spectacular legs, which were accentuated by stone-embellished spike-heeled sandals. She was wearing a short-sleeved blouse with a tropical print and gold chandelier earrings.

"Mommy!"

"Hi, sweetie." Megan's eyes traveled from Jade to him, a question in her eyes. "How are you doing?"

"We were just playing board games," he supplied.

Games a lot simpler than the one he and Megan were playing.

He reached out to take her upper arm and swept Megan's lips with a kiss. Jade, he noticed, absorbed it all with interest.

"Come on," he said to both of them. "I grill some mean steaks."

"Hamburger," Jade responded.

He feigned a long-suffering sigh. "All right, hamburger for you." He touched her nose. "But only because I feel like playing short-order cook tonight."

"What's a short-order cook?" Jade asked.

He slanted her a look. "Anyone cooking for someone who can barely reach the light switch."

Jade giggled.

He guided the little girl forward with his hand on her shoulder. "Come on, I'll explain."

"I'll join you as soon as I change," Megan said from behind them.

He turned back to her, quirking a brow. "Need some help?"

The air crackled with energy.

"No, thank you," she said, looking at him disapprovingly.

He flashed her a wicked smile. "Your choice."

"Yes."

"But I'm hoping to win the lottery one of these days."

She gave him a quelling look before heading for the stairs.

Later, they wound up having dinner on the patio, where they were able to watch the lowering sun. He grilled on his outdoor range, and Jade got her wish when he served up a Cuban-style burger seasoned with chorizo.

Jade's questions and requests peppered the dinner conversation, and Stephen realized this was what he should expect from now on.

They were a little family, the three of them, he thought, and it felt good. More than good.

It should have taken him longer to adjust from being a practiced playboy with honed predatory skills to protective father and husband. But instead it felt like coming home.

After dinner, he and Megan sat back and watched Jade explore and play on the patio.

"You're good with her," she remarked.

He leaned back farther in his chair. "She seemed a little hesitant when I came home today, though."

"That's natural."

He looked over at Jade. "Yeah, but I'm wondering whether something more is going on."

When Jade eventually came back over to join them, Megan leaned toward her. "Did you have a good day today, sweetie?"

Jade nodded, hopping back into her chair and taking a drink from her cup.

"Did you have fun at preschool?"

"Yes."

"Did something happen at school?" Megan prompted some more.

This time, Jade looked at him from the corner of her eyes.

"Jade?"

Jade looked down at her now-empty plate, and said in a rush, "I told Emily I had a daddy because you got married. She said no, I had a *stepfather.*"

Oh, damn, Stephen thought.

He looked at Megan. It seemed as though their conversation with Jade was upon them faster than they'd anticipated.

Megan opened her mouth, but Stephen silenced her with a look.

"Jade, I *am* your daddy," he explained gently. "I was away for a little while, but I'm here now and will love you forever."

Jade looked up at him, such hopefulness in her eyes, it almost killed him.

"Do you understand?" he asked.

The little girl nodded. "Uh-huh."

"And even if I was your stepfather, I wouldn't love you any less."

Jade blinked, then blurted, "Can I call you Daddy?"

His heart did a weird twist.

"Of course," he said, his voice coming out unexpectedly hoarse.

"You'll never know how much I regret not being around when you were a baby," he said.

Jade got down from her chair and threw her arms around him.

His eyes met Megan's over Jade's dark head, and he thought he saw a sheen of tears in them.

Nine

On Saturday, Stephen took them out on his yacht, a sixty-foot Sea Ray.

Jade had pleaded to see the boat, and though Megan had her suspicions about how her daughter had gotten the idea in her head, she gave in.

Stephen had been so good with Jade this past week. The three of them had even toured the Garrison Grand early one evening, seeing the suite that Stephen kept there for his—now their—personal use. She couldn't deny him or her daughter the fun of an outing on Biscayne Bay.

From what she remembered, the yacht, named *Fishful Thinking,* was Stephen's prized possession.

The two of them had spent many carefree hours on it, making love and just relaxing and enjoying each other...until she'd discovered she wasn't the only woman he'd been entertaining aboard.

Now, as she stood in the stateroom, running a brush through her hair near a small mirror, she pushed the uncomfortable thought aside.

Stephen had killed the engine and dropped anchor so that the boat bobbed in the water.

After she and Stephen had taken turns diving and swimming off the side of the boat, they'd had lunch. Then Jade—worn out by the excitement of being on a yacht for the first time—had lain down for a nap.

Her daughter was asleep now on the bunk in the guest stateroom, so there was no innocent little girl around to run interference between her and Stephen. Megan sought to quell the nervousness that seized her.

As if conjured by her thoughts, Stephen appeared. He looked relaxed, fit and tanned in swim trunks and a short-sleeved navy T-shirt he'd donned after his swim.

"Hey, there," he said, resting his hand on the top of the door frame.

"Hi." She hated that he looked so at ease when she was a bundle of nerves. She'd intentionally put on a short skirt over her halter-top emerald bathing suit, but she still felt exposed.

It didn't help she'd seen amusement in the depths of Stephen's eyes when she'd done so, as if he saw right through her maneuver.

Now, as he looked her up and down, her body hummed in reaction. She prayed her nipples wouldn't harden, betraying her even more.

Despite the ease with which he'd assumed a fatherly role in Jade's life, she had to remember he was a rat and their relationship was *all business,* including this marriage.

"What are you doing?" he asked.

"Trying to get some knots out of my hair." Her hair had dried from her dip in the water earlier, but despite having had it in a ponytail, it had gotten tangled by the wind and water.

He continued to watch her with the same searing gaze he'd had when she'd stripped down to her bathing suit earlier.

"Jade wants to learn how to swim," she blurted.

His lips curved in the lopsided smile that never failed to send heat shooting through her. "I want to teach her. If she'd grown up here, near the water, she might already know how."

Surprisingly, she couldn't detect a hint of reproach in his voice. "She'd love to learn."

He stepped forward. "Here, let me help you."

She lowered the hand with the brush to her side.

"What?" she asked, though she'd heard him perfectly well. Her mind had just stopped at the image of Stephen touching her hair.

He grasped her wrist and gently removed the brush from her nerveless fingers. Then he stepped behind her, and she felt the movement of thick bristles from her scalp to the curling edges of her wavy hair.

She also felt his presence as he shifted against her—saw it in the small mirror in front of her—and her pulse picked up.

His skin gave off the scent of fresh air, salty water and sunscreen—and healthy male sweat.

They stood in silence. He lifted first one lock of hair, then another, pulling the brush through from root to tip.

She felt the air around her grow hot and heavy, until she had to concentrate on keeping her breathing even.

"Just like a mermaid," he murmured, arranging one curling edge over her shoulder before lifting another section of hair.

"No fins," she said automatically, and couldn't believe how breathless she sounded.

He chuckled, then sobered.

"I've been thinking about your accusation, and I've done some research," he said. "I looked back over my business diary from four years ago to try to refresh my memory about the night you were talking about."

She stiffened. "I'm surprised you didn't attempt hypnosis."

He laughed shortly before going on. "We hosted a party that night for an up-and-coming British rock group, and there were plenty of celebrity hangers-on involved. The woman you saw that night was there on a lark. She must have followed me back from the Garrison Grand, or gotten a tip from someone there that I owned a yacht."

"I wonder how she could have gotten the impression you were open to a brief encounter," she remarked acerbically.

He didn't react, apparently refusing to be baited by her sarcasm. "I admit I had a reputation as a player, and since you weren't around that night, someone thought I was fair game."

"I bet," she said unbendingly.

"But I did not sleep with that bottle blonde," he continued inexorably. "She sneaked aboard, but I sent her packing the second it became clear why she was there."

"How do you explain the fact she was still straightening her clothing when I saw her?" Megan asked. She didn't want to give him a chance to clarify things, but curiosity got the better of her.

In the mirror, she saw Stephen's lips twist. "I'm betting she saw you coming—maybe even recognized you—and decided to put on a show out of spite."

She finally felt herself relax a little at his words, despite her best intentions.

"You already think I'm a cheater," he said, as if

reading her mind. "I'm not about to compound my problems by becoming a liar, too."

"How do I know you won't cheat now?" she asked, her eyes meeting his in the mirror. "You're still the head of the Garrison Grand and—" she gestured around her "—you've still got this yacht. Women will want to come on to you."

He showed her the hand with his wedding ring. "This is your insurance."

She looked at his plain platinum band. "A wedding ring isn't considered an obstacle by some women."

"I just admitted that *at the time* you met me I had a reputation—"

She raised her eyebrows. "Really? The fact that you had to jog your memory speaks volumes." Though her words were sharp, it was getting hard to maintain her edge when he was practically giving her a scalp massage. "You couldn't even remember the woman who showed up that night."

"But I could never forget you," he said against her temple. "That's why I turned her away."

She felt his words with shattering force. Her walls where he was concerned—never sturdy to begin with—crumbled some more.

"I want to make love," he stated, and her insides turned to mush.

"That's not a good idea," she managed to say through a constricted throat.

"On the contrary," he responded, tossing the brush aside. "I think it's the best idea I've had in a *long* time."

He spun her around to face him, and her hands fell against his chest.

He dipped his head, and his mouth plundered hers.

Tongues touched and lips moved, shifted, caressed, and just like that, the dam burst.

She moaned low in her throat.

His fingers delved into her hair, undoing his handiwork as he pulled her head back. His mouth skimmed along the side of her neck.

"I want you so damn much," he muttered.

Her hands moved to grip his shoulders, anchoring herself in a world gone topsy-turvy.

When his mouth met the obstacle of her bathing suit, his fingers went to the clasp of the halter top and released the bonds that kept her from him. Her breasts spilled forward, and his hands came up to palm and stroke them, rubbing folds of nylon across sensitized nipples.

The force of their desire came roaring to life, the way it always had.

They couldn't get enough of each other. Mouth fused to mouth, and his hands shot down, skimming under her skirt to grasp her buttocks and bring her flush against him to feel the strength of his need.

The past had been a glorious ride before she'd been thrown, but it had brought her Jade, and now suddenly she wanted to reach out again with both hands to grasp the sunshine, feeling reckless—no, feeling like a gambler.

She felt the strong beat of his heart and felt the thrilling excitement of wanting to be joined with him.

Her skirt hit the floor, and their hands roamed with increasing urgency. Her fingers stroked and delved, retracing every luscious inch of him that had been imprinted on her memory.

During the years they'd been apart, she'd still dreamed about him—fantasized about him. It hadn't mattered that she'd thought he was a cheat. Her heart at night was free to roam where her mind would not allow itself to go when she was awake.

Now, he pulled away from her and yanked his shirt over his head, exposing a chest she'd itched to touch ever since he'd stripped down to his bathing trunks for their swim earlier.

Her fingers danced over defined muscle, until she gave in to the urge to place openmouthed kisses where her hands had just been. His skin tasted warm, salty and sun-kissed.

With an oath of frustration, he bent and pulled down his swim trunks.

His impressive erection sprang free, exciting her even more.

She quivered, her body tightening—a reaction that echoed those she'd felt whenever they were together.

"I've got to have you," he said, and her senses ran riot.

He hooked his thumbs under the fabric of her swimsuit and pulled it off her.

His mouth came down to ravage hers. After a moment, he hooked his foot behind her ankle, sliding her leg forward and throwing her off balance so they both tumbled onto the bed next to them.

He feasted on her breasts, then found all her pleasure points: the hollow behind her ear...the curve of her breast...her inner thigh...her instep. All the while she did a slow slide to mindless desire.

And still he played with her.

He was a master at bringing her vibrantly to life.

She raked her hands down his back as he kissed her hip bone, then the indentation it formed.

When he touched her welcoming wetness with his hand, she sucked in a breath, tensing.

"Relax," he murmured.

How could she relax when she could hear the dark intent in his voice? She could feel his breath against her, and her pulse accelerated.

The first touch of his mouth sent waves of sensation surging through her.

"Stephen."

He growled against her damp heat, then delved in to pleasure her with his mouth.

She turned her head toward the mattress, her hands grasping the sheets.

She moaned, sighed and careened toward release. Within moments, she trembled against him before sinking back against the mattress, weak and fulfilled.

Seconds later, she watched as he moved up next to her and looked over at a nearby drawer. "Damn it. I just realized I don't have any protection."

"I haven't been with anyone since our affair." She was desperate for him, otherwise she'd never have been so direct. Her body was still wet and wanting.

He looked at her questioningly, then his eyes kindled.

"With a small child, there hasn't been time for anything," she explained.

"I'm healthy," he said.

She nodded.

"But you could get pregnant," he went on, holding her gaze.

Her heart flipped. "Or not. It's the wrong time of the month."

The truth was there were times when she'd been sad that Jade might not have any siblings. She'd foreclosed other possibilities when she'd married Stephen. *Why not take this?* her heart whispered.

"We're married," he said, his erection resting against her. "This time it's you and me in it together, either way."

"We've already made that bargain," she responded in a low voice, though she knew another child hadn't factored into their arrangement.

Her green light was the last encouragement he needed.

His mouth claimed hers, and with his lead, their need for each other was stoked to a blistering height once more.

When he finally sank into her, she expelled a breath on a long sigh.

"I know, baby," he murmured, soothing her. "Let me give you what you want—what we both need."

She caught his rhythm as effortlessly as she always had. It was a dance they'd always performed well, moving with primal instinct.

He thrust, sending her higher and higher. She clung to him, moaning, reaching, and leaving herself open to feeling.

Then, just when she thought the tension couldn't build up anymore, the coil within her released, and she shattered.

She felt him strain back, thrust one final time, and with a guttural groan, climax after her.

"Everyone, this is Jade," Stephen said, his hand resting on his daughter's shoulder.

Stephen's siblings stepped forward in turn to greet Jade.

Megan wet her lips nervously.

All the Garrisons had gathered, including Parker and Anna. Anna had said she'd show up to give moral support, and now Megan was glad for it.

Though Stephen's family had seen Jade at the wedding, this Sunday-night dinner at the Garrison estate would be their first opportunity to really interact with her.

This was also her own very first visit to the Bal Harbour estate, Megan reflected. She'd never stepped inside Stephen's parents' mansion during their fling, but she was here now as his wife and the mother of their child.

She let her gaze travel over her surroundings with a designer's practiced eye. The foyer was designed to impress—intimidate even—as was the entire estate.

The double-height foyer was dominated by an immense stone fireplace, before which were arranged various armchairs and sofas. Thick stone Corinthian columns supported graceful archways. To one side, a wide stone staircase led to a second level, where a gallery, bracketed by more stone columns, ran around the perimeter of the room and gave a glimpse of the rooms on the upper level.

Four years ago, she'd met all the Garrison siblings at one event or another. Parker, of course, she'd worked for, and she and Stephen had partied at

Adam's nightclub, where she'd also met the twins, Brittany and Brooke.

She wished, however, that she'd also met Stephen's mother back then. The matriarch of the clan had greeted her stiffly at the wedding and now held back, surveying the scene.

When all of Stephen's siblings had stopped fussing over Jade, Stephen's mother looked down at her granddaughter.

"Come here, little girl," Bonita said, and after a slight hesitation, Jade stepped forward.

Megan could feel Stephen tense beside her.

She'd dressed Jade in a sleeveless emerald-green dress, tying her daughter's hair back with a ribbon. She'd wanted Jade to make the best impression possible. She could deal with rejection for herself, but she wanted Jade to be accepted—embraced even—by the Garrisons.

So far, to her relief, all of Stephen's siblings had reacted warmly, surpassing expectations that she'd tried to keep in check so as not to be disappointed.

Now, though, she held her breath as Bonita grasped Jade's chin and tilted her face up so she could examine the little girl's face.

Seconds ticked by, and Megan felt as if everyone else in the room was holding their breath right along with her.

"There's no mistaking the fact you're a Garrison," Bonita stated finally. "The image of your father, in fact."

Though there was no visible softening of Bonita's features, everyone seemed to relax slightly. The lack of censure in Bonita's voice made it likely this evening at least might pass without incident.

"I'm your grandmother," Bonita said. "You may call me Grandmother."

Bonita dropped her hand, and Jade nodded, wide-eyed.

Megan's shoulders lowered. Stephen had filled her in on the fact that Bonita had a drinking problem that had become exacerbated recently. She'd stated that his mother could prove difficult about accepting what were, in her view, a mistress and out-of-wedlock child into the family.

Yet, it seemed Bonita's affection for her son had won the day, and Megan felt her tension ebb some more.

As people began to mingle and talk, waiting for dinner to be served in the dining room, Stephen moved away to speak with Adam, and Brittany approached her.

Stephen's sister squeezed her arm. "I'm so happy for you and Stephen."

Megan put a smile on her face. "Thanks, and likewise for you and Emilio." She looked over Brittany's shoulder. "Where is he by the way?"

Brittany laughed. "Busy with El Diablo."

Megan nodded. "He must work hard. That restaurant has gotten great reviews for its food and ambience."

Brittany leaned in. "Between you and me, I think it's just as well he isn't here. We're still easing our way with the family."

"Tell me about it," she responded ruefully. "I was nervous about coming tonight. Everyone had to be on their best behavior for the wedding, but tonight is a different matter."

"You're doing great," Brittany said, then looked across the room at Stephen. "You know, I suspected Stephen was carrying a torch for you after your breakup."

Megan felt a flutter, but then reminded herself that Brittany was hardly an impartial party.

"Not our playboy action hero," she said glibly.

"He matured, too," Brittany insisted. "Since you left, he built up the Garrison Grand even more. I think he poured himself into it, and in the process, he took a good hotel and made it great."

"I can't disagree there," Megan murmured, looking across the room now, too. Stephen had studied her plans for the hotel's conference and business center and made some modifications to make the renovation even more state-of-the-art. She had to admit he knew his stuff.

"My only concern was that he was becoming just a little too focused and ruthless," Brittany went on, turning to look at her again. "Now that he's married, I can stop worrying."

If only Brittany knew the half of it, Megan thought.

Of course, Brittany wanted to believe she and Stephen had found a happily-ever-after—she was in love herself. From what Stephen had told her before the wedding, Megan knew Brittany was newly engaged to Emilio Jefferies and planning a splashy wedding.

But she also knew her own situation was far different. Stephen's ruthlessness hadn't ebbed a bit, and she and Stephen had married for convenience.

She almost blurted out the latter to Brittany, but she contented herself with saying, "Jade's certainly had an effect on him."

After Stephen's sister had moved off to speak with her twin, Megan found herself mulling over the weekend's events.

Yesterday, when they'd gotten home from their outing on the yacht and put Jade to bed, she'd fallen asleep herself atop her own bed. After changing into her sleep tee, she'd meant to lie down only for a few minutes before doing some work-related reading. Instead, in the morning, she'd woken up under some blankets. She'd realized Stephen must have come in at some point and covered her up, and a wave of awareness had washed over her, despite her best efforts.

Then today, she and Stephen had both been so

busy with Jade, there'd been no time to talk. In many ways, though, she'd been grateful for the distraction.

True, yesterday the sex between her and Stephen had been fantastic. Their unbridled need had proven to her once again that, where Stephen Garrison was concerned, she had no self-control.

Yet though she believed Stephen's explanation of what had happened—or, rather, what had *not* happened—that night four years ago on his boat, she wasn't sure what they had between them now was more than just good sex.

Yes, he wanted her back in his life, but it was because he thought the two of them should raise Jade together. He wanted to be fully involved in his daughter's life, and the only way to do that was to include Jade's mother in a package deal.

Undeniably, on the yacht yesterday, she'd had a moment of recklessness that might have made her pregnant again—though the possibility was unlikely. At least this time, though, she was married and had already committed to raising one child with Stephen.

But she knew better than to risk her heart again. Stephen had never said he loved her, and given the long line of women in his life—despite Brittany's claim about his newfound maturity—she doubted he ever would. She might be the most memorable in his long line of conquests, but he'd given her no reason to believe she'd ever been more.

Still, because she'd rejected him four years ago, he saw her as a sexual challenge now. She belatedly realized she'd all but waved the red flag in front of him when she'd announced she wouldn't sleep with him.

Stephen had a strong sex drive, and she was his wife. If no longer in name only, she reminded herself, still just out of convenience.

Ten

Stephen had the chance to speak to his mother alone after the family dinner. He stopped her at the base of the foyer staircase.

Good thing that today she seemed more sober than usual. Still, he had a good hunch she'd been heading upstairs to her stash of liquor.

"You're out of control," he said without preamble.

She raised an eyebrow haughtily. "Excuse me, but I have no idea what you mean."

He had to give his mother credit. Even struggling with an addiction to alcohol, she was still the grand dame. But he knew where the truth lay.

"Let's dispense with the subterfuge," he said.

If possible, Bonita seemed to freeze even more. "I'm your mother. I won't have you speaking to me this way."

With her hand on the railing, Bonita took a step up, but he placed his hand over hers, halting her progress.

"I'm talking about your drinking, Mother. It's started to affect the entire family, and it's consuming your life."

Bonita straightened, her spine stiffening with outrage. "How dare you? Wasn't I polite and cordial to your wife and daughter? Didn't I welcome them into my home?"

"Your drinking is upsetting the whole family," he continued implacably.

Bonita's eyes snapped with anger. "How dare you speak to me about *upsetting* this family? Your father cheated and imperiled the family fortune, and you've decided to follow in his footsteps."

He sighed. The family peace that had prevailed tonight appeared to be over. He'd figured Megan would come into this at one point or another.

"Your accusations are off the mark. I didn't cheat on my wife—" Though Megan had thought he'd cheated on her before they were married, he decided his mother didn't need to know about a false accusation "—and I sure didn't jeopardize the family fortune. Parker and I are working to get this situation with the woman in the Bahamas straightened out. The *only* parallel with Dad is that I had a child out of wedlock, but I don't regret Jade's existence for a second."

His mother's lips thinned. "And now your mistress has joined the family, too. You outdid your father in that department, Stephen."

He held on to Bonita's hand when she tried to ascend. "Make no mistake, Mother. Megan *is* part of this family, and she's here to stay. I won't tolerate your being rude to her."

Then because of his purpose in seeking out his mother tonight, and because he could read the turbulence and pain in her eyes unusually well at the moment, he softened his voice. "Get yourself some help, Mother. Otherwise, we'll have to do it for you."

After a tense moment during which neither of them spoke, Bonita extricated her hand from his and went up the stairs without a look back.

Watching his mother depart, Stephen reflected on her accusations, and his thoughts naturally turned to the status of his relationship with Megan.

Yesterday had been fantastic. He'd taken Megan and Jade for an outing aboard his prized yacht and had been able to share one of his favorite pastimes with his daughter for the first time. Life didn't get any better.

On top of it all, his and Megan's lovemaking had been as explosive as ever. He meant to repeat the experience as soon as possible. Tonight, if he could arrange it.

Yesterday, when Megan hadn't seemed to mind the possibility of getting pregnant again, he'd nearly blown his cool right then with his blinding need to have her.

Now, the thought of having more children with her made his pulse quicken all over again. This time he wanted to be around for all of it. He wanted to experience the wonder of pregnancy with her. He wanted to be there when their child was born.

He wanted Megan in his bed, in his life. Period.

If Megan didn't realize it already, he was going to set out to prove it to her.

Their marriage in name only was about to become a marriage in every possible way.

When they got home from Bonita's estate, Megan helped Jade get ready for bed, then tiptoed out of her daughter's room while Stephen read a bedtime story.

Returning to her own room, she thought about how wonderful it would be to luxuriate in a warm bath for half an hour. She'd survived the evening, and all she wanted to do now was relax.

Instead, however, she opted for a quick shower in the adjoining bathroom. A hot shower would do the trick almost as well to relieve her tight muscles. And it had the added benefit of being relatively fast—no need to worry too much about Stephen moving around in the next room.

She stripped, then walked into the bathroom and got the water running in the shower. Stepping into the stall, she sighed and closed her eyes as hot jets of water pounded her.

All in all, she had to admit the evening hadn't gone *badly*. Bonita—judging from what Stephen had told her beforehand by way of warning—seemed to have behaved fairly well.

And Stephen's siblings had been warm, welcoming and nonjudgmental. They appeared to accept that whatever her relationship with Stephen had been, and whatever reasons she'd had for not telling Stephen about Jade, it was all water under the bridge now that she and Stephen were married.

She sighed again.

"Need me to do your back?"

She gasped and jerked around.

Stephen stood outside the shower stall, and from his lazy, amused tone, he'd gotten quite an eyeful.

"What are you doing here?" Surprise made her tone sharp.

His lopsided grin emerged. "I knocked on your bedroom door, and when I got no response, I came in." His eyes crinkled. "I thought you might have fallen asleep on the bed—again."

"Well, as you can see, I'm taking a shower!"

His eyes traveled downward. "Yeah, I can see all right—"

"What do you want?"

His eyes came back to hers. "Take a guess."

She regretted her choice of words. "I'll be out soon."

She made her tone repressive. They needed to talk, that was for sure—but not here and now! She used her pointed tone to mask her susceptibility.

She felt vulnerable and exposed, not to mention that standing before him naked was doing strange things to her insides.

Stephen's grin only widened. "Sure about the back scrub?"

"No, thanks."

"I'll try to get over the devastating rejection."

"I know it doesn't happen much, but join the masses."

His eyes glinted at her humor. "Do you remember the showers we took together?" he murmured. "We'd wind up late for work."

She certainly *hadn't* forgotten. How could she? She'd replayed those scenes in her mind too many times over the years.

She moved to turn off the shower. "I've grown up," she responded.

"So have I," he drawled, turning toward the door, "but that doesn't exclude indulging in some fun."

Judging by their encounter yesterday, she'd have to agree with him. Mercifully, though, she was spared a response as he walked out of the room.

* * *

Twenty minutes later, she wandered downstairs in her bare feet, a satin robe over a matching knee-length gown. Damp tendrils of hair lay against her shoulders. She hadn't completely succeeded in keeping her hair dry despite tying it up for the shower.

She found Stephen in the spacious living room. The lights were turned down low, and the voice of Harry Connick, Jr. crooning "Only You" sounded softly in the background.

Stephen stood holding two wineglasses filled with red wine. He held one out to her.

A little flame she was all too familiar with ignited inside her.

She'd sought him out for a talk—the recent episode in the shower had convinced her they were past due for one—but this wasn't quite the ambience she was expecting.

"Relax," he said, as if reading her mind.

She realized her only hope rested with appearing cool and nonchalant. Stephen would exploit any hint of responsiveness to his advantage.

With that thought, she took the wineglass from him—ignoring how the brush of their hands sent a tingling through her—and sat with him on the couch.

"Thanks for coming to the family dinner tonight," he said. "I know it was stressful for you."

"It's important for Jade to meet your family," she

said, glad to be on a safe topic. "She is the first grand-child, after all."

She took a sip of her drink. She'd expected him to immediately begin putting the moves on her, so he'd thrown her off with his comment.

Still, it was hard not to be aware of him. He was impossibly masculine in black pants and an open-collar white shirt. His shirtsleeves had been rolled back to expose the dark hair of his arms.

Now, he nodded. "I know some of my siblings would have bet good money against my being the father of the first grandchild. We almost beat Parker and Anna to the altar, too."

She looked down into her glass. "Your mother behaved well."

She hadn't gotten a warm, fuzzy feeling from Bonita Garrison, but she was happy the woman had been polite and accepting of Jade.

"For a change," Stephen said.

She looked up at him again. "Do you ever worry about drinking yourself?"

He shook his head. "No, I set clear limits to when I'll drink, and I can stick to them. Besides—" he shot her a significant look "—I get into enough trouble without bringing alcohol into it."

She knew he was thinking about their relationship and, specifically, about the child they'd produced.

"You haven't told me about your years in Indianapolis," he said abruptly.

She shrugged. "There isn't much to tell. I was raising a child with help from my family."

She talked then about her life in Indiana. She told him about her family and friends, and the funny little things that had happened to her.

"How did you support yourself?" he asked.

"I did small contract jobs for family, friends and neighbors." She shrugged again. "You know, helping someone remodel a kitchen or add on to a house."

His lips tightened.

"I know what you're thinking," she said. "Don't say it."

"We're married now," he responded. "That's what counts."

"Yes, about that—"

She wet her lips, then stopped as she saw he'd focused on the action.

"Are you going to express regrets about accusing me of cheating?" His eyes held hers steadily. "You should have faced me four years ago with your suspicions."

"I was wrong not to face you," she admitted, knowing she owed him that, at least. "You'll never know how many times I've wondered over the years whether I made the right decision for Jade."

He looked mollified.

She took a deep breath. "But I've also come to

the realization that meeting that woman that night was just the catalyst for my leaving. I knew what your life was like—"

His brows snapped together.

"—and we were having a no-strings affair."

He leaned forward to place his wineglass on the end table. "Oh, there were strings, baby, make no mistake about it."

She put down her wineglass, too, and rose. "That's why yesterday shouldn't set a pattern."

He got to his feet, too. "I agree."

"You do?" She couldn't keep the surprise from her voice. Well, *that* was easy.

His arms snaked around her. "Next time, it's going to be dry land or nothing. A small cabin like that isn't big enough for our kind of—" his eyes gleamed "—physically demanding lovemaking."

She nearly choked.

"Hey, I'm a *big* guy."

This time, she did splutter, but she could see from the amusement on his face that he was enjoying toying with her—enjoying having her wonder exactly what he meant by *big*.

A smile teased his lips. "Four years ago, we were closer to being kids. We could have made do with a park bench. Now, as you've pointed out, we're seeing the wrong side of thirty."

"I said *I* was grown-up—"

His head came down, and he claimed her mouth.

Behind her eyelids, the world erupted in color. Her mind swam.

Pressing his advantage, he plundered her mouth, making her open to him. Making her feel.

She moaned low in her throat, even as a part of her mind fought for control.

After several moments, she tore her mouth from his. "Stephen—"

In response, he bent her backward, and her robe fell open. He trailed his lips down her throat, lingering over the pulse under her jaw.

Pulsating awareness sang through her veins and gathered at the juncture of her thighs.

Oh. "We have to talk—"

"Trust me on this one, Meggikins," he said thickly. "There are actions more valuable than words right now."

"I'm not sure that's the saying," she said somewhat breathlessly, raising her head. He used to call her Meggikins all the time before she left Miami. This was the first time he'd used her old nickname in his previous sweet, unsarcastic way.

"Whatever," he responded. "There are times when we guys call it right."

He was getting it more than right, she thought. He was playing her like a virtuoso handling a Stradivarius.

He stared at the silky nightgown revealed by her

open robe. She could tell he'd focused on her nipples, which had tightened and now jutted against the thin material of her gown.

His eyes darkened, his face growing taut with desire. "Do you know I fantasized about you?" He shook his head slowly. "It used to drive me crazy that I kept thinking about you when you'd been the one to walk away."

"That's why you want me now. I'm a novelty. The one who dumped you." She guessed this wasn't the time to tell him she'd dreamed about him, too. It would be like adding fuel to the fire. She could feel his erection pressed against her.

He shook his head again, his brows coming together. He gave her a little shake. "Don't give me that garbage. You're the mother of my child."

Her heart plummeted, even as she told herself she shouldn't care whether he saw her as just a mother or not at all.

"We can barely be in the same room without wanting to get it on," he said huskily.

Her heart skipped a beat. "Lust."

"Sexual attraction," he contradicted. "It's more than a lot of other people have."

But it wasn't enough for her. "What happens when it all fades?"

"It hasn't in four years."

She shook her head in denial.

His eyes gleamed. "Do you need me to show you again just how much it can be worth?"

His hand skimmed up her thigh, raising her gown and robe. His head lowered.

"We shouldn't," she whispered.

"What?" he muttered against her mouth. "We're married. We're legal. We're not inebriated."

"This isn't what I signed up for."

"Hell, me, too, but sometimes you just have to run with it."

He hoisted her up and fastened his mouth to hers.

Oh, damn. She'd underestimated just how hard it would be to live under the same roof and resist him. And he wasn't making it any easier on her.

In the background, Harry Jr. had faded into the slow, sultry tones of Norah Jones.

Without breaking contact, Stephen used one hand to pull her panties off, then sat back on the couch with her.

Her legs came down on either side of him, straddling him.

He rubbed her sensitized nipples and made a guttural sound of pleasure.

Yes, her mind whimpered.

She'd gone so long without. So long without him. Yesterday, the dam had burst, and now all her desires came pouring forth.

He kissed her jaw, then pushed the robe off her shoulders so that it dropped to the floor. He kissed her neck, her shoulder and her collarbone, then gave her a little love bite.

She fumbled with the buttons of his shirt, sliding against him, needing him to fill the dull ache inside her.

Eventually, with a groan, he stilled her hands against his shirt. He grasped the bottom of her gown and pulled her last article of clothing over her head before tossing it aside.

Turning back to her, he reached between them. He delved, testing her with his fingers and finding her wetness.

And she savored his touch. Her eyes closed, her back arched, and her breathing became shallow. She clenched around him.

"That's right," he muttered. "Come to me, my mermaid."

She opened her eyes and looked at him.

From the harsh, intent look on his face, she knew he was ready. *She* was ready.

He withdrew his hand, and with quivering fingers, she helped him undo his belt and free himself.

She held his gaze as she sank down on him, joining them and making them both sigh with pleasure.

She rode him then with sweet rhythm while he whispered encouragement in her ear.

Slowly, slowly, they climbed to the pinnacle together.

When she peeked at him and saw his jaw was

locked, she realized only iron control kept him from taking her wildly. She knew he was waiting for her— trying to make this good for her.

And with that awareness, all her nervous tension broke and she found a magnificent release.

He caught her when she came, taking over in the last few moments and thrusting up to meet her with a deep groan as he shook and strained one last time.

Eleven

On Friday, Megan met Anna for lunch at La Loggia, near Elkind, Ross's offices downtown.

After they'd ordered, Anna said, "Marriage seems to agree with you."

"Does it?" Megan remarked, lifting her water glass.

"Mmm-hmm," Anna persisted, a teasing light in her eyes. "You look as if you've been having lots of sex—and enjoying it."

She choked on a sip of water. *"What?"*

"Are you okay?" Anna responded, laughing.

"How would you know that?" She felt as if she were wearing an *H* for *horny* emblazoned on her knit top.

Anna gave another tinkling laugh. "Simple.

I'm married to a Garrison, too, and I'm also a newlywed."

Megan resisted the urge to cup her hot cheeks.

The past week had been crazy. She and Stephen were married parents of a young child, and they were conducting a passionate affair.

The couch…the desk…the breakfast table. They were sneaking around a three-year-old. They'd even put his gift of lingerie to good use.

Just last night, after they'd put Jade to bed, Stephen had bent her forward over the desk in his study and had intercourse with her.

Anna took a sip from her water glass, seemingly reading Megan's silence for the admission it was. "Mmm-hmm. Persuasive, was he?" she murmured.

Megan groaned and hid her face behind her hands.

"Oh, Anna," she said when she looked up, "we've been on a roller coaster this past week."

Her friend laughed again. "So you're having wild, uninhibited sex with your husband. What's wrong with that?"

Everything.

"He… We…"

Anna's lips twitched. "I understand. Stephen's an attractive guy with a healthy sex drive and he wanted to get it on with you."

Megan expelled a breath and nodded. "The rat. He's reneging on the terms of this marriage."

Her friend placed a hand over her heart melodramatically. "How? By wanting to have sex with you, his wife, rather than someone else?"

"When you put it that way, it sounds so reasonable."

"It *is* reasonable."

Rather than concede, however, she held on doggedly to her position, which she nevertheless knew was fast becoming unsustainable.

Still, she felt compelled to set the record straight on one score. "It turns out he wasn't having sex with anyone else four years ago, either."

Anna raised an eyebrow, and Megan recounted Stephen's story to her.

"And I believed him," she said when she finished.

"So," Anna said, "everything should be great now, right?"

She shook her head. "*No*. Don't you see?" she said, her voice almost a wail. "I was vulnerable to believing that woman four years ago because Stephen had such a reputation as a player, and nothing has changed, and—and, oh God, I may be falling for him again!"

Panic roiled her stomach.

She was in love with him. Maybe had always remained a little in love with him.

Anna patted her hand.

She looked at her sister-in-law, her eyes pleading. "Why, why, why did he have to insist on this marriage? We could have come to an arrangement that allowed him to see Jade!"

Anna shook her head. "Megan, Megan, look around!" Anna glanced to one side of them, then to the other. "Do you know how many men have looked over at us—at you—since we arrived? You're a tall, gorgeous redhead who attracts more attention than a neon sign in the desert. Of course Stephen wanted to slap a ring on your hand as soon as possible!"

Megan closed her eyes, sucked in some deep, controlling breaths, then looked at her friend again.

"You're fearful right now, that's all," Anna said. "Believe me, I understand. I was just there. Falling in love is scary. And then there are all those trust issues."

"I know," she said matter-of-factly.

Trust. Anna and Parker didn't have the lengthy tortured history she and Stephen did and yet Anna knew about the importance of that little word.

Just then, the waiter approached with their food.

All through lunch, however, Megan wondered about her new discovery and how she was going to handle it.

She was in love with Stephen Garrison. Again.

A storm was on the way. Stephen looked up at the sky from the deck of *Fishful Thinking*. Fortunately, the storm wasn't a hurricane—at least for now.

Still, it would hit over the weekend, and he wanted to make sure his yacht was prepared.

Though the staff at the marina could do the work for him, *Fishful Thinking* was his baby, and he liked to get personally involved when he could.

The yacht needed to be tied up with longer, sturdier lines, and as a precaution, he needed to clear out some of his personal possessions.

He headed below deck, then turned at the sound of someone clambering aboard.

Retracing his steps, he felt a smile rise to his lips. Megan was early.

They'd agreed last night to meet at the marina after work and have a Friday night out. He'd been looking forward to it all day.

But as he came up on deck again, he saw his visitor wasn't Megan, but their babysitter.

Tiffany was dressed as if she was heading out for a night on the town. She was wearing a sheer blouse, black miniskirt and heels, and her face was more made-up than usual.

He remembered now mentioning to the babysitter that he'd have to tie up his boat at the Miami Beach Marina after work today.

"What's up, Tiffany?" His thoughts automatically went to his daughter. "Is something wrong with Jade?" he asked, his voice coming out sharp.

"No, no, no," Tiffany said on a breathless laugh,

walking toward him. "I dropped her off at her friend Gillian's birthday party earlier."

He relaxed. "Well, if you're thinking you need to babysit, there are crossed wires. My sister-in-law, Anna, is supposed to pick her up from the party—" he consulted his watch "—in a little over an hour."

He and Megan had agreed Anna and Parker would take Jade for the evening while they went out for a quick dinner, just the two of them. Anna had been thrilled at the prospect of babysitting.

"No crossed wires," Tiffany said easily, her gaze focused on his face, "and there's plenty of time for what I came to discuss."

"Oh, yeah?"

She nodded to the stairs. "Can we talk somewhere more private?" She hugged herself and looked around. "It's windy out here."

"Yeah, with good reason. There's a storm coming ashore," he said, but nevertheless turned to lead the way.

"I've never been aboard before," Tiffany said from behind him once they were in the narrow corridor below deck. "Is this where you nap?"

He turned around to see Tiffany peering into the master cabin.

"Yup," he said, then braced his hands on his hips. He'd dressed in pants and an open-collar shirt for work today because he'd known he'd be heading over to the yacht to meet Megan for dinner. "Now why don't you tell me what this is about?"

Tiffany straightened and peeked up at him through her lashes. "Better yet, I'll show you."

She stepped forward and fastened her mouth to his.

It happened so fast, he didn't have a chance to react. In the tight confines of the yacht's passageway, there wasn't much room to move.

Still, it was the last thing he'd been expecting from Tiffany, so for a second he remained immobile.

She pressed closer, going up on tiptoe, her arms snaking around his neck.

"Mmm," she murmured.

As she moved her mouth over his, his brain snapped on. *What the hell.*

He reached for her arms and tugged them from his neck.

She touched his chest, looking up at him pleadingly. "Do me."

He opened his mouth, flabbergasted.

"Excuse me."

He and Tiffany both turned to look at the end of the passageway.

Megan stood rigidly, silhouetted by the light, then spun on her heel.

Stephen cursed. "Megan, wait!"

He started after her, but Tiffany fisted her hand into the back of his shirt, stopping him.

He turned back, his brows snapping together. "What the hell are you doing?"

"Let her go, Stephen."

"She's my wife!"

Tiffany smirked. "C'mon, I know you're not sleeping with her. She's been in the guest bedroom."

Oh, hell. Yes, Megan's stuff still remained in the guest bedroom, but he'd been having a damn good week, seducing Megan at every opportunity—making headway, or so he thought. And now this.

Tiffany trailed a hand down his chest. "I know a virile guy like you must have a difficult time doing without," she said, lowering her voice invitingly. "So, here I am."

He removed her hand from his chest. "You don't know a thing," he said coldly.

The first glimmer of uncertainty entered the babysitter's eyes. "C'mon, Stephen. Everyone knows you play the field—"

"Past tense there, honey." In fact, in the last couple of years, his reputation had been based more on past public perception than on reality.

He glowered at her. "What's your game?"

Tiffany affected a pout. "Nothing! You're one of the sexiest, hippest guys in Miami. Everyone knows about the Garrison brothers. I wanted to see what all the fuss was about."

Stephen sighed inwardly. He'd been reduced to a

notch on the bedpost, and the irony wasn't lost on him. Aloud, he said, "You're going to explain to Megan *exactly* what happened here."

"That we were kissing?" Tiffany smirked again. "I think she saw that for herself."

"No, that you came on to me unexpectedly."

Tiffany's jaw set mulishly. "I can't do that."

"You *can,* and you *will.*" He resisted the urge to shake some sense into her.

"If I say that, I'll never get another child-care job! I have to stick to the story it was mutual."

He was surprised and even a bit impressed at how much she'd thought this through. It made him wonder, though, just how many guys Tiffany had come on to in the past. He'd been at the receiving end of enough conniving women to be sort of jaded about the type.

"You won't get a job based on the recommendation I'd give you," he gritted.

She folded her arms. "At least my way I'll have a fighting chance. It'll be my word against yours."

Tiffany had cost him, and cost him big, with Megan, but Stephen suddenly felt an iota of sympathy for the babysitter. She was young and impressionable, and obviously looking for love in all the wrong places.

"Stop chasing a rainbow. Fame and being hip isn't all it's cracked up to be," he advised.

Then he turned away to try to find his wife.

* * *

Megan blindly found her way back to her car. She got behind the wheel and her brain went on automatic pilot as she steered out of the parking lot.

It was just like four years ago. A wild affair where she couldn't see straight, then blindsided by a betrayal.

She should have known. She should have known.

Once a cheater, always a cheater, the naysayer within her chanted.

She made herself relive the pain of catching Tiffany and Stephen in an intimate embrace.

At least four years ago she'd been spared the visual evidence. Then she'd gone only on the word of a woman she hadn't met before. *That,* and Stephen's playboy reputation.

This time, she'd witnessed the cheating herself.

As she made a left turn at a stoplight, she realized she couldn't go home—or rather, to Stephen's estate near South Beach. He'd be there, and she needed time to think.

Her cell phone rang, and she ignored it. She recognized the ring as Stephen's,

Her mind raced ahead. The Garrison Grand was also off-limits for obvious reasons. Under other circumstances, she might have turned to Anna for help, but Anna was now married to Stephen's brother.

With that thought, her mind went to Jade. At least

she wouldn't need to worry about her daughter tonight. She knew Anna would be happy to take care of Jade for as long as needed.

Her cell phone rang again, and she turned it off with one hand.

She realized after a moment that she could always go to the little house in Coral Gables. She had the lease until the end of the month, and some of her furniture and belongings were still in the house.

Her mind made up, she turned the car west.

A short time later, when she reached her former home, she let herself in, kicked off her sandals and turned her phone back on.

The screen on her cell flashed information on several missed calls from Stephen. Cynically, she wondered what explanation he'd come up with this time.

Then she searched for and found Anna's number. When her sister-in-law picked up, she said, "Anna, it's Megan."

"Hi! I was just about to go get Jade—"

"Listen, would you mind keeping her until tomorrow?"

"Of course I don't mind," Anna responded. "We'll just run by the Garrison Grand on the way home and pick up some stuff for her from your suite."

Like Stephen, Megan knew, Parker and Anna maintained a suite at the Garrison Grand for personal use.

"Thanks," Megan said, relief making her relax. "I

left some clothes over there when Jade got a tour of her father's hotel."

The father who had just proved once again he was a lying, cheating, untrustworthy rat.

"You and Stephen want the evening to yourselves, hmm?" Anna asked teasingly.

"Something like that." Megan heard her voice wobble. "Just tell Jade I love her and I'll see her tomorrow."

"Is something wrong?" Anna asked, her voice suddenly tinged with worry. "You sound a little strange."

Sudden, unexpected tears clogged her throat. Damn it. She'd thought she had this under control.

"Everything's fine," she managed. "See you tomorrow."

After disconnecting, she looked around.

She was beginning to rethink her idea of staying in Coral Gables tonight. It might not be the first place Stephen thought to look for her, but it might occur to him if he reflected on it a bit.

With that thought, she strode purposely into her former bedroom and gathered up some clothes. She packed an ancient overnight bag.

She needed to ponder what to do, she thought, feeling sick to her stomach. This time, it would be hard for her to cut and run. She and Stephen were married, and there was a three-year-old child involved.

She knew he'd come after her—because of Jade, of course.

She couldn't believe she'd opened her heart to him again. *The jerk.*

She swung her overnight bag off the bed with more violence than necessary. *The philandering snake.*

This time, though, she decided her reaction would be different—not only because it had to be, but because she wanted it to be.

She walked toward the front door.

She wasn't going to be a passive victim. She wasn't meekly going away.

Outside, she locked up the house, tossed her overnight bag into the car, and got behind the wheel.

Jaw set, she knew exactly where she was going. First steps first.

She was checking into one of the Garrison Grand's rival hotels. It was just too bad the Hotel Victoria wasn't open yet.

Twelve

By the time Stephen got to the marina's parking lot, Megan was gone. Annoyed with himself for letting Tiffany slow him down, he whipped out his cell to try to reach Megan by phone.

When she didn't pick up then or on subsequent calls, he held out slim hope the reason was because she was driving. More likely, she'd drawn her own conclusions about the scenario that had apparently played out before her eyes.

He swore under his breath. He had to find her and fix this situation. He knew appearances were damning, but he had to convince her of the truth.

Just the thought she might walk away from him again made him nearly break out in a sweat.

He strode to his car, which was parked nearby. He was willing to do this the hard way—by process of elimination.

First, he headed to the most likely place he'd find her—his estate near South Beach.

When he didn't find her there, he grimly headed back out to his car. He decided to check his suite at the Garrison Grand next.

Before pulling out of his drive, however, he called Anna. It occurred to him Megan wouldn't do anything without making sure Jade was taken care of. Parker's wife might therefore be able to give him some leads.

When his sister-in-law picked up, he said, "Hi, Anna. Is Jade with you?"

"Yes, she's right here. I just got back from picking her up."

At least he knew where Jade was, Stephen thought, some of his tension easing. "Is Megan there?"

There was a pause on the line, and he could practically see Anna frowning.

"I thought she was with you," his sister-in-law said.

"There's been a...misunderstanding. Has she tried to contact you?"

"As a matter of fact, she did—"

Stephen's hand tightened on the phone.

"—but she didn't say where she was. She asked if I could keep Jade until tomorrow. Of course I said it was okay. I just stopped by your suite at the Garrison Grand on the way home and picked up some clothes for Jade."

Damn. Still, now he knew Megan wasn't at the hotel.

"Thanks, Anna," he said. "I'll be in touch. Give Jade a kiss for me."

"You know," Anna put in, "Megan said nearly the same thing when I talked to her. She wanted me to tell Jade she loved her."

At least, Stephen thought, there was one thing he and his wife agreed on at the moment. They were united in their love and concern for Jade.

"Are you sure everything is all right?" Anna asked.

"It will be soon," Stephen assured her.

When he ended the call, he sat and gazed down his driveway for a moment.

Now he knew Megan wasn't at the Garrison Grand, he was at loose ends. He'd covered the most logical bases, and Megan wasn't answering her phone.

He squinted into the distance, then realized there was one place he hadn't tried yet.

After turning the key in the ignition, he pulled away from the house and headed to Coral Gables.

Megan woke up disoriented.

She was in a strange room. A *hotel* room.

Then the drama of the previous evening came rushing back, and along with it, the queasy feeling there was no way to fix what was wrong with her life.

It was a feeling she'd had once before, when she'd found herself pregnant and alone, having realized the father of her child thought of her as nothing more than a fling.

Luckily, she'd found a hotel room yesterday. With the impending storm, there had been a number of last-minute cancellations of weekend reservations.

While she'd been tossing and turning in bed last night, she'd also come to a resolution.

The last time she'd caught Stephen cheating, she'd turned and run. She hadn't even sought an explanation from him. This time, though the evidence against him was damning, she wouldn't make the same mistake.

Now, after she showered, dressed and ate a light breakfast delivered by room service, she put in a call to Tiffany.

When the babysitter picked up, she announced without preamble, "You're fired."

"Megan?"

"Yes, it's me," she said crisply. "As of today, your services are no longer required."

"I can explain—"

"I'm sure you can," she responded, "but I don't want to hear it."

Afterward, she checked herself out of the hotel and headed for Stephen's estate.

She'd bolted, just like four years ago. But now, she was turning around and fighting.

Last night had to rank as the most miserable night of his life, Stephen reflected. Megan hadn't come home, and he hadn't been able to find her.

He poured himself another morning cup of coffee and paced back and forth in his kitchen.

He'd been up since six—not that he'd gotten much sleep. Though it was only late morning, he'd showered, dressed in jeans and a casual shirt, and been prowling around restlessly for what seemed like eons.

Yesterday, when he'd arrived at the house in Coral Gables, he'd discovered Megan wasn't there. However, he'd run into a neighbor who said she'd thought she'd seen Megan's car parked in front of the house not too long before.

Cursing his bad timing, but realizing he'd run out of options, he'd returned to his estate near South Beach.

Now, he looked outside at gray storm clouds and a steady rain.

Damn it. The storm was closing in, and if he didn't find Megan soon, he'd have to ride out the storm here—alone and without resolution.

The only silver lining was that Megan had asked

Anna to hold on to Jade only until today. That meant—at least he hoped it did—that Megan was bound to show up sooner rather than later.

He'd already phoned Anna this morning and told her to give him a call if Megan stopped by to pick up Jade. He'd sensed that his sister-in-law had questions but was refraining from asking them.

He knew Megan couldn't just take off this time. She had a partnership in her firm and a three-year-old who couldn't be uprooted easily. There was also a storm coming ashore. And most importantly, he'd find her—no matter how long it took—and make her see the truth.

Itching to do something *now,* however, he dialed the sitter. Perhaps Megan had contacted Tiffany. She'd seemed angry enough last night to let loose with some choice words aimed at the both of them.

When Tiffany picked up, he said, "It's Stephen. Have you heard from Megan?"

There was a pause. "You know, for no longer being in your employ," Tiffany drawled, "I sure do get a lot of calls from Garrisons."

Suddenly alert, he asked, "What do you mean you're no longer employed?"

"By you and your wife. She fired me."

Stephen felt his spirits lift, but he nevertheless asked sarcastically, "Even after your explanation that it was supposedly mutual?"

"It didn't get that far. She didn't even give me time to explain!"

At a sound behind him, he swung around and his eyes locked with Megan's.

"Talking to the other woman?" she asked, arching a brow.

"Gotta go, Tiffany," he said absently, then disconnected. He stared at Megan, willing her to be more than a figment of his imagination.

She looked like a mermaid that had been washed ashore and up to his doorstep. She was wearing a rain-splattered flower-print sundress, the shoulder straps of which cleverly continued beneath her breasts, outlining them. Her long red hair hung down her back, drops of rain reflecting the light cast by the overhead in the kitchen.

The way she looked right now, she took him back four years. Back to when she was still willing to play the seductress and he was her eager victim. Back to when things had been right between them.

He fought the urge to grab her and pull her into his arms. He settled for setting down the phone and walking toward her. "I didn't know where you were."

"Then let me put your mind at ease," she said, planting her handbag on a nearby chair. "The Tides Hotel."

Ouch. "You know how to hit a guy when he's down, don't you?"

"Funny, I thought I was the one who was down, and you—" her eyes went to his crotch "—were the one who was up."

She was taking no prisoners, he thought with an inner grimace. Still, ridiculously, he felt turned on.

"I thought you were going to bolt like before," he said.

"Can't." She shrugged and held up her hand. "I'm married to you this time."

He was close enough to glimpse uncertainty beneath her cool reserve, and he pressed forward. "I'm not letting you go."

Her eyes flashed. "You strong-armed me into this marriage—"

"Damn right, I did."

"I fired Tiffany."

"But you can't fire me."

"But I can divorce you," she said, her chin coming up.

His jaw set. *Like hell.*

"Were you carrying on with her?" she asked.

The question hung in the air between them. "Would you believe me if I said no?"

"Would any reasonable person?" she tossed back.

"I'm not giving you a divorce," he said implacably, "so forget it."

Megan watched the man she loved walk toward her, and held her breath.

His eyes were like hot coals, belying an expression carved in granite.

Yet beneath his hard, uncompromising attitude, she sensed a hint of vulnerability, and her heart somersaulted.

"I fired Tiffany before she gave me an explanation," she said.

He nodded. "I know. She told me. Why?"

"Maybe I learned from my mistakes," she said in a low voice. "Maybe I decided this time that if I was going to exact payment, it should fall on both guilty parties."

He nodded. "*Maybe,* but is that the real reason?"

He stopped in front of her, and she shook her head slowly, holding his gaze.

Her lips parted. "I didn't want an explanation. I was talking to Anna recently, and she mentioned the issue of *trust.* It's what was lacking the last time in our relationship. I like to think I learn from my mistakes."

"It looks bad—"

"Incriminating. So incriminating, in fact," she said, "that after the initial shock, I realized no one could be that stupid."

His face relaxed, his shoulders lowering.

"Who'd try to have a romantic encounter on his yacht when he knew his wife was due to meet him there soon?"

"When he'd gone to all the trouble of strong-arming the same wife into marrying him," he supplied.

"Exactly." She'd thought this through the night before—when she'd had a chance to calmly assess what had happened.

"I'm getting rid of *Fishful Thinking*," he said hoarsely.

Her eyes widened. "But you love that boat."

He stepped forward. "I love you more."

A crazy joy swept through her.

He raised his hand and pushed hair away from her face. "The yacht doesn't suit my lifestyle now, but there's an acquaintance who's expressed interest in buying it on more than one occasion."

His lips quirked in the lopsided smile that she'd always loved. "He used to be a rival of mine in Miami's playboy sweepstakes."

"You don't say," she said, a teasing tone creeping into her voice.

"I'm also stepping away from being the public face of the Garrison Grand."

She went still. "*What?* You can't do that."

"I can and I will," he responded, looking at her tenderly. "I don't need to be partying when what I really want is to be home."

It was a grand gesture, and sudden tears choked her.

"Are you going to say it?" he asked. "Because I'm prepared to wage a campaign if I have to."

"I love you!" She flung the words at him, even her vision blurred. "There, I said it. Are you happy now? You arrogant, ruthless—"

He yanked her into his arms. "I'm all those things and worse," he muttered, "but I love you."

Then he silenced her with a kiss. He didn't ask, he took, and they both gave themselves up to the kiss with wild abandon.

She'd taken the long way, she thought, but she finally had what she'd been looking for.

When his lips eventually moved away from hers, he trailed kisses along her cheek and to the hollow of her throat.

"You know," she joked breathlessly, her heart feeling lighter than it had in years, "if this keeps happening, I'm going to have to lock you up to keep women away from you."

"Don't worry, Meggikins," he said, his fingers searching for the zipper to her dress, "I intend to become the most family-oriented guy around. I want more kids, and I'm definitely going to enjoy making them."

She pretended to look shocked. "We can't spend all our time in bed!"

As if in response, he nuzzled her neck.

"Is this how men communicate their feelings?" she teased, her breath catching.

"What can I say? I'm a man of action."

His response elicited an involuntary laugh, even as he nibbled along her shoulder, sending waves of lush desire through her.

"We need to pick up Jade from Anna's before this storm really hits," he said reluctantly, kissing the tops of her breasts.

"Mmm," she responded. "I called Anna and Parker right before I got here. They're bringing over Jade shortly."

"In that case, we'll have to hurry."

Another laugh escaped her. "At this rate, I'll be pregnant in a month."

He raised his head to look at her seriously. "We talked about it in an 'if it happens' sort of way, but we can wait if you want to."

She shook her head. "I don't want to. Jade is going to be four, and I'd like her to have a sibling or two before she gets too much older. Now I'm a partner at Elkind, Ross, I've got some leverage as far as organizing my work schedule and taking a leave. I'll just have to space my projects further apart."

He smiled. "You'll have no problem getting clearance from your current client."

Then he lifted her onto the nearby kitchen table, bunching her dress around her hips in the process.

"The kitchen table—?"

"We haven't used it yet. Let's tick it off our list."

She slid back on her elbows to keep her balance. He was aroused, and she was weak-kneed.

"It's been one of my fantasies for a long time," he admitted, grasping her hips to pull the panties off her.

"How long?" she asked throatily.

"Too damn long," he responded. "Since you left."

She watched as he divested himself of some clothing. "Ah, those fantasies of yours…"

He looked at her, passion dilating his eyes. "We're about to make one of them come true."

"I'd dream about you, too, you know. I couldn't stop myself."

He stilled, looking at her. "Oh, yeah?"

His pose was all male swagger, tinged with hunger. She nodded.

He smiled. "Care to share?"

She shook her head. Just the thought made her—

"You're blushing." He leaned forward with wicked intent, bracing his arms on either side of her. "I'll just have to make you—"

"Nothing will make me spill my secrets," she said on a breathless laugh.

But he was already tracing a hot path to her cleavage, making her gasp.

"Whisper them to me…"

And she did, as they had grinding, pulse-throbbing sex on the kitchen table.

Later, as they were straightening their clothes, Stephen said, "After you saw Tiffany kissing me on the yacht, I thought I'd lost you for good."

"Was *she* kissing *you?*"

He nodded.

Megan was glad for the confirmation that her faith hadn't been misplaced. "I overheard you on the phone asking Tiffany about her explanation that it was supposedly mutual."

His lips twisted. "Yeah, that's her story, and she's sticking to it."

"It wouldn't have mattered," she responded. "I'd already made up my mind, but accidentally hearing your part of the phone conversation earlier was nice validation."

Stephen shook his head. "She's fairly savvy for a mixed-up kid."

Megan wondered whether she'd missed some signs where the babysitter was concerned. "I hired her through a child-care agency. She was available to babysit during the hours I needed because she's an aspiring dancer and attends classes in the evenings."

"Well, I'll be around to help now," Stephen said. "We'll continue adjusting our schedules to accommodate Jade, and I'll hire a live-in housekeeper. When I was a single guy, I didn't feel the need for permanent staff, but that's changed now."

She thought about Stephen's statement earlier. "I don't want you to give up the yacht for me."

"Not for you. For us."

"But we'll need *Fishful Thinking* to entertain all those kids you're planning to have," she teased.

He looked at her for a moment, then slipped his hands around her waist. "Do you know how much I love you?"

"Tell me again," she said, smiling as she placed her hands on his chest.

He gave her a quick kiss. "I don't think I ever got over you."

"Definitely likewise," she responded.

"You were right, you know," he added. "Until you walked away, I'd never had the experience of being dumped. It was a bitter pill, especially since I'd been crazy about you."

Her heart swelled. "Walking away from you was one of the hardest things I've ever done, even though I believed at the time that you'd cheated."

"I got a necessary dose of humility," he admitted. "After that, I toned down the playboy lifestyle and focused on building up the Garrison Grand."

"And got wonderful results for it," she said. "The Garrison Grand is considered the premier hotel in South Beach."

"Thanks, but I consider my greatest accomplishment to be Jade."

Her heart spilled over. "I feel the same way," she said softly.

He gave her a lingering kiss. "You hold my heart in your hands. You always have."

She raised her hand and stroked his face. "I never would have guessed. You looked so forbidding the day you walked into my office at Elkind, Ross."

"I was angry," he said, giving her a lopsided smile, "but I was determined to get you back in my bed."

"Oh?" She arched a brow.

"No woman has turned me on as much as you do," he said. "I was determined to reignite our affair and break it off only when I wanted to this time. Of course, I wasn't yet admitting to myself that time might be *never.*"

"Silly man," she said, her eyes misting. "So desperate, you had to blackmail me into marrying you."

"Not one of my finer moments," he admitted. "I wanted to believe I was in control, but the reality was the opposite."

He was laying himself bare for her, and joy bubbled up inside her again. Before either of them could say anything else, however, the doorbell rang.

"Jade," she said.

Stephen nodded. "I'll get it."

Moments later, he walked back into the kitchen, trailing an exuberant Jade. Parker and Anna followed behind.

"Mommy!" Jade rushed forward, and Megan bent and wrapped her daughter in her arms.

"I played board games with Aunt Anna and Uncle Parker! And I got ice cream! And Gillian's party was great, and—"

Everyone laughed.

"Slow down there," Stephen said, ruffling Jade's hair.

Megan watched as Anna looked at her, a question in her eyes.

"Is everything okay?" Anna asked, her gaze going from her to Stephen.

"Perfect now," Megan said.

Stephen slipped his arm around her and pulled Jade close to him with his other.

Megan smiled at Anna, trying to communicate that everything truly was fine now. The message seemed to come across because, after a moment, her sister-in-law smiled back and squeezed Parker's hand.

"Now that I've been to Gillian's house, I know what I want!" Jade piped up.

"What?" she and Stephen asked in unison.

"A little brother or sister," Jade announced, then ducked under Stephen's arm and skipped away. "*I* get to tell them what to do!"

Megan felt herself heat, and Stephen laughed.

Anna and Parker looked amused but knowing.

"Uh-oh," Stephen said. "I think we're in trouble."

"She's definitely *your* daughter," Megan teased, looking up at him with her heart in her eyes, "and we've definitely come home to stay."

* * * * *

STRANDED WITH THE
TEMPTING STRANGER

by
Brenda Jackson

Dear Reader,

I hope you are enjoying the stories in the Desire™ series, THE GARRISONS. I enjoyed working closely with the other five authors to bring you a scintillating tale of a family's hidden secrets, sky-rocketing passion and endless love.

In my story, Brandon Washington was a man with a plan…or so he thought. Until he meets the heroine, Cassie Sinclair-Garrison. Then he finds out the hard way that no matter what your intentions are, when emotions get in the way even the best-laid plans can get kicked to the kerb.

I love writing romance stories in which the hero and heroine are pitted against each other, but in the end true love prevails.

I hope you enjoy Brandon and Cassie's story and their journey to finding everlasting love.

Best,

Brenda Jackson

BRENDA JACKSON

is a die "heart" romantic who married her childhood sweetheart and still proudly wears the going-steady ring he gave her when she was fifteen. Because she's always believed in the power of love, Brenda's stories always have happy endings. In her real-life love story, Brenda and her husband live in Jacksonville, Florida, and have two sons.

A *USA TODAY* bestselling author, Brenda divides her time between family, writing and working in management at a major insurance company. You can write to Brenda at PO Box 28267, Jacksonville, FL 32226, USA, by e-mail at WriterBJackson@aol.com or visit her website at www.brendajackson.net.

To Gerald Jackson, Sr.
Thank you for thirty-five years of love
and romance.
To my Heavenly Father for giving me
the gift to write.
My beloved *is* mine, and I *am* his: he
feedeth among the lilies.
Song of Solomon 2:16 II

One

October

Cassie Sinclair-Garrison released an uneven breath when she rounded the corner in the lobby of her hotel. She stopped, totally mesmerized by the man standing at the counter to check in to the Garrison Grand-Bahamas. It had been a long time since any man had captured her attention like this one. He was simply gorgeous.

He stood tall at a height of not less than six-three with an athletic build that indicated he was a sportsman or someone who made it his business to stay in great physical shape. He was an American, she knew at once, studying his coffee-brown skin, his dark brown eyes and closely shaved head. And he wasn't here on business, she thought, noting the way he was immaculately dressed in a pair of dark brown trousers and a tan shirt that brought out the beautiful coloring of his skin.

She didn't know what, but there was something about him that demanded attention and from the way other women in the lobby were also staring, it was attention he was definitely getting.

Deciding she had more to do with her time than to practically drool over a man, Cassie pushed the button to the elevator that would take her to her office on the executive floor. It was an office that once belonged to her father.

Five years ago, when she was twenty-two, her father had made her manager and there hadn't been a time when he hadn't been pleased with the way she had handled things. That's why she wasn't surprised that upon his death he had left full ownership of the hotel to her. In doing so he had only confirmed what some of her employees had probably suspected all along—that she was John Garrison's illegitimate child.

A flutter of pain touched her heart as she thought of her parents. She stepped inside the elevator, glad it was vacant because whenever she encountered these types of moments, she preferred being alone. Although she had tried putting on a good front over the past five months, it had been hard to first lose her mother in an auto accident and, little over a month later, lose her father when he'd died of a heart attack…although it was probably more of a broken heart.

She had wondered how he would be able to go on after her mother's death. The last time she had seen her father—just days before he passed when he had come to visit her—Cassie had seen the depths of pain in his eyes and she had wondered how he would get over the loss. He had said more than once that losing his Ava was like losing a part of him.

Even though he was a married man that hadn't stopped him from falling in love with her mother, the beautiful and vivacious Ava Sinclair. And she had been John Garrison's true love for more than twenty-eight years.

According to her mother, she had met the wealthy and very handsome American in the States when he had been a judge and she a contestant in the Miss Universe beauty pageant as Miss Bahamas. Their paths had crossed a few years later, when he had visited the Bahamas to purchase land for this grand hotel he intended to build.

Although he had a family in Florida consisting of five kids, he was an unhappy man, a man who was no longer in love with his wife, but too dedicated to his children to walk away from his marriage.

Cassie hadn't understood their relationship until she was older, but it was beyond clear her parents had shared something special, something unique and something few people had. It was a love of a lifetime. Ava never made any demands on John, yet he had freely lavished her with anything and everything, and provided her and the child they had created with complete financial support.

Cassie knew that others who'd seen her parents together over the years had formed opinions on what the relationship was about. He was a married American and Ava was his Bahamian mistress. But Cassie knew their relationship was so much more than that. In her heart she believed they had been soul mates in the truest form. She had loved her parents deeply and they had loved her, a product of their love, and there hadn't been a day they hadn't let her feel or know it.

She had resented those times when her father would leave them to return to his family in Miami, a family she'd only found out about when she became a teenager. The truth had hurt, but then her mother and father had smoothed away the pain with the intensity of their love and had let her know that no matter what the situation was, the one thing that would never change or diminish was their love for her, as well as their love for each other. From that day forward, whether others did or not, Cassie understood and accepted her parents' unorthodox love affair.

She stepped off the elevator and walked into her office, stopping to smile at her secretary while picking up her messages off the woman's desk. "Good morning, Trudy."

"Good morning, Ms. Garrison."

Cassie liked the sound of that. She had begun using her father's last name within a week of his death. With both of her parents deceased, there were no secrets to protect and she had no reason to continue to deny herself the use of his name.

"Any additional messages?" she asked the older woman whom she had hired a few months ago.

"Yes. Mr. Parker Garrison just called and would like you to return his call."

Cassie forced the smile to stay on her face while thinking that no matter what Parker liked, he wouldn't be getting things his way since she wouldn't be returning his call. She could not forget the phone conversation they had shared nearly four months ago. He'd called within a week of the reading of John Garrison's will and he'd kept calling. Eventually, she had taken his call.

At the time she had been very aware that he, his siblings and mother had been shocked to discover at the reading of the will that John Garrison had an outside child. Of the five Garrison offspring, Parker had been the most livid because the terms of their father's will gave her and Parker equal controlling interest in Garrison Inc., an umbrella corporation that oversaw the stocks and financial growth of all the Garrison-owned properties. He wasn't happy about it.

Their telephone conversation hadn't gone well. He had been arrogant, condescending and had even tried being intimidating. When he'd seen Cassie would not accept his offer to buy her out, he had done the unthinkable by saying she had to prove she was a Garrison, and had threatened her with a DNA test as well as the possibility of him contesting the will. Parker's threats had ticked her off and she was still angry.

"Ms. Garrison?"

Her secretary's voice recaptured her attention. The forced smile widened. "Thank you for delivering the message."

Cassie entered her office. She would think Parker would have more to do with his time these days. It didn't take long for news to travel over the hotel grapevine that the handsome and elusive playboy had gotten married. And not that she cared, but she'd also heard that another Garrison bachelor, Stephen, had gotten hitched, as well.

She had no intention of ever meeting any of her "siblings." She didn't know them and they didn't know her and she preferred things stayed that way. They had never been a part of her life and she had never been a part of theirs. She had a life here in the Bahamas and saw no need to change that.

As she sat behind her desk her thoughts shifted back to the guy she'd seen in the lobby. She couldn't help but wonder if he was married or single, straight or gay. She shrugged her shoulders knowing that it really didn't matter. The last thing she needed was to become interested in a man. Her man was the beautiful thirty-story building that was erected along the pristine shoreline of the Caribbean. And "her man" was a beautiful sight that took her breath away each time she entered his lobby. And she would take care of him, continue to make him prosper the way her father would want her to do. Now that her parents were gone, this hotel was the only thing she could depend on for happiness.

Brandon Washington glanced around the room he had been given, truly impressed. He had spent plenty of time at the Garrison Grand but there was something about this particular franchise that left him astonished. It was definitely a tropical paradise.

The first thing he'd noticed when he had pulled into the parking lot was that the structure was different from the sister hotel in South Miami Beach, mainly because it was designed to take advantage of the tropical island beach it sat on. And it was nested intimately among a haven of palm trees and a multitude of magnificent gardens that were stocked with flow-ering plants.

The second was the warmth of the staff that had greeted him the moment he had walked into the beau-tiful atrium. They had immediately made him feel welcome and important.

And then it was his hotel room, a beautiful suite with a French balcony that looked out at the ocean. It had to be the most stunning waterscape view he'd ever seen.

Brandon was more than pleased with his accommo-dations. And since he planned to stay for a while, his comfort was of the utmost importance. He had to remind himself that this was not a vacation, but he'd come here with a job to do. He needed to uncover any secrets Cassie Sinclair-Garrison might have that could be used to persuade her to give up her controlling interest in Garrison, Inc., his most influential client. Not to mention that members of the family were close friends of his.

His father had been John Garrison's college friend and later his personal attorney for over forty years and Brandon had been a partner in his father's law firm. When his father was killed in a car accident three years ago, instead of transferring the Garrison business to a more experienced and older attorney, John had retained Brandon's firm, showing his loyalty to the Washington family and his faith in Brandon's abilities.

Brandon had known John Garrison all of his thirty-two years and he was a man Brandon had respected. And he considered Adam Garrison, one of John's sons, his very best friend. Now Brandon was here at the request of Parker and Stephen Garrison. It seemed

John's illegitimate daughter refused to deal with the corporation in any way and had refused to discuss any type of a buyout offer with Parker.

Before resorting to a full-blown court battle, the two eldest brothers had suggested that Brandon travel to the Bahamas, assume a false identity to see if he could get close to Ms. Garrison and dig up any information on her present or her past, which would give them ammunition to later force her hand if she continued to refuse to sell her shares of Garrison, Inc. Another smart thing John had done was retain exclusive control of this particular hotel, the one Cassie had managed and now owned. No doubt it had been a brainy strategic move to keep his secrets well-hidden.

Brandon pulled his cell phone from his coat jacket when it rang. "Yes?"

A smile touched his lips. "Yes, Parker, I just checked in and just so you'll know, I'm registered under the name of Brandon Jarrett."

He chuckled. "That's right. I'm using my first and middle name since I want to keep my real identity hidden." A few moments later he ended his phone call with Parker.

Brandon began unpacking. He had brought an assortment of casual clothes since it was his intent to pose as a businessman who'd come to the island for a short but very needed vacation. That shouldn't be hard to do, because since John Garrison's death and his secrets had been revealed, Brandon had been working long hours with the Garrison family to resolve all the unwanted issues.

Contesting the will had been out of the question. No

one wanted to air the family's dirty laundry. Doing so would definitely send John's widow, Bonita, over the edge. There were a number of people who would not sympathize with the woman, saying it was her drinking problem that had sent John into the arms of another woman in the first place and that he had stayed married to her longer than most men would have.

Then there would be others who would think that John's extramarital affair is what had driven the woman to drink. As far as Brandon was concerned, there was no way Bonita hadn't known about John's affair, given the amount of time he spent away from home. But from the look on her face during the reading of the will, she had not known a child had been involved. Now she knew, and according to Adam, his mother was hitting the bottle more than ever.

Brandon rubbed his chin, feeling the need of a shave. As he continued to unpack he knew that sometime within the next couple of days he would eventually cross paths with Cassie Sinclair-Garrison. He would make sure of it.

Cassie stood on one of the many terraces on the east side of the hotel, which faced Tahita Bay. It was late afternoon yet the sky was still a dazzling blue and seemed to match the waters beneath it. There were a number of yachts in the bay and several human bodies were sunbathing on the beach.

She smiled and waved her hand when a couple she'd met yesterday when they'd checked in recognized her and gave her a greeting as they glided by on a sailboat. At least she had met the woman yesterday; the man she already knew from the numerous times when his family's corporation—Elliott Publishing Holdings; one of the largest magazine conglomerates in the world—had utilized the hotel to host their annual business conference. Their main office was located in New York and the Garrison Grand-Bahamas was the ideal place to hold a seminar during the winter months.

Teagan Elliott was here vacationing with his wife of eight months, a beautiful African-American by the name of Renee. An interracial couple, the two looked very good together and reminded Cassie of what she thought every time she would see her parents together. And just like her parents, it was easy to see their love was genuine.

Thinking of her parents sent a feeling of forlornness through her. Now that the business of the day had been handled, she decided to stay at the hotel for the night instead of taking the thirty-minute drive to her home, which was located on the other side of the island. Maybe later she'd take a leisurely stroll along the shoreline in an area that wasn't so crowded.

She thought of the Diamond Keys, an exclusive section of the hotel that had beachfront suites with parlors and French doors that opened directly to the water, providing a commanding view of endless beach and ocean. The rooms, which were extremely expensive but definitely worth it, were nestled in the hotel's most intimate settings.

Cassie headed back inside, making her way to her bedroom to change out of her business suit and slip into a pair of silk lounging pants and matching camisole with a print design. It had been a long time since she'd carved out some time for herself. Over the past months she had spent the majority of her time wallowing in work and mourning the loss of her parents, as she tried to move on through life, one day at a time.

She had been at her mother's funeral, standing beside her father, who'd remained in shock over their unexpected loss. What hurt so much even now was that she hadn't attended her father's funeral. By the time she had received word of his death, the funeral had already taken place. All she had was the memory of the last time they had spent together, a few days before his death.

He had shown up on the island unexpectedly, not at the hotel but at her condo, waiting for her when she had arrived home from work that day. The handsome and charismatic man she'd always known and loved had held sadness in his eyes and pain in his features.

That night he had taken her out to dinner and before he had returned to Miami, he had placed in her hand the deed to the beautiful ten-acre estate in the exclusive Lyford Cay community that he had purchased for her mother fifteen years ago. It was the home she now occupied and called her own.

Cassie took a glance around as she stepped out onto the sandy shores. Daylight had faded and dusk had set in. But that didn't bother her. In fact she much preferred it. She always thought the beach at night was breathtakingly beautiful. In the background she heard the band from the lounge as it mixed with the sound of the waves crashing against the shore. She leaned down and took off her sandals, wanting to feel the sand beneath her feet. Being on the beach always made her feel better. It helped her momentarily forget her pain, and made her feel carefree, energized and invigorated.

She bit back a smile and glanced around again, just to make sure she was alone, before pretending to play hopscotch on the sand. She laughed out loud when she almost slipped as she continued to hop around on one foot from one pretend square block to another. What a wonderful way to work off the day's stress, she thought, and today had definitely been a busy one. The hotel's capacity was at an all-time high, with requests for extended stays becoming the norm. They even had a waiting list for weeks not considered as prime time. The man she had chosen to succeed her as a manager, Simon Tillman, was doing an excellent job, and now she was able to concentrate on doing other things, such as expanding her business in various ways.

She had received a call from her accountant that profits for the hotel were surging. Once it had become official that she was the owner of the Garrison Grand-Bahamas, she had begun implementing the changes she had submitted to her father in a proposal just a month before his death. Over the last dinner they had shared together, he had given his blessing to move ahead with her plans. Today after meeting with her staff, she had a lot to be happy about, for the first time in months.

"May I play?"

Cassie lowered her leg as she swung around at the sound of the deep, masculine voice, angry at the intrusion. She narrowed her eyes, at first not seeing anyone, but then she watched as a man seemed to materialize out of the darkness.

She recognized him immediately. He was the man

she had seen earlier today when he had checked into the hotel. He was the man every woman in the hotel had been watching, and a man who even now was taking her breath away.

Two

Brandon stared at the woman standing a few feet from him. He had been watching her, barely seeing her features in the shadows, and now with her standing so close, he thought she had to be the most beautiful woman he had ever seen. He immediately wanted to know everything about her.

He glanced at her left hand, didn't see a ring and inwardly let out a relieved breath. But that didn't necessarily mean she didn't have a significant other, even perhaps a boyfriend. What were the chances of her spending time at this hotel, one known for rest, relaxation and romance, alone?

But still, that didn't stop his hormones from going into overdrive when he stared into her face, seeing the cocoa color of her complexion, the dark curly brown hair that fell to her shoulders, the darkness of her brown eyes and the shape of her curves in the outfit she was wearing.

Disgusted, he was reminded of why he was there, which was not to concentrate on a woman whose looks were so striking they could almost blind him, but to get close to a woman who was causing problems to his biggest client—a woman he had yet to meet, although he'd hung around the hotel the majority of the day hoping that he would. When he had discreetly asked about her, he'd been told that Cassie Sinclair-Garrison had been in meetings all day and chances were she had already left for her home, which was on the other side of the island.

In that case, since it wasn't likely he would be running into Ms. Garrison anytime tonight, why not spend time with this beauty…if she was free and available.

He watched how she tilted up her chin and narrowed her eyes at him. "You intrude on my privacy."

Her Bahamian accent was rich, just as rich as the curly brown hair that flowed around her shoulders, he thought. With the lifting of her chin he zeroed in on more of her features. In addition to her creamy brown skin, she had high cheekbones, a cute dimple in her chin, a straight nose and lips so full and generous they were downright sexy. There was something so feminine about her it actually made him ache.

"And I apologize," he said quietly, accepting what she felt was her need to take him to task. "I was out for a walk and couldn't help but notice the game you were playing. "

"You could have said something to let me know you were there," she said directly, eyeing him.

"And you're right, but again, I got so caught up in watching you that I didn't want to interrupt, at least not for a while. If I upset you, I'm sorry."

Cassie realized she really shouldn't make such a big deal out of it. After all it wasn't just her section of private beach, but belonged to anyone who was staying at Diamond Keys, and evidently he was. "Since there hasn't been any harm done," she said in a muffled voice, "I will accept your apology."

He smiled. "Thank you. And I hope you will let me make it up to you."

"And how do you pose to do that?"

"By asking you to be my guest at dinner tonight," he said lightly, watching the look of surprise skim her features at his request.

She shook her head. "That's not necessary."

"I think it is. I offended you and want to make it up to you."

"You didn't offend me. You just caught me off guard."

"Still, I'd like to make it up to you."

Cassie bent her head, trying to hide the smile that suddenly touched her lips. If nothing else, he was persistent. Shouldn't she be as persistent, as well, in turning down his offer?

She lifted her head and met his gaze and for a period of time she was rendered speechless. He had moved into into her line of vision and she thought he was so incredibly handsome, she could actually feel a rush of blood flow through her veins. She doubted that very few women turned down anything coming from him.

"Maybe we should introduce ourselves," he said,

taking a step forward and smiling. He extended his hand out to her. "I'm Brandon Jarrett."

"And I'm Cassie Sinclair-Garrison."

It took everything Brandon had to keep the shock that rocked his body from showing in his face. This was Cassie Garrison? The woman who was causing Garrison, Inc., all kinds of trouble? The woman who had been giving Parker heartburn for the past four months? The woman who was a sibling to the Miami Garrisons whether she wanted to acknowledge them or not? The woman who was the main reason he was here on the island?

"Hello, Cassie Sinclair-Garrison," he said, forcing the words out of his mouth and hesitantly releasing her hand. It had felt good in his, as if it had actually belonged there. He had looked forward to meeting Cassie, but without this element of surprise. He didn't like surprises and this one was a biggie.

"Hello, Brandon Jarrett," she said, smiling. "I hope you're enjoying your stay here."

"I am. Are you?" he asked, not wanting to give anything away that he recognized her name or knew who she was, although she carried the same last name as the hotel.

"Yes, I'm enjoying myself."

No doubt at my expense, he thought, when he saw she had no intention of mentioning that she was the hotel's owner. "I think you might enjoy it even more if you have dinner with me."

A feeling of uneasiness crept over Cassie. The moment her fingers had slid into the warmth of his when they had shaken hands, she had felt a surge of

sensations that settled in the middle of stomach. This
guy was smooth and the problem was that she wasn't
used to smooth guys. She dated, but not frequently, and
definitely not someone like Brandon Jarrett. It was
quite obvious he knew how to work *it* and it was also
quite obvious that he thought he had a chance of
working her. That realization didn't repulse her like it
should have. Instead it had her curious. He wouldn't
be the first man who'd tried hitting on her, but he was
the first who had remotely triggered her interest in
over a year or so.

"We're back to that, are we?" she asked, chuckling,
feeling a little more relaxed than she had earlier.

"Yes, I'm afraid we're back to that, and I hope you
don't disappoint me. We can dine here at the hotel or go
someplace else that's close by. It will be your choice."

She knew if would be crazy to suggest to a perfect
stranger to take her someplace other than here, but the
last thing she wanted was to become the topic of conversation of her employees. Some of them hadn't yet
gotten over the shock that John Garrison was her biological father and that he had left the hotel to her.
Making a decision she hoped that she didn't later regret
she said, "I prefer going someplace else that's close by."

She could tell her response pleased him. "Is there
any place you want to recommend or do you prefer
leaving the choice to me?" he asked.

Again putting more trust in him than she really
should, she said, "I'll leave things to you."

"All right. Do you want us to meet in the lobby in
about an hour?"

She knew that wouldn't work. "No, we can meet

back here, at least over there on that terrace near the flower garden."

"Okay."

If he found her request strange he didn't let on. "Then I'll see you back here in an hour, Cassie Sinclair-Garrison," he said, smiling again.

Her heart missed a beat with his smile and, holding his gaze a bit longer than she should have, she said goodbye and then turned and quickly began walking back across the sand to her suite.

As Brandon headed back toward his room, he felt more than the October breeze off the ocean. A rush of adrenaline was pumping fast and furious through his veins. What were the chances of the one woman he had been attracted to since his breakup with Jamie Frigate a year ago to be the woman he had purposely come here to get to know?

Jamie.

Even now he had to steel himself against the rising anger he always felt when he thought about his fiancée's betrayal. How any woman could have been so shallow and full of herself he would never know. But more than that, she had been greedy as hell. She hadn't been satisfied with just having the things he could give her. While engaged to him she'd had an affair with a California businessman. He had found out about her duplicity when he had returned to Miami un-expectedly from a work-related trip to find her in bed with the man.

He entered his suite, not wanting to think about Jamie any longer, and instead his thoughts shifted back to Cassie. Any information he shared about himself to her would basically be false. But under the circumstances, that couldn't be helped. Tonight things had fallen into place too nicely for him and for some reason he was bothered by it. The woman he had seen playing a game of hopscotch had had an innocent air about her, definitely not what he had expected. And he had detected some sort of vulnerability, as well.

And he couldn't dismiss just how incredibly beautiful she was. With her striking good looks he would think she would have a date every night of the week. So the question that was presently popping in his mind was why didn't she?

In just the brief time he had spent with Cassie he had a feeling she was extremely bright. Maybe it had been the way she had studied him before making the decision to join him for dinner tonight that had given him that perspective.

A chuckle welled up inside of Brandon. He would find out just how bright she was at dinner when he really got into the game of wining and dining her. Whatever it took, he needed her to feel comfortable enough with him to share things about herself; things that could possibly damage her reputation if they became public knowledge.

He was suddenly unnerved by what he had to do and if he dwelled on it too long he would probably find the entire thing disgusting. But he could not let personal feelings or emotions intervene. He had a job to do and he intended to do it well.

Cassie glanced at herself in the mirror once more. She had taken another shower and changed outfits.

This one was a dress her mother had bought her earlier in the year that she had never worn until tonight.

It was a slinky thin-strapped mini-dress, fuchsia in color, and what made it elegant was the silver-clasp tie neck. She nervously smoothed the dress down her body, wondering if perhaps in trying to make a good impression she was making some sort of a statement, as well.

She ran her fingers though the long, dark brown curls on her head, fluffing them around her face. A face she thought had a remarkable resemblance to both of her parents, but mainly her father. She had her mother's eyes but her father's mouth, nose and cheekbones. And then there was that cleft in her chin that definitely came from him.

Her skin coloring was a mixture of the both of them, but her smile was that of John Garrison. She chewed her bottom lip nervously, thinking her smile was something she hadn't shown much of lately. But tonight she had smiled more than once already, although she had lowered her head so Brandon wouldn't see it the first time she'd done so.

She inhaled deeply, thinking for the umpteenth time that Brandon Jarrett was so drop-dead gorgeous it was a shame. No man should be walking around looking like he did and with a well-toned muscled body in whatever clothes he wore, made him downright lethal. He had to be the most beautiful man she'd ever met. On the beach he had been wearing a pair of jeans and a white shirt. And like her, he had removed his shoes. The outfit would have been casual on any other man but not on him.

Evidently he was single. At least he hadn't had a

ring on his finger, but that meant nothing since her father had rarely worn his wedding ring, either. She wondered if Brandon had someone special living in the States. A businessman traveling alone often forgot certain details like that. As owner of the hotel she was observant and perceptive and knew such affairs were going on under her roof, but as long as they were of mutual consent it was no business of hers.

Cassie reached for the matching shawl to her dress and placed it around her shoulders. The air tonight was rather breezy. Forecasters had reported a tropical storm was stirring up in the Atlantic. Hopefully, it wouldn't become a hurricane, and if it did she hoped that it would not set its course toward the islands.

She glanced at her watch. It was time to meet the very handsome Brandon Jarrett.

Brandon stood near the flower garden, his body shadowed by numerous plants and an abundance of palm trees. He watched Cassie as she left her suite and strolled along the private brick walkway. Like earlier, she hadn't detected his presence and this gave him a chance to study her once again.

The dress she was wearing seemed to have been designed just for her body and was definitely working for her, and for him as well. Just watching her made his pulse rate increase. The lantern lights reflecting off the building highlighted her features. Her hair flowed around her shoulders, tossing around her face with every step she took.

Sensations he hadn't felt in a long time gripped him and they were of a degree he'd never experienced before. John Garrison's youngest daughter was definitely a looker and was having an impact on his senses as well as his body. He inhaled deeply. He had to regain control. He had to remember his plan.

Deciding it wouldn't be in his best interest to catch her off guard for a second time, he deliberately cleared his throat. When she glanced his way their gazes met. He almost forgot everything, except the way she was looking at him. He had never been swept away by a woman, but he felt that he was now standing in sinking sand and quickly decided, just for that moment, he would forget the real reason he was on the island. The woman was too stunningly beautiful for him to do anything else.

"I hope you haven't been waiting long," she said, coming to stand directly in front of him, giving him a close view of her outfit.

"Not at all, but any time I've spent waiting has been worth it," he said, taking her hand in his and feeling the way her hand trembled beneath his fingers. In response, he felt his insides quiver and primitive emotions began stirring in his gut. He was discovering just how strong his sexual attraction to her was.

"Have you decided where we're going?"

Her question invaded his thoughts and he wished he could respond by telling her they were going to find the nearest bed. "Yes, the Viscaya Restaurant. Have you ever heard of it?"

"Yes, I've heard of it," Cassie answered, drawing in a deep breath. "It has an astounding reputation."

"I heard that, as well," he said, holding firm to her hand as he led her through the gardens and toward the parking lot where his rental car was parked. It was a beautiful October night and the breeze off the ocean made it somewhat cool.

"You look nice," Brandon said, opening the door to the Lexus.

She glanced up at him and smiled as she slid onto the car seat. "Thanks. You look nice yourself."

He smiled back at her. "Now it's my time to thank you."

"And you are welcome."

Cassie watched as Brandon crossed in front of the car to get into the driver's side. He did look nice in his dark trousers and crisp white shirt and looked the epitome of sexy. Everything about him appealed to her female senses. His walk was smooth and self-assured.

Before starting the engine he glanced over at her. "The lady at the front desk said the restaurant is only a five-minute drive from here."

Cassie nodded. "All right."

He pulled out of the parking lot and she leaned back into her seat, her body relaxed. She was looking forward to this evening; especially his company. There was a lot she wanted to know about him and decided that now was the time to ask. "So where are you from?"

"I'm from Orlando, Florida," he answered.

"Disney World."

He chuckled. "Yes, Disney World. Have you ever been there?"

"Yes, when I was about ten my mom took me there. We were there for a whole week."

"What about your father?"

A small smile touched her lips. "Dad traveled a lot

and joined us later, but for only a few days." And then, as if she wanted to know more about him, she asked, "And what sort of work you do?"

"I'm an investment broker. My motto is 'If you have any monies to invest then entrust them with me and I'll do the rest.'"

"Umm, that's clever. I like it."

"Thanks. And where are you from, Cassie, and what do you do?" he asked.

Brandon had come to a traffic light and he glanced over at her and saw her nervously rubbing her palms against the side of her dress. Her actions caused him to look at her thighs, the portion her minidress wasn't covering. It took everything within him to force his eyes back on the road when the light changed.

"I was born here on the island and I'm in the hotel business," he heard her say.

Deciding not to put her on the spot by asking her to expound more regarding her occupation he said, "The Bahamas is a beautiful island."

He could tell she had relaxed by the sound of her breathing. "Yes, it is. I take it that this is not your first visit here."

He smiled, liking the sound of her sexy accent. "No, I've been to the island several times, but this is the first time I've stayed at the Garrison Grand-Bahamas."

He didn't think it would be appropriate to mention that he had flown here last year with Jamie in his private plane. It had been then that he had asked her to marry him. She had accepted and they had spent the rest of the week on a yacht belonging to one of his clients, who was also a good friend.

He was grateful when they pulled into the parking lot of the Viscaya Restaurant. For a little while he was getting a reprieve from having to weave more lies.

Less than an hour later Cassie had determined a number of things about Brandon. In addition to being breathtakingly handsome, he was also incredibly charming and outrageously smooth. She'd discovered during dinner that he was also someone who was easy to talk to; someone who had the ability to make her feel comfortable around him. And she noticed he had a tendency to treat all people—from the restaurant's manager to the waiter to the busboy who'd come to clear off their table—with respect. He had made each individual feel important and appreciated.

"That was kind and thoughtful of you," she said when they were walking out of the restaurant.

He glanced over at her. "What?"

"The way you treated everyone back there. You didn't hesitate to let them know how much you appreciated their services. You would be surprised at how many people don't do that," she said, thinking how rudely her hotel workers were often treated by people who thought they were better than them.

He shrugged. "It's something I got from my father. He believed it wouldn't take much for a person to let others know when they've done something right, especially when we are quick to let them know when they've done something wrong."

"It sounds like your father is a very smart man."

"He *was* a smart man. Dad passed away a few years ago," he said.

She glanced over at him and a look of sorrow touched her features. "I'm sorry. Were you close to your father?"

"Yes, we were extremely close. In fact we were partners at our firm," he said truthfully. "My mother died of cancer before I reached my teens so it had been just my dad and I for a long time."

She nodded and then said, "My father passed away a little over four months ago and my mom a month before that."

Brandon heard the pain of her words in her voice and from the light from the electrical torches that lit the parking lot, he actually saw tears in her eyes. He stopped walking just a few feet from where their car was parked and instinctively pulled her into his arms. She offered no resistance when he gathered the warmth of her body against his. He briefly closed his eyes, regretting this cruel game he was playing with her.

"I'm sorry," he whispered in her ear, in a way for both her loss as well as his lies. Her loss was sincere and he actually felt her pain. She had loved both her parents immensely. For the first time since John's death, Cassie Sinclair-Garrison had become a real person and just not a name on a document on a file in his office. And not just the person with whom Parker had a beef.

"I didn't mean to come apart like that," Cassie said, moments later, stepping back out of Brandon's arms, looking somewhat embarrassed.

"It's okay. I can understand the depth of your pain. I've lost both of my parents, but when my mom died at least I had my dad to keep things going, providing a sense of stability in my life. But your parents died fairly close to each other. I can't imagine how you endured such a thing. Do you have other siblings?" he asked, wondering if she would acknowledge the Miami Garrisons.

She gave him a distracted look, as if thinking deeply on his question. Then she said, "My father had other children but I've never met them."

"Not even at the funeral?" he asked, already knowing the answer.

She shrugged. "No, not even then." Then she quickly said, "I'd rather not talk about it anymore, Brandon. It's rather private."

He nodded. "I understand. Sorry for prying."

She reached out and took his hand. "You weren't prying. Everything's sort of complicated right now."

"Again I understand, but if you ever need to talk or need—"

"A shoulder to cry on again," she said, trying to sound cheerful.

He chuckled. "Yes, a shoulder to cry on. I am available."

"Thank you. How long will you be staying at the hotel?"

He paused to open the car door for her. "A week. What about you?"

She waited until she was inside and glanced up at him and said. "Indefinitely. I work at the hotel and depending on how my days are, I sometimes spend the night there instead of driving all the way home. I have a private suite. My home is on the other side of the island."

"I see," Brandon said before closing the door. He

had given her another opportunity but she had yet to tell him she owned the hotel.

After walking around the car and getting inside he turned to her before starting the ignition. "I'm glad you came to dinner with me tonight. What are your plans for tomorrow?"

She smiled. "I have a meeting in the morning and then I'll be leaving for my home. I won't be returning to the hotel until Thursday morning."

Brandon leaned forward and smiled. "Is there anyway I can weasel another dinner date out of you?"

Cassie laughed. "Another dinner date?"

"Yes, I'll even be happy if you wanted to treat me to some of your good cooking."

"And what makes you think I can cook?"

"A hunch. Am I wrong?"

She shook her head. "No, you're right. Not to sound too boastful or conceited, although I don't spend a whole lot of time in the kitchen since I usually eat at the hotel, I can cook. That was one of my mom's biggest rules. And because of it, I was probably one of the few girls in my dorm at college who could fend for herself."

He chuckled. "And where did you attend college?"

"I went to a school in London and got a degree in business administration."

Brandon was still smiling when he finally decided to dig deeper by asking, "And just what is your position at the hotel? You never did say."

From her expression he could tell she was somewhat startled by his question. He was forcing her to make a decision as to whether or not she trusted him enough to tell him that much about herself.

"Evidently," she finally said, "you didn't make the connection when I gave my name earlier tonight."

He lifted a dark brow. "And what connection is that?"

Cassie held on to his gaze. "Garrison. I own the Garrison Grand-Bahamas."

Three

"You own the hotel?" Brandon asked, seemingly surprised by what she'd said and trying not to place much emphasis on what she'd just revealed and raise her suspicions about his motives for being there.

"Yes, my father left it to me when he died."

Brandon brought the car to a stop at a traffic light and used that opportunity to look directly at her. "Then you must feel proud that he had such faith and confidence in your abilities to do such a thing."

The smile she gave him extended straight from her eyes and he suddenly felt his gut clench from the effect those dark eyes had on him. "Thanks. And he did know of my capabilities because I'd managed the hotel for the past five years."

He nodded when the car began moving again. "That

might be true but I'm sure managing a hotel is a lot different than owning it. It's a big responsibility to place on anyone's shoulders and evidently he felt, and I'm sure justly so, that you could handle the job."

"Thank you for saying that," she said softly. "That was very kind of you."

"I'm just telling you the way I see it," he said, bringing the car to a stop in the parking lot of the hotel. "Now getting back to the subject of seeing you again tomorrow…" he said smoothly.

She shook her head, grinning. "You don't give up, do you?"

"Not without a fight," he said sincerely. "And if you don't feel like having me try out your cooking skills, I'd love to take you to another restaurant tomorrow evening. I understand several in this area come highly recommended."

Trying to ignore the urge to laugh from the intensity of his plea, she smiled. Since she'd taken ownership of her mother's home a few months ago, no man had crossed its threshold and she hadn't planned for one to cross over it anytime soon. But for some reason the thought of Brandon visiting her home didn't bother her, which could only mean one thing. She really liked him.

Pushing her hair away from her face she said, "I would love having dinner again with you tomorrow and I insist it be my treat. At my home. And I will proudly show you just what a good cook I am."

Brandon grinned. "I'll look forward to it."

He got out of the car and walked around it to open the door for her. What he'd said was true. He was looking forward to it but not for the reason that he should be. A part of him wished like hell that her last name wasn't Garrison.

"Thank you, Brandon," she said when he offered her his hand. "I'll leave a sealed envelope with directions to my home for you at the front desk tomorrow," she added when they stood at her door. "It's in Lyford Cay."

"And is there a particular time you prefer that I show up?"

She tilted her head back to look up at him. "Anytime after four will be fine. I won't be serving dinner until around six but I think you might enjoy taking a walk through the aquarium."

He lifted a brow. "The aquarium?"

She smiled. "Yes, my mother loved sea life and ten years ago for her fortieth birthday my father had a beautiful indoor aquarium built for her."

"You live in your mother's home?" he asked when she had lowered her head to get the door key out of her purse.

She glanced back up at him. "It used to be Mom's, but Dad signed it over to me when she died. I really had thought he was going to sell it, but I think the thought of parting with it bothered him since the place held so many special memories."

Brandon didn't know what to say to that. He did know there was no mention of John Garrison owning a home in the Bahamas in any of the legal papers he had. It was a moot point now since, according to Cassie, John had signed it over to her.

"I enjoyed your company tonight," she said, unlocking her door.

Cassie's words drew back his attention. "And I, yours. I'm looking forward to tomorrow."

"So am I. Good night, Brandon."

Although they had just met tonight, he had no intentions of letting her escape inside her suite without them sharing a kiss. All night he had focused on her lips, wondering how they would taste and how they would feel beneath his. He could feel the sizzling tension between them and took a step closer to her, deciding to draw it out and pull it in. He was powerless to do anything less.

He reached out, cupped her chin gently in his hand and studied the dimple she had there. "Nice place for a dimple," he said in a husky voice.

She smiled up at him. "My dad said it's a cleft. He had one, too."

So do his other five children, Brandon thought. "I'm going to have to disagree with your father on that. I have it on good authority that on a man it's a cleft but on a woman it's a dimple."

"Nothing wrong with disagreeing," Cassie said.

His hand felt warm and when he moved it from her chin and took the backside of his hand and caressed the side of her face, she felt her entire body tingle from sensations that not only flooded her mind but also her senses. Without any self-control she released a deep sigh and closed her eyes, thinking his touch felt so soothing. And before she could reopen her eyes she detected the warmth of his lips close to hers, and then she felt it when he placed them softly against her own.

She released another sigh and her lips parted, giving his tongue the opportunity to slip inside and capture hers. She had thought of tasting him all night and she was getting more than she had bargained for. His taste was manly, sexy, delicious—everything she had imagined it would be and more. She couldn't stop the quiver that passed through her body or the moan she heard from low in her throat. He was a master at his game, definitely an expert at what he was doing and how he was making her feel.

Her fingers gripped the sleeve of his shirt when she felt weak in the knees, and in response his arms wrapped themselves around her waist, pulling her closer to him. And she could actually feel his heat, his strength, everything about him that was masculine. Moments later when he broke off the kiss, she opened her eyes.

"Thank you for that," he whispered hoarsely, just inches from her lips. And before she could draw her next breath, he was kissing her again and the pleasure of it was seeping deep into her bones. Instinctively she responded, feeling slightly dizzy while doing so, and she could hear the *purr* that came from deep within her throat.

Moments later he ended the kiss and she regretted the loss, the feel of his mouth on hers. Her gaze latched onto his lips and she felt a warm sensation flow between her legs. Without much effort, he had aroused impulses within her that she had never encountered before. It was like her feminine liberation was threatening to erupt.

"I'm looking forward to seeing you tomorrow, Cassie," he said, taking a step even closer.

The light that shone in her doorway cast the solid planes of his face into sharp focus. She watched as his gaze moved slowly over her features before returning to her eyes. And while his eyes held hers, she studied the deep look of desire in them. For some reason the look didn't startle her, nor did it bother her. What it did do was fill her with anticipation of seeing him again.

"And I'm looking forward to seeing you, as well." When she realized she was still clutching his sleeve she quickly released it, turned and, without wasting time, opened the door and went inside.

A few moments later Brandon entered his own suite as he took a mental note of what had transpired that night. Frankly, he wasn't sure what to make of it. Cassie Garrison was definitely not what he had anticipated. He had expected a woman who was selfish, spoiled, inconsiderate and self-centered. Definitely temperamental at best. However, the woman he had spent time with tonight, in addition to her physical perfection, had possessed charm, style and grace, warmth and sensuality, even while not knowing she was eluding the latter. Then there was her keen sense of intelligence, which was definitely obvious. She was not a woman who acted irrational or who didn't think through any decision she made. Even when she had ordered dinner she had expounded on the advantages of eating healthy. And when she had spoken of her parents he could feel the pain that she'd endured in losing them, pain she was still mending from.

He shook his head, remembering how comfortable she had gotten with him. Surprisingly, they had discovered over the course of their conversation that they had a lot in common. They enjoyed reading the same types of books, shared a dislike of broccoli and had the same taste in music. And when she had opened up to him and revealed she had owned the hotel, he had seen the trusting look in her eyes.

A part of him wished the circumstances were different, that she hadn't lost her parents; that the two of them had met before John's death. And more than anything a part of him wished that he wasn't here betraying her.

In truth, he didn't want to think about that part—he really didn't want to think about Cassie Garrison at all. If only he could let it sink into his mind, as well as his body, that his only reason for being here was purely business and not personal. He of all people knew how it felt to be betrayed. How it felt to have your trust in someone destroyed. And that was not a comforting thought.

He walked out on the balcony and took a moment to stare out at the ocean, hoping he could stop Cassie from whirling through his thoughts. It was a beautiful night, but instead of appreciating the moon and the stars, his mind was getting clouded again with thoughts of a pair of long, gorgeous legs, a mass of curly brown hair cascading around a strikingly beautiful face and the taste of a mouth that wouldn't go away. Kissing her, devouring her lips, had been better than any dessert he'd ever eaten.

Closing his eyes, he breathed in the scent of the ocean, trying to get his mind back in check. That wasn't easy when instead of the ocean's scent filtering through his nostrils it was the scent of Cassie's perfume that wouldn't leave him.

A feeling of uneasiness crept over Brandon. He definitely didn't need this. He was not a man known to get wimpy and all emotional over a woman. Okay, so he had enjoyed her company, but under no circumstances could he forget just who she was and why he was here.

With that thought embedded into his mind and back where it belonged and where he intended for it to stay, he turned and went into his suite.

Craning her neck, Cassie stood at the floor-to-ceiling window in her living room and looked out, watching Brandon's car as it came through the wrought-iron gates that protected her estate.

As the vehicle made its way down the long winding driveway she forced back the shivers that tried overtaking her body when she remembered the night before—every single thing about it. For the first time in a long time she had spent an evening very much aware of a man. No only had she been aware of him, she had actually lusted after him in a way she had never done with a male before. But somehow she had managed to maintain her sensibility and control—at least she had until he had kissed her. And it had been some kiss. Even now those same shivers she tried forcing away earlier were back.

A part of her mind relayed a message to move away from the window when Brandon's car got closer, or else he would see her and assume she was anxiously waiting for him. She lifted her chin in defiance when another part of her sent a different message. Let him think what he wants since she *was* anxiously waiting.

He brought his car to a stop in front of her house and from where she stood she had a very good view of him; one he wouldn't have of her until he got out of the car and halfway up her walkway. She studied his features through the car window and in the light of day he was even more handsome. And when he got out of the car he was dressed as immaculately as he had been the night before.

Today he was wearing a pair of khaki trousers and a chocolate-brown polo shirt. The man was built. He exuded so much sensuality she could actually feel it through the window pane.

She watched him walk away from his car toward her door and suddenly, as if he somehow sensed her, he looked toward the window. His eyes held hers for a moment and then he lifted his hand in a wave, acknowledging her presence.

The heat she had felt earlier in her body intensified and the shivers she couldn't fight slithered through her once more. She lifted her hand to wave back, wondering what it was about him that affected her so. What was there about this man that had her inviting him to her home, her private sanctuary, her personal domain, the place where she felt the presence of her parents the most? Why was she sharing all of that with him?

She discovered she didn't have time to ponder those questions when he disconnected his eyes from hers and headed toward her door. She sighed deeply, her nerves stretched tight. The air she took into her lungs was sharp, and the quickening she felt in her veins was absolute.

Not waiting for a knock at her door, she moved away from the window and headed in that direction, very much aware of the magnetism, the attraction and the lure of the man who was now standing on her doorstep.

* * *

"Welcome to my home, Brandon."

Brandon gazed at Cassie, telling himself that just like last night, his reaction to her was strictly sexual, which accounted for the ache he suddenly felt below the belt. The effect did not surprise him. He accepted it although he didn't like it.

He immediately picked up her scent, the same one that had tortured him through most of the night as if it had been deeply drenched into his nostrils. Reaching out, he took her hand in his, leaned closer and placed a light kiss on the dimple in her chin and finally said, "Thank you for inviting me, Cassie."

He released her hand and she smiled before taking a step back, letting him inside her home. The moment he crossed the threshold he beheld the stunning splendor of the décor. It wasn't just the style and colors, there were also the shapes and designs that combined traditional flare with that of contemporary, colonial and Queen Anne. The mixture in any other place would look crammed, definitely busy. But in this monstrosity of a house it demonstrated a sense of wealth combined with warmth. It also displayed diversity in taste with an unmistakable look of sophistication.

"You have a beautiful home."

Her smile widened. "Thank you. Come let me give you a tour. I haven't changed much since Mom died because she and I had similar taste."

She led and he followed. "Do you take care of this place by yourself?" he asked, although he couldn't imagine one person doing so.

She shook her head. "No, I have a housekeeping

staff, the same one Mom had when she and Dad were alive. My staff is loyal and dedicated and," she said grinning, "a little overprotective where I'm concerned since they've been around since I was twelve."

They came to a spacious room and stopped. He glanced around, appreciating how the entire width of the living room had floor-to-ceiling windows to take advantage of the view of the ocean. He also liked the Persian rugs on the floor.

Beyond the living room was the dining room and kitchen, set at an angle that also took advantage of the ocean's view. The first thing he thought when they walked into the kitchen was that that she had been busy. Several mouthwatering aromas surged through his nostrils and he successfully fought back the grumbling that threatened his stomach.

Both the dining room and kitchen opened to a beautiful courtyard with a stunning swimming pool and a flower garden whose design spread from one area of the yard to the other. Then there was the huge water fountain that sprouted water to a height that seemed to reach the roof.

"Did you live here with your mother?" he asked, moving his gaze over her, taking in the outfit she had chosen to wear today, tropical print tea-length skirt and matching peasant blouse that was as distinctly feminine as she was. The way the skirt flowed over her curves only heightened his sexual desire and made him aware, and very much so, just how much he wanted her.

"Until I left for college," she said, leading him up the stairs. "When I returned from London I got an apartment, but a year later for my birthday Dad bought me a condo. When he gave me the deed to this place, I moved back."

Moments later after giving him a tour of the upstairs, she said with excitement in her voice, "Now I must show you the aquarium."

Once they returned downstairs and rounded corners he saw other rooms—huge rooms for entertaining, a library, a study and room that appeared lined with priceless artwork. He suddenly stopped when he came to a huge portrait hanging on the wall. The man in the painting he recognized immediately, but the woman...

"Your parents?" he asked, staring at the portrait.

"Yes, those are my parents," he heard Cassie say proudly.

Brandon's gaze remained on the woman in the portrait. "She's beautiful," he said. He was so taken by the woman's exquisiteness that he took a step closer to the painting. Cassie followed and glanced over at his fixed look and smiled.

"Yes, Mom was beautiful."

When Cassie began walking away, he strolled beside her, noticing several other photographs of her parents together and some included her. In every one of them John was smiling in a way Brandon had never seen before. To say the man had found true happiness with Ava would be an understatement. The image portrayed on each picture was of a couple who was very much in love, and the ones that included Cassie indicated just how much they loved their daughter, as well.

When they approached another room she stood back to let him enter. His breath literally caught in his throat. On both sides of the narrow but lengthy room

were high mahogany cabinets that encased floor-to-
ceiling aquariums, each one designed to hide the
aquarium frames and waterlines, they were filled with
an abundance of tropical and coldwater sea life, seemingly behind a glass wall.

"So what do you think?"

The sound of her voice seemed subdued, but it had
a sexy tone just the same. He turned to her. "I think
your mother was a very lucky woman to have your
father care so deeply to do this for her."

Cassie chuckled. "Oh, Dad knew what would make
Mom happy. She had a degree in marine biology and
for years worked as a marine biologist at the largest
mineral management company on the island."

"Your mother worked?" he asked before he could
stop himself.

Cassie didn't seem surprised by his question. "Yes,
Mom worked although Dad tried convincing her not
to. She enjoyed what she did and she refused to be a
kept woman."

At his raised brow, she explained. "My parents
never married. He was already married when they
met. However they stayed together for over twenty-
eight years."

Surprised she had shared that, he asked, "And he
never got a divorce from his wife?"

"No. I think at one time he intended to do so when
their children got older, but by then things were too
complicated."

"Your mother never pushed for a divorce?"

Cassie shook her head. "No. She was comfortable
with her place in my father's life as well as his love

for her. She didn't need a wedding band or a marriage certificate."

He nodded slowly and deliberately met her gaze when he asked. "What about you? Will you need a wedding band or marriage certificate from a man?"

She grinned. "No, nor do I want one, either. I'm married to the hotel."

"And what about companionship?" he murmured softly, his head tilting to one side as he gazed intently at her. "And what about the idea and thought of a man being here for you? A person who will be there for you to snuggle up to at night. Someone with whom you can get intimate with?"

If the intent of his latter questions were meant to arouse her, it was definitely working, Cassie thought, when a vivid picture flashed through her mind of the two of them sharing a bed, snuggling, making love. Shivers slid down her body and the passion she saw in his eyes was incredibly seductive, too tempting for her well-being.

Trying to maintain her composure with as much effort as she could, she said, "Those happen to be ideas or thoughts that don't cross my mind."

He lifted a dark brow. "They don't?"

"No."

"Umm, what a shame."

"I don't think so. Now please excuse me a moment. I need to check on dinner."

She turned and swiftly left the aquarium.

The moment Cassie rounded the corner to her kitchen she paused and leaned against a counter and inhaled deeply. She had quickly left Brandon because her self-confidence would have gotten badly shaken had she stayed.

He had asked questions she'd only recently thought about herself, but only since meeting him. Last night she had gotten her first experience of a real kiss. She had been filled with the intensity of desire and had never felt such passion. And for the first time in her life she had longed for male companionship, someone to snuggle up close to at night. Someone with whom she could make love. The very thought sent heated shivers down her spine.

Grabbing the apron off a nearby rack and tying it around her waist, Cassie moved away from the counter and went to the sink to wash her hands. She then walked over to the stove where she had a pot simmering…the same way she was simmering inside. It was a low heat that if she wasn't careful, could escalate into a full-fledged flame. And truthfully, she wasn't ready for that.

Four

Following the smell of a delicious aroma, Brandon tracked his way to the kitchen and suddenly paused. He had seen a lot of feminine beauty in his day, but Cassie Garrison took the cake. Even wearing an apron while standing at a stove stirring a pot, she looked stunning.

She was wearing her hair up but a few errant curls had escaped bondage and were hanging about her ears. Because of her peasant blouse, the top portion of her shoulders was bare and a part of him wanted to cross the room and kiss her, then take his lips and move downward toward her throat and place butterfly kisses along her shoulder blades.

"Something smells good," he said, deciding to finally speak up to remove such lusty thoughts from his mind.

She turned and smiled and not for the first time he

thought she had a pretty pair of lips, ones that had felt well-defined beneath his.

"I hope you're hungry."

He chuckled. "I am. I missed lunch today."

She lifted a brow. "And how did that happen when our brunch buffet is to die for?"

It wouldn't do to tell her that he had missed lunch because he had gotten a call from one of the Miami Garrisons, namely her brother Stephen. "I can believe that. In the two days I've been here I've found your hotel staff to be very efficient at everything they do. The reason I missed out on what I'm sure was such a very delicious meal was I got a call from the office on a few things I needed to finalize."

"Don't they know you're on vacation? My father's rule was to tell the office to hold the calls when you're taking a much-needed break from work, unless it was an extreme emergency."

"Sounds like your father was a smart man."

"He was," Cassie said proudly as her lips formed into another smile. "You would have liked him."

I did, Brandon quickly thought. He leaned against one of the many counters in the kitchen and asked. "So what are you cooking?"

"A number of dishes for you to enjoy. Right now I'm stirring the conch chowder. I've also prepared crab and rice, baked macaroni and cheese and potato salad. For dessert I decided to give you a taste of my grand-mother's famous recipe of guava duff."

Brandon felt his lips curve, thinking he wouldn't mind having a taste of her, too. That thought instantly sent his pulse thumping wildly. "Anything I can do to help?" he asked, thinking the best thing to do to keep his mind from wandering was to get busy.

"Let me see…" She said glancing around the room. "I've already washed everything if you want to put the salad together in a bowl."

Relief swept through him, glad she had found him something to do. If he were to continue to stand there and look at her while having all kinds of sexual thoughts, he couldn't be held responsible for his actions.

"Considering my skills in the kitchen, doing what you asked should be reasonably safe," he said, moving toward the sink to wash his hands.

Moments later he was standing at the counter putting the lettuce, tomatoes, cucumbers and onions in a huge bowl for their tossed salad. Knowing he needed to use all the time he had to get to know her, or to find out everything he could about her, he asked, "So, why are you still single, Cassie?"

"Why are you?"

Brandon could tell by her tone that he had once again put her on the defensive. To counter the effect he decided to be honest with her. "Up to a year ago I was engaged to get married."

She stopped stirring the pot and slanted him an arch glance. "If you don't mind me asking, what happened?"

He did mind her asking, but since he initiated the discussion, he would provide her an answer. "My fiancée decided a few months before the wedding that I wasn't everything she needed. I discovered she was unfaithful."

He watched her expression. First surprise and then regret shone in her eyes. "I'm sorry."

"Yes, so was I at the time, but I'm glad I found out before the wedding instead of afterward." Not wanting to discuss Jamie any further, he said, "Salad's done."

She turned back to the stove. "So is everything else. Now we can eat."

Brandon leaned back in his chair after glancing at his plate. It was clean. Cassie hadn't joked when she'd said she knew her way around a kitchen. Everything, even the yeast rolls that had been so fluffy they almost melted in his mouth, had been totally delicious.

He glanced across the table at her. She was finishing the last of the dessert, something that had also been delectable. "The food was simply amazing, Cassie. Thanks for inviting me to dinner."

"You're welcome and I'm glad you enjoyed everything."

"You never did answer the question I asked earlier, about why you're still single. Was I out of line in asking?" he asked, studying the contents of his glass before glancing back at her.

She met his gaze. "No, but there's not a lot to explain. After high school I left home for London to attend college there. I spent my time studying, more so than dating. I didn't see going to college as a way to escape from my parents and start proclaiming my freedom by exerting all kind of outlandish behavior."

"You mean you didn't go to any naked parties? Didn't try any drugs?" He meant the comment as a joke and he could tell she had taken it that way by the smile he saw in her eyes.

"No, there were no naked parties, no drugs and no

eating of fried worms just to fit in with any group." She grinned and added, "I mostly hung alone and I lived off campus in an apartment. Dad insisted. And the only reason he agreed that I have a roommate was for safety reasons."

"So you never dated during college?"

"I didn't say that," she said, taking a sip of her wine. "I dated some but I was very selective when I did so. Most of the guys at college enjoyed a very active sex life and didn't mind spreading that fact or the names of the girls who helped them to reach that status. I didn't intend to be one of them. I had more respect for myself than that."

Brandon stared down at his wine, considering all she had said. He then looked back up at her. "Are you saying you've never been seriously involved with anyone?"

She smiled warmly. "No, that's not what I'm saying." She paused for a moment before adding softly, "There was someone, a guy I met after college. Jason and I dated and thought things were working out but later discovered they weren't."

"What went wrong?"

The memory of that time filled Cassie's mind and for some reason she didn't have a problem sharing it with him. "He began changing in a way that wasn't acceptable to me. He would break our dates and make dumb excuses for doing so. And then out of the clear blue sky one day he broke off with me, and it was then that he told me the reason why. He had taken up with an older woman, a wealthy woman who wanted him as a boy toy, and he felt that was worth kicking aside what I thought we had."

Brandon stared at her. "How long ago was that?"

"Almost four years ago."

"Have you seen him at all since that time?" he asked.

She took another sip of her wine and suddenly felt quite warm. "Of course we haven't dated since then, but yes, I've seen him. He was thoughtful enough to attend my mother's funeral."

And then Cassie said, "And when I saw him I knew that our breakup was the best thing and I owed him thanks. That was a comforting thought and I no longer could hate him."

Brandon stared down into his wine, absently twirling the glass between his fingers, wondering if she ever discovered the truth about him—who he was and why he was there—would she end up hating him, too.

"You've gotten quiet on me," she said.

He glanced back up at her, held her gaze and then reached across the table and took her hand in his. "Have I? If so, it's because I can't imagine any man letting you go," he said softly, tightening his hold on her hand.

A shiver ran down Cassie's spine. She felt the sincerity in Brandon's words and they touched her. She stared at him, totally aware of his physical presence, and with his hand holding hers she felt his strength. Warmth flooded her from the heat she saw in his eyes and for a tiny moment a wealth of meaning shone in them.

"And while you were telling me about your ex-fiancée," she said, her eyes holding steady on his face, "I couldn't help thinking the same thing. I can't imagine any woman letting you go, either."

It seemed the room suddenly got quiet. The only sounds were that of their breathing in a seemingly

strained and forced tone. And he was still holding her
hands and she felt his fingers move as they brushed
across her hand in soft, featherlike strokes. The beating
of her heart increased and his gaze continued to hold
hers. The expression on his face was unreadable but
the look in his eyes was not.

He slowly stood and pulled her out of her seat. Word-
lessly, he brought her closer to him. Heat was thrum-
ming through her and she drew in a slow breath. She
slid her gaze from his eyes and lowered them to his lips.
He leaned in closer, inching his mouth closer to hers.

Cassie felt the heat within her intensify just seconds
before he brushed his lips across hers, causing a colossal
sensation that she felt all the way to her toes, before
spreading to areas known and unknown. And when a sigh
of pleasure escaped her lips, easing them apart, with a
ravenous yet gentle entry he began devouring her mouth.

Brandon felt the rush of blood that started in his
head, and when it got to his chest it joined the rapid
pounding of his heart. This was what energized passion
was all about. And as he deepened the kiss all kind of
feelings reverberated through him, searing awareness
in his central nervous system. When he took hold of
her tongue, he was filled with intense yearning and a
craving that for him was unnatural.

He slightly shifted his stance and brought her closer
to the fit of him, and to a body that was getting aroused
by the minute. By the moans he heard coming from her
he could tell she was enjoying the invasion of his
tongue. That realization had him sinking deeper and
deeper into the taste and texture of her mouth.

Her body pressed against his hard erection, making him want to sweep her into his arms and carry her to the nearest bedroom. He knew it would be sheer madness. And it would also be wrong. She deserved more than a man making love to her for all the wrong reasons, a man who had walked into her life without good intensions. A man who was even now betraying her.

That thought had him ending the kiss but he couldn't let her go just yet, so he pulled her closer into his arms. How had he allowed himself to get into this situation? How had he let Cassie get to him so quickly and so deeply?

She pulled slightly back, glanced out the window and then back at him and smiled. "Do you want to take a stroll on the beach before it gets too dark?"

"I'd love to," he said, releasing her.

"It will only take a minute for me to get my shawl. You can wait for me on the terrace if you'd like."

"All right."

She shifted to move past him and he suddenly reached out and gently locked his hand on her arm. Then he raised his hands to her hair and brushed back the strands that had fallen in her face. He felt the shiver that touched her body the moment he leaned down and brushed a kiss against her lips. "I'll be waiting," he whispered.

A few moments later Cassie quietly slipped out on the terrace to find Brandon standing with his back to her, staring out at the ocean with both hands in the pockets of his trousers.

His stance radiated so much sex appeal it should

have been illegal. He seemed to be in deep thought and she couldn't help wondering what he was thinking about. Had talking about his ex-fiancée opened up old wounds? Having someone you loved betray you wasn't easy to take. She had discovered that with Jason.

"I'm ready."

He turned at the sound of her voice and across the brick pavers she met his gaze. He then looked at her from head to toe, zeroing in on her bare feet for a few seconds.

She laughed. "Hey, don't look surprised. You never walk on the beach with shoes on. That's an islander rule, so please remove yours."

He chuckled as he dropped into a wicker chair to take off his shoes and socks. She thought the feet he exposed were as sexy as the rest of him. Placing his socks and shoes aside, he stood and smiled at her. "Happy now?"

"Yes, extremely. Now we can make footprints in the sand." She held her hand out to him. "Let's go."

Brandon took the hand she offered and together they walked down the steps toward the private beach.

"So, tell me about your life in Orlando."

Her question reminded him of the lies he had planted, as well as those he had to continue to tell. He glanced over at her and asked, "What do you want to know?"

Smiling curiously, she asked, "Is there someone special in your life waiting for your return?"

"No," he responded with no hesitation. "I date occasionally but there's no one special."

Seconds ticked by and when she didn't say anything he decided to add, "And it isn't because I mistrust all women because of what my ex-fiancée did. I got over it and moved on. I buried myself in my work because while with her I spent a lot of time away from it. That's what she wanted and what I thought she needed."

"But you found it wasn't?"

"Yes, I found it wasn't, especially when it wasn't for the right reason. Jamie had an insecurity complex and I fed into it. But that wasn't enough. She had to feel doubly safe by having someone else in her life, besides me."

"Did she not care how that would play out once you discovered the truth?"

He shrugged. "I guess she figured she would never get caught. She even went so far to admit that she would not have given up her lover after we married."

"Sounds like she was pretty brazen."

His jaw tightened. "Yes, she was."

When they reached the end of the shore they stopped and looked out at the ocean. Standing beside her Brandon could feel Cassie's heat, and even with the scent of the sea he inhaled her fragrance. He allowed the rest of his senses to appreciate her presence, being with her at this time and place.

She turned and flashed him a brilliant smile. "The sunset is beautiful, isn't it?"

"Yes, and so are you."

She lowered her head as if to consider his words. She then looked back at him. "Are you always this complimentary with women?"

"No, not always."

"Then I should feel special."

"Only because you are."

She turned and pressed her lithe body against his aroused one, and he was tempted to lower his head and connect to the lips she was so eagerly offering him. Instead he stepped back and said, "I think it's time for me to leave and go back to the hotel now."

He saw the questions in her eyes and really wasn't surprised when she asked, "Why, Brandon?"

He understood her reason for asking. But there was no way he could be completely honest with her. "I don't think we're ready for that step yet," he murmured softly, moving forward to pull her in his arms.

She leaned back and looked at him as her lips curved into a smile. "Are you talking for yourself or for me?"

He ignored the underlying challenge in her words. "I'm trying to be a gentleman and speak for the both of us."

"I'm a grown woman, Brandon. I can speak and think for myself."

He looked down at her, studied her eyes and saw the deep rooted stubbornness glaring in them. "I know that, but I want you to trust me to know what's best for the both of us right now."

She paused then said, "All right, but only on one condition."

He raised a dark brow. "And what condition is that?"

"That we have dinner again tomorrow night."

It was on the tip of Brandon's tongue to tell her that he was thinking seriously about returning to Miami tomorrow. Parker and Stephen would know soon enough that his mission hadn't been accomplished. The thought of spending time with Cassie one more night over dinner was something he couldn't pass up. But then, he would give her an out by suggesting a place she probably wouldn't go along with.

"Dinner will be fine as long as we can dine at the hotel," he said.

He was surprised when she nodded and said, "All right."

Brandon nodded. "Come on, let's go back."

When they reached the terrace he stopped and turned to her. "And I might have to go back to the States on Thursday. Something has come up that needs my attention."

He could see the disappointment in her face and it almost weakened his resolve.

"I understand. I'm a businesswoman, so I know how things can come up when you least expect them to…or want them to."

He eased down in the wicker chair to put back on his shoes and socks. He waited and then said, "I'm looking forward to having dinner with you tomorrow."

"So am I."

He glanced up at her, intrigued by the eagerness in the tone of her voice, and wondered if perhaps she was plotting his downfall. He wanted her with a fierce passion and it wouldn't take much to push him over the edge.

Brandon stood, knowing it was best for him to leave now. Hanging around could result in more damage than good. "Will you walk me to the door?"

He reached for her hand and she didn't resist in giving it to him. When they reached her front door he gazed at her, thinking he wouldn't be forgetting her for a long time. "Thanks again for a beautiful evening and a very delicious dinner."

The smile that appeared on her face was genuine. "You are welcome." And then she leaned up on tiptoes and brushed a kiss across his lips. "I'll see you at dinner tomorrow, Brandon. Please leave a note at the front desk regarding where you want us to meet and when."

Brandon held her gaze for a moment, and then nodded before turning to walk down the walkway to his car.

Five

Brandon glanced at the table that sat in the middle of the floor. Room service had done an outstanding job of making sure his orders were followed. He wanted Cassie to see the brilliantly set table the moment she arrived.

He had tried contacting Parker earlier today to let him know his trip hadn't revealed anything about Cassie that they didn't already know. He shook his head, thinking that he stood corrected on that. There was a lot about her that he knew now that he hadn't known before, but as far as he was concerned it was all good, definitely nothing that could be used against her.

Parker's secretary had told him that his friend had taken a couple of days off to take his wife Anna to New York for shopping and a Broadway show, and wouldn't be returning until the beginning of next week. Brandon couldn't help but smile every time he thought about how the former Anna Cross had captured the heart of the man who had been one of Miami's most eligible bachelors and most prominent businessman.

He turned at the sound of the knock on the door and quickly crossed the room. As he'd expected, she was on time. He opened the door to find Cassie standing there, and smiled easily. As usual she looked good. Tonight her hair was hanging around her shoulders. He studied her face and could tell she was wearing very little makeup, which was all that was needed since she had such natural beauty.

His gaze slid down her body. She was no longer wearing the business suit he had seen her in earlier that day when he had caught a glimpse of her before she had stepped into an elevator. Instead she had changed into a flowing, slinky animal-print dress that hugged at the hips before streaming down her figure. A matching jacket was thrown over her arm. A pair of black leather boots were on her feet, but how far up her legs they went he couldn't tell due to the tea-length of her dress. He knew she was wearing the boots more for a fashion statement than for the weather.

"May I come in?"

He pulled his gaze back to her face and returned her smile. "Yes, by all means."

Her fragrance filled his nostrils when she strolled by him and after closing the door he stood there and stared at her with his hands shoved in the pockets of his trousers. He had placed them there so he wouldn't be tempted to reach out and pull her into his arms. That temptation was becoming a habit.

"You look nice," he couldn't help but say because she did look nice, so nice that he felt the fingers inside his pockets beginning to tingle.

"Thank you. And you look nice yourself."

When he lifted a skeptical brow he saw her smile widen, and then she said, "You do look nice. I thought that the first time I saw you."

"That night on the beach?"

"No, that day you checked in to the hotel. I happened to notice you and immediately knew by the way you were dressed that you were an American businessman."

He nodded, not wanting to get in to all the other things that he was, especially when his conscience was getting pinched. He decided to change the subject. "I hope you're hungry."

"I am." She glanced around and saw the table. "They've delivered already?"

Freeing his hands from his pockets, he moved away from the door to cross the room to where she stood. "No, they've just set up everything. I didn't want to take the chance of ordering something you didn't like."

He reached for the menu he had placed on the table. "You want to take a look?"

She shook her head. "No, I have every entrée on it memorized."

He chuckled. "I'm impressed."

She grinned. "Just one of my many skills. And if I may…"

"And you can."

"Then I would recommend the Salvador. It's a special dish that's a combination of lobster, fish, crawfish and various other seafood that's stewed and then served over rice."

"Sounds delicious."

"It is, but I have to warn you that it's kind of spicy."

A smile curved his lips. "I can handle a little bit of spicy. And please make yourself comfortable while I phone room service."

Cassie placed her jacket across the back of the sofa and sat, crossing her legs. She hadn't missed the look of male appreciation in Brandon's eyes when he had opened the door. His already dark gaze had gotten darker and his seductive look had sent heat flowing through her body.

Deciding she needed to cool down, she glanced around. The layout of this suite was similar to one she used whenever she stayed overnight at the hotel. However since hers was an executive suite, it was slightly larger and also had a kitchen, although she never used it.

"Our dinner will be delivered in about thirty to forty-five minutes," he said, sitting on the sofa beside her and shifting his position to face her. "So, how was your day?"

She rolled her eyes and shook her head. "Crazy. Hurricane Melissa can't seem to make up her mind which way she wants to go, so we're taking every precaution. Just yesterday she was headed north, but now she's in a stall position as if trying to decide if she really wants to go north after all. We had a number of people who decided not to take any chances and have checked out of the hotel already."

Brandon nodded. He'd been keeping up with the

weather reports as well and understood her concern. Being a native of Miami, he had experienced several hurricanes in his lifetime, some more severe than others. Earlier that day he had spoken with his secretary, Rachel Suarez. A Cuban-American, Rachel had been working for his firm for over thirty years, and had started out with his father. When it came to handling things at the office she could hold her own—including the possibility of an oncoming hurricane.

"And if the hurricane comes this way I'm sure your staff knows what to do," he said, tempted to ease over toward her and run his hands up her legs to see how far up her boots went.

"Trust me, they know the drill. Every employee has to take a hurricane awareness course each year. It prepares them for what to do if it ever comes to that. Dad mandated the training after we went through Hurricane Andrew."

Brandon remembered Hurricane Andrew, doubted he would ever be able to forget it. It had left most of Miami, especially the area where he had lived, in shambles. "Well, hopefully Lady Melissa will endure a peaceful death before hitting land," he said mildly.

He then asked, "Would you like anything to drink while we wait? How about a glass of wine?"

"That would be nice. Thanks."

He stood and Cassie watched as he did so. She watched him walk across the room, thinking he was so sinfully handsome it was a shame. His gray trousers and white shirt were immaculate, tailored to fit his body to perfection. Last night he had done the gentlemanly thing and had stopped anything from escalating further between them, and after he had left her home she had felt grateful. Now she felt a sense of impending loss. He would be leaving tomorrow and chances where they would never see each other again.

For the past two days she had felt alive and in high spirits, something she hadn't felt in the last five months—and all because of him. He hadn't pushed for an affair with her. In fact when he'd had a good opportunity to go for a hit, he had walked away. Had he exerted the least bit of pressure, she would have gladly taken him into her bed. There had never been a man who'd had her entertaining the idea of a casual fling before. But Brandon Jarrett had.

"Here you are."

She looked up. Their gazes connected and she reached out to take the wineglass he offered, struggling to keep her fingers from trembling. "Thanks." She immediately took a sip, an unladylike gulp was more like it. She needed it. The heat within her was intensifying.

"You okay?"

She favored him with a pleasing smile. "Yes, I'm fine." She held on to the look in his eyes and then asked, "And are you okay?"

He returned her smile. "Yes."

She lowered her head to take another sip of her drink, trying to ignore the towering figure standing in front of her. She sensed his movement away from her, but refused to lift her head just yet to see where he had gone. Moments later when she did so, she drew in a quick breath. He was standing across the room with a wineglass in his hand, leaning against the desk and staring at her. Not just staring, but he seemed to be stirring up the heat already engulfing her. Then there were pleasure points that seemed to be touching various parts of her body. She was a sensible woman but at the moment she felt insensible, deliriously brazen. She knew what she wanted but inwardly debated being gutsy enough to get it. But then, as awareness flowed between them, she was compelled to do so.

With his eyes still holding hers, she stood and slowly began crossing the room to him. His strength, as well as his heat, was filtering across to her, touching her everywhere, and putting her in a frame of mind to do things she'd never done before. He watched her every step, just as she watched how the darkness of his eyes did nothing to cloak the desire in his gaze. It was desire that she felt in every angle of her body, in every curve and especially in the juncture of her legs. Especially there.

When she reached him she stood directly in front of him, still feeling his strength and heat, and still radiating in desire. With great effort she held on to the wineglass in her hand, needing another sip to calm her nerves, to quench her heat.

She lifted the glass to her lips and after taking a quick sip, Brandon reached out and took the glass from her, leaned in and placed his lips where the glass had been.

Brandon's heart was pounding furiously in his chest and every muscle in his body ached. Fire was spreading through his loins and a quivering sensation was moving through him at a rapid pace. Her mouth had opened beneath his and he tasted her with a ravenous hunger that was gripping him, conquering with a need he could no longer contain.

Pulling back, he placed both of their glasses on the table, and with his hands now free he took her into his arms and quickly went back to kissing her with a passion that was searing through him. With very little effort his mouth coaxed her to participate. Once he took hold of her tongue, he strived to reach his goal of ultimate satisfaction for the both of them.

What they were exchanging was a sensual byplay of tongues that was meant to excite and arouse. Their bodies were pressed so close that he could feel the tips of her breasts rub against his chest. He could feel the front of her cradle his erection in a way that had his heartbeat quickening and his body getting harder. A need to make her his was seeping through every pore. He lowered his hand and pulled her even closer to his aroused frame, as he was in serious danger of becoming completely unraveled.

She pulled back and breathed in deeply, her arms wrapped tightly around his neck. It only took a look into her eyes to see the fire burning in their depths. That look made him feel light-headed. The room seemed to be revolving, making him dizzy with smoldering desire. The experience was both powerful and dangerous. His lungs released a shuttering breath and a part of him knew he should do what he'd done last night and walk away. But his wants and needs had him glued to the spot.

And then she rose on tiptoe and whispered. "Make love to me, Brandon."

Her words, spoken in a sexy breath, broke whatever control he had left, every single thread of it. With a surge of desire that had settled in his bones, he swept her off her feet and into his arms and headed straight for the bedroom.

Cassie's heart began thumping in her chest when Brandon placed her on the king-size four-poster bed. And when he stood back and gave her that look, like she was a morsel he was ready to devour, she automatically squeezed her legs together to contain the heat flowing between them. There was an intensity, a desperation bursting within her, but not for any man. Just this one.

Since meeting him she hadn't been able to put him out of her mind. Even as crazy as today had been, periodically he had found a way to creep into her thoughts. And she had felt herself getting flushed when she thought about the kisses they had shared. The memories had been unsettling on one hand and then soothing on the other. His kisses had easily aroused her and had made every nerve in her body quiver...like they were doing now.

She watched as he slowly began unbuttoning his shirt before shrugging broad shoulders to remove it. Her gaze zeroed in on his naked chest and suddenly her mind began indulging in fantasies of placing kisses all over it. She held her breath watching, waiting for him to start taking off his pants. However, instead of doing so, he walked back over to the bed.

"Do you know what I want to know? What I have to know?" he asked, staring at her from top to bottom.

Her mind went blank. She didn't have a clue. "What," she murmured, feeling the sexual tension that had overtaken the room.

"I have to know how far up your legs those boots go."

That definitely was not what she had expected him

to say and couldn't help but smile. "Why don't you find out," she challenged silkily.

Brandon took a couple of steps toward the bed, reached out and slowly raised her dress. He sucked in a deep breath as he lifted it higher and higher. The top of the boots ended just below her knee, giving him a tantalizing view of her thighs.

"Satisfied?"

He shifted his gaze from her legs and thighs back to her face. "Partially. But I will be completely satisfied in a moment."

Cassie swallowed when Brandon unzipped her boots and began removing them, taking the time to massage her legs and ankles and the bottom of her feet. "Do you want to know something else?" he asked her.

"What?"

"I stayed awake most of the night just imagining all the things I'd like doing to you if ever given the chance," he said in a husky tone.

"Now you have the chance."

He smiled. "I know." He took a step back. "Scoot over here for a second."

She eased across the bed to him on her knees and he tugged her dress over her head, leaving her clad in a black satin bra and a pair of matching panties. He tossed the dress aside with an expression on his face denoting he was very pleased with what he had done.

Cassie was very pleased with what he had done, too. "Not fair," she said sulkily. "You have on more clothes than I do."

He chuckled. "Not for long." His hands went to the snap on his pants.

Reasonably satisfied with his answer, as well as more than satisfied with what she was seeing, Cassie watched as Brandon begin easing down his zipper, her gaze following every movement of his hand. This wasn't her first time with a man, but it had been a while. And this was the first time one had gotten her so keyed up. What she was seeing was sending shivers rippling down her spine.

She nearly groaned when he stepped out of his pants. The only thing covering his body was a pair of very sexy black briefs—briefs that could barely support his huge erection, but were trying like hell to do so. She stared when he removed them. Then she blinked and stared some more. And in a move that was as daring as anything she had ever done, she scooted to the edge of the bed, reached out and stroked over his stomach with her hand before moving it lower to cup him.

She glanced up when she heard his sharp intake of breath. "Am I hurting you?" she asked softly, as she continued to fondle him in a way she had never done with a man before. Even with Jason she hadn't been this bold.

"No, you're not hurting me but you are torturing me," she heard Brandon say through clenched teeth. "There's a difference."

"Is there?"

"Yes, let me show you." He reached his hands behind her back and undid her bra clasp. He eased off her bra and tossed it aside and his hands immediately went to her naked breasts. And then he began stroking her as precisely and methodically as she was stroking him. A startled gasp erupted from her throat when he took things just a little further and leaned over and caught a nipple between his lips.

Suddenly, she understood the difference between pain and torture. She understood it and she felt it. This was torture of the most exhilarating kind. It was the type that filled you with an all-consuming need, an intense sexual craving. When he switched his mouth to the other breast she released a deep moan, thinking his tongue was wonderfully wicked.

"I can't take much more," she muttered in an abated breath.

"That makes two of us," he said, lifting his head. "But I'm not through with you yet."

He moved to grab his pants off the floor, pulled a condom packet from his wallet and put it on. He then eased her back on the bed and gently grabbed a hold of her hips to remove her panties. She heard the deep-throated growl when she became completely bare to his view. She saw the look in his eyes; felt the intensity of his gaze, and immediately knew where his thoughts were going. He glanced at her, gave her one hungry, predatory smile and before she could draw in her next breath he lifted her hips to his mouth.

Cassie screamed out his name the moment his tongue invaded her and she grabbed on to the bedspread, knowing she had to take a hold of something. He was taking her sensuality to a whole new dimension and shattering her into a million pieces, bringing on the most intense orgasm ever. She continued writhing under the impact of his mouth while sensations tore through her. And while her body was still throbbing, he pulled back and shifted his body in position over hers. Their gazes locked, held, while he eased into her, joining their bodies as one.

Brandon sucked in sharply as he continued to sink deeper and deeper into Cassie's body, fulfilling every fantasy he'd had about her. Securing his hips over hers he then used both hands to lock in her hair as he lowered his head to capture her mouth. He began rocking against her, thrusting into her as she gave herself to him, holding nothing back. He felt her inner muscles clench him, while a whirlwind of emotions washed over the both of them.

"Brandon!"

When he felt her come apart under him, he followed suit and exploded inside of her. He felt heaven. He felt overwhelmed. He felt a degree of sensuality that he knew at that moment could only be shared with her.

Moments later he gathered her closer into his arms, their breathing hard, soft, then hard again. He slowly moved his hand to caress her thigh and stomach, still needing to touch her in some way.

Deep down Brandon knew he should not have made love to her without first telling her the truth of who he was and why he was there. He didn't want to think about how she would react to the news and hopefully, she would hear him out and give him time to explain. More than anything, she deserved his honesty. "Cassie?"

It took her a long time to catch her breath to answer. "Yes?" She lifted slightly and looked at him for a moment before saying, "Please don't tell me that you regret what we shared, Brandon."

He shook his head. Boy, was she way off. "I have no regrets but there's something I need to tell you."

She lifted a brow. "What?"

He opened his mouth to speak at the exact moment there was a knock on the door. A part of him felt temporary relief. "Dinner has arrived. We can talk later."

Like Cassie had said it would be, dinner was delicious. But it would be hard for any man to concentrate on anything when he had a beautiful woman sitting across from him wearing nothing but a bathrobe. And the knowledge that she was stark naked underneath was not helping matters.

He had assumed, when he had slipped back into his shirt and trousers to open the door for room service, that she would put back on her clothes, as well. He had been mildly surprised, but definitely not disappointed, when she had appeared after the food was delivered wearing one of the hotel's complimentary bath robes.

Deciding to take his mind off his dinner guest and just what he would love to do to her...again, he glanced out the French doors and onto the terrace. In the moonlight he could tell that the ocean waves were choppy and by the way the palm trees were swaying back and forth, he knew there was a brisk breeze in the air. Even if Hurricane Melissa decided not to come this way, she was still stirring up fuss.

"Brandon?"

He glanced over at Cassie. She had said his name with a sensual undercurrent, making him get aroused again, especially when he saw the top of her robe was slightly opened, something she'd evidently taken the time to do while he had been looking out the French doors. A smile tugged at his lips. She was trying to tempt him and he had no complaints. In fact, he more than welcomed her efforts. When it came to her he was definitely easy. "Yes?"

"Right before dinner you said you needed to talk to me about something."

He nodded. He had dismissed the thought of discussing anything over dinner. The last thing he'd wanted was the entire meal flung at his head. And in a way he didn't want to talk about anything now since he knew how the evening would end once he did so. But he couldn't overlook the fact that he owed her the truth.

She was giving him a probing look, waiting on his response. He was about to come clean and tell her everything when a cell phone went off. From the sound of the ringer he knew it wasn't his and she jumped up and walked quickly to grab her purse off the sofa and pulled her cell phone out.

"Yes?" After a few moments she said, "All right, Simon. Let me know if anything changes." Cassie held the phone in her hand for a moment before putting it back in her purse.

"Bad news?"

She glanced up and met Brandon's gaze. "Nothing that surprises me. Forecasters predict Hurricane Melissa will escalate to a category three whenever she makes it to shore."

Brandon nodded. "So she's moving again?"

"No, she's still out in the Atlantic gaining strength. Wherever she decides to land is in for a rough time."

And more than anyone Cassie knew what that meant. Because of the uncertainty, more people would be checking out of the hotel. She really didn't blame them and didn't begrudge anyone who put their safety first. But that also meant chances were Brandon would be leaving tomorrow, as well, possibly earlier in the day than he had planned. If Hurricane Melissa turned its sights toward the Bahamas, the airports would be closing, which wouldn't be good news to a lot of people.

Today things at the hotel had been crazy, but she had a feeling tomorrow things would get even crazier. She would probably be too busy to spend any time with Brandon before he left, which meant tonight was all they had. The thought of never seeing him again pricked her heart more than she imagined it would. And she knew what she wanted. She wanted memories that would sustain her after he left. They would be all she would have in the wee hours of the morning when she would want someone to snuggle close to, someone to make love to her the way he had done earlier. Those nights when she would ache from wanting the hard feel of him inside of her, she would have her memories.

He had said that he had something to tell her and a part of her had an idea just what that something was. A disclaimer that stated spending time with her, sharing a bed with her, had been an enjoyable experience, but he had to move on and he wouldn't keep in touch. She couldn't resent him for it because he hadn't made any promises, nor had he offered a commitment. What they were sharing was an island fling and nothing else and chances were he wanted to make sure she understood that.

She did.

And she wouldn't have any regrets when he left. Knowing all of that, she knew what she wanted. More than anything, tonight she wanted to spend the rest of her time making love and not talking.

Deciding not to be denied what she wanted, and knowing his eyes were on her, she untied the sash at her waist to remove her robe and dropped it where she stood. She brazenly moved to cross the room to him stark naked. He stood and began removing his clothes, as well. For the second time that night she felt daring and the look in his eyes while he pulled a condom out of his pocket and put it on over his huge erection, once again made her feel desirable.

They stood in front of each other completely naked and their mouths within inches of each other, emanated intense heat. He leaned down and captured her mouth. Unlike earlier that night, there was nothing gentle about this kiss. It conveyed a hunger that she felt as he plunged deeply and thoroughly in her mouth, at the same time he wrapped her arms tightly around her. His taste was spicy and reminded her of the food they'd eaten for dinner. The flavor of him exploded against her palate when her tongue began tangling with his.

Her body began quivering, all the way to her bones, and she felt heat collect in the area between her legs. Only Brandon could bring her to this state, escalating her need for passion of the most intense kind. She felt the powerful beating of his heart in his chest, sending vibrations through her breasts, tantalizing her nipples and making them throb, the same way she was throbbing in the middle.

She pulled back, hauled in a gasping breath, and before she could recover, he began walking her backward toward the sofa. She was glad when they finally made it there since her knees felt like they would give out at any moment. She sank back against the sofa cushions, and then he was there, his mouth and hands everywhere, and it took all she had not to give into the earth-shaking pleasure and scream.

And then he did the unexpected, he pulled her up with him turning her so her back pressed against his chest. He leaned over and began placing kisses along her throat and neck while his hand moved up and down her stomach before capturing her breasts in his hand. He cupped them, gently squeezed them, teased her sensitive nipples to harden beneath his fingertips.

"Open your legs for me." He murmured the request hotly against her ear while his hands moved from her breasts and traveled lower to the area between her legs. He stroked her while breathing heavily in her ear. Electric currents, something similar to bolts of lightning, slammed through her with his touch. Moments later another orgasm exploded within her but she had a feeling he wasn't through with her yet.

"Lean forward and hold on to the back of the sofa," he said with a raw, intense sexuality in his breath.

As soon as she stretched her arms out and grabbed hold of the sofa, she felt him grind the lower part of his body against her. He took his hands and tilted her hips before easing his shaft into her. He went deep, and she felt him all the way to her womb.

"Brandon!"

He began thrusting back and forth inside of her, sending sensations rippling all through her. Establishing a rhythm that was splintering her apart both inside and out, he grabbed hold of her breasts again and used his fingertips and thumb to drive her over the edge.

She cried out his name when her body exploded and when he plunged deeper inside of her she could feel the exact moment an explosion hit him, as well. She groaned when a searing assault was made on her senses, and when he pulled her head back and took control of her mouth she felt his possession.

Before she could get a handle on that feeling, she felt him scoop her into his arms and carry her into the bedroom.

The ringing phone woke Cassie and, instinctively, she reached over and picked it up. When she heard Brandon's voice engaged in a conversation with someone, she quickly recalled where she was and realized that he had gotten out of the bed earlier to take a shower and had picked up the bathroom's phone.

She was about to hang up when she recognized the voice of the man he was talking to. She immediately sat up straight in bed, knowing she was right when she head Brandon call the man by name. Why would Brandon be talking to Parker Garrison? How did they even know each other? Just what was going on?

Hanging up the phone, she angrily slipped out of bed. Ignoring the soreness in the lower part of her body, she glanced around, looking for her clothes, and hurriedly began putting them on. Her mind was spinning with a thousand questions as she tried getting her anger under control. She had just tugged her dress over her head when she heard Brandon enter the room.

"Good morning, sweetheart."

She swung around after pulling her dress down her body. Trembling with rage, she tried remaining calm as she crossed the room to face Brandon. A part of her didn't want to believe that this man, who had tenderly made love to her last night, who had taken her to the most sensuous heights possible in his arms, could be anything other than what she saw. Utterly beautiful. The epitome of a perfect gentleman, who was thoughtful and kind.

Something in her eyes must have given her away, and when he reached for her hand, she took a step back. "What's wrong, Cassie?" he asked in a voice filled with concern.

Instead of answering his question she had one of her own. Swallowing the lump she felt in her throat and with a back that was ramrod straight, she asked, "How do you know Parker Garrison, Brandon?"

Six

There was a long silence as Brandon and Cassie stood there, staring at each other. Tension in the room was thick, almost suffocating. Brandon inhaled deeply, wishing like hell that he'd told her the truth last night as he had intended and not have her find out on her own. Apparently, she had listened to his phone conversation long enough to know the caller had been Parker.

"I asked you a question, Brandon. How do you know Parker?"

Her sharp tone cut into his thoughts and he could tell from her expression that she was beginning to form her own opinions about things. He didn't want that. He took another deep breath before saying, "He's a client."

She turned her face from him with the speed of someone who had been slapped and the motion made his heart turn over in his chest. He had hurt her. He could actually feel it. The thought that he had done that to her appalled him and at that moment he felt lower than low. "Cassie, I—"

"No," she snapped, turning back to him.

She reached up as if to smooth a strand of hair back from her face, but he actually saw her quickly swipe back a tear. Brandon winced.

"And just what do you do for Parker, Brandon? Are you his hit man? Since I'm not being cooperative did he decide to do away with me all together?"

"I'm his attorney, Cassie," he asserted, his brows drawing together in a deep frown, not liking what she'd said.

"His attorney?" she whispered, her eyes widening in disbelief.

His stomach tightened when he saw the color drain from her face. "Yes," he said softly. "I represent Garrison, Inc."

She didn't say anything for a few moments but the shocked eyes staring at him appeared as jagged glass. Then they appeared to turn into fire. "Is Brandon Jarrett even your real name?" she blurted.

He exhaled a long breath before answering. "Yes, but not my full name. It's Brandon Jarrett Washington."

Cassie frowned. She recalled seeing the name of Washington and Associates law firm on a letterhead sent to her on Parker's behalf a few months ago when she had refused to acknowledge any more of his phone calls. "I should have known," she said with anger in her voice. "Anything that's too good to be true usually isn't true. So what sort of bonus did Parker offer you to make me change my mind about the buyout? He evidently told you to succeed by using any means necessary. You wasted your time in law school since you would make a pretty good gigolo."

"Don't say that, Cassie."

"Don't say it?" she repeated as intense anger radiated from every part of her. "How dare you tell me not to. You came here pretending to be someone you are not, to get next to me, to sleep with me to change my mind because Parker paid you to do it?"

"That's not the way it was."

"Oh? Then what way was it, Brandon? Are you saying you didn't come here with me as your target, and our meeting had nothing to do with Parker wanting me to give up my controlling share of the company?"

Brandon felt the floor beneath him start to cave in, but he refused to lie. "Yes, but that changed once I got to know you."

That wasn't good enough for Cassie. She shook her head and began backing away from him. She felt both hurt and anger when she thought of all the time they had spent together, all the things they had done. And all of it had been nothing more than calculated moves on his part.

That realization filled her with humiliation. "You bastard! How dare you use me that way! I want you out of here. Out of my hotel," she all but screamed. "And you can go back and tell Parker that your mission wasn't accomplished. Hell will freeze two times over before I give him anything!"

It only took her a minute to snatch her boots off the floor and then she stormed past him and went to the sofa to grab her jacket and purse. Brandon was right on her heels.

"Listen, Cassie, please let me explain. I told Parker just now that I was going to tell you the truth."

She whirled on him. "You're lying!"

"No, I'm not lying, Cassie. I tried telling you the truth last night."

"It doesn't matter. You lied to me, Brandon, and I won't forget it. And I meant what I said. I want you out of my hotel or I will order that my staff put you out."

With that said and without taking the time to put on her boots, a barefoot Cassie opened the door and raced out of the suite.

Brandon studied the roadway as he drove toward Cassie's home, barely able to see due to the intense rain pouring down. By the time he had made it out of the suite after Cassie, she had gotten into her car and driven off. He had gone back inside and done as she'd demanded by packing, and within the hour he had checked out.

He had called his pilot to cancel his flight off the island. He refused to leave the Bahamas until he had a chance to talk to her again, to clear himself. Nothing mattered other than getting her to believe that although his intentions might not have been honorable when he'd arrived on the island, after getting to know her, he had known he could not go through with it. And he had tried telling her the truth last night.

But deep down he knew that none of that excused his behavior in her eyes. He also knew that she had a right to be angry and upset. He owed her an apology, which he intended to give her, and nothing would stop him from doing so. Not even the threat that Hurricane Melissa now posed since she had decided to head in this direction.

The hotel had been in chaos with people rushing to check out. No one wanted to remain on an island that was in the hurricane's path. But even with all the commotion, Cassie's staff had everything under control and was doing an outstanding job of keeping everyone calm and getting them checked out in a timely manner. For Cassie to be at home and not at the hotel was a strong indication of how upset she was and just how badly he had hurt her.

He inhaled a deep sigh of relief when he pulled into Cassie's driveway and saw her car was there. He hoped she had no intentions of going back out in this weather. From the report he'd heard on the car's radio, the authorities were saying it wasn't safe to travel and were asking people to stay off the roads since there had been a number of major auto accidents.

He glanced at her house when he brought the car to a stop. Judging the distance from where he was to her front door, chances were he would be soaked to the skin by the time he made it, but that was the least of his concerns. He needed to clear things up between them and he refused to entertain the thought that she wouldn't agree to listen to what he had to say.

He opened the car door and made a quick dash for the door. The forecasters still weren't certain if Hurricane Melissa would actually hit the island or just come close to crossing over it. Regardless of whether it was a hit or a miss, this island was definitely experiencing some of the effects of her fury. He was totally drenched by the time he knocked on Cassie's door. He had changed into a pair of jeans and the wet denim material seemed to cling to his body, almost squeezing him.

The door was snatched open and he could tell from Cassie's expression that she was both shocked and angry to see him. "I can't believe you have the nerve to come here."

"I'm here because you and I need to talk."

"Wrong, I have nothing to say to you and I would advise you to leave," she said, crossing her arms over her chest.

"We have a lot to say and I can't leave."

She glared at him. "And why not?"

"The weather. The police asked drivers to get off the road. If I go back out in that I risk the chance of having an accident."

Her glare hardened. "And you think I care?"

"Yes, because if there's one thing I've discovered about you over the past few days, it's that you are a caring person, Cassie, and no matter what kind of asshole you undoubtedly think I am, you would not send me to my death."

She leaned closer and got right in his face. "Want to bet?"

From the look in her eyes, the answer was no. At that particular moment he didn't want to bet, but he would take a chance. "Yes."

She glared at him some more. "I suggest that you go sit in your car until the weather improves for you to leave. You're not welcome in my home."

"If I do that then I run the risk of catching pneumonia in these wet clothes."

Evidently fed up with what she considered non-sense, she was about to slam the door in his face when he blocked it with his hand. "Look, Cassie, I'm not leaving until you hear me out, nor will I leave the island until you do. If you refuse to do so here today then whenever you go back to the hotel I'll make a nuisance of myself until you do agree to see me."

"Try it and I'll call the police," she snapped.

"Yes, you could do that, but imagine the bad publicity it will give the hotel. I'd think the last thing you'll want for the Garrison Grand-Bahamas is that." He knew what he'd said had hit a nerve. That would be the last thing she would want.

Except for the force of the rain falling, there was long silence as she stonily stared at him before angrily stepping aside. "Say what you have to say and leave."

When he walked across the threshold he glanced around and saw what she'd been doing before she'd come to answer the door. She had been rolling the hurricane shutters down to cover the windows. "Where's your staff?"

She glared at him. "Not that it's any of your business but I sent them home before the weather broke. I didn't want them caught out in it."

"But you have no qualms sending me back out in it," he said, meeting her gaze.

"No, I don't, so what does that tell you?" she stormed.

He crossed his arms across his chest and gave her a glare of his own. "It tells me that we really do need to talk. But first I'll help you get the shutters in place."

Cassie blinked. Was he crazy? She had no intention of him helping her do anything. "Excuse me. I don't recall asking for your help," she said sharply.

"No, but I intend to help anyway," he said, heading toward the window in the living room.

She raced after him. "I only let you in to talk, Brandon."

"I know," he agreed smoothly, over his shoulder. "But we can talk later. A hurricane might be headed this way and John would roll over in his grave if he thought I'd leave his daughter defenseless," he said, taking hold of the lever to work the shutter into place.

A puzzled frown crossed Cassie's brow and she stopped in her tracks. "You knew my father?"

He glanced over at her, knowing he would be completely honest with her from here on out and would tell her anything she wanted to know, provided it wasn't privileged information between attorney and client. "Yes, I knew John. I've known him all my life. He and my father, Stan Washington, were close friends, and had been since college."

He saw the surprised look in her eyes seconds before she asked, "Stan Washington was your father?"

"Yes. You'd met him?" he asked, moving to another window.

"I've known him all my life, as well," she said. "But I never knew anything personal about him other than he and Dad were close friends. He was the person Mom knew to contact if an emergency ever came up and she needed to reach Dad."

Brandon nodded. He figured his father had been. As close a friendship as the two men shared, Brandon had been certain his father had known about John's affair with Ava. Besides that, Stan had been the one who'd drawn up John's will and who had handled any legal matters dealing with the Garrison Grand-Bahamas exclusively. Once Cassie had taken ownership of the hotel she had retained her own attorneys.

"What about all the other windows?" he asked, after securing the shutters in place.

"I had my housekeeping staff help me with them before they left."

"Good," he murmured as he glanced over at her. She was still barefoot but had changed into a pair of capri pants and a blouse. And like everything else he'd ever seen on her body, she looked good. But then she looked rather good naked, too.

"Now you can have your say and leave."

His eyes moved from her body to her face. He had been caught staring and she wasn't happy about it, probably because she had an idea what thoughts had passed through his mind.

"I'd think my help just now has earned me a chance to get out of these clothes."

Her back became ramrod straight. "You can think again!"

He suddenly realized how that might have sounded. "Calm down, Cassie," he said, running his hand down his face. "That's not what I meant. I was suggesting it would be nice to get out of these wet things so you can dry them for me. Otherwise, I might catch pneumonia."

Cassie bit down on her lip to keep from telling him that when and if he caught pneumonia she hoped he died a slow, agonizing death, but then dished the thought from her mind. She wasn't a heartless or cruel person, although he was the last human being on earth who deserved even a drop of her kindness.

"Fine," she snapped. "The laundry room is this way," she said, walking out of the room knowing he had to walk briskly to keep up with her. "And I suggest you stay in that room until your clothes are dry."

"Why? Don't you have a towel I could use while they're drying?"

She shot a look at him that said he was skating on thin ice and it was getting thinner every minute. "I have plenty of towels but I prefer not seeing you parade around in one."

"Okay."

She abruptly stopped walking and turned to face him. "Look, Brandon. Apparently everything you've done in the last three days was nothing but a joke to you but I hope you don't see me laughing. You don't even see me smiling."

The humor that had been in Brandon's eyes immediately faded. When he spoke again his voice was barely audible. "No, I don't think the last three days were a joke, Cassie. In fact I think they were the most precious I've ever spent in my entire life. The only thing I regret is coming to this island thinking you were someone you are not and because of it, I screwed up something awful. The only thing I can do is be honest with you now."

She refused to let his words affect her in any way. There was no way she could trust him again. "It really doesn't matter what you say when we talk, Brandon. I won't be able to get beyond the fact that you deliberately deceived me."

"Not all of it was based on deceit, Cassie. When I made love to you it was based on complete sincerity. Please don't ever think that it wasn't."

"You used me," she flung out with intense anger in her voice.

He reached out and gently touched the cleft in her chin and said in a low voice, "No, I made love to you, Cassie. I gave you more of myself than I've ever given another woman, freely, unselfishly and completely. "

Knowing if she didn't take a step back from him she would weaken, she said, "The laundry room is straight ahead and on your right. And since you're so terrified of catching pneumonia, there's a linen closet with towels in that room. But I'm warning you to stay put until your clothes dry. I have enough to do with my time than worry about a half-naked man parading through my house. I need to fill all the bathtubs with water in case I lose electricity."

"And if you do lose electricity, the thought of being here in the dark won't bother you?"

"For your information, I won't be here. As soon as your clothes dry and you have your say, I'm going to the hotel to help out there."

"You're going out in that weather?" he asked in a disbelieving tonc.

"I believe that's what I said," she said smartly.

"Weren't you listening when I said the authorities are asking people to stay off the streets?" he asked incredulously, refusing to believe anyone could be so pigheaded and stubborn.

She lifted her chin. "Yes, I was listening with as much concentration as you were when I was telling you to leave." She narrowed her eyes and then said, "Now if you will excuse me, I have things to do. When your clothes are dry and you're fully dressed again, you should be able to find me in the living room."

Narrowing his eyes, Brandon watched as she turned and walked away.

Cassie kept walking on shaky legs, refusing to give in to temptation and glance over her shoulder to look at Brandon once again. The man was unsettling in the worst possible way and the last thing she needed was having him here under her roof, especially when the two of them were completely alone.

She shook her head. At least he was taking off those wet jeans. She hadn't missed seeing how they had fit his body like a second layer of skin. She was glad he hadn't caught her staring at him when he had been putting the shutters up to the windows. Every time he had moved his body her eyes had moved with it. Not only had his wet jeans hugged his muscular thighs but they had shown what a nice tush he had, as well as a flat, firm stomach.

She sighed deeply, disgusted with herself. How could she still find the man desirable after what he had done? And she'd had no intention of accepting his help with the shutters but he hadn't given her a choice in the matter. He did just whatever he wanted. Even now his behavior and actions were totally unacceptable to her.

After filling up all the bathtubs and making sure there were candles in appropriate places and extra batteries had been placed beside her radio, she called the hotel. Simon had assured her that he had everything under control and for her to stay put and not try to come out in the weather. The majority of the people who had wanted to leave had checked out of the hotel without a hitch. The ones that had remained would ride the weather out at the Garrison Grand-Bahamas. If the authorities called for a complete evacuation of the hotel, then they would use the hotel's vans to provide transportation to the closest shelters that had been set up. Simon had insisted that she promise that if needed, she would leave her home and go to the nearest shelter, as well.

Satisfied her staff had everything under control, she walked into the living room, over to the French doors and glanced out. The ocean appeared fierce and angry, and the most recent forecast she'd heard—at least the most positive one—said that Melissa would weaken before passing over the Bahamas. But Cassie had lived on the island long enough to know there was also a chance the hurricane would intensify once it reached land as well.

She glanced up at the sky. Although it was mid-afternoon the sky had darkened to a velvet black and the clouds were thickening. Huge droplets of rain were drenching the earth and strong, gusty winds had trees swaying back and forth. She rubbed her arms, feeling a slight chill in the air. Even if Melissa did become a category four, Cassie wasn't afraid of losing her home. Her father had built this house to withstand just about anything.

Except pain.

It seemed those words filtered through her mind on a whisper. And she hung her head as more pain engulfed her, disturbed by the emotions that were scurrying through her. She drew in a deep breath, thinking she hadn't shed a single tear for what Jason had done to her, yet earlier today she had cried for the pain Brandon had caused her. Inwardly her heart was still crying.

Cassie lifted her head. She smelled Brandon's scent even before she actually heard him. She knew he was there and had known the exact moment he had entered the room. However, she wasn't ready to turn around yet, at least not until she had her full coat of armor in place. For a reason she was yet to understand, Brandon Jarrett Washington had gotten under her skin and even with all the anger she felt toward him, he was still embedded there.

"Cassie?"

She stiffened when the sound of his voice reached her. She tried ignoring the huskiness of his tone and the goose bumps that pricked her skin. Saying a silent prayer for strength, as well as the retention of her common sense, she slowly turned around. Because all the windows were protected by shutters, the room appeared slightly dark, yet she was able to make him out clearly. He stood rigid in the doorway and thankfully, fully dressed. He took a step into the room and heat coursed through her, and to her way of thinking she might have been thankful way too soon.

Although she didn't want to admit it, even in dry jeans and a shirt, Brandon looked the picture of a well-developed man. And she was reacting to his presence in a way she didn't want to and that realization was very disconcerting. The silence shrouding them within the room was a stark contradiction to the fury of the storm that was raging outside.

She tightened her hands into fists at her side when he slowly crossed the room to her. His gaze continued to touch hers when he reached out his hand to her and said in a soft voice, "Come, Cassie, let's sit on the sofa and talk."

Seven

Cassie glanced down at the hand Brandon was offering her. That hand had touched her all over last night, as well as participated in their no-holds-barred lovemaking. Finding out about his betrayal had hurt and she wasn't ready to accept anything he offered her. She would listen to what he had to say and that would be it.

Refusing to accept his hand, she returned her gaze to his face and said, "You can sit on the sofa. I'll take the chair." Her lips tightened when she moved across the room to take her seat.

Brandon was still considering Cassie's actions just now when he headed toward the sofa. It was apparent she didn't intend to make things easy for him and he could accept that. He had wronged her and it would be hard as hell to make things right. He wasn't even sure it was something that could be done, but he would try. Nervous anxiety was trying to set in but he refused to let it. Somehow he had to get her to understand.

Once he was settled on the sofa he glanced over at her, but she was looking everywhere but at him. That gave him a chance to remember how she had looked that first night he'd seen her on the beach. Even before knowing who she was, he had been attracted to her, had wanted to get to know her, get close to her and make love to her.

He shifted in his seat. Intense desire was settling in his loins, blazing them beyond control. Now was not a good time for such magnetism and he figured if she were to notice, she wouldn't appreciate it. Not needing any more trouble on his plate than was already there, he shifted on the sofa again and found a position that made that part of his body less conspicuous, although his desire for her didn't decrease any.

"Before you get started would you like something to drink?"

He glanced up and met her gaze, surprised she would offer him anything. "Yes, please."

She left the room and that gave him a few moments to think. In a way it was a strange twist of fate that had brought him and Cassie together. Their fathers' friendship had extended from college to death and unless he cleared up this issue between them, he and Cassie could very well become bitter enemies. He didn't want that and was unwilling to accept it as an option.

She returned moments later with two glasses of wine, one for him and the other for herself. Instead of handing him his wineglass directly, she placed it on the table beside him. Evidently, she had no intention of them touching in any way. He picked up his glass and took a sip, regretting he was responsible for bringing their relationship to such a sorrowful state.

"You wanted to talk."

Her words reminded him of why she was there, not to mention the distinct chill in the air. He took another sip of his wine and then he began speaking. "As you know, the Garrisons didn't know about your existence until the reading of John's will. I'm not going to say that no one might have suspected he was involved in an affair with someone, but I think I can truthfully say that no one was aware that a child had resulted from that affair. You were quite a surprise to everyone."

When she didn't make any comment or show any expression on her face, he continued. "But what came as an even bigger surprise was the fact that John left you controlling interest to share with Parker. That was definitely a shocker to everyone, especially Parker, who is the oldest and probably the most ambitious of John's sons. It was assumed, as well as understood, that if anything ever happened to John, Parker would get the majority share of controlling interest. Such a move was only right since John had turned the running of Garrison over to Parker on his thirty-first birthday. And Parker has done an outstanding job since then. Therefore, I hope you can understand why he was not only hurt and confused, but also extremely upset."

He could tell by the look on Cassie's face that she didn't understand anything, or that stubborn mind of hers was refusing to let her. "As I told you earlier," he continued, "my father is the one who drew up John's will, so I didn't know anything about you until I read over the document a few days before I was to present the will to the family. Once I discovered the truth, I knew the reading of it wouldn't be pretty."

He took a deep breath and proceeded on. "Pursuing normal legal action in this case, we took moves to contest the will but found it airtight. And—"

"I guess Parker smartened up and thought twice about pushing for a DNA test, as well," she interrupted in a curt tone.

Brandon nodded. "Yes, I advised him that nothing would be gained from it. John claimed you as his child and that was that. Besides, there was no reason to really believe that you weren't. You and Parker made contact and he offered to buy out your share of the controlling interest. You turned him down."

"And that should have been the end of it," she snapped.

Brandon couldn't help the smile that touched the corners of his lips. "Yes, possibly. But that's where you and Parker are alike in some respect."

At the lifting of her dark, arched brow, he explained. "You're both extremely stubborn."

She narrowed her eyes at him. "That's your opinion."

He decided not to waste time arguing with her by telling her that was what he knew, especially after spending time with her. Although she and Parker had never officially met, the prime reason they didn't get along was because they were similar in a lot of ways. Besides being stubborn, both were ambitious and driven to succeed. Apparently John had recognized that quality in the both of them and felt together they would do a good job by continuing the empire he'd created.

"I'm waiting, Brandon."

He glanced over at Cassie and saw her frowning in irritation. "I want to apologize for assuming a lot of incorrect things about you, Cassie, and I hope you will find it in your heart to forgive me."

Cassie wasn't ready to say whether she would or would not forgive him. At the moment she was close to doing the latter. However, she was curious about something. "And just what did you assume about me?"

Brandon inhaled before speaking. "Before answering that, I need to say that when you decided to be a force to reckon with by not responding to my firm's letters or returning any more of Parker's phone calls, it was decided that I should come and meet with you and make you the offer in person. It was also decided that I should first come and see if I could dig up any interesting information on you and your past, to use as ammunition to later force your hand if you continued your refusal to sell."

By the daggered look she was giving him, he knew she was surprised he had been so blatantly honest. He could also tell she hadn't liked what he'd said. "You might be stubborn, Cassie, but I'm a man who likes winning. I'm an attorney who will fight for my clients, anyway that I can…as long as it's legal. Garrison Incorporated is my top client and I had no intention of Parker not getting what he wanted. My allegiance was to him and not to you."

Cassie straightened in the chair and leaned forward. Her eyes were shooting fire. "Forget about what's legal, Brandon. Did you consider what you planned to do unethical?" she snapped.

He leaned forward, as well. "At the time, considering what I assumed about you, no, I didn't think anything I had planned to do as being unethical. By your refusal to even discuss the issue of the controlling shares in a professional manner with Parker, I saw your actions as that of an inconsiderate, spoiled, willful, selfish and self-centered young woman. And to answer your earlier question, that's what I assumed about you."

That did it. Cassie angrily crossed the room to stand in front of him. With her hands on her hips, she glared at him. "You didn't even know me. How dare you make such judgments about me!"

He stood to face off with her. "And that's just it, Cassie. No one knew you and it was apparent you wanted to keep things that way, close yourself off from a family that really wants to get to know you. And if my initial opinion—sight unseen—of you sounds a bit harsh then all I have to say in my defense is that's the picture you painted of yourself to everyone."

Cassie turned her head away from him, knowing part of what he said was true. She'd still been grieving her mother's death when she'd gotten word of her father's passing. He had been buried without her being there to say her last goodbye and a part of her resented that, and had resented them for letting it happen. But then the truth of the matter was that they hadn't known about her, although she had known about them. They would not have known to contact her to tell her anything.

"Imagine my surprise," she heard Brandon say,

"when I arrived here and met you. You were nothing like any of us figured you to be. It didn't take long for me to discover that you didn't have an inconsiderate, spoiled, willful, selfish or self-centered bone in your body. The woman I met, the woman I became extremely attracted to even before I knew her true identity that night on the beach, was a caring, giving, humane and unselfish person."

He took a step closer to her when Cassie turned her head and looked at him. "She was also strikingly beautiful, vivacious, sexy, desirable and passionate," he said, lowering his voice to a deep, husky tone. "She was a woman who could cause my entire body to get heated just from looking at her, a woman who made feelings I'd never encountered before rush along my nerve endings every time I got close to her."

He leaned in closer. "And she's the woman whose lips I longed to lock with mine whenever they came within inches of each other. Like they are now."

An involuntary moan of desire escaped as a sigh from Cassie's lips. Brandon's words had lit a hot torch inside of her and as she gazed into his eyes, she saw the heated look she had become familiar with. And she couldn't help but take note that they were standing close, so close that the front of his body was pressed intimately against hers, and the warm hiss of his breath could be felt on her lips. Another thing she was aware of was the hardness of his erection that had settled firmly in the lower center of her body.

She shuddered from the heat his body was emitting. Luscious heat she was actually feeling, almost drowning in. And then there was the manly scent of him that was sending a primal need escalating through her. It was a need she hadn't known existed until she had met him and discovered that he had the ability to take her to a passionate level she hadn't been elevated to before.

She knew he was about to kiss her. She also knew he was stalling, giving her the opportunity to back up and deny what the two of them wanted. But that wasn't what she wanted. Although they still had a lot more talking to do, a lot more things to get straight, she felt at that particular moment that they needed time out to take a much needed break from their stress.

And indulge in a deliriously, mind-boggling kiss.

When to her way of thinking he didn't act quickly enough, she stuck out her tongue, and with a sultry caress, she traced the lining of his lips from corner to corner. She saw the surprise on his face and the darkening of his pupils just seconds before a deep guttural groan spilled forth from his throat. He reached out and wrapped his arms around her waist, and like a bird of prey, he swooped down and captured her lips with his.

He had a way of devouring her mouth with the finesse of a gazelle and the hunger of a wolf, sending shivers all the way through her. And when he began mating with her tongue with a mastery that nearly brought her to her knees, she released a moan deep in her throat.

He tasted of the wine he had drunk and had the scent of man and rain. And he was consuming her with such effectiveness that she could only stand there and purr. His kiss was turning her into one massive ball of desire and she felt a dampness form between her legs.

He pulled his mouth free. His breathing was heavy

when he said huskily, "If you don't want what I'm about to give you, stop me now, Cassie. If you don't, I doubt I'll be able to stop myself later."

She had no desire to stop him. In fact she intended to help. To prove her point, she pulled his shirt from where it was tucked inside his jeans, before freeing the snap and easing down his zipper. And with a boldness she'd only discovered she had last night, she slipped her hand inside his jeans and felt her fingers grip the rigid hardness of him. She cupped him, fondled him and felt him actually grow larger in her hand.

"I want to be inside of you, Cassie," he whispered hotly in her ear. "I want to feel your heat clamp me tight, squeeze me and pull everything I have to give out of me. I want to make love to you until neither of us has any energy left. And then, when we regain our strength I want to do it all over again. I want to bury myself inside you so deep, neither of us will know at what point our bodies are connected."

His erotic words sent fire flaming through her body. The dampness between her legs threatened to drench her thighs. "Then do it, Brandon. Do me. Now."

As far as Brandon was concerned, her wish was his command and he eased her down on the Persian rug with him and quickly began removing their clothes. The logical part of his brain told him to slow down, she wasn't going anywhere, but another part, that part that was throbbing for relief said he wasn't going fast enough.

When he had her completely naked he turned his attention to removing his own clothes. And she was there helping him by pulling his shirt over his head and tugging his jeans down his legs after she had removed his shoes and socks.

He made a low growl in his throat when she straddled him and began using her tongue to explore him all over, starting with the column of his neck. She worked her way downward, tasting the tight buds on his chest before easing lower and giving greedy licks around his navel. She left a wet trail from his belly button to where his erection lay in a bed of tight, dark curls.

Cassie paused only long enough to raise her head to look at Brandon before gripping the object of her desire in her hands again. Lowering her head, she blew a warm breath against his shaft before clamping her mouth over him. Then she simply took her time, determined to give him the same kind of pleasure he had given her last night.

His body arched upward, nearly off the floor, and he released a deep groan before reaching down and grabbing hold of her hair. She thought he was going to jerk her away from him. Instead he entwined his fingers in her hair and continued to groan profusely. And then he started uttering her name over and over from deep within his throat. The sound had her senses reeling and made the center part of her wetter than before.

"No more," he said, using his hands to pull her upward toward him to capture her lips. And then he was kissing her with a need she felt invading her body. And suddenly she found herself on her back, her legs raised over his shoulders, nearly around his neck. He then lifted her hips and before she could catch her breath, he swiftly entered her, going deep, embedding himself within her to the hilt.

And then he began those thrusts she remembered so well, she tried grabbing hold on his buns, but they were moving too fast, pumping inside of her too rapidly. So she went after the strong arms that were solid on both sides of her and held on to them.

Their eyes met. Their gazes locked. The only thing that wasn't still was the lower part of their bodies as he kept moving in and out of her, filling her in a way that had sweat pouring off his forehead and trickling down onto her breasts. And then she felt her body shudder into one mind-blowing orgasm, the kind that made her go wild beneath him while screaming out his name and digging her fingernails into his arms.

And then he threw his head back and screamed out her name, as well. She felt him explode inside of her and she clenched her muscles, pulling more from him and knowing what had just happened could have very well left her pregnant with his child if she weren't on the pill. But the thought of that didn't bother her like it should have because she knew at that moment, without a doubt, that she had fallen in love with him.

"The power's out."

Cassie's head snapped up when she felt a movement beside her. She quickly remembered where she was. On the floor in the living room in her home, naked. She had dozed off after making love to Brandon, several times and then some.

She squinted her eyes in the darkness, missing the warmth of his body next to hers. "I put the candles out. I just need to get up and light them."

"Can you see your way around in the dark?"

"With this I can," she said, reaching for a large flashlight nearby. She smiled. "I figured we might lose power so I was ready."

She turned the light toward him and, seeing his naked body, she deliberately aimed it on a certain part of him. She chuckled. "Does that thing ever go down?"

He grinned. "Not while you're around." He walked over toward her. "Where's your radio?"

"On that table over there."

"Let me borrow this for a second. I don't know my way around in your house in the dark as well as you do." He took the flashlight and slowly moved around the room. When he located the radio he turned it on. It was blasting a current weather report that turned out to be good news. The island had been spared the full impact of Melissa but another tropical island hadn't been quite as lucky. The worst of the storm was over and everyone without power should have it restored by morning.

Cassie crossed the room. "I want to call to make sure everything is okay at the hotel."

"All right. I'm going to get dressed and check to see how things are outside."

By the time Brandon returned he found Cassie in the kitchen. She had put back on her clothes and was standing over a stove…with heat. Seeing his raised brow she said, "Mom preferred gas when it came to cooking, so if nothing else, we won't starve."

He nodded as he leaned in the doorway. "How are things at the hotel?"

"Fine. The power went out but the generator kicked

in," she replied. "A few fallen trees but otherwise nothing major. How are things outside?"

"The same. A few fallen trees but otherwise nothing major. And it's still raining cats and dogs." He crossed the room to look into the pot she was stirring. "What are you cooking?"

She smiled up at him. "The conch chowder from the other night. I grabbed it out of the freezer. You said you liked it."

"I do. It's good to know you plan on feeding me."

She chuckled. "That's not all I plan to do to you, so I have to keep your strength up."

He came around and grabbed her from behind and pressed her against him. "For you I will always keep my strength up. What can I help you do?"

"Put the bowls and eating utensils on the table and pour some tea into the glasses."

Moments later they sat to eat and Brandon decided to use that time to finish the talk he had started earlier. "So now you know why I did what I did, Cassie. I'm not saying it was right." At her narrowed eyes he changed his strategy and said, "Okay, it was wrong but you weren't making things easy for anyone."

She leaned back in her chair. "Tell me, Brandon. What part of 'no' didn't Parker understand? No means no. He asked to buy me out and I said no, I wasn't interested. What was the purpose of him calling when my answer wasn't going to change?"

"The reason he refused to let up is because he's a staunch businessman, Cassie. Parker is a man who is used to going after what he wants, especially if it's something he felt was rightfully his in the first place. Besides, you never took the time to hear what he was offering."

"It would not have mattered. What Dad left me was a gift and there's no way I'd sell my shares, no matter how much Parker offered me. And if he keeps it up, you'll be representing him on harassment charges."

Brandon stared at her for a moment, knowing she was dead serious. He chuckled. She lifted a brow. "What's so funny?"

"You, Parker and all the other Garrison siblings, but specifically you and Parker. At first I wondered what the hell John was thinking when he put that will into place. Now I think I know, although I didn't before coming here and meeting you."

"Well, would you like to enlighten me?"

"Sure. Like I said earlier, you and Parker are a lot alike and I think John recognized that fact. Besides the fact that both of you are stubborn, the two of you have an innate drive to succeed. Apparently John recognized that quality in both of you and felt together you and Parker would do a good job by continuing the empire he'd started."

She shook her head. "That can't be it. Dad knew how much I loved it here. He of all people knew how I missed the islands while attending college in London. To do what you're insinuating would mean moving to Miami and he knew I wouldn't do that. I told him after returning from college that I would never leave the island again. It's my home and where I want to stay."

"Then why do you think he gave you and Parker sharing control?"

Cassie inhaled deeply. "I wished I knew the answer."

Brandon's face took on a serious expression before

he said, "Then hear me out on my theory. John loved all of his children, there's no doubt in my mind about that. I also believed that he recognized all of their strengths…as well as their weaknesses. Not taking anything away from the others, I think he saw you and Parker as the strongest link because of your business sense. Parker is an excellent businessman, a chip off the old block. He's done a wonderful job of running things while John was alive, so John knew of his capabilities. And I understand that you did a fantastic job managing the hotel, so he was aware of what you could do, as well. Personally, I don't think it was ever John's intent for you and Parker to share the running of Garrison, Inc. Both of your personalities are too strong for that and he knew it. I think he put you in place to serve as a check and balance for Parker whenever there's a need."

She gazed at him thoughtfully before saying, "If what you're saying is true then it would serve no purpose if I were to sell my share of control to Parker. I wouldn't be accomplishing what Dad wanted."

"No, you wouldn't."

She studied him for a moment. "You haven't forgotten that you're Parker's attorney, have you?"

He smiled as he shook his head. "No, and I wasn't speaking as Parker's attorney just now. I was speaking as your friend…and lover." After a brief moment, he said, "I'd like to make a suggestion."

"What?"

"Take a few days off and come to Miami with me. Meet Parker, as well as your other sisters and brothers. I know for a fact that they would love to meet you."

"I'm not ready to meet them, Brandon."

"I think that you are, Cassie. And I believe John would have wanted it that way. Otherwise, he would have given you ownership of the hotel and nothing else, but he didn't do that. He arranged it where sooner or later you would have to meet them. And why wouldn't you, want to meet them? They're your siblings. Your family. The six of you share the same blood."

He laughed. "Hell, all of you certainly look alike."

She raised a surprised brow. "We do?"

"Yes. All of you have this same darn dimple right here," he said, leaning over and reaching out to touch the spot.

She tilted her chin, trying to keep the sensations his touch was causing from overtaking her. "It's a cleft, Brandon."

He chuckled, pulling his hand back, but not before brushing a kiss across her lips. "Whatever you want to call it, sweetheart."

His term of endearment caused a flutter in her chest and the love she felt for him sent a warm feeling flowing through her. A few moments passed and then she said in a soft voice, "Tell me about them."

Knowing her interest was a major step, Brandon bit back a smile. "All right. I think I've told you everything there is about Parker. He's thirty-six. No matter how arrogant he might have come across that time when you did speak to him, he's really a nice guy. He used to be a workaholic but things have changed since he's gotten married. His wife Anna is just what he needs. She was his assistant before they married."

He took a sip of his tea and then said, "Stephen is

thirty-five. Like Parker, he's strong-willed and dependable. He's also compassionate. He's married and his wife is Megan. They have a three-year-old daughter named Jade."

Cassie lifted her brow. "Correct me if I'm wrong but it's my understanding that he got married a few months ago."

Brandon smiled. "You are right."

"And he has a daughter that's three?"

Brandon chuckled. "Yes. He and Megan had an affair a few years ago and she got pregnant. He didn't find out he was a father until rather recently. Now they're back together and very happy."

A huge smile touched Brandon's lips when he said, "And then there's Adam. He and I share a very close friendship and I consider him my best friend. As a result, I spend more time with him than the rest. He's thirty and operates a popular nightclub, Estate. And last but not least are the twins, Brooke and Brittany. They're both twenty-eight. Brittany operates a restaurant called Brittany Beach, and Brooke operates the Sands, a luxury condominium building."

Cassie took a sip of her own tea before asking, "What about my father's wife?"

Brandon glanced at her over the rim of his glass. "What about her?"

"I'm sure she wasn't happy finding out about my mom," Cassie said.

Brandon put his glass down and met her gaze. "No, she wasn't. But finding out about you was an even bigger shock. A part of me wants to believe she had an idea that John was having an affair with someone, but I think finding out he had another child was a kicker. Needless to say, she didn't take the news very well."

Brandon decided not to provide Cassie with any details about Bonita, especially her drinking problem. He would, however, tell her this one thing. "If you decide to come to Miami with me, I want to be up front with you and let you know that Bonita Garrison won't like the fact that you there. Trust me when I say that it wouldn't bother her one bit if you decided to drop off the face of the earth."

Cassie almost choked on her tea. Once again Brandon had surprised her. Now that he had decided to tell her the truth about everything, he was being brutally honest. "If she feels that way then I'm sure the others—"

"Don't feel that way," he interrupted, knowing her assumptions. "Their mother doesn't influence how they treat people in any way. Come to Miami with me, Cassie, and meet them."

She ran her hands through her hair as she leaned back in her chair. "I don't think you know what you're asking of me, Brandon."

"And I think I do. It's the right thing to do. I know it and I believe you know it, as well. This bitter battle between you and Parker can't go on forever. Do you think that's what John would have wanted?"

She shook her head. "No."

"Neither do I." He paused, then he asked, "Will you promise that you will at least think about it?" He reached across the table and took her hand in his.

"Yes, I promise."

"And will you accept my apology for deceiving

you, Cassie? I was wrong, but I've told you the reason I did it."

She thought about his words. He had tried telling her the truth last night, and if sex was all he'd wanted from her, he'd had a good opportunity to get it the night she had invited him to her home for dinner. But he had resisted her advances. And even last night, she had been the one to make the first move.

She stared into his face knowing the issue of forgiveness had to be resolved between them. She could tell he was fully aware that he had hurt her and was deeply bothered by it. "Yes, now that you've explained everything, I accept your apology." She saw the relieved look that came into his eyes.

He hesitated a moment. "And another thing. I didn't use any protection when we made love, so if you're—"

"I'm not. I've been on the pill for a few years now, and I'm healthy otherwise."

Brandon nodded. "So am I. I just don't want you to think I'm usually so careless."

"I don't." She smiled, thinking of the way he handled their lovemaking, always making sure she got her pleasure before he got his. "In fact, I think you are one of the most precise men that I know."

Later that night Cassie lay snuggled close to Brandon in her own bed. She was on her side and he was behind her in spoon position, holding her close to the heat of him. The power had come back on a few hours ago and they had taken a shower together before going to bed and making love again.

He was sleeping soundly beside her, probably tired

to the bone. He had taken her hard and fast, and she had enjoyed every earth-shattering moment of it. Her body trembled when she remembered the mind-splitting orgasm they had shared. Brandon was undoubtedly the perfect lover.

And she appreciated him sharing bits and pieces about her siblings, satisfying a curiosity she hadn't wanted to acknowledge that she'd had. And then he had been completely honest with her about how her father's wife would probably feel toward her if she decided to do what Brandon had suggested and go to Miami with him.

She inhaled deeply. A part of her wanted to go and resolve this issue between her and Parker once and for all, and then another part didn't want to go. What if Brandon was wrong and they really didn't want to meet her like he thought?

Deciding she didn't want to bog her mind with thoughts of them anymore tonight she let her thoughts drift to the issue of her and Brandon. She knew that true love was more than a sexual attraction between two people. It was more than being good together in bed. It was about feelings and emotions. It was about wanting to commit your life to that person for the rest of your life.

It was about the things she and Brandon didn't have.

She loved him. That was a gimme. But she knew he didn't love her. He was attracted to her and he enjoyed making love to her. For him it had nothing to do with feelings and emotions. Her heart turned in her chest at the realization, but she couldn't blame him for lacking those things. He hadn't made her any promises. He hadn't offered her a commitment. She was okay with that. She had no choice.

Moments later when she discovered she couldn't get to sleep, she knew the reason why. She quietly eased out of bed, put on a robe to cover her naked body and slipped down the stairs. She entered the room where her parents' huge portrait hung on the wall and turned on the light. Whenever she had problems and issues weighing her down, she would come in here where she would feel their presence and remember happier times.

A few moments later she went to the aquarium, sat on a love seat and observed the many species of marine life in the tanks all around her. The sight and sound created a relaxing atmosphere and she sat there with her legs tucked beneath her and enjoyed the peaceful moments.

She left the aquarium a short while later and when she eased back in the bed, Brandon tightened his arm around her, pulled her closer to his warmth and whispered in her ear, "Where were you? I missed you."

She cuddled closer to him. "Umm, I went downstairs to think about some things."

"About what?"

"Whether I should go to Miami with you to meet my sisters and brothers and resolve the issue between me and Parker." She cupped Brandon's face in her hand. "I've decided to go, Brandon."

And then she leaned up and kissed him, believing in her heart that she had made the right decision.

Eight

Cassie glanced over at Brandon, who was sitting across from her in his private plane. They had boarded just seconds ago and already his pilot was announcing they were ready for take off from the Nassau International Airport.

The last week had been spent preparing for this trip, both mentally and physically. As strange as it seemed, she was a twenty-seven-year-old woman who would be meeting her siblings, all five of them, for the first time. And surprisingly enough, once Brandon had told them of her decision to visit, she had heard from each of them…except for Parker. However, his wife Anna had contacted her and had seemed genuinely sincere when she'd said that she was looking forward to meeting her.

After remnants of Melissa's presence had left the island and the sun had reappeared, it was business as usual. Cassie had gone to the hotel that first day to check on things, and her other days she had spent with Brandon.

They had gotten the trees taken care of that had fallen on her property and then the rest of the time had been used taking care of each other. She'd given him a tour of the island and had introduced him to some of her mother's family. They had shopped together in the marketplace, had gone out to dinner together several times and had taken her parents' boat out for a cruise on the ocean. But her favorite had been the times she had spent in his arms, whether she was making love with him or just plain snuggling up close.

She would be spending two weeks in Miami as a guest in his home. After that, she would return to the Bahamas and resume her life as it had been before he'd entered it. She tried not to think about the day they would part, when he would go his way and she would go hers. In reality, they lived different lives. He had his life in America and she had hers in the islands.

And even now, she still wasn't sure of Brandon's feelings for her, but she was very certain of her feelings for him. She loved him and would carry that love to the grave with her. Like her mother, she was destined to love just one man for the rest of her life.

She continued to stare at Brandon, and as if he felt her eyes on him, he glanced up from the document he was reading and met her gaze. "You okay?" he asked, with concern in his voice, as he put the papers aside.

"Yes. I'm fine." And she truly was, because no matter how things ended between them, he had given her some of the best days of her life and she would always appreciate him for it.

"How about coming over here and sit with me."

She took a perusal of his seat. It couldn't fit two people. "It won't work."

He crooked his finger at her. "Come here. We'll make it work."

The raspy sound of his voice got to her and she unsnapped her seat belt and eased toward him. He unsnapped his own and pulled her down into his lap. "Don't be concerned with Gil," he said of his pilot. "His job is to get us to our destination and not be concerned with what's going on in here."

She snuggled into his lap, thinking this was what she would miss the most when he left—the closeness, the chance to be held tight in a man's arms, to be able to feel every muscle in his body, especially the weight of that body on hers. Not to mention the feel of him inside of her. Then there was his scent…it was one she would never forget. It was a manly aroma that reminded her of rain, sunshine and lots of sex.

"I spoke with Parker before we left."

She'd heard what he said but didn't respond. She was still thinking of lots of sex.

He tightened his arms around her as he glanced down. "Cassie?"

She tilted her head and looked up at him. "I heard you."

He didn't say anything for a moment, just reached out and softly caressed the cleft in her chin. She swallowed with his every slow, sensuous stroke. He was trying to get next to her. And it was working.

"What did he want?" she asked, forcing the words out from her constricted throat. His hand had moved from her chin and was now stroking the side of her face, the area right below her ear.

He pretended not to hear as he continued to trace a path from her ear to her neck. "Brandon?" she said, to get his attention.

"I heard you," he answered, meeting her gaze and grinning.

She grinned back. "What did Parker want?"

"He has summoned you to the compound for Sunday dinner."

She raised up and glanced at him with a perturbed look on her face. "He did what!"

He laughed. "I was joking. I knew you wouldn't like the word *summoned.* I like getting a rise out of you."

She eased her hands between his legs to his crotch. "I like getting a rise out of you, too. Now stop teasing and tell me what Parker wanted."

He pulled her hand back and drew her closer into his arms. "He wants to *invite* you to Sunday dinner at the Garrison Estate. It's a weekly affair for the Garrison family."

She nodded as she thought about what he'd said. "And what about Bonita Garrison? The woman who wouldn't care if I dropped off the face of the earth."

Brandon inhaled deeply. "I wondered about that myself, but knowing Parker he'll have everything under control."

Cassie glanced up at him. "You don't sound too convincing."

He lowered his head. "Maybe this will help," he

breathed against her lips while his hand lifted her skirt to stroke her thigh. He then stroked his tongue across her lips the same way his hand was massaging her thigh, gently, pleasurably and methodically. And if that wasn't enough, he inserted his tongue into her mouth and the impact shattered her nerve endings. Her lips parted on a sigh, which gave him deeper penetration, something he was good at taking advantage of. And he was doing so in a way that had her moaning from the sensations escalating through her. His exquisite tongue was doing wild and wonderful things to hers. Devouring her mouth. Deepening her desire.

"Buckle up for landing."

He lifted his head when his pilot's command came across the speaker. And then as if he couldn't resist, he lowered his head and kissed her again. This time it was Cassie who pulled back and whispered against his moist lips. "I think I need to go back to my own seat."

"Yes, you do," he agreed, tracing his tongue around her mouth before finally releasing her from his lap.

She eased back to her seat and quickly buckled in. She lifted her head. Their gazes met. She smiled. So did he.

The thought that suddenly ran though her mind was that they hadn't missed making love one single time since that first experience and they hadn't gone a day without sharing a kiss, either. Those would be memories that would have to sustain her. Memories she would forever cherish.

"Cassie?"

She glanced over at him. "Yes?"

"Welcome to Miami."

* * *

"Do you mind if I make a quick stop by my office to check on things?" Brandon asked Cassie as he drove his car down Ocean Drive. Her attention was on the happenings outside the car's window. During this time of the day, it wasn't unusual to spot models, vintage cars, Harleys and people on Rollerblades mixing in with the many tourists that visited South Beach.

She turned to him, smiling. The sun coming through the window seemed to place golden highlights in her hair. "No, not at all. I'm sure you want to check to make sure nothing was damaged during the storm, although from the looks of things, all this city got was plenty of rain."

"Which seem to have grown more people," Brandon said, chuckling. "This area gets more popular every day. Daytime is bad enough but wait until darkness falls and all the nightclubs open. South Beach becomes one big party land."

"Umm, sounds like fun."

He chuckled. "It is, and Adam's nightclub is right there in the thick of things. It's doing very well. Before you return to the Bahamas, I plan to make sure I take you out on the town one night, and Adam's club is just one of the many places we'll visit."

Cassie slanted a smile over at him. "Don't tell me you're one of those party animals."

He laughed. "Not anymore, but I used to be. Adam and I have a history of spending many a nights out partying and having a good time. We were intent on experiencing as much of the wilder side of life as we could. But after Dad's death I had to buckle down and get serious when everything fell on my shoulders. I will always appreciate your father for having faith in my abilities and retaining our firm after Dad died. John didn't have to do that, but by doing so, he gave me a chance to prove my worth."

Cassie nodded as her smile deepened. "So you settled down, but is Adam still the party animal?"

"Not to the degree he used to be," he said. "He's become a very serious businessman. You're going to like him."

"You would say that because he's your best friend," she said.

"Yes, but I think you're going to like all the Garrison siblings."

She gave him a doubtful look. "Even Parker?"

"Yes, even Parker. Once you get to know him you'll see he's really a nice guy, and like I told you before, his marriage to Anna has changed him in a lot of ways. He loves her very much. I would be the first to admit that I never thought I'd see the day he would settle down. After all, he was one of the city's most eligible bachelors, a status he liked having."

Cassie considered his words and wondered if there would ever be a woman in Brandon's life that he would fall in love with and want to marry and spend the rest of his life with.

"We're almost there, just another block. And you'll be able to see the Garrison Grand once I turn the corner. It's on one corner of Bricknell and my office is on the other."

No sooner had he said the words than she saw what had been her father's first hotel. A sense of pride flowed through Cassie. It was a beautiful high-rise, a stately structure.

"It's beautiful," she said, getting to study it in more detail when they came to a stop at a traffic light right in front of the grand-looking building. The Garrison Grand was a perfect name for it.

"Stephen's in charge of running it now and he's doing an excellent job. He has exemplary business skills, but he's going to have his hands full when the Hotel Victoria open its doors."

Cassie glanced at Brandon. "The Hotel Victoria?"

"Yes, it's a hotel that's presently under construction and is being built by Jordan Jefferies. It will be a competing hotel that will be slightly smaller in size but will rival the Garrison Grand in luxury and prestige and attract the same type of clientele. Jeffries is a shrewd businessman who can be rather ruthless at times. He's a person who's determined to succeed by any means necessary."

"Sounds a lot like Parker."

Brandon chuckled. "Yes, which is probably why the two can't get along. There's a sort of family rivalry going on between the Garrisons and the Jeffrieses and has been for a while. However, a couple of months ago, Brittany defied the feud and recently became engaged to Emilio, Jordan's brother."

"I can imagine Parker not being too happy about that," Cassie said.

"No, and neither is Jordan. But Brittany and Emilio seem very much in love and intend to live their lives the way they want without family interference."

"Good for them."

Brandon glanced over at her as he pulled the car to a stop in a spot in a parking garage. A name plate indicated the spot was designated for his vehicle only. "You sound like a rebel."

She unsnapped her seat belt, stretched over and placed a kiss on his lips. "I am. My mom told me how her family was against her dating my dad since he was a married man. She defied them and dated him anyway."

"What about you? Would you date a married man?"

She shook her head. "No, I'm more possessive than my mom ever was. I couldn't stand the thought of sharing. That's why I feel somewhat sympathetic to Bonita Garrison. I can only imagine how she must have felt finding out her husband had had a long-term affair with another woman. But then another part of me, the part that knew my father so well and knew what a loving and loyal man he was, feels there was a reason he sought love and happiness elsewhere."

Brandon shrugged. "Perhaps."

Cassie really didn't expect him to say any more than that. Even if he knew anything about her father and his wife's relationship, he wouldn't say. No matter what she and Brandon had shared, he was very loyal when it came to the Garrison family.

A few moments later they entered the lobby of the Washington Building. "My father purchased the land for this building over forty years ago from your father. At the time a young John Garrison, who was in his early twenties, was on his way to becoming a multimillionaire. He was single and one of the most eligible bachelors in Miami. My father was his attorney even then."

Cassie nodded as she glanced around before they stepped on the elevator. "Nice building."

"Thanks. My firm's office is on the twentieth floor," he said, pressing a button after the elevator door closed shut. "I lease out the extra office space to other businesses."

When the elevator came to a stop on the twentieth floor they began walking down a carpeted hall. Brandon's law firm's glass doors had his named written in bold gold script. The receptionist area was both massive and impressive, and a young lady who sat at the front desk smiled and greeted them when they entered.

Passing that area they rounded a corner that contained several spacious offices, where she noticed people working at their desks. Some looked up when she and Brandon passed their doors and others, who were busy working or talking on the phone, did not. Cassie figured since it was Friday, most were probably trying to bring their work week to an end at a reasonable time so their weekend could begin.

She admired the layout of the offices. She knew that every office was made up of three fundamental elements—architecture, furniture and technology—and it appeared that Brandon's firm emphasized all three. The interior provided a comfortable work environment where anyone would want to spend their working hours. The painted walls, carpeted floors in some areas and marble tile floors in others, modern furniture and state-of-the-art equipment all provided an upscale image of what she'd thought Brandon's place of business would be like and she hadn't been wrong.

"I should have warned you about my secretary,

Rachel Suarez," he said in a low voice. "She's been here for ages, started out as my dad's first secretary, and she thinks she owns the place. But I have to admit she does a fantastic job of running things. I have ten associates working for me and she keeps everyone in line, including my other thirty or so employees."

Cassie glanced over at him, not realizing his firm was so massive. "You have a rather large company."

"Yes, and they are good people and hard workers, every one of them."

"The layout is nice and no one is cramped for space," she openly observed.

Brandon's secretary's desk appeared to be in the center of things. The sixty-something-year-old woman's face broke into a bright smile when she saw her boss. "Brandon, I wasn't expecting you back until sometime next week."

He smiled. "I'm still officially on vacation. I just dropped by to see how everything faired during the storm."

The woman waved off his words with her hands. "It wasn't so bad. I'm just glad it didn't get worse. I understand the islands got more rain that we did."

She then glanced over at Cassie and gave her a huge smile. "Hello."

Cassie smiled back. "Hello to you."

Brandon began introductions. "Rachel, this is—"

"I know who she is," the woman said, offering Cassie her hand. "You look a lot like your daddy."

Cassie raised a surprised brow as she took the hand being offered. Her surprise had nothing to do with being told that she looked like her father since she knew that was true. Her surprise was that the woman knew who she was.

At Cassie's bemused expression Rachel explained. "I was Stan Washington's secretary when you were born."

Cassie nodded. In other words the woman had known about her parents' affair and, like Brandon's father, had been sworn to secrecy.

"I'm going to give Cassie a tour of my office, Rachel. And like I said, I'm still on vacation so I won't be accepting any calls if they come in."

Rachel grinned. "Yes, sir."

Brandon ushered Cassie down the carpeted hall to his office. When they entered he locked the door behind him. She only had time for a quick glance around before he pulled her into his arms. "Now to finish what we started on the plane," he said, before lowering his head for a kiss.

Their mouths had barely touched when Brandon's cell phone rang. Muttering a curse, he straightened and pulled it out of his pocket. He rolled his eyes upon seeing whose telephone number had appeared. "Yes, Adam?" he said, a split second from letting his best friend know he had caught him at a bad time.

"Yes, Cassie is here and yes, she's with me now." A few moments later he said. "No, she's not staying at the Garrison Grand. She'll be a guest in my home." He winked his eye at Cassie before she moved to sit on the sofa across the room, crossing her legs in a very sexy way.

"And, no," he continued, trying to concentrate on what Adam was saying and not on Cassie's legs, "you won't be able to meet her until dinner on Sunday. You might be my best friend but I can't let you use that fact to your advantage since Parker has requested that the family all meet her at the same time. Besides, I'm taking her to dinner tonight and tomorrow I plan to give her a tour of the town."

Brandon laughed at something Adam said and replied, "Okay, Adam. I'll let Cassie know." He then clicked off the phone and placed it back in his pocket.

"Let me know what?" she asked, returning to where he stood.

Brandon smiled. "If you want to go ahead and make him your favorite brother, he's fine with it."

A smile touched Cassie's lips. She had a feeing she was really going to like him. "He seems nice."

"He is. Like I told you, all of them are, including Parker. The two of you just rubbed each other the wrong way in the beginning."

"And what if he doesn't agree with the counteroffer I intend to make him? I want you to know that I won't back down. He can either take it or leave it."

Brandon grinned. Sunday dinner at the Garrisons would be interesting, as usual. "I wouldn't worry about it if I were you. Like I said, Parker is a sharp business-man and I believe he wants to end the animosity between the two of you and come up with a workable solution as much as you do."

He reached out and caressed the cleft in her chin. "Every time I touch this I get turned on."

Cassie smiled, shaking her head. "I think you get turned on even when you're not touching it."

He laughed. "That's true." And to prove his point he lowered his mouth and joined it with hers. Their lips locked. Their tongues mated. Desire was seeping into both of their bones. Brandon thought he would never get enough of this woman no matter how much he tried.

Moments later he lifted his head and drew back from the kiss, his gaze on her moist lips. "I better get you out of here. It's not safe to be in here alone with you. I've never made love to a woman in my office, but I might be driven to do that very thing with you."

On tiptoe she stretched up and brushed a kiss across his lips. In a way she wanted him to take her here. That way when they did go their separate ways, her presence would always be in here, a place where he spent the majority of his time working.

"Maybe not today, but promise you'll do it before I leave to return home."

He lifted a brow. "Do what?"

"Make love to me in here," she said, stepping closer and sliding her fingers to his nape to caress him there.

He released a shuddering sigh at her touch before asking, "Why would you want me to make love to you in here?"

"So you could always remember me, especially in here."

He was taken aback by her words, and then murmured softly, in a husky tone, "Do you honestly think I could forget you, Cassie? Do you think I'd be able to forget everything we've shared together?"

Before she could answer he bent his head and claimed her lips, kissing her with so much passion it made her stomach somersault. It made the lower part of her body feel highly sensitive to his very presence.

Reluctantly, he pulled his mouth away and gazed at her in a way that sent sensations rushing all through her. He took her hand in his. "Come on and let's get out of here before I do just what you ask and not care that I have an office full of people working today."

A smile touched his lips when he added, "They're a smart group of people who will get more than suspicious about all the noise we'll make."

"Umm, you think we'll make a lot of noise?" she asked when he unlocked the door.

"He glanced over at her before opening it and chuckled. "Sweetheart, we always do."

Later that night Cassie could feel the soft pounding of Brandon's heart against her back. His arms were wrapped around her as he slept. The warm afterglow of their lovemaking had lulled her to sleep, as well, but now she was awake.

And thinking.

He had a beautiful home, and after showing her around, she had felt the love he had for it while he'd given his tour. She had watched him carefully when he had shown her with pride the things that were his. They were possessions he had worked hard to get and he was still working hard to retain. He'd told her that a number of his father's clients had dropped his firm after his father's death, citing Brandon's youth and lack of experience. John Garrison had been one of the few who'd kept him on, and had gone even further by recommending him to others. With hard work Brandon had rebuilt the legacy his father had started.

When Brandon stirred in his sleep, she glanced over her shoulder and her gaze touched his sleeping face. She wanted him. She wanted to marry him. She wanted to have his babies. But most of all, she loved him. However, this would be one of those situations where she couldn't have any of the things she wanted.

Because he didn't love her in return.

And she could never spend her life with a man who didn't love her. She had grown up in an environment that was filled with too much love to want something less for herself.

She closed her eyes to blot out the advice her mind was giving her. *Get out while you can do so without getting your heart shattered. Take your memories and go.*

Cassie opened her eyes, knowing she would take the advice her mind was giving her. This was Brandon's world and hers was in the Bahamas. Instead of staying the two weeks she'd originally planned, she would let him know after dinner on Sunday that she would be leaving in a week. It was important that she and Parker resolved the issues between them, and she was looking forward to meeting her other siblings. After that it was time to move on. The more time she spent with Brandon, the more she yearned for things she could not have. Already her love for him was weakening her resolve and undermining her defenses.

It was time for her to make serious plans about returning home. There was no other way.

Brandon walked off the patio and back into his home to answer the ringing telephone. He stood in a spot where he could still see Cassie as she swam around in his pool.

The two-piece bathing suit she was wearing was sexual temptation at its finest, and he was quite content to just stand there and stare at her. But when his phone rang again, he knew that wasn't possible. He reached on the table to pick it up. "Yes?"

"Brandon, this is Parker."

He wondered when Parker would get around to calling him back. They had been playing phone tag for the better part of the day. He understood Parker had been in meetings most of yesterday, and Brandon and Cassie had left the house early this morning when he had taken her to breakfast and later on a tour of South Beach.

When she had mentioned that she had a taste for Chinese food, they had dined for lunch at one of his favorite restaurants, an upscale and trendy establishment called the China Grille. After lunch, instead of taking in more sights, he had done as she requested and had taken her to the cemetery where her father was buried. He had stood by her side when she'd finally got a chance to say goodbye and then he had held her in his arms while she cried when her grief had gotten too much for her.

Afterward, they had returned to his place to take a swim in the pool and relax a while before getting dressed for dinner and the South Beach night life.

"Yes, Parker, I'm glad we finally connected."

"I am, too. How's Cassie?"

Brandon turned and glanced out the bank of French doors to stare right at her. She was no longer in the water but was standing by the edge of the pool, getting ready to dive back in. It was his opinion—with the way she looked with the sunlight made the wet strands of her hair gleam, and her body made his breath catch every time he saw it, naked or in clothes—Cassie was every man's fantasy. That was definitely not something her oldest brother would appreciate hearing from him.

"Cassie's fine and is out by the pool. She wanted to take a swim before we go out to dinner."

"Everyone is looking forward to meeting her tomorrow," Parker said.

"Glad to hear it. I had a hard time convincing her of that, but I did, which is the main reason she's here in Miami."

"Just so you know, I haven't mentioned it to Mom."

Something in Parker's voice forced Brandon to ask, "But you will, right?"

"I don't think that will be a wise thing to do at this point."

Brandon didn't like the sound of that. Chances were Bonita would be home since she rarely left the house on Sundays. And, for that matter she was rarely sober after lunchtime, as well. "And why not, Parker? I've been totally up front with Cassie since she discovered our association and I'm not going to have her start doubting my word or intentions about anything. If Bonita will be at dinner tomorrow, before I agree to bring Cassie, I need a good reason why you won't be telling Bonita she's coming. That wouldn't be fair to either of them." He knew Cassie could hold her own against anyone, but in this particular situation, he felt she shouldn't be placed in a position where she had to.

For the next ten minutes Parker explained to Brandon why he'd made the decision he had, and after discussing it with his siblings, they felt Bonita being caught unaware would be the right approach to use. "That might be the right approach for Bonita, but what about Cassie? I can see an ugly scene exploding, one I don't like and wouldn't want to place her in."

Brandon rubbed his hand down his face. "I'm going to tell her, Parker, and explain things to her the way you have explained them to me. It's going to be her decision as to whether or not she still wants to come."

"And I agree she should know, which is the reason I wanted to talk to you. So when will you tell her?"

Brandon sighed deeply. "I'd rather wait until in the morning. I don't want anything to ruin the plans I have for dinner," he said, fighting for control of his voice. He still wasn't sure not telling Bonita was the right thing, although he understood Parker's reason for it.

"Please inform me of Cassie's decision one way or the other," Parker said. "If she doesn't want to join us for dinner at the Garrison Estate tomorrow evening, then we can all get together and take her out somewhere else. Mom will wonder why we're not eating Sunday dinner at her place though, so either way, she's going to find out Cassie's in town and that we've made contact with her. I just think it's best if we all stand together and face Mom as a united front."

"I understand, Parker, but like I said, it will be Cassie's decision."

Nine

Frowning, Cassie stared over at Brandon. "What do you mean Bonita Garrison doesn't know I was invited to dinner?"

Brandon sighed. He had known she would not like the news Parker had delivered yesterday. "Considering everything, the Garrison siblings felt it would be best if she didn't know," he explained.

From where he was standing, with his shoulder propped against the bookshelves in his library, he could tell that Cassie, who was sitting on a sofa, was confused by that statement.

"But it's her house, right?" she asked, as if for clarification.

"Yes, it's her house."

"Then am I to assume she's out of town or something and won't be there?"

"No, you aren't to assume that." He saw the defiant look in her eyes, a strong indication as to what direction this conversation was going.

"Then I think you need to tell me what's going on, Brandon."

He sighed again, more deeply this time. What he needed was a drink, but that would have to come later. He really did owe her an explanation. Straightening, he crossed the room to sit beside her on the sofa. His gaze locked on her face when he said, "Bonita Garrison is an alcoholic and has been for years. She's always had a drinking problem and John's will only escalated the condition. Like I told you before, considering the state of their marriage, I think she had an idea he was having an affair, but she didn't know anything about you. That was one well-kept secret."

Cassie's frown deepened. "Have any of her children suggested that she seek professional help?"

"Yes, countless times. I understand John even did so, but for the longest she wouldn't acknowledge she had a problem. She still hasn't."

Cassie nodded. "But what does that have to do with me? Wouldn't seeing me in her home uninvited, the person who is living proof of her husband's unfaithfulness, push her even more over the edge?"

He reached for her hand. "Parker and the others are hoping it doesn't. Their relationship with her is strained and has been for some time. I'm talking years, Cassie. They'd decided, and unanimously I might add, that they want to meet you, build relationships with you, include you in the family mix, and they refused to sneak behind their mother's back to do so. They believe it's time to mend the fences and move on, and want Bonita to see that as a united group they plan to do just that, with or without her blessings."

He chuckled. "I've known those Garrisons most of my life and this is the first time they've ever been in complete agreement about anything."

Brandon got quiet for a moment and then said in a serious tone, "John would be proud of them. And knowing the type of man he was, a man who loved his children unconditionally, I want to believe that had he lived, he would have eventually gotten all of you together. He was a man who would have made it happen."

His words had Cassie staring at him thoughtfully. What he'd said was true. She believed that, as well. She had learned about her siblings' existence from her father, and she had known he had loved them as much as he had loved her. He had said so a number of times.

"But…" she said, frowning still. "What if things get ugly?"

"And there's a possibility that they might," he said honestly, needing to make her aware of that fact. "But Parker wants you to know that no matter what, they intend to finally bring things to a head, a forced-feeding intervention, so to speak."

Cassie inhaled a deep breath. She just hoped Parker and the others were right. The last thing she wanted was to be responsible for Bonita Garrison getting pushed over the edge. But then her children knew her better than anyone and Cassie was sure that no matter how strained their relationship, that they loved their mother. And if they felt what they had planned for this afternoon was the right approach to use then she would trust their judgment.

She met Brandon's gaze. "Okay, thanks for telling me."

"Are you still going?"

"Yes. I'm going." After a moment, she asked, "You will be there, too, right?"

A smile touched the corners of his lips. "Yes, I was invited, as well, and I will be there," he said. Tugging on the hand he still held he pulled her closer to him and whispered, "But even if I weren't invited I would still be there, Cassie. You would not be alone."

Cassie glanced around when Brandon brought the car to a stop in front of the massive and impressive Spanish-style villa that was the Garrison Estate. Everywhere she looked she saw a beauty that was spellbinding. From the brick driveway to the wide stucco stairs that led to the entrance, she thought there weren't many words that could be used to describe the house that could sufficiently do it justice.

She inhaled a reverent breath in knowing this is where her father had lived, the place he considered home when he wasn't in the Bahamas with her and her mom. And even now a part of her could feel his presence. What Brandon had said earlier that day was true. Her father would want his offspring to meet.

"You've gotten quiet on me. Are you okay?"

She glanced over at Brandon, hearing the concern in his voice. From the moment his plane had landed in Miami, he had been attentive, considerate of her well-being and so forthcoming with his affection. More than once she'd had to stop and remind herself that his affection had nothing to do with love, but was a result of his kindness. There was a natural degree of warmth and caring about him. Those were just two of the things that had drawn her to him from the first.

"Yes, I'm okay. I was just thinking about Dad and how much I loved him and how much I miss him, and how today I can feel his presence more so than ever."

"And you never resented him for having another family besides you and your mom?"

"I never resented Dad, but when I was a lot younger, after having found out he was a married man with another family, for a long time I resented them. In my mind, whenever he would leave me and Mom it would be to return here to them. I never gave thought to the fact that whenever he was in the Bahamas with me and Mom, he wasn't with them, either. I was too possessive of him in my life to even care."

"But now?"

"But now I want to believe that somehow he was able to give all six of us equal time, special time, as special as he was," she said softly.

"I think he did," Brandon said in a quiet tone. "I believe he knew what each of his kids needed and gave it to them. He was an ingrained part of each of their lives and they loved him just as much as you did."

Her eyebrows lifted. "Do you think that even now? After finding out he'd had a long-term affair while married to their mother? You don't think that love was tarnished because of it?"

Brandon shook his head. "No. Adam is the only one

I've spoken to in depth about it, basically to garner his personal feelings. He said they all knew their parents' marriage was on the rocks for years. Bonita's abuse of alcohol led to a friction that couldn't be mended."

Cassie nodded, then dragged in a deep breath and said, "It's time we go inside, isn't it?"

"Yes. Nervous?"

"I would be lying if I were to say no. But I can handle it."

Brandon chuckled as he unbuckled his seat belt. "Cassie Sinclair-Garrison, I think you can handle just about anything."

He exited the car and came around to open her door for her, admiring what she was wearing. Although it was the middle of fall, the weather was warm and the sky was clear and she was casually dressed in a pair of black slacks and a velvet plum blouse. The outfit not only brought out the natural beauty of her skin coloring, but added a touch of exuberance to her brown eyes, as well. She smiled at him.

He offered his hand and she took it. The sensation that immediately flowed through him was desire that was as intoxicating as the strongest liquor.

After closing the door, he placed her hand on his arm and walked her up the wide stucco stairs that led to the front door. Before he could raise his hand to knock, the door opened and Lisette Wilson stood there smiling at them. The woman had been the Garrison's housekeeper for as long as Brandon could remember and, according to Adam, Lisette was a force to reckon with when he'd been going through his mischievous teen years. Now she seemed older, and although a smile was bright on her face, she looked tired. She was probably worn out from having her hands full these days with Bonita's excessive drinking. With none of the Garrison siblings living at home, they depended on Lisette to keep things running as smoothly as possible on the home front.

"Mr. Brandon, good seeing you again, and I want to welcome the both of you to the Garrison Estate."

Brandon returned the woman's smile. "Thanks, Lisette. Have Parker and the others arrived yet?"

"Yes, they're on the veranda," she said, stepping aside for them to enter. "I'll take you to them."

Lisette led the way. Brandon could feel the tenseness of Cassie's hand on his arm. He smiled over at her as they passed a wide stone column that marked the entrance to the living room. After passing through several beautifully decorated rooms, they walked through a bank of French doors to the veranda. The Garrison siblings were there. All five of them. Along with three of their significant others.

"Your dinner guests have arrived," Lisette announced.

The group immediately ended whatever conversation they were engaged in and turned, seemingly all at once. Eight pairs of eyes stared at them, mainly at Cassie. They appeared stunned. The look on their faces confirmed that they were thinking what Brandon already knew. She was definitely a Garrison.

It was Parker who made the first move, crossing the veranda with an air that was cool and confident. He came to a stop in front of them. He continued to stare at Cassie, studying her features, probably with the same intensity that she was studying his.

For her it was like seeing what she figured was a younger version of their father. He looked so much like John Garrison it was uncanny. All three Garrison men did. That was the first thought that had crossed her mind when they had looked at her. But Parker, the first-born, had acquired nearly every physical feature their father had possessed, including his height, build and mannerisms—especially how his dark brow creased in a deep, thoughtful frown when he analyzed anything.

Not feeling at all intimidated, Cassie tilted her head back as she met his intense stare. Then she watched his eyes soften speculatively when he said, "Umm, the famous Garrison cleft. Was there ever a time you thought it was a curse rather than a blessing?"

Refusing to let her guard down, not even for a second, Cassie said, "No, that never occurred to me. Anything I inherited from my father I considered a blessing."

A semblance of a smile touched his arrogant lips and he said, "So did I." Extending his hand out to her, he said, "I'm Parker, by the way."

She accepted it. "And I'm Cassie."

He nodded before glancing over at Brandon. "Good seeing you again, Brandon."

"Likewise, Parker."

Parker's eyes then returned to Cassie. "There's a group of people who're anxious to meet you. Please come and let me introduce them."

"All right," she said, giving Parker the same semblance of a smile that he'd given her as she held his gaze steadily. Their opposing wills seemed to be squaring off, but in a sociable way. "I'd love to meet everyone," she said.

Cassie glanced over at Brandon and he smiled at her, and immediately his strength touched her, gave her the added confidence she needed. She fell in love with him even more.

She inhaled deeply as the two men escorted her across the veranda to meet the others. As much as she didn't want them to be, butterflies were flying around in her stomach at the round of introductions she was about to engage in.

She forced herself to relax and smiled when they came to a stop before a woman she quickly assumed to be Parker's wife, from the way he was looking at her. He might have been a happy bachelor at one time, but from the way he gently placed an arm around the beautiful woman with shoulder-length dark hair and green eyes, it was quite easy to tell he was a man very much in love.

He smiled affectionately at his wife before returning his gaze to Cassie. "Cassie, I'd like you to meet my wife, Anna."

Instead of shaking her hand, Anna gave her an affectionate hug. "It's nice meeting you, Cassie, and welcome to the family."

"Thank you."

Without taking more than a step, Cassie came to stand in front of two men she immediately knew were her other two brothers, since their clefts were dead giveaways. The woman standing between them had green eyes and wavy red hair. And just like Parker's wife, she was gorgeous.

"Cassie, welcome to Miami and I'm Stephen," the man standing to her left said, making his own introductions while slanting a smile at her and taking the hand she offered. "And this is my wife, Megan."

Like Anna, Megan automatically reached out and hugged her. "It's nice to finally get to meet you," Megan said, smiling at her with sincerity in her eyes. "And you have a three-year-old niece name Jade who I'm hoping you'll get to meet before you return to the Bahamas."

"I would love that and can't imagine leaving Miami before I do."

She then glanced at the other man, who was tall, dark and handsome—common traits, it seemed, with Garrison men. "And you must be Adam," she said.

A broad grin flitted across his face and suddenly two words came to her mind regarding him—loyal and dedicated. He reached out and gave her a hug and a kiss on the cheek. "Yes, I'm Adam, and remember, I'm to be the favorite brother."

She met his gaze and had a feeling that he would be. "I'll remember that."

She then turned and saw two women and a very handsome man of Cuban descent. She knew immediately that the two women were her identical twin sisters.

"Cassie, I'd like you to meet Brooke, the oldest of the twins by a few minutes," Parker said of the tall, attractive, model-thin woman with long dark brown hair and brown eyes. "And this is Brittany and her fiancé, Emilio Jeffries."

Cassie faintly raised a brow at the derision she'd heard in Parker's voice when he had introduced Emilio. She then remembered what Brandon had shared with her about there being bad blood between the Garrisons and the Jefferieses, and how Brittany had basically fallen in love with one of her brother's enemies. But still, she couldn't help but admire

Brittany for her bravery, as well as her good common sense. No woman in her right mind would let a hunk like Emilio slip through her fingers, regardless of how her family felt about it.

"It's nice meeting all of you," Cassie said, glancing around at everyone and very much aware of the moment Brandon came to stand next to her side.

"It's good to know I'm no longer the baby in the family," Brittany said, grinning.

The next few minutes Cassie mingled with everyone while answering numerous questions about her life in the Bahamas, without any of the inquiries getting specific about the relationship between their father and her mother. Stephen asked about the activities at the Garrison Grand-Bahamas and complimented her on the great job she was doing.

For the most part Parker didn't say anything, and knowing the astute businessman that he was, she figured he was hanging low and listening for any details regarding her business affairs that might interest him.

"Dinner is ready to be served."

Everyone glanced over in Lisette's direction before the woman disappeared back inside.

"Would you give me the honor of escorting you in to dinner?" Adam asked as he appeared at her side. "I'm sure Brandon won't mind," he added, winking an eye at the man he considered his best friend.

Cassie smiled serenely, wondering how much her siblings knew...or thought they knew of her and Brandon's relationship. Did they assume they were friends, lovers or what? Did she care? She knew the terms of their relationship, the boundaries as well as the life span of it.

She smiled over at Brandon before returning her gaze to Adam. Before she could open her mouth to say anything, she felt Brandon's hand at her back when he said in a low tone, "I think we will both do the honor, Adam. I've appointed myself her escort for the evening."

She saw the two men exchange meaningful looks. She was aware, as much as they were, that Bonita Garrison had not yet made an appearance. "I think having two escorts is a splendid idea," she said.

When they reached the dining room she noted Parker had taken the chair at the head of the table. Brandon took the chair on one side of her and Adam took a chair on the other side. Emilio was sitting across from her and they shared a smile. She suspected that he felt as much an outsider as she did. There was the easy and familiar camaraderie the others shared, including Brandon. He'd evidently shared Sunday dinner with the group before because he seemed to be right at home.

"So when can I come visit you in the Bahamas?" Brooke asked, smiling over at Cassie.

Before she could respond, Adam said, "Trying to get the hell out of Dodge for some reason, sis?"

She rolled her eyes at him. "Not particularly," she said, not meeting his gaze as she suddenly began concentrating on the plate Lisette set in front of her.

"You're welcome to visit me any time," Cassie said and meant it. When Brooke glanced up, Cassie could have sworn she'd seen a look of profound thanks in her eyes. That made Cassie wonder if perhaps what Adam had jokingly said was true and Brooke was trying to escape Miami for a reason.

Conversation was amiable with Adam, Brooke and Brittany telling her about the establishments they owned and ran under the Garrison umbrella. Stephen discussed the Miami Garrison Grand and even asked her advice on a couple of things that he'd heard she had implemented at her hotel.

When Brooke excused herself for the second time to go to the bathroom, Cassie overheard Brittany whisper to Emilio that she thought her twin was pregnant. Cassie was grateful everyone else had been too busy listening to Megan share one of her disastrous interior decorating experiences to hear Brittany's comment.

Suddenly, the dining room got deathly quiet and Cassie knew why when Brandon reached for her hand and held it tight in his. She followed everyone's gaze and glanced at the woman who was standing in the entrance of the dining room. Regardless of what curiosity she had always harbored about her father's wife, she never in a million years thought such disappointment would assail her body like it was doing now.

It was easy to see that at one time Bonita Garrison had been a beautiful woman, definitely stunning enough to catch a young John Garrison's eye. But the woman who appeared almost too drunk to stand up straight while holding a half-filled glass of liquor in her hand looked tired and beaten.

"Mother, we weren't sure you would be joining us," Parker said, standing along with all the other men at the table.

"Would it have mattered?" Bonita snapped, almost

staggering with each step she took. She made it to the chair on the other side of Parker and sat.

Resuming his seat, Parker glanced at Lisette, who had entered, and said, "Please bring my mother a plate as well as a cup of coffee."

The woman glared at her oldest son. "I don't need anything to drink, Parker. I have everything I need right here," she said in a slurred voice, saluting her glass at him.

"I would say you've had too much, Mom."

The comment came from Stephen and whereas Bonita Garrison had glared at Parker just moments earlier, she actually smiled at Stephen. She didn't say anything to Stephen directly, but instead announced, "Maybe I'll have a cup of coffee after all."

Cassie knew it was then that Bonita noticed her presence. She saw Brandon sitting beside her and holding her hand, and said, "Brandon, how nice, you've brought a date."

Brandon didn't say anything but merely nodded, while Bonita continued to stare. Cassie figured that it wouldn't take long before her identity became obvious with her sitting so close to Brittany. Other than the color of their skin, the two women favored. In her drunken state such a thing could go over Bonita's head.

But it didn't.

Cassie found herself the object of the woman's intense attention and then suddenly Bonita rose on drunken legs and, not speaking to anyone in particular, she asked, "Who is she?"

It was Parker who spoke. "Cassie. Cassie Sinclair-Garrison."

The woman snatched her gaze from Cassie and glared at Parker. "That woman's child? You invited that *woman's* child to our home?"

"No, I invited our *father's* child to our home, Mother. Cassie is our sister and we thought it was time we met her," Parker answered with the same mastery in his voice that Cassie was certain he used in the boardroom.

Bonita's features took on a stony countenance. "Meet her? Why would you want to meet her after what your father and her mother did to me?"

"Whatever happened between you and Dad was between you and Dad," Adam said firmly, his jaw set.

"And no matter what happened, Mother, or the participants involved, nothing changes the fact that Cassie *is* our sister and we want to get to know her," Stephen added.

Bonita slowly glanced around the table and saw a look of conformity on the faces of Brooke and Brittany as well. Angrily, she slammed her glass down. "Don't expect me to be happy about it." She then stormed out the room.

"Maybe we should consider cancelling her sixtieth birthday party," Brittany said softly.

No one agreed or disagreed. Instead, Parker met Cassie's gaze and said, "I want to apologize for my mother's behavior."

Cassie shook her head. "You don't have to apologize. I just regret upsetting your mother."

"Don't sweat it," Adam said, smiling as he took a sip of his wine. "Everything upsets Mother. We're used to it and have been for a long time. Over the years we've learned to deal with it. Some better than others."

Dinner resumed and the tension eventually passed. Cassie, like everyone else, indulged in the shared discussions, murmurs, chuckles and laughter around the table. Feeling more comfortable, she began to relax and more than once she glanced over at Brandon to find him staring at her.

When dinner was over everyone retired to the family room. Moments later, Brandon asked to speak with Parker privately. She knew he would be telling them of her wish not to discuss any business today, and that she preferred meeting with Parker tomorrow.

Moments later, she found herself alone with Brittany, Brooke and Emilio. Anna and Megan, who were close friends, took a walk outside to admire one of the many flower gardens surrounding the estate, and Stephen and Adam had excused themselves to speak with Lisette.

"I see your brother still doesn't care for me," Emilio said, chuckling to Brittany.

She leaned up and kissed his cheek. "Doesn't matter, since I like you."

Fascinated, Cassie decided to ask, "Do you think he'll ever soften up?"

Brooke lifted an arched brow. "Who, Parker? No. That would be too easy," she said, with more than a trace of annoyance in her voice.

"And he's really upset now that he knows that Jordan has acquired a piece of land he had his sights on," Emilio said. Then since he thought Cassie didn't know, he added, "Jordan is my brother."

"Excuse me, please. I think I'll join Anna and Megan in getting some fresh air," Brooke said rather tersely before turning and walking out the French doors.

Brittany watched her twin leave. "I wonder what that was about?" she said thoughtfully. "Something's up with her."

"Pure speculation on Brittany's part," Emilio added. "She thinks Brooke's been acting strange lately."

"It's not what I think, sweetheart. It's what I know. She's my twin, so I can't help but notice certain things."

Before Brittany could speculate any further, Brandon, Parker, Stephen and Adam returned. Brandon came up to her and slipped his hand around her waist. "Ready to leave?"

Cassie smiled up at him. "Yes, if you are."

She promised Brittany she would drop by her restaurant this week and gave Brooke her word she would visit the condominiums that Brooke owned.

Before leaving she made more promises. Adam wanted her presence at his club at least once and Stephen asked her to come by the Garrison Grand so he could give her a tour. Parker hadn't asked her to promise him anything since he was meeting with her first thing in the morning at his office. The most important thing to him was for them to come together and find a resolution to what was keeping them at arm's length.

When she and Brandon walked to the car she smiled over at him. "Dinner wasn't so bad."

He grinned. "No, I guess not. What did you think about Bonita?"

"I hope that she'll get professional help, and soon."

"What about your siblings?"

She tilted her head and said, "To be quite honest, I like them."

He opened the car door for her. "I told you that you would. Even Parker softened up some."

When he came around and got inside the driver's side he glanced at his watch. "I know just the place I want to take you now."

She glanced over at him upon hearing the sensual huskiness of his tone. "Oh, really? Where?"

"My office."

Ten

After walking down the carpeted hallway holding hands, they reached Brandon's office. There was no guesswork as to why they were in an empty office on a Sunday night.

Cassie could unashamedly remember her request to him a couple of days ago, and there was no doubt in her mind that he was going to give her just what she'd asked for.

She chewed her bottom lip, not in nervousness but in anticipation. Goose bumps had begun forming on her arms, desire was making her panties wet and her tongue ached to mingle with Brandon's in a hot-and-heavy kiss. From the time he had announced just where he would be taking her and they had pulled out of the brick driveway of the Garrison Estate, sensations, thick and rampant, had flowed through her, making her shift positions in her seat a few times.

Cassie's thoughts shifted back to the here and now when Brandon released his hold on her hand and she immediately felt the loss of his touch. Opening the office door, his touch was back when he guided her inside before closing the door behind them. He tugged on her hand and brought her closer to him.

She felt weak in the knees, and to retain her balance, she placed her hands on his chest and gazed up at him, remembering the last time they had made love. It had been early that morning when they had awakened. And his lovemaking last night had given her a good night's sleep and been the very thing that had lulled her awake that morning as well. She'd wanted more of what he had the ability to give her. He had been more than happy to oblige her in the most fervent and passionate way.

She knew she should tell him of her decision to return to the Bahamas sooner than she'd originally planned, but at the moment she couldn't. The only thing she could do while standing in his embrace was get turned on even more by the gorgeous brown eyes looking down at her. Being the sole focus of his attention was causing all sorts of emotions to run through her; feelings that were intimate and private, feelings that could only be shared with him.

"Do you know what I think about whenever I look at you?" Brandon asked in a low husky voice, taking his forefinger and tracing the dimple in her chin.

She shook her head. She only knew what she thought about whenever she looked at him. "No. Tell me. What do you think when you look at me, Brandon?"

He took a step back and his gaze flicked over her from head to toe, and then he met her eyes. "I think about stripping you naked and then kissing you all over. But I want to do more than just kiss you. I want to taste you, to savor your flavor, get entrenched in your heated aroma, and to get totally enmeshed in the very essence of you."

Cassie was caught between wanting to breathe and not wanting to breathe. His words had started her heart to race in her chest and was making heat shimmer through all parts of her. Whenever they made love he had the ability to let go and give full measure, holding nothing back and making her the recipient of something so earth-shattering and profound.

With a heated sigh, she recovered the distance he had placed between them and reached out and wrapped her arms around his neck. She stared into his face, studied it with the intensity that only a woman in love could do, taking in every detail of his features—the dark brown eyes, sensual lips and firm jaw. Despite her determination to return to the island and live her life alone, she knew there was no way she would ever forget him and how he made her feel while doing all those wonderful things to her.

"On Friday you said you wanted me to make love to you in here because you didn't want me to forget you. Why do you think I'd forget you, Cassie?"

Chewing her bottom lip, she met his gaze knowing his inquiry demanded an answer, one she wasn't ready to share with him. If she did, she would come across as a needy person, a woman wanting the love of a man who wasn't ready to give it. A man she figured had no intention of ever getting married after what his fiancée had done to him. But then, hadn't she figured that same thing about her own life after Jason?

"Cassie?"

Giving him an answer that was not the complete truth she said, "Because I know this is just a moment we are sharing, Brandon, and nothing more. I know it and you know it, as well. But I want you to remember me like I will always remember you. And since this is where you spend a lot of your time, I want you to remember me here."

He smiled with a touch to his lips that made more heat flow through her. "Especially in here?" he asked in a deep, throaty voice.

"Yes, especially in here," she replied silkily. "I want to get into your mind, Brandon." What she wouldn't say is that she wanted to get in his heart, as well, but she knew that was wishful thinking.

With all amusement leaving his face, he said in a serious tone and with a solemn expression, "You *are* in my mind, Cassie."

She swallowed. She had all intention of making some kind of sassy comeback, but didn't. She so desperately wanted to believe him, and in a way she did believe him. He might not be in love with her, but over the past couple of weeks they had bonded in a way that went beyond the bedroom. He had come to the island seeking her out with a less than an honorable purpose, but in the end he had come clean and had been completely truthful with her, telling her more than she'd counted on.

And he had brought her here tonight to make the

memories she wanted him to have, even when she would be across the span of an ocean from him, he would remember her in here. The happiness she felt at that moment made her feel light-headed and she automatically breathed air into her lungs, picking up his manly scent in the process. "Then let's make memories, Brandon. Let's make them together."

Brandon stared at Cassie. He wanted her with a desperation he almost found frightening. The intensity of his desire was almost mind-boggling. It had been that way each and every time they made physical contact. She was an itch he couldn't scratch enough, a meal he could never get tired of consuming.

With the way she was standing so close to him, he could feel the hard tips of her breasts pressing against his chest, and the heated juncture of her legs aroused his erection even more. And if those things weren't mind-wrenching enough, he pulled her closer to the fit of him, needing the intimacy of their bodies joined first in clothes and then without.

The thought of making love to her in his office suddenly sent a sexual urgency as strong as anything he'd ever encountered to fill him to capacity. And with a sharp hunger that could only be appeased one way, he lowered his head and greedily consumed her mouth, devouring its taste and texture. He felt her lips tremble beneath his, he knew the exact moment her tongue engaged in their sensuous play, something so powerfully erotic it made him growl deep in his throat. He knew the air conditioning was on and was working perfectly, yet he felt hot and the only way to cool off was to remove his clothes. Their clothes.

He broke off the kiss and quickly began unbutton-ing his shirt, driven by graphic images flowing through his mind of just what he wanted to do to her. The thought made his lips curl into a smile.

"What are you smiling about?" she asked when he began removing his shoes and socks.

He glanced at her and chuckled. "Trust me, you don't want to know so I'd rather not tell you."

"But you will show me?" she asked when he began removing his pants.

He nodded. "Oh, yes, I will definitely show you."

Totally naked, he stood in front of her. He wanted to take her hard and fast, then slow and easy. He wanted to brand her. He wanted to …

Sensing he was suddenly about to lose it, he took a condom out of his wallet and quickly put it on before stepping closer to her to begin removing her clothes, appreciating the fact that she was helping. Otherwise he would have ripped them off her in his haste, his greed, his obsession.

When she stood before him completely nude, he knew that this was one immaculate woman, a woman who could turn him on like nobody's business. She was elegant and sexy, all rolled into one. He reached for her hand, took it in his and began walking backward toward his desk. He'd been fantasizing about taking her on it since the last time he'd brought her here. He could imagine her legs spread wide, with him standing between them and making love to her in a way that had his body hardening even more just thinking about it.

And they would be making memories. There would never be a time that he wouldn't enter his office without thinking about her, remembering what they had done in here, and remembering her being a part of him for this short while.

When they reached his desk he picked her up and sat her on it. A hot surge of desire rammed through him and he wanted his hands all over her, he wanted his body inside of her. He wanted it all. He reached out and let his fingers trace a path all over her, and pretended to write his name on her chest, stomach, thigh, everywhere.

And then he captured her mouth, sank into it with a hunger that was more intimate than any kiss he'd ever shared with a woman. She was consuming all of him, whether she intended to or not. Deliberate or accidental, he didn't care, she was doing it, taking him to a level that was physically exciting and emotionally draining all at the same time.

And when he gently leaned her back on the desk he spread her thighs and took his place between them— a place at the moment that was rightfully his. She looked beautiful with her hair a tousled mass on her head, flowing over her shoulders and falling in her face. He pushed the soft, curly strands back, not wanting anything to obliterate her vision. He wanted her to see every single thing he would do to her.

Her warm scent assailed him and he leaned forward and took her lips with an urgency, his tongue invading her mouth the way his erection was about to invade her body. Not wanting to wait any longer, knowing he couldn't even if he did, he pressed his engorged flesh against her and then when he felt her ultrawet heat, he eased it into her, clenching his teeth the deeper it went.

The sound of her moan pushed him into moving, stroking her body with his, thrusting in and out of her while holding her hips immobile. He made love to her with a primitive hunger that had him feeling every single sensation right down to his toes. Every stroke seemed keyed to perfect precision and his heart was pounding with each and every thrust.

He felt her shudder and his reaction to it was instantaneous. He was overtaken with pleasure so intense his body exploded in a million tiny rapturous pieces. Releasing the hold on her hips, he reached up and tangled his fingers in her hair as his entire body became one huge passionate mass. He pressed into her deeper still, when he felt the essence of him shooting into her womb as her flesh still continued to throb while his senses raged out of control. It was as if this part of her knew exactly what he needed and was giving it in full measure.

When she went limp, he somehow found strength to gather her into his arms to hold her, not wanting to let her go, wondering how he would do so when she left in two weeks. Not wanting to think about their parting, he picked her up and moved to sit behind the desk with her nestled protectively in his lap.

He glanced down at her. Her face wore the glow of a woman who'd just been made love to, a woman who had enjoyed the shared intimacy of a man. Not being able to stop himself from doing so, he reached out and began touching the swollen tips of her breasts. And when he noticed her breathing change, he leaned forward and took a tip into his mouth.

He wanted her again.

He lifted his head and met her gaze and his hand

began trailing down her body, seeking out certain parts of her. He heard her sharp intake of breath when his fingers touched the area between her legs.

"Had enough yet, baby?" he asked huskily in a low voice.

She clutched at his shoulders and whispered the one single word he wanted to hear. "No."

"Good."

He stood with her in his arms and headed toward the sofa. Tonight was their night. In the coming days the Garrisons would want to spend time with her before she returned home. But tonight was theirs and they would make memories to last.

Parker's secretary glanced up and gave Cassie a thoroughly curious look as she stood from her seat. "Mr. Garrison is expecting you and asked that I escort you to his office the moment you arrived, Ms. Garrison."

"Thank you."

Cassie followed the woman, knowing she had made the right decision in deciding to meet with Parker this morning alone. Regardless of her and Brandon's relationship, Parker was still his client.

She had talked to her own attorney and taken in all the advice he had given her. He had indicated he wanted to be included—whether in person or via conference call—in any business meetings that she and Parker conducted that included Brandon, as a way of making sure she was well-represented and not being compromised in any way. She came to the conclusion that things would be less complicated and more productive if she and Parker discussed things and tried to reach an agreement without any attorney involvement for now.

The secretary gave a courtesy knock on Parker's door before opening it and walking in. He turned from the window, which overlooked Biscayne Bay, and gazed at her. With his intense eyes on her she was struck again with just how much he looked like their father.

"You're staring."

She could feel herself blush with his comment. She noticed his secretary had left and closed the door behind her, and she was grateful for that. "Sorry, I can't get over just how much you look like Dad."

He chuckled slightly. "That's funny. I thought the same thing about you on Sunday. And I hadn't expected you to look so much like him."

The guard she put up was instinctive and immediate. Tilting her head back, she asked, "Who did you expect me to look like?"

He shrugged. "I don't know, probably more like your mother, a stranger, someone I really didn't have to relate to. But seeing you in the flesh forced me to admit something I've tried not to since the reading of Dad's will."

"Which is?"

"Admit that I do have another sister—one my father evidently cared for deeply to have done what he did," he said, while motioning to a chair for her to have a seat.

"But I'm a sister you'd rather do without," she said, accepting the seat.

He moved to take the chair behind his desk and grinned sheepishly. "Yes, but don't take it personal. I've felt the same way about Brittany and Brooke one time or another when they became too annoying. It was hard as hell being an oldest brother." And then he added thoughtfully, "As well as an oldest son."

A part of Cassie refused to believe her father had been so ruthlessly demanding of his firstborn. "Did Dad make things hard for you since you were the first?" she couldn't help but ask.

He seemed surprised by her question. "No, I made things hard on myself. I admired everything about him and wanted to be just like him. He was a high achiever in everything he did—sports, business, financial success. He was a man who was well-liked and admired by many. I never knew if I'd be able to grow up and fit his shoes, but God knows I always wanted to."

He paused then said, "But one thing about Dad was that he was fair, with all of us. At an early age we were encouraged to enter the family business and that's something none of us have regretted doing."

Cassie nodded. He had encouraged her to join the family business, as well. At sixteen she had worked part-time for the hotel and when she had graduated from college he had given her the responsibility of managing it. It had been a huge responsibility for a twenty-two-year-old, but he had told her time and time again how much faith he had in her abilities.

And she hadn't wanted to let him down…just like Parker had probably grown up not wanting to let him down as well. Did he assume that since their father hadn't left him the bigger share of the pie that somehow he had?

"Dad was proud of you, Parker," she decided to say.

She saw the glint of surprise that shone in his eyes. "He discussed us with you?" he asked.

"Of course, considering the circumstances, he wasn't able to tell all of you about me, but I've always known about the five of you. He used to talk about what a wonderful job you were doing and that he had no qualms about turning the running of the entire company over to you one day."

Parker leaned back in his chair and Cassie felt him study her intently while building a steeple with his fingers. "If what you're saying is true then why are you and I sharing controlling interest?"

Cassie smiled. His arrogance was returning. "Because I'm good at what I do just like you're good at what you do. He knew both of our strengths, as well as our weaknesses, and although you can't quite grasp it now, I think he figured that over the long run, the two of us would work together for the betterment of the company. You even admitted that Dad was a fair man."

"Yes, but—"

"But nothing, Parker," she said, leaning forward in her seat. "He was a good and fair man, point blank. And I'm sure Brandon has told you by now that I won't sell my portion of the controlling shares."

"Yes, he did say that," Parker said, and Cassie smiled at the tightening of his lips. There was no doubt in her mind that Parker Garrison was used to having his way, something she hoped his wife Anna was working diligently to break him out of.

"I'm here to make you another offer, one we can both live with," she said.

The look in his eyes said he doubted it. "And what offer is that?"

"Like I've told you, the Garrison Grand-Bahamas

is my main concern, but I won't give away a gift Dad gave to me. However, I will agree to sign my voting proxy over to you with the understanding that you inform me of all business decisions, not for my approval but just to keep me in the loop on things, since I'll be in the Bahamas."

Cassie saw the protective shield that lined the covering of his gaze when he asked, "Are you saying you won't sell the controlling shares but you'll give them to me by way of proxy?"

"Yes, that is exactly what I am saying. Since I'm signing them over to you it will basically mean the same thing, except I retain ownership. Yet it removes me from having to provide my feedback and vote on every single business decision you make."

The room got quiet and she saw the protective shield become a suspicious one when he asked, "Why? Why would you do that?"

A quiet smile touched the corners of her lips. "Because I believed Dad all those times when he said you were one of the most astute business-minded persons that he knew, and because I also believe that you will do what you think is best for the company and keep Dad's legacy alive for the future generation of Garrisons."

She could tell for a moment that Parker didn't know what to say. And then finally he said, "Thank you."

She nodded as she stood. "No need to thank me, Parker. Have Brandon draw up the papers for me to sign before I leave."

He stood, as well. "You'll be here another week, right?" he asked.

"That had been my original plan but I've decided to leave at the end of the week. I haven't told Brandon of my change in plans. I will tell him tonight."

Parker came from around the desk to stand in front of her. "Cassie, Brandon is a good man. In addition to being my attorney, he's also someone that I consider a good friend. The reason he did what he did when he came to the Bahamas—"

She waved off his words. "I know, he explained it all to me. Although I was furious at the time I'm okay now." *I'm also very much in love,* she couldn't add.

"Anna and I would like to have you over for dinner before you leave. Will you be free Wednesday night?"

Cassie smiled, feeling good that she and Parker had formed a truce. She thought about all the other dinner engagements she had scheduled that week with Stephen, Adam, Brittany and Brooke, and said, "Yes, I'd like that and Wednesday night will be fine. Thanks, Parker."

Brandon sat looking at Cassie on the dance floor with Stephen, who had dropped by to see her before she left for the Bahamas. Tonight was her last night in Miami and he had brought her to Estate, Adam's night-club. It was Thursday night, which Adam had long ago designated as ladies' night.

Brandon had been surprised and disappointed when Cassie had told him a few nights ago that she would be leaving Miami a week earlier than she had origi-nally planned. He had come close to asking her not to go, to stay with him, and not just for another week but for always. But then he remembered what she had said about the Bahamas being her home and not ever wanting to live anywhere else. Little did she know that when she left she would be taking a piece of his heart right along with her.

"Brandon, got a minute?"

He glanced up at Adam. "Sure, what's up?"

Adam straddled the chair across from him and glanced around as if to make sure no one was in close listening range. He then met Brandon's curious gaze. "I've decided to run for president of the Miami Business Council."

Brandon smiled. "That's great, Adam. Congratulations."

Adam grinned. "Thanks, but don't congratulate me yet. Already there's a problem."

Brandon raised a curious brow. "What kind of a problem?" Both he and Adam had been members of Miami's elite Business Council for years, and evidently Adam felt it was time to step up and take control. Brandon saw no problem with him doing that. Like his brothers, Adam was an astute businessman and the success of Estate could attest to that.

"Some of the older members, those with clout, aren't taking me seriously. They see me as a single man who is a notorious playboy, and since I work in the entertainment field, they also see me as someone not suited to lead the business council."

Brandon stared over at Adam. Unfortunately, he could imagine the older, more conservative members saying such a thing to Adam. "So what are you going to do?"

"One of the things that someone suggested that I do is easy."

"Which is?"

Adam smiled. "Work on expanding the club's clientele beyond the young, rich and famous. But the other suggestion won't be so easy."

"And what was that suggestion?" Brandon asked, hearing a hint of despair in his best friend's voice.

"To clean up my playboy image it was suggested that I find a wife."

Brandon blinked. "A wife?"

Adam nodded. "Yes, a wife. So what do you think?"

Brandon frowned. "I think you should tell whoever told you that to go to hell."

"Be serious, Brandon."

Brandon's frown deepened. "I am serious." He then sighed as he leaned back in his chair. "Okay, what if you did consider doing something like that? What woman will marry you just to help you advance your career that way?"

Then before Adam could respond, Brandon said, "Don't bother answering that. For a split second I forgot your last name is Garrison. You'll have all kind of greedy-minded, money-hungry women lining up at your door in droves. Is that the type of woman you'd want to be strapped to for the rest of your life?"

"It won't be for the rest of my life. I'm only looking at one year, possibly two. I want a woman who'll agree to my terms. We can get a divorce at the end of that time."

Brandon took a sip of his wine and asked, "And where do you intend to find such a woman?"

Adam shrugged. "I don't know. Do you have any ideas?"

Brandon chuckled and said the first name that came to his mind. "What about Paula Franklin?"

Adam glared at him. "Don't even think it."

Paula had first made a play for Parker a few years ago and when Parker hadn't shown her any interest, she had moved on to Stephen. Stephen had avoided her worse than Parker had, and she'd finally turned her sights on Adam, determined to hook up with a Garrison.

Adam had been forewarned about Paula from Parker and Stephen and hadn't been surprised when she had shown up at the club one night, ready to make a play for him and willing to do just about anything to succeed. When he had refused her advances, she had all but stalked him for a few weeks until he had threatened her with possible harassment charges.

Brandon gazed at him thoughtfully for a minute and then smiled and said, "Okay then, what about Lauryn Lowes?"

Adam gave Brandon a look that said he'd lost his mind. "Straight-laced Lauryn Lowes?"

Brandon ignored the look and said, "Yes, that's the one. You have to admit she's a picture of propriety, something those older, conservative members would want in a wife for you, so consider it a plus. And she's not bad-looking, either."

Brandon's words got Adam to thinking. "Lauryn Lowes."

Brandon stood and clapped Adam on the shoulder. "Yes, Lauryn Lowes. And while you're giving that some thought, I'm going to steal my girl from Stephen for a dance."

"Umm, that's interesting," Adam said, looking at him.

Brandon paused. "What is?"

"That you consider Cassie *your girl*. If she's your

girl then why is she leaving town tomorrow to return to the Bahamas?"

Brandon frowned. "She said she needed to go. What was I supposed to do? Hold her hostage? The Bahamas is her home, Adam, and she doesn't want to live anywhere else. She told me that a few days after we met."

"Have you given her a reason to change her mind?" Adam asked. "Maybe it's all been for show and you really don't care about her as much as I assumed you did. But if I cared for a woman, I mean really cared for one—although mind you, I don't—I would do whatever it took to make sure we were together, and nothing, not even the Atlantic Ocean, would be able to keep us apart." Before Brandon could say anything, Adam got out the chair and walked away.

Brandon took that same chair and sat, thinking about what Adam had said and his mind began racing. Although Cassie never said she loved him, a part of him had always felt that she did whenever they made love. She would always give herself to him, totally and completely.

And although he had never told her how he felt, he knew in his heart that he loved her, as well. He loved her and he wanted her, but he didn't want her to be with him in Miami if she wasn't going to be happy. Besides, her hotel was in the islands. It wasn't like she could fly over there every day for work.

He suddenly rolled his eyes when a thought flickered through his mind and he wondered why he hadn't thought of it before. He took a few moments to consider the idea, evaluate the possibility and then decided he would make it work. He laughed out loud, pretty pleased with himself.

"What's wrong with you?"

Brandon looked into Stephen's concerned face. Instead of answering he glanced around and asked, "Where's Cassie?"

"She's still out there dancing," Stephen responded, sitting down at the table. "Another song came on and this guy asked her to dance."

"And you let her?" Brandon asked, actually feeling a muscle tick in his jaw.

The sharp tone of his voice actually surprised Stephen. "Was I supposed to stop her or something?" When Brandon didn't respond, Stephen asked, "What's going on, Brandon?"

Brandon searched the dance crowd for a glimpse of Cassie. He saw her dancing to a slow song in another man's arms.

"Brandon?"

He glanced across the table at Stephen. "What?"

"I asked what's wrong with you?"

Brandon stood again. "Nothing's wrong with me. In fact at this moment everything is right with me. I think I'll go dance with Cassie."

Stephen shook his head, hiding his grin. "She's already dancing with someone."

"Too bad."

Like a man on a mission, Brandon crossed the room and tapped the man dancing with Cassie on the shoulder. The man turned and glared at Brandon, but instead of saying anything, he graciously moved away.

As soon as he did so, Brandon took hold of Cassie's hand and pulled her into his arms.

She glanced up at him and smiled. "The song is almost over so you didn't have to cut in, Brandon."

"Yes, I did."

"Why?"

"Because I didn't like the thought of another man touching you."

This was the first time she'd ever witnessed Brandon in a possessive mood and she made a half-hearted attempt at a chuckle. "And why would that bother you?"

"Because it does."

"Why?"

The song had ended and when others began returning to their tables, he took a firm hold of Cassie's hand and said, "Come on, let's take a walk."

They went outside and moments later they walked down a group of steps that led to the beach. Cassie paused long enough to remove her sandals. Her heart was beating fast and furious within her chest. Why had Brandon gotten all possessive and jealous all of a sudden? Could it mean that he cared for her more than she'd thought? A degree of hope stirred within her chest.

She decided to break the silence surrounding them. The only sound was the waves hitting the shoreline. "Estate is a very nice club."

Brandon stopped walking and she did likewise. She looked up at him and the bright lights from all the businesses on the beach lit his features. He was staring at her, his dark gaze intense. "I didn't bring you out here to talk about Adam's club," he said.

She looked away for a moment, across the span of the Atlantic Ocean, trying to maintain her composure. When she turned back to him, glancing up at him through her lashes, she asked, "Then what did you bring me out here to talk about, Brandon?"

For a brief moment Brandon couldn't speak. All he could do was stare at Cassie while his throat was constricted. Slowly expelling a deep breath, he said, "Our feelings for each other."

She met his gaze. "Our feelings for each other?" she repeated.

"Yes. I want to know where do you see our relationship going after you leave here tomorrow?"

As far as Cassie was concerned, the question he asked wasn't a difficult one to answer. "Nowhere."

Brandon tried to ignore the sharp pain that touched his chest. "And why do you think that?"

"Why would I not think that?" she responded in an irritated tone. "You've never said anything about continuing a relationship with me."

She was right. He hadn't. "I was afraid to," he said honestly.

She met his gaze. "Afraid? Why?"

"I knew what you told me weeks ago about how much you loved your homeland and not ever wanting to leave the island again to live anywhere else. I knew I could never take you away from that so I couldn't see a future for us. I was giving in to our demise too easily. But now I know what my heart is saying."

She studied his intense features before asking in a soft voice. "And what is your heart saying, Brandon?"

He took hold of her hand and brought her closer to

him and then placed that same hand on his chest and over his heart. "Listen."

She felt the gentle, timely thump beneath her hand and then heard him when he said, "It's a continuous beat that's saying over and over again, I, Brandon Jarrett Washington, love Cassie Sinclair-Garrison, with all my heart, soul and mind. Don't you hear it, sweetheart?"

Cassie fought back the tears that threatened to fall. "Yes, I can hear it now."

He smiled. "And do you also hear the beats that are saying that I want to marry you, make you my wife and give you my babies."

She chuckled. "No, I don't hear those ones."

"Well the beats are there, drumming it out loud and clear. What do you think? And before you answer I want you to know that I have no intention of asking you to leave the island to move here to accomplish any of those things."

She lifted a brow. "You're anticipating a long-distance marriage?"

He heard the disappointment in her voice. She was probably remembering the sort of absences her parents had endured. "Not hardly. I plan for us to live together in the Bahamas as man and wife and I will use my private plane to commute to Miami each day. It's less than a thirty-minute flight. Some people spend more time than that on the highways to get to work."

Her heart was filled with even more love when she said, "You would do that for me?"

He smiled and took his thumb to touch the dimple in her chin. "I would do that for us. I love you and I am determined to make things work." He then leaned down and captured her mouth with his and she shuddered under the mastery of his kiss. Moments later, when he pulled back, she was left quivering.

"Are you with me, sweetheart?"

She reached up and placed a palm to his cheek and smiled. "All the way."

He tightened his hold on her hand and tugged her in another direction. "Where are you taking me?" she asked, almost out of breath."

"Home. And I think we need to cancel your flight in the morning. My heart is beating out plenty of other words that you need to listen to, so I think you need to stick around."

Cassie smiled, totally satisfied that her heart belonged only to this man, and that it would always be that way. "Yes, I think I will stick around for another week after all, especially since my heart has a few special beats of its own, as well, Mr. Washington. And they are beating just for you."

* * * * *

Don't miss Secrets of the Tycoon's Bride
by Emilie Rose and
The Executive's Surprise Baby
by Catherine Mann,
the next two scandalous stories in
THE GARRISONS, *available from*
Mills & Boon® Desire™ in November 2008